W9-BVG-562

DISCARDED

WHISPER NETWORK

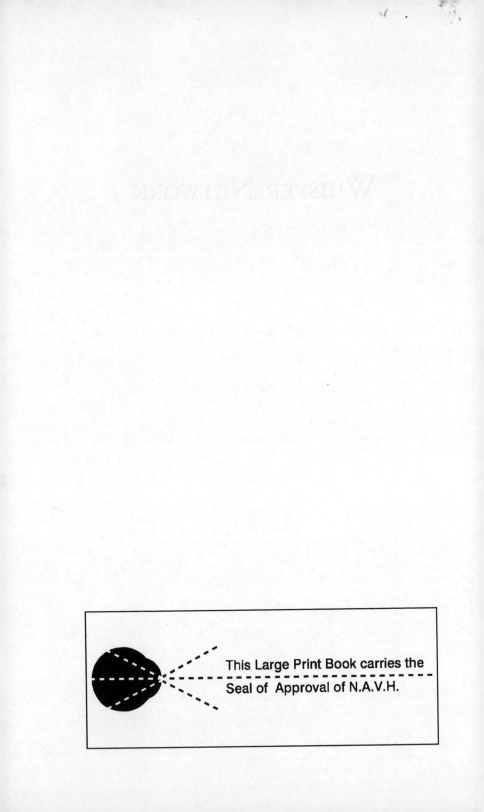

This Large Print Book carries the
Seal of Approval of N.A.V.H.

WHISPER NETWORK

CHANDLER BAKER

THORNDIKE PRESS
A part of Gale, a Cengage Company

GALE
A Cengage Company

Farmington Hills, Mich • San Francisco • New York • Waterville, Maine
Meriden, Conn • Mason, Ohio • Chicago

GALE
A Cengage Company

LIBRARY OF CONGRESS CIP DATA ON FILE.
CATALOGUING IN PUBLICATION FOR THIS BOOK
IS AVAILABLE FROM THE LIBRARY OF CONGRESS

ISBN-13: 978-1-4328-7026-3 (hardcover alk. paper)

Published in 2019 by arrangement with Macmillan Publishing Group, LLC/Flatiron Books

Printed in Mexico
1 2 3 4 5 6 7 23 22 21 20 19

For every woman who shared her story with me or with the world, and for every woman who fueled the collective voice within these pages and a movement that demands to be witnessed, we hear you.

PROLOGUE

If only you'd listened to us, none of this would have happened.

EYEWITNESS ACCOUNTS

12-Apr

Eyewitness 1: I'd just stepped outside when I saw a flash of — I don't know — something, movement, I guess, on the other side of the plaza and at first I thought it was a giant bird and then some terrorist bomb. Another split second and I realized it was a person. I couldn't tell if it was a man or woman. People in this district are all pretty old school. They still wear suits. Traditional. Black pants and blazer flapping. Anyway, it's a pretty good fall from up there.

Eyewitness 2: It was around one-thirty in the afternoon. I was just leaving lunch with a client at Dakota's. I nearly threw up my steak salad.

Eyewitness 3: I'm not saying I don't feel bad. I do. It's awful. But also you have to be pretty selfish to do a thing like that, you know? There were people on the street. It was just after lunchtime. If you really have to, if you really must, then do that on your own time without so many people around. That's all I'm saying.

CHAPTER ONE

Three Weeks Earlier:
The Day It Began
20-Mar
Before that day, our lives raced along an invisible roller-coaster track, a cart fastened to the rails through engineering and forces we couldn't wholly grasp, despite our super-abundance of academic degrees. We moved with a sense of controlled chaos. We were connoisseurs of dry shampoo brands. It took us four days to watch a complete episode of *The Bachelor* on our DVRs. We fell asleep with the heat of laptops burning our thighs. We took two-hour breaks to read bedtime stories to toddlers and tried not to calculate the total number of hours spent working as mothers and employees, confused as to which came first. We were overqualified and underutilized, bossy and always right. We had firm handshakes and hefty credit card balances. We forgot

11

our lunches on kitchen countertops.

Each day the same. Until it wasn't. The morning that our CEO died, we looked up suddenly to realize the roller coaster had a faulty wheel and we were about to be thrown off the rails.

Ardie Valdez — a patient, stoical person, with practical, well-made Italian shoes — was the first to have an inkling of the crash ahead. She heard the news and decided to take cover. "Grace?" She stood in the hallway — sterile, but with unaffordable art — and knocked on a plain closet door with a cow magnet stuck to its front. "It's me, Ardie. Can I come in?"

She waited, listening, until she heard a rustling behind the door. The legally mandated lock flipped out of place.

Ardie ducked into the small room and latched the door behind her. Grace was already settling back onto the leather sofa, her silk blouse hitched cockeyed over two plastic cones fastened to her breasts.

Ardie surveyed the room. A mini-fridge. The beat-up sofa on which Grace sat. A small television set playing *Ellen.* Outside, she could hear voices, quick steps, phones being answered and copies being made. She frowned, approvingly. "It's like your own little hideout in here."

Grace reached for the dial of the breast pump and it began its methodical, mechanic whir. "Or like my own little tomb," she said lightly.

Grace's dark sense of humor always managed to catch Ardie off guard. From the outside, Grace seemed so *uncomplicated.* She had teased, bleached blonde hair, was an active member of the TriDelta Alumni Club, and attended church at Preston Hollow Presbyterian with her tall, dark, and checkered shirt–wearing husband, Liam. They'd been on the personal invite list to the opening of the George W. Bush Presidential Library and identified as "compassionate conservatives," which Ardie took to mean that they wanted gay people to get married, but preferred to pay as little in taxes as possible. Also, they owned at least one handgun in a lock safe that they kept on a garment shelf in Grace's walk-in closet, and the fact that Ardie liked Grace in spite of all that said something.

"How much should babies eat, anyway? I am *always* pumping. I mean, *fuck,* Ardie, look at me, I'm watching *Ellen* during the day."

Grace didn't usually say "fuck."

Ardie remembered how long the days felt when her son, Michael, had slept only a few hours at a time. Her entire body had felt heavy and dirty, as if she had a thin layer of grime over her whole body, like unbrushed teeth.

She rummaged through her tote bag and pulled out two sweaty cans of La Croix. She handed one to Grace and dropped down on the floor in front of the couch. Ardie could do things like sit on floors at work because — and she'd be the first one to admit this — she had opted out. Years ago, actually. She slept in instead of spending an extra hour in the morning on hair and makeup. She went shopping almost never. She didn't spend a minute of her precious time in Pilates. It was the most liberating thing she'd ever done.

She glanced down at her phone. *Still* nothing.

"So apparently," Ardie said, "Bankole died. At home this morning when he was getting ready for work." She delivered the news matter-of-factly. Ardie didn't know another way to deliver news. It was always, *My mother has cancer* or *Tony and I are getting a divorce.*

"What? *How?*" Grace dropped the tubes she'd been busy trying to reinsert into the funnel-like contraptions poking out of her nursing bra.

14

"He had a heart attack. His wife found him in the bathroom." Ardie propped her elbows on her knees, staring up at Grace. "I just found out."

Ardie had met the company's CEO, Desmond Bankole, only once, a handshake in the elevator because he'd made a point to meet every person who worked in his building, down to the cleaning staff, at least once. His teeth were very white. He was smaller than she thought he'd be, with birdlike wrists peeking out underneath his suit jacket.

"I'm hiding, by the way," Ardie said — and before Grace could ask — "from Ames. He keeps asking where Sloane is. I told him she was probably out for lunch. He said that he hadn't approved her leaving for lunch today. I said she's the Senior Vice President of North American Legal Affairs and she doesn't need his approval to go to lunch and —"

"You said that to him?" Grace sat up. Sloane was their friend, but also technically their boss, which made Ames their boss's boss.

"Of course, I didn't really say that to him. Are you crazy?"

"Oh," Grace said, blinking. She toyed with the small diamond cross dangling from her

15

necklace. The electric whir of her pump counted off time between them.

"So I'm hiding in here like a coward," Ardie continued. "Waiting for Sloane to call me back." As a rule, men like Ames didn't care for Ardie. He hated having to listen to someone he didn't enjoy looking at. When he asked her where Sloane was, his eyes skirted over and around her and he moved on as soon as he could. She didn't mention this part to Grace.

Ardie cringed. Grace's breasts could not be ignored in this small room. "It just sucks them up so that they looked like torpedoes. Doesn't that hurt?" Ardie's son, Michael, was adopted almost four years ago, a happy end to years of infertility struggles. She'd never done any breastfeeding herself, but she'd always imagined serene suckling, coveted skin-to-skin contact, a loosely draped handwoven scarf to conceal those who were too modest. Not this violent yanking that she was now witnessing up close.

"Not as much as Emma Kate's mouth, to be honest." (Breastfeeding was supposed to be *painless* they told us. Breastfeeding was *beautiful,* they said. Well, we would like to drag their nipples over asphalt and see how painless and beautiful they thought it was.)

"God, we can invent smart toothbrushes,"

16

said Ardie. "My robotic vacuum can find its home and put itself to bed at the end of the night and we can't invent a thingamajig to suck out milk that works a little better than *that*?" The machine was sort of grotesquely mesmerizing.

"Men have teeth." Grace raised her eyebrows. "And floors."

Ardie took a long swig of grapefruit-flavored sparkling water as, on screen, Ellen DeGeneres welcomed a young man on stage. He looked like a teenager and Ardie didn't have the slightest clue who he was. She tapped her phone screen again: nothing new.

"I just had a scary thought," she said, after a beat. "Ames could be the next CEO."

"No. You think?"

"He looks like a CEO. He's tall. People like tall." Ardie clenched and unclenched her fist, stretching out the carpal tunnel that was a constant threat to her wrist. "I'm telling you," she said. "That son of a bitch could run this company and then where will we be?"

It wasn't just the rumors involving an intern. Or what had happened with his executive assistant two years earlier at the Byron Nelson golf tournament, after which guess who had been fired? Spoiler alert: not

Ames. It wasn't even the idea that corporate culture started at the top and a Truviv with Ames at its helm would be like announcing open season.

It was that Ames Garrett hated Ardie.

"I don't know," said Grace. "He's always been nice to me."

Ardie let the issue sit. Grace was a few years younger than Ardie and Sloane and still clung to the notion that someone could be a "good person" despite their actions, as though actions weren't the very indicator of one's person. And Ardie had seen Ames Garrett in action.

Still, there were issues one didn't discuss, even among friends — religion, money, and, perhaps, Ames.

Grace turned the dial on her pump to increase the intensity. One of the tubes popped out of place and quivered along the floor. A white drop spilled onto Grace's skirt. She closed her eyes and tilted her head back, her nostrils caving. When she opened them, her eyes shone. She rubbed her wrist into her nose and picked up the errant tube with purposeful calm. She missed the hole twice when she attempted to reconnect the attachments. The third try was a success. She gingerly sat back into the couch. "That really is depressing about Bankole, though."

She trained her glassy gaze on the TV screen. "Is it wrong that we're not more sad?"

Ardie didn't reply because Grace actually did seem very sad.

Ardie checked her phone again. A single bar of service.

Where the hell was Sloane?

CHAPTER TWO

20-Mar

Sloane stared at the ceiling of an elevator, willing it to move faster until the very second the doors split apart on floor fifteen, at which point she dashed through them like a racehorse.

"They're all in the conference room —" Her secretary, Beatrice, leaned over her vestibule, her coiled phone cord stretched from where she had the handset pressed to her ear.

"I know, Beatrice. I know." Sloane tore past her through the hallway. "And I am already royally screwed."

For the record, all had been *fine* a couple of hours ago when she'd sat down with her husband and her ten-year-old daughter, Abigail's, school principal. She had responsibly tucked her phone inside her landfill of a purse because she was a *good* mother, which in that place meant an *undistracted* mother. Or that was the part she'd been intent on playing in front of Principal Clark, anyway.

And now look!

She'd fished out her cell post-meeting to find the text messages from Ardie:

Desmond dropped dead this morning.
Heart attack.
Ames is looking for you.
Ok, seriously, where are you??
Sloane??

She hadn't even had time to say goodbye to her husband.

At last, she stood outside the North conference room, heart pounding so hard she worried that she, too, might have a heart attack. Number one killer of women over forty! She'd heard that somewhere. Maybe on *The View.* She pulled the handle to let herself inside.

Seven lawyers at the director level or higher sat around the table. Ames — General Counsel. Kunal from Communications, Mark for Employment, Ardie from Tax, Philip covered Risk, Joe, Litigation, and Grace was Director of Compliance. Plus another younger woman with a chestnut-colored pixie cut and Snow White cheeks

21

whom Sloane had never met before. Every face in the room turned to watch Sloane enter.

"Sorry I'm late." She slid into the empty seat beside Ames. The woman with the pixie cut smiled politely at her.

Ames glanced up from a stack of papers. A stripe of white ran a wavering line through his thick hair, otherwise the color of black coffee, save for the silvering that had begun to take root above his ears. "Where have you been?"

"I was —" Sloane paused for a fraction of a second, weighing how to finish the sentence. (We all did this. Whether in dating or at the office, we realized the power of pretending our children didn't exist. A man could say he was taking the day to go fishing with his son, while a mother was usually better off hiding the fact that she took a long lunch to run her child to the doctor's office. Children turned men into heroes and mothers into lesser employees, if we didn't play our cards right.) "I stepped out briefly." She cleared her throat.

"Without your cell phone?" Ames licked his fingertip to help him flip through the pages. Bodies shifted uncomfortably around the table.

"I was momentarily out of pocket, yes,"

22

she said. "Poor reception." Not a great excuse, in her world.

Ames made a nondescript noise and shifted the wad of Hot Tamales in his mouth.

She stared at him, resisting the urge to meet the seven pairs of eyes trained on her around the room.

Then Ames winked. Always his left eye. The delicate crow's-feet branching quickly out to his temples. He was one of the only men she knew who still reached for the wink. He could pull it off, actually. It said at once: *We're fine here,* but also: *I'm the one in charge.*

He opened his palms to the rest of the room. "Sloane Glover, everybody." As if he were introducing a comedian to the stage. Sloane bristled, though her face remained placid. Working with Ames was like sitting next to someone who was constantly kicking your shin under the table. "So nice that we can finally begin. Shall we?"

Awkward nods of acknowledgment followed. Beside her, Philip quietly pushed his legal pad and pen in front of Sloane's place. She pressed her hand to the spot between her ribs and blew out a breath. *Thank you,* she mouthed and Philip, whose tie was always crooked, simply shrugged. If only all men at the office could be more like Philip.

"I assume by now everyone has heard about the unfortunate passing of our Chief Executive Officer, Desmond Bankole," Ames began. "Memorial services will be announced in the coming days. I'm sure I'm not off base in expecting to see many of you at the funeral."

As Ames talked about Bankole's accomplishments, Sloane furiously downloaded from pen to paper the action items she'd been formulating as she drove back to the office.

Ames cut a look to her.

She set down her pen.

"Let's try to stay on the same page here." He folded his hands on the table. "I asked Grace to start us off by discussing any legal obligations Truviv has as a public company. Grace?"

Grace straightened. Sloane often wondered if her face underwent the same transformative process when *she* had to put on an air of authority about a subject at work. In her twenties, she knew, it had. Then, she could feel herself pulling on the mask of confidence, lowering her voice, removing the "likes" from her speech, stilling her knee, reminding herself that, yes, she *was* qualified. Grace's tells were subtler. In

Grace she saw a lift of the chin. A squaring of shoulders. Sloane — like most of us — rarely spotted these tiny betrayals of self-assurance in male colleagues. Was it because they weren't there? Or were we not in tune enough to see them?

"Sure," Grace said and launched into a discussion of the SEC, about 8-K filings, and updating the company's website. In a CEO's unexpected absence, transparency, Grace explained, was key. "I'll circulate a memo that will be easier to digest," she finished.

"And we're working on a statement." Kunal pointed his finger, touching it to the table for emphasis. "Until that's available, please answer any press calls by saying that we are very saddened by Desmond's loss both personally and professionally." His wide brown eyes took notice of each face in the room. "Do not respond with the words 'No comment,' whatever you do. Shareholders *hate* 'no comment.' Understood? We'll shoot for having the statement tomorrow morning. Does that sound good to you, Sloane?"

Sloane sat back in her chair. "Sounds do-able," she said decisively. Men could get away with hedging. It came across as thoughtful. If Sloane waffled it would sound like she didn't know what the hell she was doing. "We need to emphasize the firm's succession plan and look at recent examples of companies that handled a CEO's death or illness particularly well. A couple spring to mind, like Mc—"

"Actually," Ames interrupted. Sloane's toes contracted reflexively. "I think we should be looking at McDonald's. They had a similar situation. Two CEOs dying in two years. The first one was sudden. And Imation. Those are the two examples I'd go with, Kunal."

Sloane absorbed a spike of frustration. She'd used all the potential reactions by this point in her career. Her favorite was a polite: "Interesting, that sounds a lot like what I just said" in her best Southern accent. But to this she said simply, "*Great* idea, Ames."

Ames rubbed his palms together, satisfied. "All right, we all have our marching orders. My office door is always open if you need me."

They stood to go. Sloane clicked the pen closed. Ink stains peppered the inside of her right middle finger. Ardie and Grace, who had been seated side-by-side across from her, skirted the room to pass by on their way out. "Sorry," Ardie leaned in and

26

whispered while shaking her head slowly.

Grace pressed her lips together and caught Sloane's hand for a quick squeeze. Sloane noticed a damp stain on the front of Grace's silk blouse that she knew, without thinking, wouldn't come out. It was useless to wear any kind of silk while breastfeeding. She'd have to tell Grace.

"Katherine." Ames held up a finger, talking to the new woman, who still lingered while everyone else had filtered his or her way out. "You can wait in here one moment. I just need to go pull the draft announcement from my desk for Sloane." He looked at Sloane. "You don't mind stopping by my office, do you?"

Ames's office door was not actually, as he'd said, always open. Neither literally nor figuratively. Sloane had followed him as he walked two steps in front of her along the narrow corridor.

He opened the door to his office and together they stepped inside The Shrine — a gallery wall of Ames with famous athletes. Truviv, Inc., was the world's foremost athletic apparel brand, sponsoring all the country's biggest athletes. There he was playing golf with Tiger Woods. Now, here he sat courtside with an injured Kevin Durant.

Then — look! — another candid photo playing catch with Justin Verlander and his wife, Kate Upton. If Ames realized that the men and women memorialized on his wall might only be his friends because Truviv wrote a large portion of their sponsorship checks, he didn't care. Either way, Sloane considered The Shrine the semi–socially acceptable equivalent of a dick pic.

"So," he said, turning to lean on his desk. He was a middle-aged man who wore a charcoal suit well and managed to look better with age. At least this was what Sloane objectively knew to be true, though she herself had a hard time recognizing his good looks anymore. They'd become just another fact about Ames that she didn't quite believe. "Desmond's gone." He stuck his thumbs deep into his eye sockets and kneaded his eyes. "That was something I didn't see coming."

"I'm . . . yes, I'm so sorry." Sloane allowed herself to drift farther in past the threshold. Since hearing the news, it was the first time she'd mentally framed the CEO's death around condolences. It was terrible. He had children, two she thought, each only a little bit older than Abigail. She planned to process his passing tonight with her husband, Derek, over a glass of wine — the finest chardonnay their refrigerator had to offer. She would remember Desmond for his lively, attentive face as he sat in the first chair on the left side of the conference table, listening as she gave quarterly presentations to the company's executives.

"Remember how he always called you Miss Sloane?" Ames folded his arms. His shoulders shook with a quiet, good-natured laugh. "Like you were a preschool teacher?"

The memory triggered a faint smile. "Yes, god. It didn't actually bother me. Coming from him."

"He liked you." Ames pushed his weight off the desk and went around to the other side, where he began typing on the keyboard without committing to sitting down. She waited for a few moments, unsure of how much attention was required for whatever he was doing behind the computer.

"I'm sorry to change the subject, but who was that woman?" Sloane asked. "Katherine, was it?"

He slid open a drawer, shook out a couple Hot Tamales — an oral fixation to curb his smoking habit — and popped them in his mouth. "That was Katherine Bell. I'll introduce you. Slipped my mind with everything going on. One second, please." He struck a few more keys and then looked up at Sloane again.

She had the idea that Ames sometimes had a touch of selective amnesia about their early years at the firm. Other times, it was the only thing he seemed to remember about her at all. Today, he was clearly in the mood to pretend history didn't exist. "She's our new hire," he said. "Lots of corporate experience. She'll be working in your section. I think you're going to find her to be a really valuable asset."

Sloane cocked her ear toward Ames, as though she'd misheard him. "My section?" She repeated it as a question.

"That's right."

"And you didn't think to consult me about hiring someone new for *my* section?" Her voice sounded too high-pitched. *Shrill,* he might call it. "I'm SVP of that section."

It had been years since Ames had pulled something like this on her — years! And Sloane nearly undid all of them, all those months upon months of keeping her cool, of dealing with Ames and his Grade-A bullshit, with a sudden outburst of unadulterated anger.

Ames stooped to look at his computer screen again. "And I'm the General Counsel," he said. "Should we swap resumes?"

Sloane could already feel herself going

30

over this conversation tonight in the mirror while brushing her teeth, wishing it had gone differently.

"Where is Katherine's office?" She changed tacks.

"I figured you could take care of all that. After all" — he flashed a disarming smile and his chin dimpled — "you are Senior Vice President."

"Right." She took a deep breath and compartmentalized. It wasn't as though they could leave an attorney, even one Sloane hadn't asked for, idling in the conference room forever. She rested her legal pad on her forearm and added *Find Katherine an office* to the list of action items, right at the top. What an inauspicious day to begin. And hadn't she looked young, her skin so well *hydrated*? The word "ingénue" had come to mind, though that was ridiculous. She had to be at least thirty, older than Sloane was when she started here.

Sloane turned to leave, forgetting for a moment the reason she'd come in the first place.

"Sloane. The draft." Ames had finally made a decision to sit and was clicking through something she couldn't see because his screen was tilted. He nodded toward the legal pad on his desk. "I took a first stab. I

31

want to see it before it goes out."

Sloane walked back to his desk. A pair of scissors lay open atop the legal pad. Their silver blades left a violent X against the yellow pages. She felt lack of sleep and stacks of unopened bills and anger. Her fingers lingered over the cool metal. Sometimes when Sloane stood in very high places, she worried an urge to jump would seize her and she'd find herself tumbling off the side of a building. We all understood this feeling, how with just a twitch of fingers, Sloane — or any one of us — could snatch up the scissors and snip the artery in Ames's neck.

She pulled the legal pad, her fingertips sticking to the pages with faint perspiration. "I'll have this back to you in an hour," she said, a false note creeping into her voice as she escaped Ames Garrett's office, not for the first time.

DEPOSITION TRANSCRIPT

26-Apr

Ms. Sharpe: State your name, please.

Respondent 1: Sloane Glover.

Ms. Sharpe: What is your occupation, Ms. Glover?

Respondent 1: I work at Truviv as a lawyer. My formal title is Senior Vice President of North American Legal Affairs.

Ms. Sharpe: How long have you worked at Truviv?

Respondent 1: About thirteen years.

Ms. Sharpe: That's a respectable length of time. Longer than most people stay at their jobs, I imagine. What has kept you at Truviv for so many years?

Respondent 1: I hold a highly coveted position. In-house jobs, especially ones that pay well, are hard to come by. Truviv is a household name. Many people would have killed — sorry, I didn't mean — there were lots of people who would want my job.

Ms. Sharpe: And how did you come to know Ames Garrett?

Respondent 1: Ames was part of the group I interviewed with before making the move over from Jaxon Brockwell, so I suppose we first met then.

Ms. Sharpe: Did you work closely with Mr. Garrett?

Respondent 1: Not until we worked on a divestiture of an affiliate brand, I guess. He had been with the company about five years at that point, I believe. He was coordinating the diligence materials to be sent to opposing counsel and I was assisting him.

Ms. Sharpe: And how would you characterize your relationship back then?

Respondent 1: It was fine.

Ms. Sharpe: What do you mean by "fine," Ms. Glover?

Respondent 1: I thought Ames was smart and ambitious. He taught me a lot about running a sales process. We got along.

Ms. Sharpe: I see. And when did your affair begin?

CHAPTER THREE

20-Mar

We read *Lean In*. Take it from us; the book was all but mandatory in our city's female professional set. If our friends needed advice it was our honor bound duty to tell them earnestly, wisely, imploringly, Friend, what you need to do is *lean in.*

So we read it, all two hundred and forty pages of it, while we got our highlights done or listened to the audiobook as we drove the turnpike in our Land Rovers. We needed someone to tell us what we were doing wrong and how to fix it. To remind us that we weren't making enough money or rising up the ranks quickly enough or busting enough balls. We fantasized about our careers, we attended women's networking events, we looked for career risks we could take. We followed the recipe and set the timer for eighteen months and figured by then, the glass ceiling would have shattered under the weight of all the world's leaning women.

When exactly did we realize it wasn't working? Was it the election? Before then? It's hard to register differences in the status quo. Like trying to measure slight drops in temperature without a thermometer. But Ms. Sandberg was right about something. We had to lean in.

It was the only way to hear the whispers.

Every three minutes, an automatic air freshener sprayed citrus-scented disinfectant, startling Grace back into her surroundings. In a public restroom. On the toilet. Scrolling mindlessly through her Instagram feed. Her underwear a sling between her ankles.

This was what new motherhood had reduced her to. It was the lack of sleep. Everyone promised it would pass. That someday soon she would start to feel like her old self again.

She wished her old self would hurry the fuck up.

The door to the restroom swung open and two pairs of heels entered.

Grace might have announced herself by unfurling a wad of toilet paper or standing up so that the automatic flush triggered,

36

but before she could move, one pair of heels stopped in front of the mirror and said, "Danielle forwarded me that spreadsheet thingy. God, who knew there were so many sleazy guys in Dallas?"

Grace looked warily up from her phone. Squinted. Tilted her head to make out the shoes standing at the mirror: pink, pretty, but not terribly fancy. Steve Madden, maybe.

The young woman in the pink heels must be doing some midday facial maintenance at the mirror. The other girl, in leather heels, entered one of the stalls and slid the lock into place. "You should have told me. I got it, like, three days ago."

Grace was having trouble placing the voice. (Our voices were hardly more than an artifice. We were living in the days of vocal fry and verbal upticks. And we hated ourselves for it.) Talking in the restroom combined two activities that had no business taking place within the same moment, but Grace remembered being younger, when it was a symbol of closeness to traipse into a single bathroom together, chatting and taking turns squatting over a disgusting toilet seat. She felt a faint throb of longing for those days.

"The crazy thing is," Leather Heels continued, "one of the guys on there is my dad's best friend."

At the sink, Pink Heels said, "Whoa." Grace heard the snap of a compact. "And he was never, you know, creepy with you?"

Grace felt conscious of her own bow-tied Ferragamos, which she was sure could be seen below the stalls if either of the girls cared to look. Should she pick them up? Or was that going a step too far?

She couldn't decide what to do to, and so she did nothing.

"No, he's always been really nice. A normal version of nice, I'm pretty sure. My family had dinner with him last month."

"Can you imagine if it *was* your dad, though?" Pink Heels asked. "Because, that's the thing. They are. Somebody's dads, I mean. Think of getting this in your inbox and you see your dad's name and 'asked me to put a finger in his ass' next to it. Could you ever look at him the same again?" Grace thought Pink Heels was the legal intern, a first year law student, spending a couple days a week working at Truviv. Not from one of the better schools, if she remembered. *Was her name Olivia? Sophia?* One of those.

"Okay, excuse you," said Leather Heels. "Mark Souls is an honorable man. And that's not an image I need." Right, that voice belonged to Alexandra Souls, one of the young transactional attorneys Sloane had hired last year. Grace liked Alexandra. And Alexandra and Olivia-or-Sophia were friends from college, weren't they?

The interesting thing was: Grace hadn't heard anyone talk about anything *but* Bankole dying today. Maybe these girls were too young or too far down the ladder to care.

Or maybe they just thought this was bigger news.

They really *should* check beneath the stalls.

"Do you think that one is even true? The thing about the . . . ass?" asked Olivia-Sophia, sounding more titillated than scandalized.

Alexandra just laughed.

The points of Olivia-Sophia's shoes turned to face the stalls. "Did you add anyone's name?" she asked.

Grace heard the toilet flush. "No . . . I — no . . ." Alexandra was saying. The response felt like a loaded gun. The hinges squeaked as Alexandra exited the stall. "You?"

But then Alexandra must have washed her hands, because the faucet was blasting over their voices. Then the air dryer.

39

Grace kneaded her temple. She was trying to put the pieces together. There was a spreadsheet that Alexandra and Olivia-Sophia had received. And it must contain a list of sorts. A list of sleazy men, they'd said. And they were passing it between themselves. *Discussing* it. (Grace was catching up, but a number of us had already seen this list. Adding to it, too. We were using dummy email addresses, fake usernames, and blind copy like they were going out of style faster than full-body rompers and split sleeves.)

The sink suddenly shut off.

"It doesn't matter," Alexandra was saying. "That guy obviously did something to piss someone off. So, I'm sure he deserves it. They should all lose their jobs."

Grace flinched. *What about due process,* she thought, though she instantly felt like a law school goody-two-shoes, which she supposed she had actually been.

Alexandra and Olivia-Sophia were leaving and Grace couldn't hear the rest of their exchange, only the murmur of voices sliced off by the closing door behind them, leaving Grace with only a sense of unease to keep her company.

Though, on second thought, perhaps she'd had that already.

CHAPTER FOUR

None of us had time. For anything, it seemed. If time was currency, we were all going broke. Sometimes, we'd see a book hit the *New York Times* bestseller list with a promising title like *I Know How She Does It* or *Overwhelmed.* For a few weeks, we'd pass it between us, trying to use the advice like a trendy new diet plan. But for all of us, there were — how do the pundits put it? — institutional roadblocks.

First, we were working with less time than the men in our office. That was just a fact. Thirty minutes to blow-dry our hair in the morning. Ten minutes to straighten and curl it. Fifteen for makeup. Three minutes for jewelry. Sixteen minutes to pick out an outfit. Forty-five minutes of cardio in the evening, followed by the occasional fifteen minutes of abdominal work. If you think we're making this up, we suggest a quick

41

search through the staff profile pictures on the company website to see what we mean.

There were economies of scale, too. Time was a finite resource, so who should get the most of it? Those of us who were moms had the most compelling argument: *consider the children!* But what about the rest? We sat in our offices listening to the tick of our biological clocks as they counted out every missed date, missed chance encounter, missed opportunity to meet someone with whom we might actually want to become a mother. And then — the bait-and-switch. If we did become wives and mothers, the value on our time increased as the amount plummeted.

These were not fixed cost deductions. Maybe we'd decide to forgo the Christmas card photos of tartan-clad children and not have kids at all. But too often that felt like a choice for career, and career only. A tacit decision to forfeit our free time at the door, please and thank you. Someone should teach a graduate course on the intricacies of our time. We wonder if, perhaps, Shonda Rhimes is available?

Sloane had been staring at her computer screen for too long. Outside, the sun had gone down. The Dallas skyline — its glittering orb and glowing suspension bridges —

gradually gave way to the gaudy electronic billboard, spanning cement-to-sky, of the city's Omni Hotel.

She rubbed her eyes, no longer caring whether she left black smudges at the corners. When she was just out of law school, working at a firm, she would have known precisely how long she'd been reviewing the form 8-K for filing. Law firms forced their attorneys to measure their time in six-minute increments. But that was well over a decade and two offices ago. Now Sloane still sometimes found herself silently keeping a running log of her time:

.1 hours, eating pho
.2 hours, texting with Derek and Abigail
.1 hours, reading trash tabloid websites
4.5 hours, revising press release exhibits and data table exhibits to SEC filings

Her phone vibrated on her computer stand. It was Derek. She picked up on the second buzz.

"She lives!" Sloane loved the sound of her husband's voice. She pictured him, leaning over the island in their kitchen, his copper hair a bit too long around the ears, a threadbare Nirvana T-shirt — the same one he'd been wearing the day they met and which she still liked to steal at least once a week to wear to bed — stretched over his shoulders.

She had four missed calls. "I'm sorry, I'm sorry. I'm the worst. Have you considered getting a new wife?"

Years ago, Derek had imposed a rule that Sloane not be allowed to apologize for doing her job anymore. But she figured the rule was hers to break.

"No worries," he said, in his easy manner. Not that his job wasn't stressful. Derek was a middle-school teacher and preteen boys were a nightmare. But it was a different kind of stress and theirs never needed to compete. "Just calling to check on you. Oh, I sent in Abigail's forms for the walkathon next week and turned in the check for her piano recital, so you can cross those two items off your list."

"You know how I love to cross," she said, scanning a line in the filing that she'd already tried to read three times. She'd forgotten about the forms entirely. "Thank you."

There was a short silence, just enough space for them both to recall that they'd argued last night. The longer they were married, the easier it was to push "pause" on an intense disagreement and pick it up at a

44

later time — preferably one that wasn't past Sloane's bedtime. But there it was again. Like a little shared bruise that she'd only just remembered how she'd gotten.

"How is she?" asked Sloane at the same time that Derek said, "She seems fine. I've been watching her since she got home."

The fight had been about Abigail. It was always about Abigail these days. She could almost hear Derek in her head telling her, *It wasn't a fight, it was a disagreement.* Fine, but Sloane liked hyperbole and, when it came to her daughter, she felt entitled to it.

It began a couple of months ago. Abigail had grown sulky. She stopped playing with her dolls. Sloane had asked her rather innocuously to please clean them up and Abigail had yelled that — and Sloane was paraphrasing here — perhaps everyone would be happier if Abigail were dead.

Derek thought Sloane was overreacting. He taught seventh grade English, which, if you asked him, meant that he had the market cornered on early childhood development expertise. But Sloane had the market cornered on Abigail. She took her to a psychologist, who assured her a "death and dying" phase was a perfectly normal part of childhood development. "I told you, Sloane. Perfectly normal," Derek had repeated on the way home as if he, too, had a doctorate in psychology.

But then a few days later, Sloane spotted the text messages popping up on the screen of Abigail's phone. *Slut. Bitch. Cunt.* Each one felt like a bullet to the chest. Nobody told her this before she became a mother. That suddenly your diligently built-up immunity toward all these *things,* like name-calling and popularity contests, would up and leave the second someone took aim at your child.

She had shaken Abigail's phone in Derek's face and screamed, "Is this normal? Is this *peeeerfectly* normal, Derek?"

Of course, that hadn't been fair to Derek, the dad who knew the names of all Abigail's classmates and brought donuts for the homeroom teachers. When he read those messages, he'd been so terrifyingly dadlike, it had actually been a bit of a turn on.

Sloane wanted to sue the school district for what had happened. Remedial action. Adequate protection. Legal consequences, if they weren't going to take her seriously. But the school district was also Derek's employer, which meant that he wanted her to "play nice." He'd used those words specifically.

They'd presented a united front at the

meeting and Sloane let Derek take point just as he'd asked. Insisted, really. It had not felt great.

Over the phone, she heard him scratch the roughness of his chin. Sloane typed through the pause because she couldn't afford not to. "Sloane, I'm sorry, I —"

At the sound of a soft knock at the door, she twisted her chair around. Ardie leaned on the doorframe, her black blazer and pants more wrinkled than usual.

"Derek, I'm sorry, but I have to go." She heard him sigh and felt a wave of guilt. "Love you."

"Don't work too hard," he said before hanging up and Sloane knew that he really did mean it in an altruistic, please-don't-have-a-mental-breakdown type way, the way he often confiscated her laptop after eleven because he'd read that ambient blue light was bad for her sleep.

Sloane moved her phone to the other side of her keyboard. "Have you been standing there long?"

Ardie invited herself in and rested her hands on the back of Sloane's guest chair. "Long enough to see that you need to go home." She passed Sloane a brown accordion folder. "Here are the tax appeals for the Waco factory site. Sorry, another

47

thing for you to review, I know. But if it makes you feel better, I haven't even started reviewing the tax models for the subscription box acquisition."

Sloane dropped the folder onto her desk. *Thunk.* She had been meaning to talk to Ardie for a couple of weeks now, ever since it had become clear that the tiny little secret she was keeping from her friend — it was *nothing* — was becoming more of a lasting issue. But, well, today truly wasn't the day for opening up a can of worms. Of course, this did sound vaguely like an excuse, but it wasn't. More of a strategy.

"I heard Sales took the rest of the day off to mourn Bankole's passing, can you believe that?" Sloane said instead.

Ardie widened her eyes dramatically. "Listen, Sloane, you mustn't make light. Those twentysomethings' feelings are *valid.*" She pressed her palms together as if in meditation. "They can't be expected to work and feel things at the same time. *Lead* with empathy, okay?"

One of the best things about Ardie was that she could be just a little bit mean exactly when Sloane needed her to be. Sloane's most closely held tenet was that women could not be real friends unless they were willing to talk shit together. It was the closest thing she knew to a blood pact that didn't involve knives.

"I, like, so, *so* sincerely apologize." Sloane rested her palm over her heart and gave her best pouty frown, or at least she hoped she did. She'd just recently started a Botox regimen — she was ever-so-slightly on the other side of forty, after all — and she wasn't entirely sure what her face looked like at any given moment anymore. "If they were smart, they'd be trying to figure out who the next CEO's going to be."

"If they were smart they'd be worrying about the price of their stock options."

"Do you think they'll bring in an outsider?" Sloane asked.

"Your guess is as good as mine, but my bet? Bringing in someone new would take too long. Anyway," she sighed, "Michael's daycare charges a dollar for every minute I'm late to pick him up, which means I'm already going to owe . . ." She glanced at her watch. "One gajillion dollars."

"I thought we paid you to be good at math."

"Oh, you do. That's an accurate figure, I assure you —"

They stopped short.

In the doorway, Katherine had her sweater folded over one arm. She glanced between the two of them. "Sloane, if it's all right with you, I thought I might step out for the night."

She made a demure motion to tuck a lock of hair behind her ear. Odd, Sloane thought, because Katherine's hair was far too short to be tucked anywhere. It was like reaching for a phantom limb.

Despite all of her righteous indignation, Sloane had nearly forgotten about *Katherine.* She hadn't known what to do with her on her first day. Katherine was pretty in the way that meant Sloane had to remind herself to like her. The older she got, the more she found herself wanting to dislike young, pretty women. It was a terrible impulse, but one that Sloane curbed diligently.

Sloane gave an exhausted smile. "Oh, yes, please, go home, report back tomorrow and remind me what homes are like. Are they nice? Do they have beds? Down pillows? Is that where people keep their paj— ?" She stopped. She'd seen something, a long shadow in the hall. She stood up on her bare feet and tiptoed closer to the doorway to peer around Katherine. "Is someone *lurking* behind you?" she asked.

Ames poked his head in and cleared his throat. "No, no, just me." He waved at Ardie and nodded toward Sloane. "I promised Katherine I'd take her out for a drink, welcome her to the office, pick her brain about her experience, that sort of thing."

Promised. The word rang in Sloane's brain. It sounded so paternal coming from Ames.

Sloane knew she should have been saying something. Her mind was moving slowly. So much had happened today. Desmond had *died* today. Less than twelve hours earlier, in fact. His body might hardly be cold and yet now Ames was taking this new woman — Katherine — out for drinks. That couldn't be right, could it? But they were standing there looking at her, waiting, and yes, she had heard Ames correctly. She was sure of it. Ames was taking Katherine out for drinks. Tonight.

The memory surfaced unbidden.

A quiet warning Sloane received from her mentor, Elizabeth Moretti, back at Jaxon Brockwell the day she'd announced she was taking the job at Truviv. Over the two years she spent at Jaxon, Elizabeth had pulled her aside exactly twice with that look on her face, the appraising one with the subtext that read, "I am older than you, I am wiser, and I have seen things." That day, she looked at Sloane and said: *Watch out for*

Ames Garrett, and she had left it at that.

Right. Well, fat amount of good it had done her, as Sloane had confidently shaken Ames's hand on day one at Truviv, and six months later, they were screwing.

Now Ames was watching her. Ardie was watching her. And Katherine was looking back and forth between all of them, as if still trying to puzzle it through. Sloane stared at her desk. Calls she needed to return. Emails she needed to write. She pinched her eyes shut, a sign that she was about to do something colossally stupid.

"Great idea," she said. "I'll grab my purse."

Ames and Katherine stared at her. It wasn't as if she'd said she was going to join the circus, for fuck's sake.

Ames looked amused. "I thought you were buried?"

"The hole will still be here when I return." She, too, could enjoy temporary amnesia.

Ames's head bobbed slowly. "Great," he said. "We'll meet you at the elevator, then." He slapped the doorframe twice on his way past, as he and Katherine walked out.

Ardie spun on Sloane. "Are you sure about this?"

Sloane looked up at the ceiling, palms turned up. "No, of course I'm not sure about this, Ardie."

"Then do you want to tell me why — ?"

"You know exactly why."

Ardie crossed her arms and raised her eyebrow expectantly.

"I don't know," said Sloane, exasperated. She pointed at the door and lowered her voice. "I guess maybe I'd like to prevent the slaughter of the sacrificial lamb this time. You might have seen her scampering about. Five-five-ish. Pixie cut. Doll face. Happy?" She scooped up her purse and slung it over her right shoulder. "It's one drink." She held up a finger to Ardie's skeptical face.

"One," Ardie conceded. "And I'm going to call karma and put in a good word."

Sloane closed her eyes, exhausted. She felt the phantom creases wanting to burrow into the bridge of her nose. She knew that if she asked, even hinted, Ardie would go with her, daycare pickup or no. Sloane was lucky that way.

"Coming from you," she said, "that would mean a lot." She clasped her friend's wrist for a split second, wanting to linger. They still kept a half-drunk bottle of gin in the file cabinet from the last time they'd had to save a woman from Ames Garrett. Only last time, that woman had been Sloane.

Truviv Instant Messenger
21/04 — 4:31 PM

Recipient: Sloane Glover
Sender: [Blocked]

Slut.
Bitch.
Cunt.

54

CHAPTER FIVE

20-Mar
How few words we said to each other in the
elevator. We'd step in, smelling freshly of
shampoo and mouthwash. The smooth
heave against our feet, pulling us up into
the air, couriering us to our floors. Each
time the doors opened, a small portal into
another world appeared.

We got proficient at sorting each other by
our respective floors before the button was
even pushed. Marketing? Welcome to the
eighth floor graveyard of former cheerleaders in limbo as they decided whether to attend grad school. Sales account lead on
twelve? We could spot her fresh manicure
tapping at her phone screen, the designer
purse hooked over one shoulder broadcast-
ing that she must be having a really good
year. We might quietly ask a Product Development Coordinator where she got the new
glasses. Or give space to the woman in the

black suit who entered behind us and resolutely pressed the button for fifteen.

But what did we really know about each other? We were separated by steel and scaffolding. Our universes seemed disconnected, occasionally bumping up against each other because of proximity alone. Or so we thought.

We needed only to have knocked at the door to one another's worlds to find out how our histories knitted themselves together, weaving shared threads into a noose of our own making.

This was very nearly what happened when Rosalita and Crystal, the new girl, stood outside a fifteenth floor office. With alarm, Crystal hissed, "There's someone in there." She jerked back from the door as though it had burned her. Rosalita let out a slow breath that did nothing to conceal her annoyance, which was the point.

It was nine-thirty at night. Together, Rosalita and Crystal had been working through the darkened floors, vacuuming and emptying out trash cans, wiping down countertops, and replacing toilet paper. The office windows were flat black holes staring out into space. Inside, the automatic hall lights illuminated the square of office space in which the pair of women worked. After they moved on, the lights would flicker off.

The lights used to bother Rosalita. They made her feel like she was in a spotlight, being observed. Even worse, sometimes a set of lights would flicker on at the end of a corridor and she would freeze, heart beating fast, waiting for someone to appear. When no one did, she still had to finish her round, but never without checking over her shoulder every few minutes.

"Moths," her supervisor once told her. That had been years ago, when Rosalita first began cleaning, a few months after her uncle had driven her and her sister in a sweaty van up from the Valley. At some point, she let other worries replace the lights.

"It's fine," Rosalita told Crystal, placing neat check marks on the paper attached to the clipboard, noting the offices they'd completed. At the shift meeting, she'd been glad to be assigned again to her usual floors. One of the executives had died and soon there'd be the business of cleaning out his office. Rosalita wanted no part of that.

"Should I knock?" Crystal asked.

Rosalita swished past Crystal, rapped twice on the open door, and, without waiting for an answer, took efficient steps into the occupied fifteenth-floor office. She snapped up the trash and recycling bins, carrying them back into the hallway.

This was how the new girl would be taught.

Rosalita had learned that the secret to being invisible wasn't to tiptoe around the perimeters. That only drew attention and made everyone else uneasy in the process. No, the secret to invisibility was speed and purpose. Those qualities allowed others to relax and go about their jobs as if you weren't even there.

Rosalita emptied the bins into the rolling dumpster. She replaced the plastic lining and reentered the office. The blonde woman looked up from her computer screen. "How's your night going?" she asked Rosalita amicably.

Rosalita replaced the cans in the corner and brushed off her gloved hands.

She recognized this springy, blonde woman. *Sloane Glover,* the woman's name appeared on the silver plate outside her door. She reminded Rosalita of a talk show host, polished and sparkly. She was the exact right type of white woman to cause an international media firestorm if she ever went missing.

"Fine, miss," Rosalita answered. "And you?"

The woman sighed and tilted back in her chair. "How do you say 'shitty' in Spanish?"

Rosalita snorted a harsh laugh, the kind born from common misery.

Abruptly Sloane lifted her head. "Sorry. God." She shook her head and pushed her fingers into her temples. She didn't seem so springy or sparkly today. Her eyes, Rosalita noticed, were red. Not work, but a shopping website occupied her screen. "I — didn't mean. I'm such an idiot. That was such a rude thing to say. To assume, I mean." Sloane looked Rosalita directly in the eyes. "It's been a long night. Not an excuse." She held up a hand as if to stop someone from striking her.

Rosalita waited patiently until the Sloane woman was done. She had a lot of words and they all seemed to need to come out at once. *"De mierda,"* Rosalita said.

"What?"

"Shitty. *De mierda.*" Rosalita frowned, considering. "Or . . . *no vale mierda. De pura mierda.* Take your pick." She shrugged. If Rosalita should have been offended over Sloane's assumption, she didn't know why. She had dark, wavy hair and bronze skin. She spoke with a thick accent. And besides, she'd lived in Guanajuato until she was twelve. Sure, there were times when Rosalita did not like to be asked to speak Spanish — mostly when the request came from men (a fetish). But otherwise, she didn't get so offended, like some of the younger girls. It took too much energy.

Sloane smiled gratefully. "*De mierda,* indeed. Thanks." Impulsively, Sloane's eyes flitted back to her screen and then, remembering, to Rosalita.

Her smile faltered. "I'm sorry," she apologized for the second time in fewer than five minutes.

Rosalita knew she'd been dismissed. She didn't hold it against Sloane, who looked as if she should have gone home hours ago.

Returning to the hall, she ticked the box next to Sloane Glover's office on her clipboard. "Go get a bottled water for Mrs. Glover from the fridge," she told Crystal. "I'll take care of the next one." Crystal obeyed. She was young and possibly pregnant, Rosalita guessed, though she had been hiding it well beneath the baggy, company-issued polo.

Rosalita pushed the supply cart, slowly, methodically over the carpet. What she knew with the certainty of someone who'd seen it too many times before was that, tonight, Sloane Glover was drunk.

Ardie Valdez

So . . . how did it go? What did you learn? What's her story?

Grace Stanton

How did what go? What are we talking about? Who?

Ardie Valdez

Sloane had drinks with Ames and Katherine last night. Katherine is that woman that sat in on the meeting yesterday. She's new, apparently. Started in the office yesterday. Ames hired her without talking to Sloane. Classic.

Grace Stanton

Sorry, out of the loop. Drinks . . . with Ames? Really?

Sloane Glover

Sorry! Sorry! I'm here. Just now getting to the office. Anyway . . . Yes, drinks with Ames. Uneventful. Was on his best behavior. Katherine. Is. Pedigree. Think: Westminster dog show. Harvard Law. Associate at Frost Klein. Hails from Boston. (Hence the shoes?) Not a lot of "Southern warmth" if you know what I mean. May take some time to thaw. Fuck though, I'm drowning.

Thank Tina Fey she's smart.

Ardie Valdez

Hey, what are all the secretaries doing gathered around Beatrice's screen? Something about a spreadsheet. Does someone have a big Excel project going on?

Grace Stanton

I don't know, but I heard the first-years talking about a spreadsheet yesterday. Something about sleazy businessmen in Dallas. Forgot to tell you. Does anyone have a Clif Bar? I'm starving.

Ardie Valdez

No, sorry. I have SunChips in my desk, though. Help yourself.

CHAPTER SIX

21-Mar

We were always looking for the perfect man. Even those of us who were not signed up for the traditional, heteronormative experience were nevertheless fascinated with the anthropological, unicorn-like search for one. Married or single, we were either searching for him or trying to mold him from one we already had. This perfect specimen would consist of the following essential attributes:

He shared his food and always ordered dessert. When we recommended a book, he bought it without needing a friend to second our suggestion first. He knew how to pack a diaper bag without being told. He was a Southern gentleman with a mother from the East Coast who fostered his quietly progressive sensibilities. He said "I love you" after 2.5 months. He didn't get drunk. He knew how to do taxes. He never questioned our feminist ideals when we refused to squish bugs or change oil. He didn't sit down to put on his shoes. He had enough money for retirement. He wished vehemently for male-hormonal birth control. He had a slight unease with the concept of women's shaved vaginas, but not enough to take a stance one way or another. He thought Mindy Kaling was funny. He liked throw pillows. He didn't care if we made more money than him. He liked women his own age.

We were reasonable and irrational, cynical and naïve, but always, always on the hunt.

Of course, this story isn't about perfect men, but Ardie Valdez unfortunately didn't know that yet when, the day after Desmond's untimely death, Ardie's phone lit up: a notification from her dating app.

Jesus, the thing still startled her. Her phone spent so much time vibrating she wished she had saved the money on that post-divorce sex toy and waited for her phone to buzz.

Ardie looked at her screen:

You're on fire. You've got 1 new message.

There was even a "fire" icon next to the text, as if the app seemed precisely designed to remind Ardie she was too old to be *dat-*

ing. It was an emoji world now, and Ardie was just living in it.

Ardie had started at Truviv eighteen months before Sloane. Same skeptical, not easily impressed Ardie, but with much better clothes. Sloane liked to tell people that if it weren't for Sloane's ripped pencil skirt and Ardie's emergency sewing kit, they might never have become friends. But Ardie knew that wasn't true. Sloane was actually very good at picking friends and Ardie discovered shortly thereafter that Sloane always kept an emergency sewing kit in her own desk drawer anyway. Ardie had never told her that she knew.

Life was much brighter then, she'd admit that much. Full of possibilities and silly anecdotes. Before she became this new Ardie, a forty-two-year-old divorcée.

Last year, in the pickup line at Starbucks, Ardie finally worked up the courage to tell Sloane she was leaving her husband, Tony. *Another woman has been sleeping with my husband,* she'd said, in her typically sardonic fashion. *So I guess he's hers now.*

Sloane had flown into a fury on her behalf. All: *How could Tony do this? What about Michael? What about the house?*

Ardie had just turned to her, handed her a vanilla latte, and said one word: *"Don't."*

The subtext was clear: no, not you, don't *you* start.

Things were delicate between them for a brief while after that.

She'd known for years about Sloane and Ames. She wasn't like Sloane. Best friend was a person, not a tier, for Ardie. She didn't have a high school best friend, a college best friend, a law school best friend, a preschool mom best friend, and a *work* best friend, which was Ardie's assigned moniker when Sloane spoke to her other best friends. And so with one syllable — *"don't"* — Ardie had told her only best friend that, no, she had to stop, no, they would not talk about it, no, she wouldn't be allowed to commiserate over the miserable human being Ardie's husband turned out to be.

Because, as they both knew, Sloane had been the other woman too. With another man, sure, but what did that matter? That *was* a category. A tier, in fact. And there was guilt by association.

It was amazing how, even now, even in the privacy of her own head, Ardie glossed over her role in the story. The secret that was buried so deep that it registered only the smallest spike in her pulse as she skipped through the memory. A blank space. A lie.

But what did it matter now? They were

over it. Gin under the bridge, as it were. In fact, six weeks ago, Sloane insisted Ardie sign up for Match.com and Ardie, as was typical, indulged her. She'd even let Sloane type up Ardie's profile one night after work and, in the morning, Sloane presented it to her as if she were unveiling a new car in the driveway. "Derek told me I was being too pushy." Sloane had been talking too fast, describing how she'd filled out the profile next to her husband in bed. "But what does he know? He's such a man." (And what *did* men know about matchmaking, by the way? For us, it was an Olympic sport, while they hoarded single friends like they were stock-piling them for the apocalypse.)

Ardie didn't have the heart to tell Sloane that no one used Match.com anymore and she'd been using three dating apps regularly at that point. But she appreciated Sloane's intrusion into her new — it still felt new, even fourteen months after the divorce — dating life much more than she let on. It was good to get a friend's opinion.

Ardie made room for her phone on her desk. The thumbnail of the man who emailed looked promising. Her heart crept toward her throat. She liked this part. It was like opening up a little present.

Hello. My name is Colby. I am a simple guy. I like fishing and only own jeans, but I swear I have a job. I sell granite, stone, and other sorts of residential remodeling supplies. It sounds super boring so you know that I can't be making that part up. On the weekends, I take my dog walking around White Rock Lake and I'm enjoying some different shows on Netflix. I've been married once. No kids, unfortunately.

Let me know if you would like to meet up.

Best, Colby

P.S: W/E, FFA

Ardie read the email twice through. She wasn't usually drawn to "country guys," but she appreciated Colby's straightforward tone. And couldn't she picture herself learning to fish? Wouldn't Michael love that?

She didn't know what the post-script meant. These days, online dating was practically its own language. She typed the first acronym into her search bar. W/E.

The answer came swiftly: well-endowed.

Ardie let her head droop. *So close, Colby, so close.* The sense of disappointment was all too acute. Much as she and Sloane liked to make fun of millennials, online dating taught Ardie that younger people had an odd kind of resilience: impervious to some things, but completely open and vulnerable to virtually everything else.

She entered the second acronym into her browser anyway. FFA.

Fat Female Admirer.

Ardie pressed her lips together. She looked down at the curl of skin escaping over the waist of her slacks and then, for reference, at her own profile picture.

She wasn't bothered by the idea that she was fat. She was bothered that she didn't know it, as if her own body might have snuck up and changed without her noticing because she was, on the whole, alone, with nobody to track those types of changes aside from her. And what didn't seem fair, what felt horribly cruel, was that Ardie had already gone through every agonizing dating ritual in her twenties, whittled her way down through the pile of men that came and went. She had selected her person and he had selected her and that was supposed to mean she would never again have to worry about the rightness or wrongness of things like being fat, because for someone, for that one person, they were okay. She was okay. Until she wasn't.

Ardie closed her eyes. Tried to shut it out. But the thoughts were already there, filtering in like mist through a window screen.

She missed her husband. Or she missed being married. She wasn't sure she knew the difference anymore. Ardie missed talking to him while he took a shower. She missed watching television together. She missed regaling the only person in the world who cared as much as she did with a painstakingly detailed account of all the small, funny, and amazing things Michael had done that day. She missed waking up in the middle of the night beside a lump in her bed.

She just missed.

The office kitchen had a stylish finish, recently remodeled with matte green walls and stone backsplashes, sleek stainless-steel appliances Ardie wouldn't have splurged for in her own home. As a company, Truviv had a bit of a psychological complex. It was, by local accounts, a cool company, but one that would have been cooler in, say, Austin or Portland. It had a lovely but not ostentatious gym with a healthy assortment of group classes. It was a sports apparel brand, after all. It cultivated a quiet sense of health and refinement by disallowing smoking outside the building (smokers had to go up to one of the balconies — there was an image to uphold) and encouraging men to wear the signature dry-fit dress shirts under their suits. Sporty, but dignified, in Dallas, where no one had ever gone gaga for the foosball-table-and-cereal-bar craze of open-concept tech companies.

Ardie chose a ceramic mug from the cabinets. Last year, the company had also upgraded to Keurig machines, so she selected a pod that promised a pecan aroma and clamped it in. (Oh, how we loved free things like K-Cups and hand sanitizers and thanked god for purses in which to stuff them.) At home, Michael loved to operate the Keurig. He would be four in a couple of weeks and she'd been "pinning" images of superhero birthday parties and wondering if she was the sort of mom who made fake cities out of cardboard boxes. Her ex-husband's new wife, Braylee, was exactly that kind of person.

What kind of a name was Braylee, anyway? She wasn't even that young. Thirty-nine. As the scorned wife, Ardie felt entitled to mock her ex-husband's dumb bunny of a new wife. But Braylee worked in private equity and she wasn't young or dumb, which made it all the more irritating.

Braylee would be at the birthday party.

Ardie had been maintaining a vague sense of hope she'd find a date to Michael's party before the day arrived. A date! To her son's birthday!

As the Keurig groaned to life, Ardie saw Katherine coming into the kitchen. She had impeccable posture. Was impeccable posture a prerequisite to choosing a pixie cut? Ardie used her polite office smile and waved. "How are you settling in?"

The blue-white light of the refrigerator illuminated Katherine's cheeks and nose.

"Oh, um, fine. Thanks." Katherine reached in and selected a Coke Zero. "It's different, I guess," she said.

"I'm sure." Ardie could hardly think back to a time that she hadn't worked at Truviv. Even in law school, she'd known she wanted to make the switch from a firm to in-house as quickly as possible. Billable hours weren't for her. "Change can be good," she said. "If only for the Tex-Mex."

"Maybe."

"So, do you have any kids?" Ardie asked. People could be total curmudgeons at work, but get them talking about their children and they'd become suddenly human.

Katherine began opening drawers in the kitchen, searching for what, Ardie had no idea. She paused. "Are you allowed to ask me that?"

"I . . . think so, yes."

"Oh, then no. I don't." Katherine found a paper napkin, wrapped it around her aluminum can, and hip-checked the drawer back into place. "I'm not married, either." The faintest hint of a smile.

Ardie cleared her throat. "Me neither," she said. "So I guess that leaves only religion and sexual orientation to cover, then?"

Katherine squinted her eyes shut and gave a delicate laugh, then pushed her thumbs to her head. "Ow. Sorry." She shook her head as though embarrassed.

The door opened behind her, followed by the sound of men's shoes, a hiss-swish against tile, punctuated every few steps by the light tap of a heel.

"Ladies." Ames breezed past Ardie, heading for the family-sized jug of animal crackers on the far counter. Ardie was prone to noticing the most trivially human aspects of Ames Garrett. Like the tufts of gray hair sprouting on the backs of his hands. Or the fold of loose skin between his jaw and neck.

"How'd you like Savor? Cool place, right?" he asked Katherine, tilting his head back to pop one of the tiger, elephant, or lion cookies into his open mouth. "Ardie," he said by way of acknowledgment. "I actually know the owner." He chewed, looking again at Katherine.

"Yes, thanks for arranging it," Katherine replied. "It was nice of you to take the time." The noise of Ames chewing was too loud between the three of them.

"I don't know any of the cool places yet," she finished with a deferential nod. Sloane was right, of course. Katherine wasn't naturally warm or bubbly. She seemed like a woman trying to be taken seriously. This was a problem distinct to pretty, young women, Ardie had found, this carving out of a place outside of their good looks, while still wanting to take advantage of them.

"Stick with me, kid." A starburst of wrinkles spread congenially from the corners of Ames's eyes. "Feel free to stop by my office this afternoon. We can discuss next steps. We can even talk about that acquisition team you wanted to join, how about that?" Then — "Your coffee's finished," he said to Ardie, grabbing a Coke from the fridge. He hiss-swished again past her, pausing for a fraction of a second. "Only believe the nice things this one tells you about me, Katherine." And his laugh, it lingered for a split second after the door closed behind him.

Ardie glanced back at the coffee maker,

74

using her considerable expertise in the art of looking unfazed. Ames left invisible pricks on the surface of Ardie's skin and a vacuum of silence in his wake. "Well," she said, making the conscious effort to fill it and regain the sense of equilibrium. "If you need anything, don't hesitate."

Ardie turned to leave, trailing a ribbon of steam from her coffee cup behind her. As she was reaching the door, Katherine stopped her.

"Actually, Advil?" Katherine asked. "Sorry, I think I have a bit of a migraine coming on. I get them occasionally. Do you . . . happen to know if there are any painkillers around here?"

Ardie softened. She used to get migraines as a teenager. Nightmarish experiences. She could hardly function. Though was it possible, now that she thought about it, that there was more than the one drink last night? Sloane hadn't texted her when she got back to the office and Ardie had fallen asleep before she remembered to check.

Sloane had promised it would be only one. She studied Katherine.

"The cabinet on the top left." She pointed and Katherine pressed her fingers to her forehead and took a deep, relieved breath.

Ardie watched her for a moment, a pained

expression as she twisted the childproof top off a bottle of Advil. "Katherine," she said, having the sudden, pressing urge to lay claim to her before Ames did. "I'm having a birthday party for my four-year-old next weekend. Sloane and Grace will be there. Do you want to come?"

26-Apr

Ms. Sharpe: Please state your name.

Respondent 2: Adriana Valdez.

Ms. Sharpe: And how long have you been with the company, Ms. Valdez?

Respondent 2: I've worked at Truviv a little less than twelve years.

Ms. Sharpe: Impressive. How long did you know Katherine Bell before the incident?

Respondent 2: About a month, I think.

Ms. Sharpe: What was your impression of Miss Bell at the time you met?

Respondent 2: She was pleasant enough. She seemed bright, young, driven. She wasn't the super warm and bubbly type, but neither am I. I thought I understood her.

Ms. Sharpe: Would you say that over that month, you became friends with Miss Bell?

Respondent 2: I'm not sure

whether I would say that or not.

Ms. Sharpe: Can you elaborate?

Respondent 2: I believed that we developed a friendship at the time. However, certain things have come to light since.

Ms. Sharpe: Can you be more specific?

Respondent 2: Okay. Katherine lied.

CHAPTER SEVEN

21-Mar

It was lunchtime and Sloane was very close to running late to her personal training session with Oksana downstairs. She swung by her office to pick up her gym bag and collect the files she'd been intending to give to Katherine all morning. At drinks, Katherine had seemed eager, as though she could think of almost nothing *but* work. She wanted to parse the nitty-gritty details of deals on which Sloane had worked, how Sloane had started her career, the layout of the corporate legal structure. Katherine asked the same of Ames and he basked in the chance to tell war stories of long shot transactions that closed at the bottom of the ninth inning.

I want to be like you. Had Katherine really said that, as Sloane snatched a couple of mints from the hostess stand on their way out? They'd had two, maybe three drinks.

Why had she agreed to have so many? Ames had that effect on her. And then Katherine's face had been close to hers, expectant. Sloane might have misheard; she didn't want to ask her to repeat the compliment. And, well . . .

Katherine's office was empty now and Sloane's brain felt tender.

She stopped at the glass front wall of Grace's office. The glass, from which the corner-office types were conveniently exempt, was designed to make the building feel more open-concept, but was actually intended to reduce their privacy. Grace's door sat only a few paces down from Katherine's.

Sloane tapped on it. "Have you seen Katherine?" she asked.

Grace looked up. "Oh."

Grace's skin looked a little gray ever since she'd returned from maternity leave, like she'd been ill or living in an underground bunker. Not that Sloane would ever mention it. She'd once had to explain to Derek that telling a woman she looked "tired" was the same thing as telling her she looked awful. Just don't.

"She's in with Ames." Grace went back to typing. "How's Abigail doing?"

Sloane stared down the corridor at Ames's

80

closed door, Katherine behind it.

Doing what? She shook her head, frustrated. It was nothing. Ames was their boss. *Their.* All of the lawyers in the legal department. But, then, Sloane knew what could happen with Ames behind closed doors.

She ducked back into Grace's office. "Sorry, what'd you say?" Sloane turned back.

"I asked how Abigail was doing."

Sloane had been a teensy bit cagey about Abigail recently. *Well, Grace,* Sloane imagined saying, *she rolled her eyes at me for the first time this morning. Over a bowl of oatmeal, no less. At me, if you can believe it. Her super cool, super fun mother.* And Grace would laugh good-naturedly and say, *Oh, god, they grow up fast, don't they?* Only that wasn't it, because Abigail did not grow up fast. She grew up slowly. Painfully so at times, it had seemed. She didn't walk until she was eighteen months. At ten, she still enjoyed watching the Disney Channel and weaving colorful potholders on a loom. She tended to be dreamy and liked to fold herself close to the ground to push pill bugs around with sticks. And Sloane was just supposed to *believe* that this new, sulky Abigail chose to emerge directly after the school Incidents, those nasty, ugly text messages, by — *what?*

— coincidence?

She was overreacting, that was what people wanted to say to her face. Maybe she was. That was the problem with being a parent, wasn't it? All the schools of thought floating around — *Stop bullying! Prepare your child for the bullies! High fructose corn syrup will literally kill your innocent children in their sleep!* — and apparently you were just expected to pluck one from the sky and go with it.

She might have told all this to Grace, but stopped short. Grace Stanton had never been picked on. She'd been a literal pageant queen back in middle school. And though Grace was kind, telling Grace, of all people, about Abigail felt like a betrayal of her daughter. She couldn't bear the thought that, even for the most fleeting of moments, even just in her own mind, Grace might think a little less of Abigail.

"She's doing great. She's playing Bach's March in D Major for her piano recital next week." *Or maybe it was Beethoven's in G Major.* "Anyway, I've got an appointment." She turned to go and hesitated. "Oh yeah, did you ever get that spreadsheet?"

Grace pressed her knuckle into the corner of her eye and blinked. "Nothing's shown up in my inbox." She yawned. "But I forgot to ask around."

"Mine, either."

"Maybe we're not cool enough. Maybe we're too old."

"Bite your tongue," Sloane said. "Tell Katherine I was looking for her, all right? Papers on her desk. Please review with comments."

Grace pressed her lips into a thin line and saluted, but even her arm at attention looked wilted. Sloane set a mental reminder to check in on Grace, just as a friend. Sloane was Emma Kate's godmother, after all. She should tell Grace she was dying to smell Emma Kate's breath again. Before the baby got too old and sprouted teeth. Or rolled her eyes.

But Sloane knew she was terrible at keeping up with mental reminders. Her life was empty water bottles rolling around on the floorboards of her expensive car. Unopened mail on kitchen countertops. Thank you cards written but never sent. In the back of her mind, she was already moving on, adding this mental reminder to the detritus of unfinished tasks to be recycled into background stress, where it would serve as fuel for her spotty and unexplained bouts of insomnia, chin acne, and stomach bloating.

■ ■ ■ ■

Truviv's corporate gym, a yawning space of indoor track, state-of-the-art machinery, and brightly-colored mats, was located on the building's eighth floor, where it could mock us as we passed it on the elevator. We hated the gym. We loved it. We escaped to it. We avoided it. We had complicated relationships with our bodies, while at the same time insisting that we loved them unconditionally. We were sure we had better, more important things to do than worry about them, but the slender yoga bodies of moms in Lululemon at school pickup taunted us. Their figures hinted at wheatgrass shots, tennis clubs, and vagina steaming treatments. We found them aspirational.

So we sweated on the elliptical and lifted ten-pound weights, inching closer to the bodies we told ourselves we were too evolved to want. We knew the men watched us in our yoga pants, knew they believed this was why we wore yoga pants in the first place. We pretended not to notice the feeling of eyes sliding over us. If we heard "I like your form" from one more male co-worker who fiddled with his playlists for ten minutes in between sets, well, we might bash his brain in with a dumbbell.

Sloane swiped her fob on the keypad and the door to the locker room clicked open. An endless loop of *Keeping Up with the Kardashians* reruns played on the flat-screen television above the sinks.

Sloane slipped out of her black, lace-trimmed skirt and hung it inside a top locker. Derek had complimented her on it this morning, running his hands over her hips while she brushed her teeth. Then they'd had nice, married people sex — quick, satisfying, and to the point — because they were each half-listening for Abigail. Sloane had an orgasm and dropped Abigail off for band practice all before 8 AM.

"Sloane!"

She turned at the sound of her name.

The woman in the towel and flip-flops walking toward her was Ames's wife, Bobbi Garrett. Bobbi had a throaty voice and the authentic Southern drawl of someone from Oklahoma instead of Texas. She was a stay-at-home mom of twins, two boys, who filled her time with do-gooder tasks where she raised indisputably large sums of cash for worthy causes and made people like Sloane feel terrible for snarking on the annoying spectacle of charitable social events. Bobbi Garrett was a perfectly pleasant person to

85

be around for anyone but Sloane Glover.

"I just came to meet Ames for lunch and he let me sneak a quick workout." Her skin had the red, blotchy quality of someone who has taken a cool shower after a hard workout. "How are *you,* doll?" Bobbi gently pushed her arm.

"Oh, you know, hanging in there." Sloane sounded like a robot. A dull robot. But she didn't know how else to speak to Bobbi; every time Sloane saw Bobbi, she was transported back in time to an image of a shirtless Ames, hovering over her, his hips pressed into hers. And she was filled with instant shame followed by something subtler. She felt the lies stacked between her and Bobbi wrestling to get out.

"Is my husband working you too hard?" Bobbi was watching Sloane with concerned eyes. "I swear, I will get on that man. You have a husband and kids, and, lord, well, you know how men can be. They have to be *reminded.*"

There were other women in the locker room. Women padding barefoot around them, weighing themselves, poking earrings back through their lobes. But Bobbi didn't intuit the unspoken protocol of shared workspaces. Sloane gave a silent thank you to those damn Kardashians babbling in the background.

"No, no, just a crazy time," said Sloane, pulling on her Truviv-branded running shorts. "No fault of Ames, I promise."

It was never the fault of Ames. If there were ever an issue at work, Sloane was, according to him, "irrational," "hypersensitive," "ridiculous," and even, once, *"hormonal."* Funny how those words had never come up before she'd slept with him.

Bobbi's hand flew to her mouth. The fingernails were perfectly manicured in cherry red. "Desmond," she said, taking hold of Sloane's forearm. Bobbi closed her eyes and shook her head with utter dismay. "I can't believe he's gone. Are you doing okay?"

"Yes, I really am."

"Good. My Bible study met last night, purely by coincidence, and we prayed over that man's sweet family."

Sloane was trying to hold on to the memory of Derek this morning. The smell of his sandalwood shaving cream lingering on his face. She wished that Grace were here. Grace was so much better at this. She actually went to church, for one, while Sloane enjoyed her family's Sunday ritual of bacon, eggs, and lounging in front of the television. But every so often, Sloane was confronted with the particular vocabulary of the upper-middle-class Christian women in town. People were always being "called" or having things "laid upon their heart" or were "praying over" one thing or another. Sloane learned years ago to integrate work vocabulary into her own vernacular: she would "liaise directly" with someone or "reach out" or "provide color" or "digest" a report. Easy. But she'd never grown fluent in Bobbi's language. Now she felt put at a small disadvantage.

"I wanted to ask," Bobbi continued. "Have you heard anything about a meal train?"

"I haven't heard anything. But . . ." Sloane said, uncertainly, "I'm sure Desmond's family would appreciate it."

Bobbi held up her hand. "Consider it done. Listen." She pulled Sloane off to a less populated area of the locker room, where clean, folded towels were stuffed into cubbyholes. Bobbi pressed her face in closer to Sloane, as though they were used to sharing secrets. "I'm sure Ames has already told you, probably even before me. I know how closely you two work together." She imagined relaying this to Ardie later on, how Ardie would hoot with dark appreciation. "But Ames is on the short list, apparently, for potential replacements for Desmond. He was notified by the board late last night. I just know Ames would make a wonderful CEO."

Ames. CEO. Sloane felt her mind wading through quicksand; she focused all her energy on keeping her face still, a talent she'd honed a time or two when, for example, the man whose wife she was speaking to had once reminded her she was still a better lay than she was a lawyer, this despite the fact that she had, at the time, closed a twenty-*million*-dollar deal almost single-handedly on a one-month deadline. For her efforts that year, she had received only a frozen ham and a crystal coaster with the company logo emblazoned on it. Later, she learned that Ames had "forgotten" to submit the letter approving her year-end discretionary income. When confronted, he reminded her that she had — his words — *used* him to sleep her way into a high-paying position and considered the bonus snafu a karmic effort to even the score.

If only that had been the end of it.

"Honestly," Bobbi was saying, "it feels like everything has been leading up to this for us. But if there's anything you think we, or *he,* should be doing to better his odds? I know he'd appreciate your counsel, even if he's too proud to ask for it. He's just under a lot of pressure."

"Right, well." Sloane leaned back on her heels, trying to create physical distance. She felt hot. "It's a bit above my pay grade," she said.

Bobbi's expression froze ever so slightly.

"But yes," Sloane added in a rush, "of course, I'll be sure to reach out." She saw the need for an exit plan and she took it. "Bobbi, I have to — I have to get back to the office soon, so I better get to it."

Bobbi smiled her big, chemically whitened smile. "Of course, of course. You look fantastic, by the way," she said, which was a blatant lie. Sloane did not look fantastic, or even good. A lie for Bobbi, Sloane thought. Another thousand and maybe they could even the score.

Sloane snatched her gym bag and shut herself in one of the privacy changing rooms, heat crawling up her neck like a fever. She sank down, back to the wall, crouched, breathing heavily. Ames, as the freaking CEO of Truviv — why hadn't she seen it coming? She bit her teeth into her knuckles. It shouldn't matter to her, should it? She told herself it shouldn't matter. But it felt so unfair. She sounded like a pre-schooler: *but that's not fair!* But . . . it wasn't.

Bad behavior rewarded and whatnot. Of course, whose fault was that? Hers, was it? Certainly she had never been anything but a silent witness on Ames's behalf. Certainly she had made a decision to let him get away with acting however the hell he wanted to act. Though, it occurred to her, she might not be the only one. She wasn't the only one. Surely. Definitely. She had been about to call Derek when — better idea — she dialed Elizabeth Moretti's number. Elizabeth answered on the first ring. "What do you have for me, Glover?"

Back at Jaxon Brockwell, Elizabeth had a piece of the entire firm's gossip and Sloane learned quickly to temper what she told Elizabeth, who wasn't nearly as discreet as she pretended to be.

Sloane closed her eyes and took a deep breath before answering. "Nothing billable, I'm afraid." She stood up, turned her back to the locked door behind her, and hunched her shoulders protectively around her phone. "Elizabeth," she said, voice low. "What do you know about a spreadsheet?"

"I know nothing about spreadsheets other than I went to law school specifically to avoid them." Sloane could hear Elizabeth typing on the other end of the line.

"Something about a spreadsheet of men

— sleazy men maybe — in Dallas. Does that . . ." Sloane's phone vibrated and she lifted it from her ear to find a notification that her battery was about to die. Shit.

"Oh. Yes. The BAD Men List."

"*Bad* men?"

"Beware of Asshole Dallas Men. BAD Men! I may have seen it floating around."

"Where'd you get it from?" Sloane tapped the screen to silence the message that felt like an admonishment: *get your life together!*

"You know I never disclose my sources." Sloane did not actually know that at all.

She squeezed one eye shut, chewing on a nail, which was getting jagged between her teeth. She just wanted to see it, she told herself. A quick check. Then she'd know.

She heard Elizabeth stop to chew something on the other end of the line and imagined her former mentor's horse teeth grinding through her handful of afternoon pretzels. "Sloane, do you want me to get it for you? This list?"

"Only if it's not too much trouble."

"Consider it done. But don't tell anyone you got it from me." They were both quiet. Then Elizabeth started typing again. "Hey," she asked, "is it true Bankole died in his shower?"

■ ■ ■ ■

As Sloane left the locker room to meet her trainer, Ames stood at the entrance of the gym, leaning against the wall, with his arms folded over his tie, waiting for his wife. Their eyes met. He flattened his lips together into what could pass as a smile of acknowledgement without actually being one. And again, like yesterday, Sloane felt the old fury stirring at the sight of him, like a soda bottle shaken up, the cap still secured.

The thing that had done it were box seats at a Mavericks game. Ames had scored them from his boss because, back then, he wasn't quite the boss he was now. They both *hated* the crab cakes and canapés served upstairs and had wandered down to the breezeway amid a heated debate over the appropriate hotdog condiments. Sloane should have known she was in trouble right at that moment. No two people of the opposite sex argue over subjects as mundane as condiments unless they want to sleep together.

Downstairs with the masses, they purchased real basketball game fare and felt prouder of themselves than they should have. Ames used to be funny. That was something people forgot. He had been

93

handsome, too. The kind that could make Sloane's stomach flip. They had returned to the box seats, Ames clutching the neck of a champagne bottle they'd talked the bartender into selling them. Sloane's sides had ached with laughter. She wore a shiny new engagement ring, given to her by a man who loved her, trusted her, and would need her financially from now until eternity. She felt powerful. She felt like she wanted to blow shit up.

She was an idiot, of course. She hadn't been the first, she would learn. Women whose names she couldn't even remember if she tried. She'd just been smart enough to keep her mouth shut. Mostly, anyway. The damage had been maintained. Sloane played by the rules of the game. And so *she* got to stay. She got to keep her seat at the table.

But now, it was like her body was rehashing a decade's worth of experiences with Ames, right up to the closed door she'd witnessed this afternoon, with Katherine somewhere behind it. Katherine who wanted to be just like her. Up until this point, when Ames had stepped out of line, Sloane could bring him back to heel with the subtle suggestion that she could, if she were so inclined, speak to Desmond. She wouldn't, but . . . she could. Now Desmond no longer existed. And nothing felt fair. And yet Sloane felt she'd actually earned, and therefore deserved, this eventuality: Ames rising the ranks higher and, now, highest, while she watched on. Saying nothing.

Over the next forty-five minutes, Sloane channeled it all into sumo squats, dead lifts, burpees, and walking lunges until her time had run out and her trainer, Oksana, was congratulating her on one of her best workouts to date.

Sloane did feel better. Emptier. Cleaner, even. This was the thing we all loved about exercising, the way it could push everything else out except for the one pressing, present matter — the hurt.

It was only after Sloane chugged a bottle of water, cooled herself down under the shower, and had gotten dressed again that she pulled her phone out of her bag and checked for emails. There it was, at the top of her inbox, in bold type, an email from Elizabeth Moretti. Email chain, blind copy.

B.A.D. MEN: BEWARE OF ASSHOLES. ASSHOLES, BEWARE

Truviv Employee Statements

13-Apr

Lucy Davies: Of *course* it started with the spreadsheet. That thing was a disaster from day one. Honestly, I told anyone who would listen. I said that it was a terrible idea. I did! Vigilante justice, and all that. But did anyone listen to me? No. And now look!

Keith Tran: I don't know. Maybe. If it was the spreadsheet, then I guess the takeaway is that what happened could have happened to any one of us. That's what scares me.

Angie Mann: Yes, we were aware of the spreadsheet that had been circulating and we took the allegations regarding those named seriously. However, I'll add that we took the rights of our employees whose names appeared on the list equally seriously. There are two sides to every coin.

Sophia Ventura: Yeah, we were all going a little crazy. Who

wouldn't be? It was like, okay, here's this guy's name on the list and he did God knows what and, oh wait, now I have to go into his office *alone* mind you and ask him if he'd like his pages collated? But, also, I mean, think of it this way: it wasn't like this was going on in just our office. Men's names were popping up from all over the city, but I bet you're not going around asking questions at all those offices, am I right?

Alexandra Souls: I think everyone needs to start taking responsibility for their actions and stop blaming an Excel file for this entire fiasco. I mean, we're all supposedly adults here.

CHAPTER EIGHT

23-Mar

There were men in the office. They worked at desks alongside us. They populated the human resources department, accounting, compliance, and information technology, they worked above us and below us. But there was an invisible separation between the men and us. So we found each other. If the workplace was the traditional purview of the old boys' club, we responded by forming a secret sorority. We recognized the secret handshake. We saw each other as sisters in arms.

Of course, let's not forget the good men: the ones who laughed at our jokes and asked our drafting advice, who didn't think of motherhood as a handicap, who had wives that worked hour-intensive jobs, who handled their half of the housework, who were happily married or gay. They didn't open meetings by complaining about female-cast movie reboots or ask us to take just-one-call during our maternity leaves. But even the good ones — especially the good ones? — pretended not to notice the lines: how much more deference they earned on the phone for having a male voice. Or how their height and stature and morning stubble gave an authoritative weight to their ideas that ours never had. If brought to their attention, the good ones would wave off such observations with humble embarrassment and tell us how much smarter and better we were than them. They were our colleagues and some were even our friends.

But these lines did exist. And not only in our heads. No matter how expertly we pretended to be cool with dirty jokes, how convincingly we proved to be comfortable with confrontation without being confrontational, no matter how adept our impersonations of our male colleagues, there was often something in our performance of competency and belonging that the men in our offices didn't quite buy into. They thought they could see right through us. They thought they knew us. They thought they could predict us. Especially someone like Grace, whose heart so often seemed written clearly across her face.

Grace couldn't remember the last time she'd told a lie. A real, bona fide lie. Until now.

"I'm working late, Liam, an all-nighter, I'm sorry. There's breast milk in the fridge," Grace had said. Of course, her husband had been properly incensed on her behalf. How could they expect this of her? It was completely unreasonable. Hadn't she explained to them that she was a *new* mother?

People were always reminding Grace that she was a new mother.

Three weeks ago, when she confessed to Liam that, actually, *no,* she did not think she could get up anymore to feed Emma Kate, that she would rather listen to the baby cry, he'd squeezed her shoulder and said, "You're tired. It's okay to feel this way." And she had thought, along with the rest of us: how convenient to always have a man nearby to explain our pesky emotions! He kissed her temple, and told her she was an amazing mommy.

Then she and Liam took Emma Kate to her four-month checkup — weeks late — and Dr. Tanaka had handed Liam a glossy, routine pamphlet listing the warning signs for postpartum depression: Prolonged sadness, helplessness, unexplained episodes of crying. An increase or decrease in appetite.

Inability to sleep when tired. Concerns that the mother will harm the baby, herself, or others. It was all quite interesting, Grace thought. Very informative. But . . . not Grace. "You're making motherhood look easy. Your daughter is right on track," the doctor had said. So that was it. Everything was as it should be because if it weren't, surely Dr. Tanaka would have noticed. He was the best pediatrician in Dallas. She'd made sure of it.

The idea came to her a week earlier, when Liam had casually inquired as to when they'd start thinking about having another baby. Grace was no spring chicken, he'd said, though he'd used nicer words because, of course, Liam was a *good* person. Throughout her entire pregnancy, he'd been fastidious in assuring her how beautiful she was. He'd been the expectant father who went out at ten o'clock and came back with milkshakes like he was earning a merit badge for his efforts. Those late night food runs meant Liam's own gut had grown during the nearly ten months she'd carried Emma Kate, and for a CrossFit devotee like Liam, it was, Grace thought, the nicest thing he'd ever done for her.

But the talk of a second baby alarmed her. They hadn't even had sex since Emma

101

Kate's birth. The doctor cleared her for "sexual activity" several weeks ago, but she hadn't told Liam yet. Maybe she was more of a liar than she thought.

Grace realized there simply wasn't a clinical diagnosis for selfishness. And since that was apparently her affliction, she decided to fucking treat it herself.

The hotel room cost a whopping six hundred and fifty dollars for the night. A few days ago, she'd snatched one of the credit card offers from the mailbox, one marked "Pre-Approved" in obnoxious letters. She filled it out during one of her pumping breaks at the office, then slid the card into her wallet. At that moment of crucial betrayal, her baby had woken up six times the previous night, seven the one before that. She read in a *Post* article that it was sleep deprivation not waterboarding that ultimately got Al Qaeda members to talk. The promise of a nap. She understood. She gave up. Her baby had broken her.

Her brain had felt like cotton and ached between her temples. So exhausted was she that Grace had been queasy, the contents of her half-eaten breakfast swimming in the pit of her stomach. Coffee only sparked an uncomfortable buzz coursing beneath the thick, milky coat of fatigue. She now craved sleep more than she ever had cupcakes.

It was a gorgeous hotel, with an infinity pool, a celebrity-chef restaurant, and free champagne in the lobby. She hadn't seen a point in doing it halfway. If Grace Stanton were going to hell, it wouldn't be over a night at a Holiday Inn.

Last night, Grace padded around in the downy hotel slippers and thought: so this is how people begin affairs. At first she'd promised herself it would be a one-night stand. But by the time she'd opened a bottle of chardonnay (she didn't skimp here either, leaping straight for the $75 section of the room service menu), she fully intended to continue this sordid tryst with herself.

I will leave my husband for you, she'd told the aromatherapy treated bathtub. *We'll run away together. We're soul mates. There's just this one issue of my breasts keeping my child alive, but, just give me a couple months to sort things out. You'll see. I promise. I love you.*

This morning, she woke up as the sun curled around the edges of the blackout curtains. She pulled the sheets up to her nose. They were store-bought white and smelled like expensive French parfum. A shiver of satisfaction curled her toes as she thought of how much Liam must have missed her when he was changing diapers and feeding bottles at two, then three-thirty, then five AM.

At last, she sat up and ordered room service — a croissant with butter and apricot jelly and a cappuccino. Her breasts ached. Small knots had formed in the tissue. She pressed on them gently and winced.

She would be late to work, very late. *Burn it all to the ground,* she'd thought last night when she hadn't set an alarm. But as she got out of bed, she was feeling less rebellious. And as she got dressed, a clean black sheath and pearls, she felt fresh darkness spreading inside her stomach, like oil.

Grace tried to picture Emma Kate.

Her child's eyes were still strange to her. Two marbles encased in a wrinkly alien head. Constantly staring, constantly expecting the love to which she ought to be entitled. A reasonable expectation, Grace conceded, for a child who had been born into a stable family with a healthy mother in her mid-thirties. It wasn't as though Emma Kate had been a surprise. Grace kept her calendar meticulously. Even having a girl was preordained. Liam had laughed, but Grace learned all the tricks: she committed to an ungodly amount of Crystal Light and yogurt during those fertile days. And Sloane, who of course had Abigail, advised her to orgasm after Liam, which had taken some doing. After one ultrasound, when the doctor delivered an envelope to Grace, she already knew it'd be a girl. Liam had dreamed of a little girl, too, and he had actually teared up when she told him the news. And when Grace had slid the ultrasound envelope over Sloane's desk for her and Ardie to see, they had literally shrieked. Well, Sloane had, anyway. And there were immediate plans to raise girls together, use Abigail as a babysitter, and for Michael and Emma Kate to get married someday. It had all been perfectly lovely. Exactly as she'd always planned.

All this and still, sometimes she wanted to stare back at Emma Kate and caution her: don't get carried away. Against all indications, Emma Kate had most surely not won the parental lottery.

If it was any consolation, nothing had exactly been as advertised to Grace, either. In college, she'd been treasurer of her campus's TriDelt chapter and, ever since, she'd missed the natural connection shared with a large group of women. When she'd given birth to Emma Kate, she wept happily along with Liam, and even secretly rejoiced. Finally. She'd be admitted into the biggest, most important sorority of them all — motherhood. She imagined stroller exercise classes and Mommy & Me yoga. Easter egg hunts in April. A gorgeous christening gown and Grace standing at the front of the church, cradling her baby's bonneted head. The perfect family.

But Grace instead felt separated, cut off, from virtually all other mothers. She stared at the happy, loving mothers at church, holding their adorable children's hands, sweet little girls in stockings and patent leather shoes, and tried to figure out what the hell she was missing.

What was so *worth* it? Because from where Grace was standing, she couldn't square her big, saggy boobs, pudgy stomach, leaky urinary tract, dark circles, sporadic mastitis, and cracking nipples, coupled with the fact that it now took her legitimately two hours to get out of the house with her baby in tow, and she had to listen to screeching cries whenever she stole into the shower, and she was no longer welcome in restaurants with tablecloths, with the baby who was skinny, eczema riddled; she dribbled cloudy liquid from the corners of her mouth and barely even smiled. She wanted to feel that connection, but the closest she'd come was the first time Emma Kate had gripped her finger and it had lasted only that long. Grace felt like an idiot for believing that there was some magic to the math. Some alchemy that made this all, as everyone had told her, worth it.

If Grace felt a kinship with any mothers at all since Emma Kate's birth, it was with the ones that drove their minivans into a lake.

Grace only had a canvas tote bag stuffed with yesterday's clothes, along with makeup and toiletries and her manual pump. She gave a final glance to the fluffy bed, the clean, folded towels, and the assortment of Lavazza coffee inserts, dreading the return to her own house where dirty diapers clogged the genie and spit-up stained the throw pillows.

At the end of the hall, she pressed the button at the elevator bank, walked into the roving glass case, and was startled to recognize the other woman in the elevator.

"Katherine?" Grace felt a hint of delight, as if she'd run into an acquaintance at the airport or at a far-off vacation or in Target. An amusing life juxtaposition.

Katherine stood with her back to the glass, looking stiff. A spark of recognition flashed in her eyes. "Hi," she said.

"Grace," she filled in the blank for her. "Sorry, I'm sure you've met a thousand people in the last few days."

"Oh, no, I wasn't —" Katherine waved the end of the sentence away. Her skin was face-wash-commercial fresh, her hair parted neatly to the side. She wore only studs for earrings, which seemed daringly sparse and editorial amid the sea of swinging Kendra Scott jewelry, in vogue among Dallas women these days.

The elevator dinged at the lobby floor. A tame, babbling stream ran from a marbled buttress and trickled water into a glimmering blue pool filled with koi fish. The atrium smelled like an upscale Vegas casino, all recycled air and manufactured fragrance.

"What are you doing here?" Katherine asked.

Grace considered another lie, but none came readily to her. "I needed a night off," she admitted. "I have a baby who has taken up arms against sleep." A couple sleepless nights back at home with Emma Kate and Grace knew she'd again be lost in the quagmire of exhaustion, trying to bump and feel her way through her days.

The corners of Katherine's mouth curled up. "What's her weapon of choice?"

"Lungs of steel. It's obvious but ruthlessly effective." Grace paused before the sliding glass doors that led out to the valet and the city beyond. Outside, the sun blazed. "Sometimes I just can't with her. It's like I —" Grace shuddered.

"Hate her?"

"I sound horrible." And she did feel horrible — like a horrible, horrible mother — but she probably didn't feel horrible *enough,* and that made her feel even worse, though again, *not* as badly as she should feel. She had the thought that if she didn't like being a mother — and she could nearly admit that to herself now — at least she could excel at how awful she'd feel about it. She could compete in the Guilt Olympics. Maybe even medal. But, in truth, she was usually too tired even to attempt that. "I didn't exactly tell my husband," she added, sheepishly.

Katherine looked impressed. "That you weren't coming home?"

Grace flattened her hand against her cheek, partially embarrassed, partially not. "No, I told him that part. But" — she squinted one eye closed. "I might have said I had to pull an all-nighter at work." Which was so far from the truth it was almost comical. Ever since her return, she felt like Sloane and Ardie treated her with kid gloves, spared from any work of urgency or interest, as if she must be desperate to return home to her newborn. Her precious, alien newborn.

"Ah." Katherine nodded, her mouth quirking mischievously. "Your secret's safe with me."

Grace felt a pathetic tug at her heartstrings, enjoying the taste of a secret, which, when shared, in her experience, almost always portended new friendship.

"And you?" Grace asked.

"The condo that I'm moving into isn't ready yet. It's a new building. I have a friend who hooked me up. I'm crashing here until I can move in."

"The Prescott? Swanky."

"Yeah. It is. But they've put me in a room way up at the top." She tilted her chin. The center of the Prescott was a gaping hole that shot straight to the sky-lighted ceiling. "I'm terrified of heights. Those glass elevators? It's like I'm plummeting to my death."

"Want to switch places with me?" Grace asked. "I'll gladly take over your hotel room and you can stay with my husband while you try to negotiate a treaty between my daughter and bedtime. Sloane mentioned you're a bit of an expert." Grace hoped that she didn't come across as trying too hard.

Compliments could be tricky too early in a relationship and it was no different with friendship.

"At negotiation, maybe," Katherine said. "At children, definitely not. Children and I don't get along, actually."

Grace looked out again, distractedly, to where the real world was waiting. She already felt the tightness forming in her chest.

"Well," she said after a short pause. "We should probably get going. Sloane may have already reported me missing by now. A few more minutes and she'll have called out the National Guard."

Katherine reached into her purse and pulled out a pink valet ticket. "We can't have that," she said. "That would blow your cover."

"My cover?" Grace twisted the clasp of her necklace around to sit on the knots of bone at the back of her neck.

"With your husband?" Katherine wrinkled her nose like a bunny's. It was a decidedly cute expression for a woman in her thirties. "You told him you were at work."

Grace pressed the heel of her hand to her forehead. "God, you're right."

There was an edge of laughter in both their voices now. Grace felt a small spark.

As though her cord had finally reached an outlet that had been too far away. She was already looking forward to asking Katherine out for a glass of wine or to go shopping in Highland Park Village. This was why she'd always been a girl's girl — she was good at it. It occurred to her, in a moment of clarity, that maybe what she'd been looking for wasn't to connect with other mothers at all.

Katherine led them out to the valet stand. The breeze was unseasonably warm for February. The smell of grease foreshadowed client lunches, which always took place at a civilized eleven-thirty in the morning. A gunmetal Jaguar idled in the porte cochere. An unspoken advertisement for the hotel.

As the two young men sprinted off in the direction of the parking lot, Katherine folded her arms and looked out at the street. "You've been at Truviv a while?"

Grace hunted absently for her car keys before realizing they were with the valet. "Six years."

"So, is everyone always this *nice*?"

Grace laughed. "For the most part, yes. It's a good group." Southern people were almost competitively nice and Grace and her family were considered top-flight. "Not so much at your old job?"

Katherine looked, for a moment, like she

112

didn't know how to answer the question. "It's not that, exactly. Just looking for a fresh start." She began to say something else, but the valet pulled up in Grace's car with a screech. Both women jumped back, Grace's arm stretching protectively out in front of Katherine's chest.

"Sorry." Grace's cheeks pinked. The reaction had clearly been that of a carpooling mother and she'd managed to treat Katherine — Harvard Law *Katherine* — as a child incapable of looking both ways before crossing the road.

"It's fine," Katherine said, smoothing her dress. "If you'd been a colleague at my old job, you'd have pushed."

And Grace laughed because the idea was ridiculous. Of course.

SUBPOENA DOCUMENT

21-January
Ms. Katherine Bell
2337 Windsor Street
Boston, MA 02101

Ms. Bell:
Your employment with Frost Klein & Roget ("Frost Klein") will officially be terminated as of today's date.

You are hereby notified that you have been terminated for cause.

You will not receive payment for the remaining balance of leave pay you have accumulated. Your health care benefits will remain in effect for 0 days.

Please review the nondisclosure agreement you signed upon hiring. According to this agreement, you are not to disclose any firm trade secrets, practices, or methods of operation. Frost Klein is entitled to take legal action if it is revealed that you discussed trade secrets during or after employment.

Sincerely,
Alan Ziegler
Managing Partner
Frost Klein & Roget

CHAPTER NINE

23-Mar

No productive day began with a morning appointment outside of the office. Sloane knew this. She had made peace with it.

Or at least she thought she had, before she'd begun watching the unread emails stack up in her inbox, reproducing like fruit flies. That her day would be trashed was already a foregone conclusion and it wasn't even eleven AM yet. Probably some kind of record.

From where she sat, the school office smelled of cheese. The chairs were too small and too square and it was impossible not to get the sense that droves of crumbs lurked in the carpeting. A horseshoe linoleum counter separated the waiting area from the office staff, who were very busy stapling and ignoring ringing telephones.

Sloane sat with her purse squashed in her lap, already feeling chastened. "Remember,

Abigail," she told her daughter, who was poking at her smartphone. "You don't have to say anything. If you have a question, whisper it to me or Ms. Ardie." This would be the first meeting with Abigail actually *in* attendance and, while it was one thing to take up Sloane's time, it was quite another that her daughter should be expected to spend hers.

Abigail peered around her mother to look at Ardie. "Mom says I can tell you anything and you can't tell, not even to her, because you're my lawyer."

"I didn't say *exactly* that."

Abigail was a perfectly normal looking ten-year-old girl: crooked teeth, pink popsicle lips, and a smattering of freckles on her nose that Sloane guessed from experience would fade during college. She was kicking her shoes out with nervous energy. They were new Converses, ungodly expensive for a ten-year-old's sneakers, and they might as well have been included on the mandatory school supply list, right next to "composition notebook" and "Lilly Pulitzer thermos." When she was on a tear, Sloane swore to Derek that they were going to flee the Park Cities and escape to the countryside. But then there was the matter of the mortgage — secured, thanks to Sloane, at a competitive rate — and her job, three cell phone plans, car payments, and, then, Derek and Sloane truly did love the steelhead trout at Fearing's . . . so she supposed that Converses weren't such a big deal, really.

"That's exactly right, Abigail." Ardie ignored Sloane. "I'm sure we can think of lots of secrets to share."

"Like how Mom and Dad have secrets that they can't tell me!" Abigail's shoes kicked harder. "Only *we'll* be the ones who can't tell."

Ardie grinned and sat back. "I'm going to need some follow-up on those. Sounds juicy."

"Only if you're interested in where Mom and Dad hide the vodka." Sloane extracted lipstick from her purse and applied it without using a mirror. "How do I look?" She turned to Ardie and puckered her lips. Recently, Sloane noticed she had to keep her lipstick fresh, or the color seeped out into the tiny wrinkles starting to form around her lips.

Ardie, who wore almost no makeup and didn't even dye the grays in her hair, gave her best not-impressed face. One of her signatures. "You do know we're at your daughter's school, right? I think Judge Judy took the day off."

Sloane cocked her head. "I don't usually tolerate this sort of attitude from outside counsel, you know."

She was joking, but not convincingly. This thing with Abigail was a serious matter and Sloane was taking it seriously. Deadly seriously.

At their first meeting with the principal, they'd learned Abigail wasn't the only recipient of the messages. The girls in her class were *experimenting* with *new words,* apparently. That was small consolation for Sloane. Other girls may have been able to handle that brand of twenty-first-century playground cruelty, but her sensitive Abigail? "Eggshell skull syndrome," her torts professor had called it in law school. The idea that if you struck a person in the head and it broke their skull, it didn't matter that the same blow wouldn't have cracked most other people's skulls. The injured person's unexpected frailty wasn't a valid defense to the seriousness of any injury caused to them. Abigail had the eggshell skull.

Today was the follow-up, and when Derek found out he couldn't be here — a conflict with the middle school's state testing — he suggested the perfect solution: "Bring Ardie." Ardie *wa*s so much steadier than

Sloane, she agreed. Like how Ardie wore the perfume of a much older woman, dried roses and spice, while Sloane had a vague self-awareness that she sometimes gave off an unintended air of frivolity, down to the carelessly chosen sample-sized perfume choices that she cycled through every day of the week.

The door to their left swung open.

"Sloane Glover? The principal's ready for you."

Sloane stood up so quickly she felt dizzy.

"Easy," Ardie murmured beside her.

Sloane took a deep, steadying breath and the three of them filed into a small, gray office that overlooked the playground.

Sloane spoke first. She nearly always did. "Principal Clark," she said. "This is our attorney, Ardie Valdez."

Principal Clark stood, adjusted his tie, and extended a hand to Ardie. He was black and tall, purposefully bald, but with strands of white flecking his trimmed beard. Sloane found herself inexplicably checking his ring finger: unoccupied. He'd be such a cute match for Ardie. If Sloane weren't so angry with him and threatening to sue, of course.

"I'm sure her presence isn't necessary," Clark said. "This is only an opportunity for us to meet to discuss Abigail's progress."

They all stared at Abigail, whose ankles were crossed under her chair. She looked nervous and uncomfortable, like a cat doused in water.

Ardie pulled up a seat. "And the school's progress. We can't forget that part."

Sloane beamed. Point for Ardie right at the start of the match. Not that Sloane was competitive.

"Correct." He cleared his throat and stared down at a stack of papers on his desk. Sloane herself sometimes used the same stalling tactic. *Stare down, shuffle, shuffle, and, ah, here we are, finally let's begin.* "I'll start, then," he said. "The school has recently sent out flyers targeted at both parents and students to discuss the parameters on students' expected social media conduct. Parents are being asked to monitor accounts and maintain passwords."

A legal pad had appeared on Ardie's lap. "And what about enforcement?"

He nodded as though he'd been about to get there. "For the older students, misconduct on social media will result in suspension of social activity privileges, such as dances or basketball games."

"But Abigail isn't one of the older students," Sloane butted in. "She's in *fourth* grade. She doesn't even *have* social media."

"I have YouTube," Abigail added, giving a decisive and adult-like nod to Principal Clark.

"That's different, sweetie," Sloane said automatically. And then found herself thinking: Was it? She should check Abigail's account. Review what she'd been watching. She wished she, too, had brought a legal pad. That had been sloppy of her.

Principal Clark ignored Abigail. "Right. I do realize that. To that end, have you considered changing Abigail's phone number?"

Sloane let out a contemptuous guffaw. "That's your answer? Why should the onus be on her? On us? What happens when those kids get her *new* number? They shouldn't even have phones."

"There's a safety consideration there. Parents these days feel safer if their children have phones on them."

Sloane didn't think she'd mind if one of those punk kids got kidnapped once or twice.

Behind Principal Clark, kids ran with lunch boxes and aluminum water bottles and scaled the monkey bars. "Has anything new happened, Abigail?" he asked.

Abigail stuffed her hands underneath her thighs, swaying back and forth. "I don't know. Maybe," she said, her voice small and guileless. "A couple boys. They asked me to go behind the gym to get their shoes. I went, but, I guess there were no shoes." She shrugged. Her eyes were wide and blue. "I came back, but they were all laughing at me. I didn't get the joke. I screamed at them to go away in my loudest voice like Mom taught me. Then they said I was crazy."

Sloane closed her eyes and swallowed hard. Sometimes when she and Abigail were leaving Target or a movie theater together and the parking lot was mostly empty, she made Abigail practice her screaming. Derek thought the exercise would only scare her. But what did he know? Derek had never been a girl. Sloane had, and if their daughter were ever in danger, Abigail knew exactly what to do: scream bloody murder.

And now here they were.

"I don't get it," Sloane said. "Shoes? Why are kids laughing at my daughter about shoes?"

Principal Clark seemed to be hiding — *what?* — a smile behind his clasped fists, his elbows propped casually on his desk.

"Is something amusing here, Principal Clark? What are we missing?" Ardie scooted to the edge of her seat, pen poised.

He unlocked his fingers and shrugged.

"Kids," he said. "It's silly, really." His eyes darted between Ardie and Sloane. They waited.

"Sloane and I love silly."

Clark scratched the back of his neck. "It's not supposed to make sense. It's this thing the boys have been doing. It's like flirting. It means they think you're pretty. A ritual they have, I guess you could call it. They ask the girl they think is pretty to go back behind the gym and then, well, nothing. They're *children.*" He pressed his lips together and raised his eyebrows to Abigail.

"I'm sorry, what now?" Sloane felt herself doing the exaggerated blinky thing that Derek hated so much. But she only did it when she was right. And when the person to whom she was speaking was stupidly wrong. "You're telling me my daughter has been subject to some tween hazing thing?"

Ardie's stare, too, had hardened into judgmental curiosity. (Because we knew this logic: we were *always* supposed to be thankful when anyone thought we were pretty.)

Their eyes met — Sloane's and Ardie's. What more than a decade of shared work experience bought you was the same bullshit meter. Ardie's movement was so subtle. A nearly imperceptible flash of her eyes, followed by the slightest tilt of her head. *I'm sure as hell not going to stop you,* it said.

"Humiliating her," Sloane said to Principal Clark. "That's a compliment? All in good fun, I suppose."

"Mom." Abigail bounced in her seat.

"I understand what you're thinking. But I assure you, it's harmless."

"Oh! Oh! You *assure* me?" Sloane's face went white with anger.

Ardie was steady beside her. She leaned forward. "I think part of what my clients are responding to is the fact that these boys purposefully embarrassed Abigail. They then called her crazy. Do you know why that's problematic, Principal Clark?" She didn't wait for an answer. "It's problematic because when we allow young boys to so casually call a young girl 'crazy,' well, it offers everyone else permission not to believe her. Were any of these boys called crazy for inventing this made-up story about *shoes,* of all things?"

Principal Clark's residue of a smile disappeared.

Ardie continued. "I didn't think so. What makes it more problematic is that the administration here seems to think that all of this behavior — the boys, the girls — is cute. When really what it seems to be doing is fostering a dangerous behavior. It's not cute, Principal Clark. And my client, here, is legitimately concerned about the safety and well-being of her child."

"I understand that," Principal Clark said, his face now grave.

Sloane managed to find her voice and her purse at the same moment. She stood. "I agreed with the school board to do these meetings in hopes real progress would be made, and no further legal action required." She held her hand out to her side and Abigail slid off her chair and took it. "But this meeting was a complete waste of my time. Let's hope you take the next one more seriously."

On cue, Ardie, Abigail, and Sloane left Principal Clark's office without looking back. Sloane felt the vein in her forehead pulsating.

"Mom." Abigail tugged on her arm when they were outside in the hazy sunlight. "You *yelled* at Principal Clark."

"I didn't yell at him." They were now on the elementary school's bright concrete sidewalks leading out to the visitor parking. Distant shrieks pierced the air, which smelled damp with humidity and sweaty children. "I spoke up. There's a difference."

It was possible Sloane *had* been closer to yelling. The fog of self-righteousness could be a powerful drug. She would tell Derek she'd been very stoic and let Ardie do most of the heavy lifting. Ardie *had* been amazing, that much couldn't be argued with.

"So . . ." Sloane turned to Abigail and Ardie. "Can we treat you to lunch?"

"Actually" — Ardie squinted against the light reflected off the pavement — "I'm just going to Uber back to the office. I've got to finish those reports and it's my day for pickup again." She was already pulling up the app on her phone.

Sloane's shoulders drooped. "Fine," she conceded. "But only under protest. Let the record show that I attempted to pay you with the best meal between five and" — she thumbed through the crumpled bills in her wallet — "fifteen dollars could offer." She pulled Ardie into a hug. "If you wouldn't mind, though, I'd like to keep this thing with Abigail between us. It's delicate," she said, with a slight twinge of stress. The deposit of another secret into her and Ardie's friendship account. Another blending of their work and personal lives. She watched her daughter study a nearby plant and pluck two tiny buds from between its leaves. She loved her daughter so much, but she had, in her heart, imagined that she would have more friends. Was that an awful thing to think? Was Sloane a terrible mother? "And, you know, company policy and whatnot, it could get — you *quote-unquote* representing us — well, it could get a little muddy." Strictly speaking, Truviv lawyers weren't meant to represent anyone other than Truviv. It was, if they were going to be sticklers about it, a violation of the company's malpractice insurance policy and it could, *technically,* open up a whole host of issues. Though, of course, it wouldn't. A silly rule. Like jaywalking. "You understand, right?"

Ardie gave her shoulders a squeeze. "Just between us."

There was a brief moment where Sloane thought it might be the time to make her small, little nothing confession, but then Ardie's phone buzzed and her ride was pulling into the bend, and honestly, it was the tiniest betrayal. Hardly worth mentioning. After all, it wasn't exactly a matter of national security. This little social affair she was having. No, god, wait, it wasn't an *affair.* Could it be an affair if it was just platonic? Probably not. And it wasn't as though Ardie and Sloane were in a committed, monogamous relationship. They *had* other friends. They were adults. Anyway, she could always tell her later. Or better yet, not at all.

CHAPTER TEN

23-Mar

Rosalita placed the envelope addressed to "Ms. Valdez" on Ardie's keyboard. She was glad that Ardie wasn't in her office. It was simpler this way.

Ardie had offered her services to Rosalita "pro bono." At the time, Rosalita hadn't known what that meant, not exactly, but her son, Salomon, helped her to look it up on Google and what it had meant was "free." Rosalita didn't like free. Or rather, she didn't trust it. Even a free sesame chicken sample at the mall was an invitation to buy a meal. The free sample acted as bait. And Rosalita had no desire to get lured in. Her first instinct had been to refuse Ardie's help outright. She would have, were it not for the nagging sight of her little boy, leaving her no choice but to accept. So she scraped together savings from the meager money she made off this job and stuffed the envelope with dollar bills.

The biggest problem had been figuring out exactly how much she should pay. This, too, she'd searched for on the Internet and the hourly rate seemed to range from the expensive to the exorbitant. Rosalita could pay neither, so she put together what she thought was fair. A stack of wrinkled cash thinly disguised in a mailing envelope. The recklessness of abandoning that amount of money scrambled her insides like an egg.

"What are you doing?" Rosalita's entire body hitched at the sound of a man's voice behind her. She turned and there he was, the man from the corner office, the white streak of hair running away from his fore-head. Goose bumps rose on the backs of Rosalita's arms.

"Nothing." Rosalita laced her fingers together and held her hands in front of her waist. She stood for inspection, his eyes covering the length of her. "Cleaning," she corrected. He hadn't entered the office, but the weight of his body blocked her exit. Her pulse thrummed at her eardrum. She could tell him the truth, but on principle, it was none of his business. Or maybe it was, but, in either case, she had already begun the lie and so now she was stuck with it.

She thought of the envelope behind her

and how it would look if he studied more closely what was on the desk, how ridiculous it would sound to say that she was leaving the money instead of taking it. He wouldn't believe her.

"No supplies?" He scratched behind his ear, as though the question meant nothing to him when clearly it did, or else he wouldn't be asking it.

Rosalita drew herself together, mentally wrapping a tourniquet around the anger and humiliation that threatened to bleed into her voice. A man passed in the hall, casting a sideways look. She was familiar with the built-in assumption that she and the rest of the cleaning staff were dying to get their plastic-gloved hands on whatever spare shoes and noisy bracelets people left on or under their desks. Her last cleaning partner, LaTisha, told her about a memo that had been passed around the upstairs offices encouraging everyone to lock their belongings in a safe place and log off their computers to avoid theft. *Reduce temptation by hiding belongings out of plain view!*

Jesus Christ. *Temptation.*

"I don't need supplies to empty the trash cans. The other cleaning will be done during night shift." She thought to explain further but doubted whether he could pay attention for that long. Once or twice every month, Rosalita would pick up a day shift, during which there was only a skeleton crew, kept on the clock to attend to light housekeeping and the inevitable spill of an entire cup's worth of coffee that occurred at least once a morning. She wished only to end this interaction as quickly as possible.

His eyes traveled from the trash can in the corner to where Rosalita stood, directly in front of Ardie's desk. She was lying and, probably, they both knew it. She waited, like a cocked pistol, to learn what was going to happen next. One second. Two seconds.

If she had been someone else would he have —

"Everything all right?" Ardie appeared behind the man and Rosalita should have been relieved to see her.

"Everything's fine." His hand slid over his cheeks. "Just checking in on things."

"In my office?" Ardie asked with wide-eyed innocence. She squeezed past him, her oversized purse pushing against him so that he was forced, out of politeness, to move to the side. His face read visibly annoyed. But he'd ceded the ground.

He stood for a moment and then lifted an open hand to Rosalita and said, "Have a good afternoon," before striding away.

Ardie pushed the door closed without debating the matter with Rosalita. "What was that about?" she asked, foisting her bag onto one of the two guest chairs.

Rosalita twisted the ugly yellow fabric of her polo shirt between her fingers. It was rough on her skin. Her thick ponytail fell across her back. "Nothing." She felt small and inconsequential, like a child watching the adults work.

"It didn't look like nothing." Ardie plunked her rear end into the rolling chair. "Sorry. Were you looking for me?" But now, on the other side of the desk, Ardie saw the envelope resting on the keyboard. She held it up. "What's this?"

Rosalita didn't reply.

Ardie folded her hands over her stomach. She let out a long exhale as she thumbed through the contents of the envelope. Then, once finished, she tapped the edge of the envelope on her open palm and stared out the window.

The fact that the two women had struck up a friendly acquaintance wasn't as weird as it seemed. It had happened naturally, over many months. Years, by now. The first time that Ardie had spoken to her in Spanish, Rosalita worried that maybe the woman was a lesbian. But she had a little boy and a husband who later became an ex-husband and then Rosalita felt like a bitch. *¿De dónde es usted?* Ardie had first asked and it had turned out that Ardie, the daughter of two doctors, was from McAllen while Rosalita went to high school in neighboring Rio Grande City. Their conversations never lasted more than five minutes, but there was something lovely about getting to speak to another adult person in Spanish, which was usually discouraged at work for fear that the building's tenants would think the cleaning staff were gossiping about them (they were). It was the comfort of not having to funnel through the extra layer of translation, to feel that she was being understood and sounded intelligent and like herself around a person like Ardie that filled her with a sense of self-confidence that escaped her throughout most of her interactions at work, at the grocery store, at the bank, with the cable repairman.

Ardie sighed again. "Rosalita, I will accept this money on one condition," she said. "I would like to hire Salomon to help at my son's birthday party."

Rosalita met Ardie's eyes. "How much?"

"One hundred dollars," said Ardie.

This was more than the amount in the envelope. Rosalita frowned, nearly forgetting the man. "One hundred and fifty," she countered. It was her mother who had taught her never to be grateful for someone's first offer. Her mother had been a tiny woman with a nasty bout of early-onset dementia caused by a head injury suffered during a minor car accident. For the years leading up to her death, her mother's love had felt to Rosalita like barbed wire. But, as a result, Rosalita had grown calluses. And looking back, she was often surprised to find that some of the most important skills she'd learned in her life had come from that very same crazy, no-sense mother.

Ardie paused. "One hundred and twenty-five. Do we have a deal?"

"Yes." Rosalita nodded. "We have a deal."

Ardie extended her hand and Rosalita told herself that this deal was simple enough. That was what she'd told herself then, too. Of course, back then it had been about her survival and she had forced herself to boil what that meant down into facts and figures. And yet it remained, to this day, the worst thing she'd ever done. A simple transaction that forever proved to Rosalita that she was, at her core, cold-blooded. That she would choose herself and her son over everything and everyone.

It's only money, she thought today. But . . .

hadn't it been "only money" the last time that she'd made a deal?

CHAPTER ELEVEN

27-Mar

Desmond Bankole's memorial service took place seven days after his death. Those days in between had passed in the usual blur of work, car, home, punctuated by the occasional urgent phone call, quickly drawn memo, and perfunctory meeting. Sloane arrived to a veritable Who's Who, where everyone milled about in black dresses, recognizable though slightly out of context. Her heels had sunk into the manicured lawn when she'd taken a shortcut to the church entrance. She had a visceral hatred of funerals. At fifteen years old, she'd attended three in the same year. Her maternal grandmother, followed by both of her grandfathers. She'd disliked shaking the hands of elderly people, the touch of their wadded-up tissues hidden in their papery palms. The sense of uncontrollable tears, a swell of intimate emotion on display — and worse, expected.

After Abigail was born, she and Derek had drawn up a will and Sloane left instructions: cremation, please, then pour her remains in the backyard while saying a prayer to Tina Fey. And okay, yes, she may have included a slightly overbearing suggestion for Derek that he consider marrying Ardie, who Sloane was certain would care deeply about Abigail's education, remember to pack her lunch, and, a bit cruelly on Sloane's part, not overshadow her in the looks department. But other than that — the Tina Fey prayers and the marrying of one of her closest friends — Sloane planned to be a low-maintenance dead wife and mother. Honestly.

As she sat in the pew, her back aching from the hard wood, she kept her arm looped through Grace's and an Altoid pinched to the roof of her mouth.

"Last song." Ardie pointed to one of the final lines on the program.

"Hallelujah." Sloane lifted her eyes skyward.

Grace glared at them. "Is this how you two would act if *I* died?" she whisper-scolded them. She dabbed her eyes with a wadded tissue and sniffled loudly. The tip of her nose had turned an unattractive shade of red. Sloane rubbed her friend's shoulder. Grace wore a beautiful black cashmere shawl around her shoulders. Her frosted hair was pulled up into a prim French twist. Perfectly put together, as always. But goodness, she was *sensitive* lately.

"That depends," Ardie whispered back. "Would it be before or after you finished the regulatory analysis on the subscription box acquisition?" She checked her watch. "And to be fair, we've been here over an hour already."

"She's teasing, Grace. We'd be devastated."

Grace untangled her arm from Sloane's and folded it across her body.

Grace kept her eyes trained ahead at the pastor, who was offering closing remarks, and bowed her head to join the rest of the congregation in some sort of prayer.

"We'd wear black for a year," Sloane murmured. "We swear it." She placed her hand on one of the Bibles in the pew. It was quite convenient.

Grace lifted her chin. "I'm not being ridiculous, you know. It could happen." She met Ardie's eyes, too. "To any of us."

"Sure," Sloane said softly, watching her friend. *Natural,* she told herself, to confront your own mortality after the birth of your first child. "But it won't."

The organ boomed through the chapel and Sloane rose to her feet with the tide of mourners. Her ring caught on the sheer black hose underneath her dress. A short, severe run raced to the top of her kneecap. "Shit," she whispered. Louder than she thought.

"Are you okay?" Ardie turned to Sloane.

"I'm fine." There was no saving the hose. She'd simply have to live with it until she could remove them in the bathroom and hope she'd remembered to lotion her calves this morning. She wished Derek could have been here, his hand resting on her back. He had nice hands. Basketball-palming hands. "I just want to get out of here."

Outdoors, the day was glorious. The grass smelled freshly mowed. There were actual butterflies flapping about between the assortments of plants decorating the church's exterior.

As the crowd filtered out of the church like a herd of cattle, Sloane overheard collegial greetings, saw handshakes, heard lunch dates being set. She should be mingling, too. Seize the moment. Tables of refreshments were set up on the lawn and people were picking up plastic glasses of orange juice or water.

"Do you want anything?" Ardie asked, heading for the table. Ardie could never resist a free spread.

"I'm all right, thanks." Sloane's stomach felt unsettled. Grace had vanished, maybe to touch up her makeup, which was a mess after the service. Grace must be a better person than she was, thought Sloane, who had managed not to cry at all.

There was a tap on her shoulder and Sloane turned to see Elizabeth Moretti, her arms already outstretched to envelop her in a hug. Elizabeth had big brown hair and a smile that showed off too much of her gums. But she had beautiful clothes and today wore an expensive-looking, scallop-trimmed shift dress that Sloane imagined still had the tags fixed to it only a few hours before. "I thought I'd see you here."

Naturally, Sloane had thought the same thing of Elizabeth. Though it made less sense, given that she didn't work for Truviv.

Elizabeth looked around, clucking her tongue. She was so noisy. "Tragic," said Elizabeth. "Lovely ceremony, though. Flower arrangements to die for, pardon the unfortunate pun. Do you see that guy over there?"

Sloane subtly looked across a planter filled with purple and orange pansies toward two men talking beneath the shade of an oak tree. Both early forties, lucky because they still had their hair, but the telltale alleyways of shiny peach flesh had begun to stretch, making inroads past the original hairline.

"The shorter one," Elizabeth continued. "He came in as a lateral, so I don't think you knew him. Jacob Shor. He made partner at Jaxon Brockwell a couple years ago. *He* was on the BAD Men List. I thought I knew everything. But nope, right next to his name it said, 'tried to solicit sex in his office with a summer associate.' I nearly died. Sorry. God." She crossed herself, staring up at the steeple. "But can you believe it?"

Could she? Sloane looked at the man, who seemed genial enough. A friendly face. She could imagine him as a beloved PE teacher. A predator? Not as easily.

"So." Elizabeth drew out a compact, checking her reflection. Casual. "Was he on the list?"

Sloane was mad at herself for forgetting her sunglasses. The day was heating up, and she had a terrible poker face. "Who said I was looking for someone?" An edge in her voice.

"An educated guess."

Sloane was sweating underneath the hot mid-morning sun.

She could have added him herself. It was anonymous. A shared document floating in the nebulous cloud of the Internet. Anyone could add or edit and she had started to. But, then, she hadn't. Why?

"Fine, fine, you don't have to tell me. None of my business." Everything was Elizabeth's business. She snapped the compact closed. "But you should add him. Might help someone. Take the bull by the testicles." She cupped her hand to demonstrate. "Know what I mean?"

Sloane didn't want to talk about this right now, not with her. Hadn't Elizabeth been her own sort of list, back in the day?

Watch out for Ames Garrett.

"I'm sorry, Elizabeth. I have a terrible run in my hose. I need to excuse myself to the restroom." Sloane sounded too formal. What was wrong with her? She had officially lost track of both Ardie and Grace now. She needed to pull it together, though she really did hate funerals.

She hugged Elizabeth. Sloane rarely liked hugging other women she knew professionally, but she still remembered Elizabeth was the sort of person that enjoyed hugs.

"Clear nail polish," Elizabeth called after her.

Sloane turned her head back. "What?"

Elizabeth looked at her appraisingly. She cupped her hands around her mouth like a megaphone. "Will stop the run."

Sloane lifted a hand in gratitude.

Inside, the church was much emptier than before, thank goodness, with only stragglers milling and talking in low voices. Her footsteps echoed along the hall as she followed signs to the bathroom, which she'd been told was located somewhere in the East Wing.

She was rounding the corner when she saw it. That skunk streak of white through dark brown hair always stopped her short. Her heart rate quickened. Ames's head was lowered, as though in prayer. But he was talking to Katherine Bell, her slender back pressed up against the wall. Sloane's first instinct was to interrupt, but as was often the case in work-related scenarios, her mind immediately began cycling through a slew of tricky possibilities. She retreated around the corner to watch from a distance while pricks of warning shot up her arms.

What was he saying?

And then — did she really need to know

exactly? Sloane could likely transpose her twenty-eight-year-old self into Katherine's shoes and take an "educated guess." Sloane had no idea how long the two of them had been talking, but it took less than a minute for the conversation to end. A thin trickle of sweat had pooled in Sloane's bra. She felt her nostrils flaring in that repulsive way she could never quite control when she was a certain version of angry.

She waited. Katherine's face was impassive as she walked toward her down the corridor and Sloane readied herself so that when Katherine rounded the corner, she feigned alarm.

"So sorry," they both said at the same time. Though Sloane was trying to read her eyes. Had Ames been an asshole? Or was the conversation a perfectly normal occasion and Sloane was making too much of it?

That damned list. He should be on it. People should be warned. CEO. *My god.*

Katherine swept away a hair caught in her eyelashes. Sloane smiled, taking a step back so they could regain their personal boundaries. Katherine seemed to be someone who liked personal space.

Sloane had been collecting first impressions of Katherine. Sartorial choices that were, at least to Sloane's tastes, a half step off, which Sloane believed helped her to deduce *something* about Katherine. Probably that she didn't like to ask for others' opinions. Actually, she reminded Sloane a touch of Abigail — the social awkwardness complicated by prettiness. No one expected those two attributes to go together and that created a problem for people, because pretty people — for instance, blonde, blue-eyed girls like her daughter — weren't allowed to be reserved unless they wanted to be called snobbish. Pretty people were preferably supposed to act like Sloane, who was pretty, but mostly because she'd asked for lots of people's opinions over the years and really, really loved Neiman's. "Is the restroom this way?" Sloane asked, pointing.

"Yes," said Katherine, a flush visible on her apple cheeks.

"I ruined my hose," Sloane explained, as though she needed to offer up a reason. "I look like a two dollar hooker."

Katherine's mouth formed a small "o" of surprise. "I actually keep another pair in my purse if you need one." She was pulling her bag to her hip when Sloane lightly touched her forearm.

"That's okay. I think I'll just chuck these in the trash can. My daughter says hose make me look like an old lady anyway."

Katherine was wearing opaque black tights. They didn't make *her* look like an old lady. They turned her legs into an appealing silhouette.

"Let me know if you change your mind," Katherine said, moving past, her expression politely blank and closed off.

"Thanks. Yes, I will." But she was already looking past Katherine, watching Ames alone in the empty hall of the East Wing. It was a relief to hear Katherine's footsteps drift away. Ames ran his fingers through his hair, rocking back on one heel. Then he pushed the door to the men's restroom open.

Temporary insanity. Sloane might have been suffering from that rare affliction and knew it was a defense with slim chances of holding up in court. But this would never wind up in court.

Sloane followed Ames into the men's room.

"Hello?" she called, in case it was occupied by anyone other than Ames.

"Someone's in here." It was Ames's voice. The single stall to the left hung open and the line of urinals was empty aside from Ames, who had his back to her.

He turned, his eyebrows jacking up in surprise. The creases in his forehead had deepened over the years. (While we needed nips and tucks and filler injections to stay relevant, they needed only to age to become more dignified. Don't think we didn't notice.)

"Sloane?" She heard the metal zip of his fly shooting back up. "What are you doing in here?"

Good question. What was she doing in here? Acting on impulse, she supposed. Derek did say she had an impulsive streak. Like when she came home with a shelter kitten she'd seen in a pen outside the grocery store only to remember later that Derek was allergic. Or was it maternal responsibility? Or was she just too old to deal with bullshit? She was confronting her boss — *shit,* her *boss* — in the bathroom.

Calmly, she said, "I heard you're on the short list for CEO. Congratulations." She almost sounded as though she meant it. Before Ames could talk, Sloane added, "I ran into Bobbi, a few days ago, by the way."

Water gurgled through pipes embedded in the wall. But otherwise it was too, too quiet. Her voice echoed.

Ames adjusted his belt. She hated when he did that because it couldn't help but call attention to his crotch. Maybe that was exactly his intent.

"She told me." There was a subtext. It said: *Yes, my wife and I talk and I'm not a monster, thanks.* He shrugged. "A lot of things would need to fall into place before anything happened."

"But you feel your odds are good. I can tell." She refused to let her eyes wander to her own reflection in the mirror.

A half smile. A single dimple buttoning his cleanly shaven cheek. "I've always had good luck in Vegas."

"What are you doing with Katherine?" she asked, because this was the point. His was the name missing on that list, for better or for worse.

"Ah, come on, Sloane." He rolled his eyes now, tipped his head back a bit, like he was a teenager and she was reminding him to pick up his room. "I'm not doing anything. What makes you think that?"

Sloane realized she had been thinking of Ames all these years like a dormant volcano with a low chance of eruption.

"I have eyes, for starters. And ears. And . . . some relevant experience." She leveled her gaze. *You know what they say about history,* she thought.

"Not this again." There it was. The boyish annoyance. Inconvenienced. "When are you going to get *over* it? It's been years." It

148

hadn't. The affair had been years ago, but she'd been paying for it ever since and he knew it. Because every time she thought the problem of Ames Garrett had gone into hibernation, he proved her wrong. Like three years after the affair, Ames handed a high-level transaction assignment Sloane had been championing to David Kelly because Ames "couldn't trust her not to sleep with opposing counsel on this one." Five years after she had Abigail, Ames casually told her that her ass still looked decent in a suit. At seven years, he got drunk and asked to sleep with her again "for old times' sake." Dozens of these instances peppered her career. And now she saw the symptoms of another flare up. A new cycle. And without Desmond, she worried that her — their — immunity had been compromised.

"Your wife asked if I had any advice for you to help your chances," she said, slowly. "I promised her that if I did, I would offer to share it." His eyes danced with amusement and she hated him for it. "So here it is: If you want to stay on the short list, *Ames*, I would *advise* you to keep your hands and any other body part you might be tempted to use clean. Okay?"

He scoffed and shoved his hands into his pockets. "You're unbelievable, Sloane, you know that?" She thought about that word. *"Unbelievable."* Was it true? He'd hit upon the exact right word choice, even if he hadn't meant to. The concern that plagued her, as she suffered through every injustice, every slight, every entitlement to her space and her mind that he took full advantage of: that no one would believe her. All because of that short, stupid affair.

"My condolences, Ames." She turned to leave. She had said something. She'd done something. It wasn't the "BAD" list, but it was her own version, just more direct.

"If you want to hear *my* counsel, Sloane." Her heart tripped as she hesitated, hands flattened against the door. "It's this. Rising water lifts all boats. If I was offered the position, and I'm not saying I would be, but if I was, then it stands to reason that there would be a vacancy in the General Counsel position and you do have some — as you said, I think — relevant experience."

Her body stiffened. Partially because what Ames had said sounded suspiciously like a bribe. Partially because he was right.

Sloane had reached an age where anger no longer meant slamming doors or breaking glasses. Instead, her rage carried on in the vibrations of her organs. She exited without another sound, her mind lingering

150

in the bathroom, needling over the words exchanged with Ames.

Which is why she didn't immediately notice Bobbi Garrett standing in the hallway, a glass of water in each hand, staring at her.

Sloane registered her with a start. An obvious flinch. "Went in the wrong one," she told Bobbi, reaching up to smooth her hair. Of course Ames had brought his wife. Already playing at being the first family of Truviv, Inc.

Bobbi's laugh was an octave too high and the water sloshed in the plastic cups, dribbling over her fingers. "I was just looking for my husband." Her husband. Not Ames. Her husband.

Sloane's boss.

"I think he may have been in there," said Sloane. "I'm sure, *if* he was, he'll be right out."

She should have covered her tracks by entering the ladies' room. She knew that, but she'd already had as much of today as she could stomach and Ames's marriage wasn't her responsibility. She walked back toward the radiant churchyard. Cars had begun to pull out of the parking lot, their headlights flashing on in broad daylight. The run in her hose had inched its way down so that it looked like an ugly scar running over her kneecap.

Sloane hated funerals and she swore to herself that never again would she attend another one. *Unless,* she thought. . . . Unless it was for Ames.

DEPOSITION TRANSCRIPT

26-Apr

Ms. Sharpe: Ms. Glover, are you aware of how and when these unsubstantiated rumors about Ames Garrett first started?

Respondent 1: I take issue with the words "unsubstantiated" and "rumors."

Ms. Sharpe: Okay, then. Did you and your friends ever discuss Ames Garrett socially?

Respondent 1: I'm sure we did, yes.

Ms. Sharpe: In what context?

Respondent 1: He was our boss. We saw him daily. I'm sure he came up in a variety of different contexts.

Ms. Sharpe: Did you complain about him?

Respondent 1: There were plenty of things about Ames to complain about, so I'm sure we did.

Ms. Sharpe: How often would you say that you complained about Ames?

Respondent 1: I don't know. I didn't keep a log.

Ms. Sharpe: Monthly? Weekly? Daily?

Respondent 1: I don't know.

Ms. Sharpe: As part of this investigation, we have spoken to dozens of Ames Garrett's friends and colleagues who categorically support Ames, who say that he has a sterling reputation, who have known him for years and know him to be a family man, a good guy. Women he knew in college, in law school, professionally, who say definitively that they never felt uncomfortable around Ames.

Respondent 1: That logic makes no sense, Cosette. If someone is a murderer, you don't point to all the people in his life that are still alive and say, he can't be a murderer, look at all these people he didn't kill!

Ms. Sharpe: Are you comparing Ames Garrett to a murderer?

Respondent 1: No.

Ms. Sharpe: Because while we're on the subject . . . Is it true that you've recently been questioned as part of a possible homicide investigation?

Helen Yeh: Objection. Move to strike Counsel's last question from the record.

Ms. Sharpe: The respondent broached the subject.

Respondent 1: As you know, the entire office has been questioned. And no one said anything about killing anyone, did they?

CHAPTER TWELVE

28-Mar

Though it was only March, the spreadsheet turned us all into Santa Clauses. We were making the list, checking it twice, trying to figure out who was naughty or nice.

We hit "refresh." We waited for names to appear that never did. We were thrown off guard when names we hadn't expected popped up. During those weeks we stood in elevators, scanned documents in the copier, and sat in sales meetings, watching as though with X-ray vision. We saw through the closed doors and past the zipped dress pants.

We dismissed some behavior — we could take a dirty joke. Others — the men who made points to tell us about their open marriages, who followed us into restrooms, who sent explicit text messages and then claimed to be too drunk to remember, who didn't hear the word "no," who retaliated when they did, who groped our asses — we couldn't. We thanked God it wasn't us. And when it was, we felt a sick sense of comfort that it wasn't *only* us, a relief like having just vomited after a hangover.

We leaned across treadmills, theorizing with one another about what made the men on that list tick and in this, we failed inherently because we wasted more time focusing on those men's emotional lives than they had ever spent on ours.

The question was never why. It was —

"What are we going to do about Katherine?"

Sloane breezed in without knocking, shut the door to Ardie's office, and pressed her back to it as if she'd been chased there. Ardie was proofreading an email to a third-year associate at Norman, Steele & Sandoval regarding a property tax dispute, a practice — proofreading — to which the younger attorneys in the office seemed allergic. Everyone was in such a hurry.

Sloane sniffed the air. "It smells like McDonald's in here, Ardie. Please tell me you did not go to McDonald's."

"Okay, I didn't go to McDonald's."

Sloane walked over to the trash bin and pinched a fast food bag between her fingers, the remnants of a sausage, egg, and cheese biscuit that Ardie had grabbed on her way into work. It had been delicious. "I will never understand you." Sloane dumped the crumbled bag into the bin and took the guest chair opposite Ardie's desk.

"Good morning to you. Please, have a seat," said Ardie, unperturbed. Like every other woman on the planet, she'd seen the Kate Moss memes with the assertion, "Nothing tastes as good as skinny feels" and thought to herself, *Pardon me, but have you tried cheesecake?* Though Ardie suspected the real rub with respect to her eating habits wasn't that she liked food that was bad for her, but that she liked food that was cheap. Ardie could afford organic, free-range, and farm-raised, she just didn't usually want to.

"I'm having a moral dilemma." Sloane pulled her chair closer to the desk.

Ardie finished rereading her email and pressed "send." "I was under the impression that your morals were fairly flexible." Ardie noticed that her suit was shiny and worn at the elbows. It was the kind of thing that she should be more attentive to, she knew. But her mother had always told her that there was no more important physical attribute for a woman than good skin, and Ardie had very good skin, so that ought to count for something.

"My morals are complicated. There's a difference." Sloane folded her hands on her knees, sitting pin straight, like she was a pupil trying to impress a teacher. Ardie pushed her lips together and rested her temple on two fingers. "I saw Ames . . . hovering with her at the memorial service, from which you abandoned me, by the way."

Ardie had taken her finger sandwiches to go and escaped to her car. She wasn't cut out for that many people. She took walks in her neighborhood and, when she did, she would cross the street, *avoid* a whole cul-de-sac, simply to dodge the necessity of having to wave at another human being. It was a wonder she had a friend like Sloane.

"I already invited her to Michael's party." Ardie deflected the built-in question as to her whereabouts.

Sloane frowned and cocked her head. "That was uncharacteristically kind of you."

"I resent that."

"Anyway." Sloane pressed her fingertips together as she talked, too fast, as always. "I confronted Ames and —"

"You what?"

"I confronted *Ames,*" she repeated. "And he told me in no uncertain terms that if he became CEO then I'd be up for General Counsel." Sloane sat back in the chair, palms open like jazz hands. The big reveal.

Ardie furrowed her brow, a slight shake of her head. "Obviously."

Sloane, not amused. "But he was . . ."

"Hovering." Ardie had the feeling that she'd been here before. Look! The artwork on her office walls hadn't even changed. The same purple orchid arched lazily over her desk and a small rubber fig still grew in the corner, both of which she watered and cared for diligently. The picture of Tony had disappeared since the last time. Like magic. In that instance — the case of the missing Tony photograph — Ardie actually suspected Grace, though she'd never explicitly confirmed it.

"Yes." She sat forward again. "I really want that job."

"You deserve that job."

Sloane didn't argue. (False modesty was on its way out, like a bad fashion trend. But we were still slow adopters of professional confidence — like when skinny jeans were coming into fashion and we were all: *But can we even?* Yes, yes we could.)

"So as I see it," Sloane continued, "my options are: Get him fired, warn her, or kill him. Which would you choose?" Ardie didn't particularly want to let herself answer that. "I'm *kidding.* Obviously." Sloane bulldozed a path through the conversation, working herself up. Ardie wondered if the sheer act of talking made her friend sweat. "The second option seems the least complicated, what with the lack of alibis and/or maniacal scheming required. But I figure if we can get to her before he gets to her, then problem solved." She dusted her hands to demonstrate.

Ardie was silent for a moment. She folded her knuckles under her chin. "I tried warning you." This was mostly true, though it had been half-hearted. They weren't, at that point, the kind of friends that picked each other up from outpatient surgery for breast-cyst removals.

Sloane scoffed. "You were a little late."

Sloane didn't mean for those words to hurt, but they did all the same. Not badly. More the kind of dulled phantom pain one might experience years after a surgery. Real, but not real.

"And what if you're a little late?" Ardie asked. "Remember that anything you say could get back to him. Are you prepared for that?"

At this, Sloane didn't scoff, because Ardie was reminding her of a truth we all had to learn to various degrees. The office was an environment perfectly engineered to breed distrust. Every confidence, every request for advice was a leap of faith and we all had horror stories of times when we'd misplaced it.

Sloane tipped her head back and massaged the tight muscles at the back of her neck. They all had terrible posture from staring at a computer the whole day. "We can feel her out," she said, her voice croaky from having her throat arched. "We can make her one of us." She finished her stretch. "You don't really think she's involved with Ames, do you?"

Ardie considered this. "No. I don't. Not yet, anyway." She'd known practically the minute that Sloane had started sleeping with Ames. People were so obvious when they were trying to be subtle. Though it was possible that Katherine was simply more discreet.

Sloane tightened her mouth, determined. "There's the list."

Sloane had forwarded the "BAD Men" list right away. Since then, so had a colleague from her first law firm and even Tony's new wife, Braylee. Ardie had thought little about the spreadsheet list. She'd dismissed it as gossip. Like a slam notebook kids made back in the nineties. She'd always sort of liked the idea of everyone minding their own business. But she had to consider that she'd become painfully closed-minded in her middle-aged years. Maybe her feelings toward the list were a similar feeling to those that kept her from downloading the latest software update for her iPhone. But, then, sometimes the latest software updates were crap, so she wasn't totally wrong on that front. "He's not on it," Ardie said as evenly as she could.

"That could be fixed." As if this were an idea Sloane was floating at a meeting: *fixing* the problem of Ames.

"Sloane." Ardie sighed. It should probably concern her that she was always the sigher in a relationship. It was as though her God-given role were to listen to everyone around her spout off ideas and only she could foresee the millions of things that could go wrong. It would make anyone sigh. Though she worried that it didn't make her seem very fun. Maybe that was why Tony left her for Braylee. *She* seemed like a woman whose breaths were always deep, calm, and even.

"It's a good idea. You have to admit."

Ardie bobbed her head noncommittally back and forth as she mentally assessed the risk. The entry could get traced back to Sloane. She didn't know how. Sloane could

163

get sued for libel, though not if what she said was true. Sloane could get fired. But not unless the other two items came true first. It could ruin Ames's life. "It's not the worst idea."

"It hasn't just been me. There were other women before me. That intern. And his assistant, right? And it hasn't just been one or two things. You have to remember when —"

"I remember."

"Okay. Then you *know* his name should be on that list," Sloane said. "All the cool kids are doing it."

"If all the cool kids jumped off a building would you?" she asked.

One corner of Sloane's mouth tugged sideways. "God no. I'd probably give them a shove. Believe it or not, I wasn't that popular in high school."

Ardie rolled her eyes. "I absolutely don't believe that."

"Well." Sloane looked between the two of them. "Relatively speaking."

Right at that moment, behind Sloane's head, Ames passed the pane of glass at the front of her office. A twist of brown and gray and a streak of white. A dark gray suit. Stubble growing along his neck. Aging earlobes. Creases on the back of his coat. Fingertips pressed to the heels of his hands.

She couldn't remember the last time he'd looked her in the eye or the last time he'd glanced in her direction and hadn't made an expression that made clear her entire body was personally offensive to him.

Fuck it, Ardie thought. Add him.

26-Apr

Ms. Sharpe: What can you tell us about the list, Ms. Glover?

Respondent 1: Which list?

Ms. Sharpe: The Beware of Asshole Dallas Men List. I believe you're familiar with it.

Respondent 1: I didn't invent the list.

Ms. Sharpe: I never implied that you did. I simply asked that you tell us about it.

Respondent 1: It was a list. Of men that worked in Dallas, with short entries that detailed those men's sexually aggressive behavior in the workplace.

Ms. Sharpe: Did you think this list was a good idea?

Respondent 1: I thought it was an idea. I didn't come to a conclusion as to whether it was good or bad. It was clear to me that people saw a need and that they reacted to that need.

Ms. Sharpe: By "people," you're referring to women?

Respondent 1: Last time I

checked, women were people, too, Cosette, are they not?

Ms. Sharpe: Who decided which men would be included on the list?

Respondent 1: No one person decided. If a woman had experienced a man's poor behavior or had been made aware of it, she could choose to include him on the list.

Ms. Sharpe: So, effectively, what you're saying is that the women in this case not only acted as the accusers, but also as judge and jury.

Respondent 1: This wasn't a courtroom. There were no legal ramifications.

Ms. Sharpe: But Ms. Glover, last time I checked, these are, in fact, legal ramifications, *are they not?*

Ms. Sharpe: Let me ask you a more direct question. When did you decide to use the list to try to sabotage Ames Garrett?

Respondent 1: The intent of the list was never to sabotage. The intent of the list was only to warn.

Ms. Sharpe: Ms. Glover, would you mind explaining "proximate cause" to us, as you understand it, for the record?

Respondent 1: "Proximate cause" means that an event is sufficiently related to an injury such that a court will consider that event to be the cause of the injury.

Ms. Sharpe: Well put. And could you tell us the test to determine whether proximate cause exists?

Respondent 1: Proximate cause is measured by the *"sine qua non"* test. Latin for "but for." Y would not have happened but for X.

Ms. Sharpe: In this case, Ms. Glover, someone is dead. That's the "Y." My question is simple: Would someone be dead but for your actions?

CHAPTER THIRTEEN

28-Mar

Ardie was the first to reach for the tortilla chips on the table. The restaurant was kitschy Mexican, vintage boots fastened to the wall as décor. Colored twinkle lights hung from the ceiling. Groups of men leaned over taco plates, ties tucked into their dress shirts.

Around the table sat Grace, Sloane, and Katherine. Katherine didn't accept Sloane's invitation to lunch with what one might call "robust enthusiasm." She insisted that she'd brought her own, and Sloane shot back, "Objection, irrelevant" which elicited a groan from Ardie, who was fundamentally opposed to lawyer jokes of all kinds.

"So" — Sloane cracked open the laminated menu — "is it too early for margaritas?"

Grace crossed her legs. "The rule in my house was always anything goes after ten AM."

Sloane waved over the young waitress. "A margarita for everyone, then?" Sloane asked the group.

"I have to pump right after this." Grace yawned.

"I'm in." Katherine still held herself with the same impeccable posture, as though she might need to balance a set of dishes on her head at a moment's notice. Her mouth, Ardie had noticed, had a habit of twitching between a small smile and a neutral expression — back and forth, back and forth — as if it were asking for permission. Maybe the drink was a sign she was loosening up. *Fingers crossed,* Ardie could imagine Sloane singing out too loudly; thank God, the thought didn't occur to her. The waitress scribbled down the order and hurried away. "Your baby is being a bit of a buzz kill," Katherine said to Grace.

Sloane's eyes flashed wide and she flattened her hands on the tablecloth. "Oh my god, you have to *meet* Emma Kate. She's like the most gorgeous baby you've ever seen. She could be in Pampers commercials. She's that beautiful. You will just hate her. That's how beautiful she is. Though of course you can't hate babies."

A swallowed-the-canary look passed between Grace and Katherine. Grace lifted her glass ever so slightly to Katherine.

Sloane pointed her finger between them, leaning in. "Okay, you two, what are you guys, like closet BFFs? What are we *missing*? Spill."

Grace primly unfolded the black cloth napkin and draped it over her lap. "I don't know what you're talking about. Do you, Katherine?"

"Fine." Sloane examined her nails. "We can play that game, too. Ardie and I have secrets, don't we?" Her ponytail swept across her shoulder as she turned to Ardie.

Ardie set down her water glass. "And we're older than you, so we have more."

The margaritas arrived and Grace raised her water glass. "Cheers, y'all." And Ardie might have been feeling optimistic, but she thought Grace looked happier than she had in weeks.

Sloane licked a line of salt from the rim of her glass. "God, Grace, you're like the perfect mom. I'm pretty sure I drank *wine* when I was pregnant. When I was breast-feeding, which — let's be serious — was for, like, three whole months, I don't even think I knew *not* to drink." She squeezed the lime and dropped it into the drink. "And look at Abigail! She's fine!"

Ardie rolled her eyes, breaking in half another chip. "What do I always tell you? Statistics mean nothing on the individual level. And the inverse is true, as well."

Sloane reached across the table to dip a tortilla chip into the salsa. "Ardie is always trying to teach me mathematical concepts in disguise. I'm a shit pupil, though," continued Sloane. "Let's see. There's that one and, oh yeah, you shouldn't consider sunk costs when making future decisions. Hey? Hey? Pretty good, am I right?"

"Has anyone ever told you, you should write for *The Economist*?" asked Grace, sweeping a strand of hair that had escaped back into place, as she spoke through a bobby pin clenched between her teeth. "And *besides*." She expertly pinned her hair back. "This lunch is about *Katherine*. Katherine, *you* have the floor." Grace performed a Vanna White gesture with Katherine the goods on display. "We want to know everything there is to know about you."

"Or whatever you'd like to tell us," Ardie said, because it was obvious to Ardie that, like herself, Katherine was a bit of a — well, not shy, exactly, Ardie wasn't shy — a *quiet* person. Someone that couldn't quite operate on the same wavelength as those chatty, socially adept people, people like Grace and

Sloane, who naturally failed to see the signs. Sloane believed that inside every introverted person was an extrovert waiting for a friend. Seriously. She had actually said those words. It was like conversion therapy, only it sort of worked. At least for short spurts. But Ardie understood. It could all be very intimidating. Exhausting. Trying to stuff yourself into a group of friends and give off the appearance that you fit in, when really all you wanted to do was sit and eat chips so that all of your energy didn't accidentally bleed out your ears.

To this end, Ardie did notice that Katherine's stare kept trailing off somewhere just north of Sloane's head and that it took a spare moment for her eyes to catch back up to the conversation. Katherine smoothed her hands over her lap. "Oh, well. Let's see. I was an editor on Law Review."

"At Harvard, no less, I hear," Grace chimed in.

The corners of Katherine's mouth snagged ever so slightly upward. "That's correct." Katherine spoke with such precision, enunciating each syllable. "I received a scholarship to study abroad in Oxford. I —"

Sloane rapped her fist on the table, impatiently. "Okay, okay, we know all that stuff. Now get to the good parts. We want to know about your family, where you're from. What you like. All that."

"Spare yourself," Ardie said. "You'll soon learn that it's best to give in as quickly as possible. It's the more humane option."

The waitress interrupted to take their orders. Ardie realized only after she was doing it that she had been scanning the restaurant for her ex-husband. He worked in the area and it *was* a popular lunch spot. The waitress vanished again and Ardie returned her focus to her colleagues.

"Right," Katherine resumed. "I'm from Boston. I'm the youngest of five kids. I'm the only girl. I didn't have much time outside of work at my last job. To do much of anything."

"I still have PTSD from my time at a firm." Grace spun a straw in her water glass. Grace never drank liquid except out of a straw so as to spare her lipstick. "That's not an exaggeration, either."

Katherine's gaze flitted oddly upward again.

After a disconcertingly short amount of time for food to supposedly be cooked and served, plates were slipped in front of the group and Ardie breathed in the smell of hot cheese and jalapeños.

"Do you have a boyfriend?" And it was of

course only Sloane who would ask this question so baldly.

Katherine hesitated. "No," she said.

"Or a girlfriend? Or something?"

"No," Katherine repeated.

"Because I'm a bit of an expert when it comes to writing online dating profiles." Ardie and Grace both looked at Katherine simultaneously and gave small shakes of their heads — *no.* "I saw that." Sloane stuffed a bite of enchilada into her mouth. In front of her, her margarita was down to ice.

Lunch progressed in the way that lunches do. Katherine picked at her salad, while Grace described how she woke every morning with painful knots that she had to massage out in the shower. And Sloane was texting on her phone when Katherine's fork clattered sharply down against her plate. Ardie paused mid-bite, looked at Katherine's face, which was, for one single instant, collapsed in an expression of beady-eyed anger and protruding jawline.

"Are you okay?" Ardie asked. And now she turned her head to peer over Sloane to where she saw a television set up behind the bar. A baseball game played with the volume off.

Ardie settled back in her chair and ap-

175

praised Katherine, who blushed and took another sip of her margarita. "Sorry. I just — it was a bad call."

"I love the Rangers." Ardie punctuated her position with the tongs of her fork. Ardie loved baseball for the leisurely pace of the game, for the opportunity to eat hotdogs slathered with mustard, for the social acceptability of yelling at people you didn't even know. While Sloane and Grace had taken the job at Truviv barely knowing the difference between a touchdown and a goal, Ardie actually enjoyed sports. They made sense. And Truviv often gave tickets to its employees for free. "You're a Red Sox fan?" She grinned.

Katherine blew out a quick breath and raised her hand. "Guilty."

And it all seemed so perfectly innocent and collegial and we would wonder if all such moments did — seem that way — until later colored by events no longer in anyone's control.

We would look back on this moment months later and wonder many things. We would look for signs. And we would find them.

"Finally somebody for me to watch games with!" Ardie hooted.

And Sloane would say, "Let's have one

more" and then lean across and whisper —
"Katherine, have you seen the BAD Men
List?"

CHAPTER FOURTEEN

28-Mar

"Naughty." That was such a pervy word. A porn word. And yet it was the first one that came to Grace's mind. *Oh, Grace, you're being so naughty.* Thank goodness her thoughts weren't broadcast for public consumption.

After lunch, Grace slipped into the pumping room and locked the door behind her, checking it twice to make sure that it was firmly latched. She entered and slipped off her high heels. In the corner, she had stowed a plastic, lidded bin, with her name written in Sharpie across the side. Her little smuggled stash. She patted it fondly.

Grace hadn't started the whole thing intentionally. Only following the tryst at the hotel, that wild night of aromatherapy and room service. She opened the container and began pulling out her treasures. A sleep mask, French hand cream, cashmere socks, a pair of silk pajamas, a down pillow in a fresh linen case, and a blanket made from merino wool. Grace changed into the pajamas and tugged the socks over her tired feet. She moaned audibly. The pads in her nursing bra were damp with milk but she left them in, stretching onto the cracked leather sofa and fluffing the pillow into a mound beneath her head. Meanwhile, the parts of her electric pump still floated in a bowl full of soapy water beneath the kitchen sink.

To keep up with Emma Kate's demand, Grace should pump at least three times a day. Then, one afternoon she thought, *Screw it,* and lay down to take a nap instead. She woke with red lines creasing her cheek and drool dried into the corner of her mouth, but for a short time after she felt suddenly *human.*

Her milk supply had already begun to dwindle and yet she couldn't bring herself to quit the now daily nap. Every afternoon, she was like a woman who, upon embarking on a new diet, was dismayed to find her willpower tapped out when faced with a chocolate cupcake. The pumping room was Grace's chocolate cupcake.

And, because Grace was a perfectionist, she'd set to work perfecting her craft. To think that a few short weeks ago, she felt trapped inside this very same room, put out by the lack of cellphone service and loss of her precious time.

It was so easy.

Grace knew her rights, too. For a whole year after Emma Kate's birth, Truviv was required to provide her with a private space in addition to breaks sufficient for her to express milk. Truviv was *not* required to allot her any time to sleep, but really, shouldn't they be? Maybe just a little?

Grace pulled the sleep mask over her eyes and tried to shut the world out. The beauty of it was that no one suspected Grace Stanton would lie at all, much less about feeding her infant daughter. No one suspected a thing, which made Grace wonder, what else might she be capable of pulling off?

DEPOSITION TRANSCRIPT

26-Apr

Ms. Sharpe: In your initial complaint, you alleged a decade-long culture of sexual harassment. A decade is a long time. Why didn't you say something? Surely, you were afforded the opportunity to report your concerns at some point during that timeframe. At least once. But I will tell you, we didn't find a single instance of complaint on record from you.

Respondent 1: I obviously feared for my job and the future of my career. I feared retaliation from Truviv. A fear, which, as you can see, has turned out to be quite valid.

Ms. Sharpe: Ms. Glover, in that case, you've now sat on this alleged information for at least ten years, by your own account. Why now?

Respondent 1: To believe that I was the only incident of sexual harassment would have been naïve. But I wasn't comfortable with the same thing that had happened to me happening right under my nose. I could no longer, in good conscience, stand by and watch without speaking up.

Ms. Sharpe: Mr. Garrett was poised to become Truviv's next CEO. You were aware of this, weren't you?

Respondent 1: I was.

Ms. Sharpe: Your conscience has impeccable timing.

Ms. Sharpe: When you say that you recently believed there was another target of Mr. Garrett's alleged behavior, to whom exactly were you referring?

Respondent 1: Katherine Bell.

Ms. Sharpe: And what exactly did you see Mr. Garrett do to Katherine Bell?

Respondent 1: I saw him singling her out for attention, attention that was not commensurate with her current position within the company. I saw him ushering her into closed-door meetings in his office.

Ms. Sharpe: Does the company have

a policy against closed-door meetings?

Respondent 1: Of course not, but —

Ms. Sharpe: So in sum, you are alleging that Ames Garrett paid attention to one of his employees and had meetings in his office.

Respondent 1: No, Cosette. It got worse. Much.

CHAPTER FIFTEEN

29-Mar

The following day, outside of Ames's office, Sloane cradled a stack of accordion folders against her hip. She knocked gently, leaning in close to the door to listen for signs that he was on the phone.

But in moments, Ames's muffled voice sifted through the wood. "Come in." Sloane turned the knob, the metal insides of the lock twisting out of place. The shades were drawn over the floor-to-ceiling windows, masking the view of the Margaret Hunt Hill Bridge and turning the natural light gray.

Katherine stood behind Ames's desk, her weight leaning onto the hand resting against the hard surface. Sloane was more surprised to realize that she wasn't all that surprised to find Katherine there. Katherine had been following along with whatever was happening on Ames's screen. Sloane had been trained in a similar fashion behind countless partners' desks when she was a young associate, enough separate points of reference that this particular one shouldn't turn the switch on any alarm bells. Which just went to show how context mattered.

Katherine looked up. "Hi, Sloane." And Sloane tried to read the hidden messages that might be written there. But she found that Katherine's own shades were drawn, the view masked.

Sloane made no hurry as she walked over to the chair opposite the desk and took a seat. She crossed her legs. "I brought the disclosure requests for the subscription box acquisition," she told Ames. "I highlighted what I thought we should push back on. You want to take a look or do you want me to pull the trigger?"

Ames's forehead creased, his eyes following her without moving his head. A stash of Hot Tamales protruded from within his cheek. The scent of cinnamon clung to the air.

Who's afraid of the big bad wolf? Sloane thought.

Because while Katherine's expression was a blank, Ames's said one thing: power.

"I can come back," Katherine said, straightening. She glanced between Ames and Sloane. Sloane couldn't quite get used to the way Katherine's short hair left her entire neck exposed.

Sloane watched Ames, but didn't budge. When Ames nodded, Katherine collected a legal pad and pen previously stranded on the desk and left.

The photographs of a dozen famous athletes smiled down at them from the walls. Sloane tapped her heel on the thin layer of carpet. The chair in which she sat wasn't company-issued. It was mid-century. Navy leather. Comfortable. Probably pricey.

Sloane, who had a natural aversion to silences, let this one stretch.

Ames cleared his throat. "I'll take a look at them before they go out."

Sloane kept the accordion folders on her lap. "What's Katherine working on?" she asked.

Ames leaned back in his chair, rubbed his middle finger and thumb across his brow line. "I was teaching her to use Edgar," he said, as if suddenly tired. "Looking at some of the SEC filings and regulatory matters." He ran his fingers over the length of his tie, straightening it on top of the buttons of his shirt.

"How very hands on of you." She drummed her nails across the folder. They were short and unkempt. She couldn't remember the last time she'd had a manicure other than what she and Abigail managed in an empty bathtub, their limbs hiked up over the sides as they took turns swiping polish over their fingers and toes.

He intertwined his fingers on his stomach, which bore only the subtlest hint of age in the form of a pocket of fat sitting right above his belt. "She's writing a memo for me on the SEC laws of disclosure surrounding cybersecurity breaches."

"Shouldn't Grace be doing that?"

He tapped his fingers together. "Grace won't mind. She's just back from maternity leave. You might say I'm being considerate." He looked pleased with himself.

Sloane sat forward, resting her elbow on the folder in her lap. Her chin on her fist. "Because, funny enough, I thought she was supposed to work under me?"

He tilted his head to stare up at the ceiling. *Yes, Ames, thank you, it's plenty obvious that you're annoyed with me, but I'm not going away.* "I'm delegating to where there's a need, Sloane."

She narrowed her eyes. "You can't keep your hands off the new merchandise."

He brought his chair back to straight. "Look who's objectifying now."

"You know what I mean."

187

"Go take a Midol, Sloane."

She clenched her teeth, her lower jaw jutting forward into an underbite. She actually was on her period, so this irked her more than it should have. If there was one monthly obligation we dreaded, it wasn't the backing up of operational databases or the handing in of audit collection sheets or the checking of updates to the management packs — it was our periods. No number of commercials in which women dove into pools wearing white swimsuits could convince us that our periods were a thing of swanlike beauty. On our best days, we maintained a grudging allegiance with our bodies. We knew we shouldn't be ashamed. We *weren't* ashamed. We were grown-ass women — which is obviously why we paraded to the restrooms with tampons secretly stuffed into our cardigan sleeves as though we were spies delivering encrypted information. Other times, we had to fish quarters out of the bottom of our purses, searching for change to feed the feminine hygiene dispensers that had yet to be updated in the past twenty-five years. We took birth control in an attempt to assert a modicum of control over our uncontrollable hormones. We unbuttoned our pants at our desks. We rattled the kitchen Tylenol bottle into our hands. We ate chocolate. We pretended that all of this was a myth. That we had neither fallopian tubes, nor menstrual cycles, nor breasts, nor moods, nor children. And then we took it as a compliment when one of the men in the office told us we had balls. So, tell us again how this wasn't a man's world.

"But while we're on the subject." Ames pushed his sleeves up his forearms. "I guess I should let you know that Bobbi wanted you gone. After the little stunt you pulled at Desmond's memorial."

"It wasn't a stunt."

He shrugged. "Thinks we're having an affair, trying to have an affair, I don't know what the fuck." His jaw worked. "Point is, she doesn't trust you anymore."

Sloane laughed mirthlessly. "I would think it's you she shouldn't trust."

"Women." He laced his fingers behind his head and leaned all the way back. "Anyway. Look, the deal's always been that I'd have your back as long as you didn't make things hard for me. I thought you understood that. I'm doing this out of the kindness of my heart, Glover. We have history. I get that. I try to respect it, really I do. But you pull stuff like that again and, well . . . I'm not going to protect you." Idly, he pulled a golf ball from his desk drawer and tossed it up in the air and caught it. "I'll feed you to the wolves and it won't fucking bother me. We clear?"

Sloane surveyed her surroundings, took note of where she was, of the environment she'd chosen to inhabit. Of the man sitting behind the desk. Of her position. "I wasn't aware we had a deal." She reached a conclusion. "In that case, I want a bigger office."

He let the chair come crashing back to upright. Balanced the ball on top of a stack of Post-its. "What?" His cheek tightened with, not a smile, but somewhere in that family. As though he'd just heard a ridiculous punch line.

"And I want job security," she said. "A contracted time period with a buyout clause."

He crossed his arms. What were the things she had liked about him again? Sloane couldn't remember.

"Have you lost your mind?"

She ignored him. "I want a larger 401(k) contribution. Double."

He rolled his chair so that his legs were hidden underneath the desk and his arms rested on top of it. Good. He was coming to the table. She knew him too well and, it had suddenly occurred to her, that he might, before long, consider Sloane to be a liability.

"If I didn't know you better, I might think you were blackmailing me."

"I'm negotiating. Isn't this what you taught me to do?"

He looked to his side, but there was no one there to buy his *Can-you-believe-this-woman* schtick.

"I already told you," he said. "If I'm appointed CEO, then I will be sure to recommend that you succeed me as General Counsel." He steepled his fingers.

"And I am telling *you* that I'm here to protect myself. Plain and simple."

He scoffed. "From what, Sloane? You suddenly think I'm the boogeyman?" He elicited a faux shiver. She wasn't amused. "We've worked together for, what, twelve years? I think we've done all right."

She wondered if that were true. If in the novel of his own life, as his very own point-of-view character, Ames Garrett believed that he and she had done "all right." He wasn't wrong. Not entirely. Weeks, even months, could go by in which Ames didn't make her blood boil or undermine her authority or make an inappropriate comment or hold over her head that they'd slept together. She felt a weird sense of loyalty to the man with whom she'd worked for most of her professional life. He thought they'd done all right. *All right.*

She often found herself saying: *He doesn't know any better.* It was this thought that had flashed through her mind the moment she added his name to the BAD Men List. *Issues with physical and interpersonal boundaries at the office; pursued sexual relationships with subordinate co-workers; sexist.* That was what she'd written beside his name. She worried she'd been unfair to him in some way. Leaving him unable to defend himself. That whether or not he knew better mattered. And it was as though she'd just woken up and realized that it was she who had been allowing herself to be the defenseless one and that of course Ames *knew* better. He was fifty years old. She'd added him to the list as her mea culpa to other women out there. But now Sloane needed to make sure that if Ames became CEO, she didn't find herself cut out of a job and replaced with a newer model. And so he needed to understand that she could make things difficult for him at a time when he didn't want them to be difficult.

"A bigger office, Ames. Job security. A 401(k) and your pay stub."

"My *pay stub?*" He shook his head incredulously.

"That's right. What you were making when you were in my position. I want that immediately. And what you're making now. So that I know what to ask for when I'm made General Counsel."

He ran his hand through his hair. She remembered when she thought the white streak through it — a symptom of something called Waardenburg syndrome — was so interesting. Hair couldn't make someone interesting. And neither could an office and famous friends. Ames fucked missionary-style, like a jackrabbit. "You women all think the system is out to screw you."

"You are the system, Ames." She stood, stared down at him, thought about how her stilettos could poke cleanly through his eye sockets if she wanted them to. "And in case you've forgotten, we screwed."

The decision had had nothing to do with Derek, and Sloane should have felt bad about that. It was just that she had wanted to sleep with Ames and now she didn't. What she wanted was to marry Derek, she'd decided, as though Ames were a flu virus she'd needed to get out of her system. She was over it. And she wanted to stop. A decision that she'd shared with Ames earlier in the week.

The response had been chilly, at best. Angry, at worst.

"Oh, sure, now you want out," he'd said in one of their talks since. "You opened up your *legs* and *used* me to get ahead in your job, but now you want out."

"That's not fair."

"Oh, *really*? You were the youngest attorney on the Tread Ops deal, Sloane. You're telling me you think that was all you? Enjoy your bonus for that. You're welcome."

"We're both adults here," she'd said, like that had anything to do with it.

They'd been having the same conversation for a week. A continuous loop. In the interim, she focused on what she was good at — work — because twenty-nine-year-old Sloane hadn't yet decided how to punish herself for the affair with Ames, now that she'd had her cake, now that it was being shoved down her fucking throat.

Don't make this weird, she'd said to him, repeating words she'd once heard from a college boyfriend.

At five-thirty, her office line rang and it was Ames's voice on the other end. "Can you come down here?"

Once she'd replaced the receiver, Sloane

had stared at her desk. It was only a breakup. Breakups were supposed to be awkward. That didn't change whether you were sixteen or nearly thirty. So Sloane carried a legal pad to Ames's office, where he greeted her good-naturedly.

"Shut the door, please," he said, waving his hand to demonstrate.

She took a seat in the chair in front of him. It was mid-century. Navy leather. Comfortable. Expensive.

Ames moved around to her side of the desk and sat on top of it, knees splayed so that she was eye level with his crotch. He rested his elbows on his knees. "We're fine, right?"

Sloane relaxed. They were adults. "Yes, absolutely. We're fine."

"No hard feelings?" His eyebrows lifted boyishly. She could imagine, with some distance, she might find him charming again. Just not in a way that made her want to kiss him.

"Of course not." She smiled, wanting to put him at ease. "I just want things to get back to normal."

His head bobbed up and down, up and down. "Me, too. Me, too. That's what I want, too."

And then she blinked and his hand was

on her thigh. His mouth on her neck. His fingers tangled in her hair.

She gasped. "I meant —" Her voice was breathy — sexy? God, she hadn't meant to sound sexy. "Ames," she said.

He pulled her head back. His lips covered her throat, where her heart pounded at the surface.

"Stop." This time she knew there was no mistaking what she said or how she said it. His weight pressed down on her thigh. His tie trailed her lap. A wet tongue slipped into the crevice of her ear.

The sound that squeezed from her chest was strangled. In the back of her mind, she remembered that she was at work. At the office. *Don't make a scene.*

Sloane used the force of her legs to shove the chair back. The lace trim of her skirt ripped at the hem releasing the sickening noise of a small laceration in the fabric as it split. But Sloane freed just enough distance between their bodies to duck beneath his arm. She didn't look back as she swung open the door to his office. She didn't have to. She already knew what he looked like with ruffled hair.

The path from Ames's office to Sloane's was a straight shot and she walked the distance briskly, chin up, eyes trained at her target, as if she were walking the plank with careful dignity. Tears dripped from her eyes.

From down the hallway, Ardie glanced up from a printout, and then did a double take.

"Sloane?" Ardie walked toward her, but Sloane didn't stop. She couldn't. "Are you o—" Sloane looked straight through her and passed her in the hall.

Through sheer force of inertia, Sloane reached her office and slumped into the familiar desk chair. Rage roared in her chest, but it was muted by so many other emotions.

Ardie was in her office, around the desk, crouching beside her chair.

"What happened?" Ardie's voice was a low, threatening rumble.

"Nothing." Sloane closed her eyes. It pushed a flood of tears over the hills of her cheeks.

Footsteps came from the hallway and Ames Garrett appeared in the door. "Sloane." His voice teetered along the edge of a command and a plea.

Ardie stood slowly from behind Sloane's desk. Sloane would remember the look in her friend's eyes until the day she died. It was the look nightmares were made of. Just not Sloane's.

She would remember the way that Ardie

walked around the desk and how Ames's Adam's apple leapt. She would remember how Ames held out his palms.

"Ardie. I didn't —"

No words were exchanged — or were they? Sloane couldn't remember that part. Only that Ames began to walk backward. That somehow the force of Ardie was enough for him to leave Sloane's office and that once Ardie had closed the door on their boss, there was silence and the questions that would linger for months thereafter: Would he have left his wife? Did he love Sloane? Did he hate her? What would happen to her? Had she hurt him?

That evening, Ardie had pushed a stiff drink into Sloane's hand and Sloane had hoped that would be the end of it.

But there were phases to stopping sleeping with a man you no longer liked and the final one could last more than a dozen years. But Sloane *was* okay. They'd done "all right," as Ames had put it.

Ames would give her what she wanted. But, in the end, would it really be enough?

CHAPTER SIXTEEN

30-Mar

We never cried at work, almost never, although when we did cry, once at home or maybe before that, in the car with our sunglasses on as we corkscrewed slowly down through the parking garage floors, it was usually about work.

Everything was about work, even the things that weren't: Would we continue to work after children? Would we put our work goals ahead of having a family? Were we working enough? Were we working too much? Were we being paid the amount our work was worth? What were we doing this weekend, did we want to have brunch or did we have to work?

Inescapable low-grade thought spirals that manifested in the at-least-once-a-week clammy feeling that spread out in our guts while we rode the elevator down to the lobby, the slow sense of dread building, that we'd left something undone, mishandled a situation, or fucked up royally. Not that we could quite put our finger on what, exactly, it was that we'd done wrong. And that made it worse because it left 480 minutes of possibilities to rifle through, searching for the root of the problem that poisoned the memory of our day.

And then the next morning, we would stuff Dr. Scholl's pads into the bottoms of our high heels and sign up to chair another Junior League luncheon and pretend the only emotions we felt were happy, pleasant, and competent.

And maybe that was why none of us grasped the importance of Bankole's death to the extent that we should have. We were too busy doing the happy-pleasant-competent dance, smiling while we prayed no one would notice if we missed a step.

But we couldn't go on that way forever. What's amazing now is that everyone expected us to.

When Grace finally cried at the office, it was over spilled milk — literally. By the time she noticed the damp spot seeping through the fabric of her monogrammed tote, it was too late. Her pencil skirt and blouse were wet, not that she cared about that. She dropped to her knees in the middle of the hallway. The texture of the rough carpet punctured her kneecaps as she pulled out the storage bag from which a trickle of breast milk streamed silently through a leak in the plastic.

"No, no, no, no," she murmured.

Her brain rifled through expletives, but none rose to the surface. Instead, she felt her heart bleeding out as she cupped her hand beneath the bag. She tried cradling it to the kitchen sink, getting there only in time to realize that there was nothing sterile in which to store the milk as the final few milliliters of it dripped through the cracks between her fingers. *Liquid gold.*

And that was it. One hour of pumping. Lost. Please, God, just rip her freaking breasts off and give them to someone else who was more responsible. She blamed the manufacturing company. She blamed her husband. She even blamed her daughter. And if that was wrong, she didn't care.

Grace would like to outsource the whole thing — what was that called again? Oh, right, *"formula"* — but she just knew that the second she did, Emma Kate would develop childhood diabetes or terrible allergies and the doctor would turn to Grace and ask: *Were you breastfeeding?* And Liam would look at her all: *I support your decision* while silently wishing he'd had a baby with somebody else.

She rested her elbows on the edge of the stainless-steel sink and clawed her fingers through the base of her chignon. She knew that if she looked into a mirror, her eyes and nose would be red. This was the thing about crying in the office. The more you wanted not to cry, the more likely it was that you would.

"Excuse me, Grace?" The voice of Ames Garrett came from behind her. "Is this yours?"

She turned her chin barely past her shoulder, noting the wet, traitorous tote with her initials stitched to the front. "Yes. Sorry."

The two of them stood there for an uncomfortable moment. An employee obviously on the verge of some completely-inappropriate-for-work emotional breakdown and her boss. *Congratulations, Grace, you are singlehandedly sabotaging the cause of your gender.*

Before she and Emma Kate were two separate people, she'd always been slow-burn furious when someone had asked her, "Will you come back to work after the baby's born?" No one asked Liam that, so why should they ask her? But, *behold!* Here was Exhibit A.

Ames rocked back on his heels. Coins shifted in his trousers pocket. "You know what you need?" he asked. *Sleep,* she thought, immediately. *Definitely sleep.* "A smoke," he supplied.

She turned her back to the sink and ran her fingernail along her lower eyelids. "I'm breastfeeding. I can't."

"Looks to me like you just finished. You've probably got, what, another three hours? You're fine." Ames extracted a pack from the inside of his jacket pocket and tapped it twice against the heel of his hand. "Trust me. I've got two kids who slept but never at the same time and a wife who saw being a new mother as a competitive sport." Ames lowered his voice. "It wasn't pretty."

Grace touched the damp spot on her skirt, wondering when she'd manage to make it to the dry cleaners. Probably not before she wore the skirt again. She could buy a new one online, which would be easier, even have it overnighted, but Grace liked to pretend — especially to herself — that she had normal, working-woman financial concerns. Because the only socially acceptable reason a woman could work as hard as Grace did was out of necessity. She blew out a slow calming breath while Ames waited patiently in front of her.

A chance for one-on-one time with the General Counsel didn't come around every day. And even if it did, Grace wouldn't have known how to turn down the offer. So she left the drained bag in the sink, collected her tote, and followed Ames up to the eighteenth floor balconies.

Truviv relegated smokers to balcony corrals, little squares of outdoor space that echoed those near-extinct airport lounges and similarly reeked of lung cancer.

The building cast a shadow over the square of open space, leaving a slight chill in the air. She squinted out at the sun-soaked city beyond. She would kill for a bit of that sun. She felt so clammy since having a baby. The film of urine and runny feces and spit-up and drool and milk never quite washed from her body.

Ames pulled out a cigarette and handed it to Grace. She'd never smoked one before, but reasoned that if fifteen-year-olds loitering in front of malls could do it, a thirty-eight-year-old woman with a doctorate degree ought to be able to figure it out, too. She placed the papery tube in the "V" between her fingers and held it to her lips, like she'd seen done in movies. Ames spun his thumb over the lighter and a flame erupted. She leaned forward to meet it and the end of the cigarette smoldered. A satisfying curl of smoke slipped out from the tip.

She sucked gently, careful not to breathe in the smoke, while Ames expertly balanced a cigarette in his own mouth and lit it.

It was remarkable, really. One puff, and his body visibly relaxed, his shoulders retreating from his neck. He glanced sideways at her and raised his eyebrow, his mouth toying with the idea of a smile, as if to acknowledge his vice with a chagrined, *What can I say?*

It struck her that he didn't know about the list yet. She felt a bit bad now standing directly across from him one-on-one, knowing that his name was being passed around Dallas behind his back. Though Grace knew enough to know not to be the messenger.

Ames drew another breath through the cigarette and let the smoke fall out of his mouth. "My mother was babysitting the twins once and left a container of Bobbi's breast milk on the counter all day so that Bobbi had to throw the entire thing away. I thought she was going to punch my mother in the face. Instead, she just refused to speak to her for two weeks. It was almost as bad."

Grace laughed. The smoke stung the inside of her nose, making her eyes water again. "I would have punched her for sure."

She caught a glimpse of the diamond — three carats — on her left finger. It would definitely draw blood if she punched someone.

He frowned. "You probably feel like you're losing your fucking mind, don't you?" He took another drag.

Grace didn't say anything. She could feel the thin layer of ash on the balcony floor, gritty beneath her Cole Haans.

"Never mind," he said. "You don't have to answer that." He tapped his cigarette on the railing, letting the ashes fall. Grace, realizing that her ashes were flaking onto her skirt, followed suit. "Bobbi cried all the time. Bobbi never cries. She's like a living Hallmark card, this eternal ray of sunshine and optimism." He smiled and Grace could see that his wife made him happy, which was *refreshing.* There was this weird fad between men within the office to see who could complain more about their wife. *Oh my effing god, she's making me go to Disney World with the kids, kill me. I get home from work and she hands me the baby before I can even take my wallet out of my pants. I'll have to work an extra twenty years to pay for her Birkin bag.* That sort of thing. It was like they were pretending they were kidnapped from their native villages and forced to buy twenty-five-thousand-dollar cushion-cuts from Tiffany's against their will. Like, who did they think they were convincing and why did they believe the illusion that they'd made shitty life choices was such a badge of honor?

Maybe this was the real reason why Grace insisted on working despite the fact that Liam, a successful venture capitalist (along with her trust fund), could easily take care of them. She didn't want to be one of *those* wives.

"I thought the Body Snatchers had come in the middle of the night and switched her out," Ames continued. "It was like the Twilight Zone. So much crying. I'm not saying that to be mean. The stuff your bodies go through. I couldn't do it, that's for sure."

Grace folded her arms and rested her elbow in the crook of her left wrist to support her smoking arm. She had a smoking arm now, apparently. The nicotine was already buzzing through her, making her head feel heavy. A gentle ache had picked up somewhere in the center of her skull.

But as the edge dulled on her frustration over the spilled milk, she began to worry what Sloane would think of her being up here with Ames.

"Did you smoke with Bobbi?" she asked,

distracting herself. She didn't want to think about Sloane. Ames wanted to spend time. With her. She felt, she admitted, special.

"I think there's some rule that says I'm not allowed to incriminate my wife, isn't there?"

"Rule of Evidence Section 504." Grace had a memory like a steel trap.

"She doesn't find my blue-collar roots nearly as charming as she should." He winked, a gesture that should have been cheesy, but Ames had those squinty eyes that burst into wrinkles when he smiled. It was a good look.

She'd known Ames for six years and she didn't actually mind him. Even before this. She knew he and Sloane didn't exactly get along. But she'd always harbored the distinct hunch that Sloane bore at least some of the responsibility for blurring the lines between them. That and, well, nothing Ames had done was exactly *egregious*. More like open for interpretation. There were rumors. Okay, yes, there were *definitely* rumors. But weren't there rumors about everyone? Everyone had someone who didn't like them. Maybe not Grace, in particular, but most people. He was rough around the edges, at times, sure, but this was a corporate executive who smoked cigarettes and wore his sleeves rolled to the elbows.

Grace walked to the railing, flattened her forearms on the narrow beam. Boxes of grass appeared as miniature putting greens down below. Cars the size of her thumb waited at stoplights, swerved around each other, and disappeared into parking garages. Her heart rate sped as she gazed vertically down at the concrete. It was impossible to look down and not think about falling. Moments earlier, she might have considered throwing herself over the side of the building.

"You're going to be fine," Ames said. "You have a good doctor, right?"

"Emma Kate has the best pediatrician I could find. Dr. Tanaka." A soggy flake of paper came off on her tongue and she realized she'd been chewing the end of the cigarette like a thumbnail.

"For you, I mean."

Grace turned her back to the rails. "I'm fine. Just tired."

"Of course." He shuffled up next to her, a respectable distance away, leaned his own elbows against the railing. "Bobbi had postpartum depression." He shrugged. "More common with twins, I guess. She had to go on medication, but thank God

209

she did. I'll be honest," he said. "I thought it was some made-up, hippy-dippy shit. A glorified word for 'tired.' But I did my research when her doctor diagnosed it. Mood swings. Anxiety. Whole body exhaustion. Suicide. All that from having a baby. Seems like a flaw in the system."

A flaw in the system.

Yes, Grace supposed it was.

"I hardly think I'm depressed." She tilted her head. "I'm wearing Rebecca Taylor." The back of her nose felt dry from the smoke. She hoped to veer the subject away from her fragile mental state. She appreciated the concern, but the last impression she wanted to leave her boss with was that she was one sleepless night away from a mental breakdown. She waited a beat. "So," she began, "is there anything you wish you'd done differently here at Truviv?" Grace knew that men loved these kinds of questions and, in this case, the answer might actually be useful. He looked up quickly at her. "Professionally, I mean."

He settled his weight onto the rail again and dragged on the cigarette. "I don't think so." He exhaled and hitched his left cheek into a pleased half-grin. "I think I'm in pretty good shape these days."

"Then how about advice for someone like

me? What if, say, I wanted to head up a larger section within the department? You would tell me to do . . . what, exactly?"

There'd been times in Grace's life during which she'd let her ambition show, only to have it received amusedly, like a party trick, a cute young girl who knew all her state capitals and could say them on demand. Others when it had felt like a gust of wind had blown up her skirt, revealing her ambition and causing all the men in the room to become simultaneously aroused and embarrassed for her. But she no longer cared.

He nodded thoughtfully, flicked the remaining nub onto the ground, and extracted another finger-length cigarette. "Okay." He pointed the unlit cigarette at her. "First thing we need to do is to get you some more interesting work. Challenging assignments. Make sure you can run a deal not just from the regulatory side. I can help with that." Grace felt a spark of promise. A glimmer of unexpected hope. Maybe she could be more of the Marissa Mayer–type mother. Chronic overachiever. Mom on the side. "Keep a file of any compliment you receive in your inbox." He set fire to the roll. "Anytime someone tells you in writing that you've done a good job, save it. Send an email to me once a quarter with whatever's in that file and the type of work you've been doing for the last few months."

"You want me to brag?"

He scratched his hairline with his thumb. "I want you to build a case, a case as to why you deserve a promotion. You do all that and in a year we'll talk about next steps."

Grace swallowed a smile. She was proud of herself. And just a teeny-tiny bit less exhausted. Though she should probably put a moratorium on the word "teeny-tiny," a phrase which she must have picked up from Emma Kate's nanny.

There was a short pause and then — "Want to see a picture of my kids?" Ames asked.

"I thought you'd never ask." Near-strangers were always asking Grace to produce pictures of Emma Kate like they needed evidence Grace cared enough to take them. It was nice to be on the other end of it.

Ames held up his finger and balanced the cigarette bud on a nearby ashtray while he wriggled his wallet out of his back pocket. "I'm old school. Still like to keep them in here." He flipped through a couple plastic inserts and held it up to show two side-by-side school photos of his twins. Big smiles.

Not at all identical. One of the boys had red hair, the other the dark brown of his father. "Neither of them got my . . ." He pointed at this streak in his hair. It had become less noticeable since his hair had begun to gray in the last couple of years. "Waardenburg. Fifty-fifty shot." He shrugged.

His finger held open the leather. A shiny card behind one of the pictures caught her attention and she leaned in closer, pretending to admire his sons. She held her hair back.

"So handsome," she said in the tone of a college girl hired to watch a child for four hours. The top of a hotel keycard had been slid into place. The name on it: The Prescott.

She straightened and smiled. He clapped the wallet shut and stuffed it into his slacks again.

"I think so, too," he said in reply to her compliment. "But how would I ever really know? Everyone thinks that about their kids."

He rescued the cigarette and sucked on the end one more time. He laughed gently, puffing out white smoke like a dragon. "Hey, I was thinking." He dropped the stub and crushed it under the sole of his black leather shoe. "Could you do me a favor?"

CHAPTER SEVENTEEN

31-Mar

Rosalita sat on the edge of Salomon's bed. A Spider-Man bedspread was tucked beneath his armpits and he smelled like the yellow Johnson & Johnson soap she'd been using in his baths since he was a baby. "Did you finish your workbook problems?" Rosalita forced herself to use English because he'd need English more than he would need Spanish. It hurt her, this invisible communication barrier already cropping up between them.

He nodded, his thick eyelashes like curtains drawing over the crown of his cheeks. When he was a toddler, her uncle and his wife laughed and said it was a good thing that Salomon came out of her, otherwise she might not believe that he was hers. But Rosalita saw herself marked on Salomon in dozens of tiny but important ways. The flat spots on the ridges of his ears. His toler-

215

ance for extremely spicy foods. His allergic reaction to scented soaps.

She patted the solid lump of his chest. "Did you get all the answers right?"

He nodded again and she gave him a hard look in return. "Yes," he said, out loud. Sometimes she had to coax out the words that the hearing loss he'd been born with had tried to steal from him, words they'd fought hard to dig up from deep inside her sweet boy.

In the end, it had not been so painful to ask Salomon's father for the money to pay for her son's speech therapy and then for the expensive hearing aid. Rosalita was proud, but she measured her actions against only one question: What was best for Salomon? And so she asked then and she would ask again, once Salomon got into the private school program. Which he would, she told herself. Because it was her goal as much — if not more — than his.

It amazed Rosalita to watch her little boy's hands scrawling words quickly across a page, to see that he knew American history and could do fractions. Rosalita wasn't stupid, but she'd never learned to read or write English as well as she would have liked. Before the office building job, Rosalita had cleaned the houses of women who tended to send last minute text messages about where they'd left the broom or to ask if she could let the dog out and she was always embarrassed by the crude messages she sent in return, knowing they weren't right, but also not knowing how to fix them. She'd completed middle school in Mexico before moving across the border and nearly finished high school here in the U.S. She still loved to read. But those had become such small pieces of her that she knew the people in the office building where she worked would never be able to see them, not even if they had a microscope.

"I have something to show you." Salomon's body wriggled underneath the covers as he dug for some buried treasure hidden at his feet. "Ms. Ardie gave this to me." Then he was grinning and holding out his palm and in it rested a shiny gold-and-blue pin. "She said an airplane captain wears it and that I can have it."

Rosalita's cheeks flushed and she ran the back of her hand across her hairline.

"I might be a pilot one day," he said. "And then the good thing will be that I'll already have this badge."

"Perhaps," she said, placidly. She'd never been on a plane. Ardie Valdez had been on one so frequently she didn't need to save the wing pin for her own son.

And what did it matter? This was what she told herself because it was sensible and true. There was no competition. Though the meaner part of her conscience couldn't help but add that the reason there was no competition was because Ardie Valdez was already so far ahead.

And now a piece of the office and of Ardie lived in her house. A small thing. And yet, small things had broken her before.

"Or maybe even someone that *builds* airplanes." Her voice turned suddenly tired, as though she were returning home after third shift instead of leaving for it. "But only" — she dragged the covers up to his chin — "if you study hard. Give that to me," she said. "I don't want you poking yourself in your sleep."

He pushed it into her hand. It was only a piece of junk. Weightless. But it made her boy smile and that was what scared her.

The mattress sighed with the release of her weight. She flipped off the switch, leaving only the glow of the moon-shaped nightlight in the corner. With his good ear pressed into the pillow, she knew he didn't hear her when she whispered, "Te amo, Salomon."

■ ■ ■ ■

Rosalita drove to work and parked in the lot across the street from the Truviv building. The cleaning staff wasn't allowed to park inside the office garage, despite the fact that it was nearly empty at this time of night. The distance kept the cleaners from walking out with anything that wasn't nailed down.

After collecting their cart of cleaning supplies, Rosalita and Crystal rode the elevator up the building's spine and onto an office floor so devoid of life, she felt that she'd landed on the moon. Detecting the women's movements, the lights flickered on with a spitting crackle followed by the low-grade hum of fluorescent bulbs.

Crystal's baggy socks sulked around her ankles as she walked over to the empty receptionist's desk and fished through the candy bowl with raggedy nails. Rosalita swatted her hand away. "What?" Crystal snatched her hand to her chest.

"Those aren't *for* us," Rosalita said, returning to the cart where her clipboard hung.

"What, like they count them?" Crystal eyed the bowl hungrily.

"They might."

Crystal dropped the issue.

Rosalita began to work the floor with clinical efficiency. When she cleaned the east bathroom, she slipped her hand into her pocket while Crystal bent over a toilet bowl inside one of the stalls and pulled out Salomon's wing pin, then dropped it into the paper towel bin before changing the bag. She told herself she measured her actions by only one question: What was best for Salomon? She told herself that, but she also knew how to lie.

And so they continued along the fifteenth floor. Hours passed differently in the middle of the night. The simultaneous thrill and depression that came from being awake when everyone else was asleep. The sharpness of the light against the dark. The way time became only a construct and yet also the only thing that Rosalita could think about. It still reminded her of the days after Salomon's birth, when she held him to her breast as she gazed into the television, deep into the darkness, when nothing worth watching was ever on. And in the morning, she would call her sister and catalogue the night's events in minute detail — how much Salomon ate, how many hours he slept, how many hours she slept — as if this minutia needed to be documented, witnessed. And she knew that the memory of those nights would never leave her body until the day she died.

It felt like a lifetime ago that Rosalita had climbed into the web of motherhood and allowed it to stick, to weave itself into her hair in shades of gray, to crawl beneath her skin where it turned to blue and purple spider veins, to draw a shiny, taut line just above her pubic bone. Since then, the cobweb had only grown in complexity, the needs of her life only enmeshing her deeper and deeper into the silk strands until one day she might at last be gobbled up.

Alongside her, Crystal still wasn't exactly proficient but was improving and she kept the cart organized enough so that Rosalita could speed through her rounds. At this point, Rosalita was sure Crystal was pregnant by the way her fingers rested idly on her stomach and when they did, Rosalita could just make out the small mound protruding there. Probably a boy, because Crystal was skin and bones everywhere except for her belly. That was how Rosalita had been, too. And her body remembered this also by the pearly riverbeds that crawled along her sides and out from her belly button like a sun. It remembered.

Rosalita emptied the shredder and the wastepaper basket in the offices of Sloane Glover and Ardie Valdez and a new employee — Katherine Bell. When she reached the end of the hall, the corner office was closed, lights off. She knocked twice and entered.

The mistake was obvious. A yelp, quickly stifled. A rough huff of air. Rosalita caught sight of a woman with dark, short hair staring, open mouthed, at her in the strip of light cast over her from the cracked-open door, eyes wide and shining in the dark like a raccoon exposed in the beam of a flashlight. Rosalita lost her breath in a gasp that made hardly any sound at all. And then the moments that followed were quiet, too. So quiet that the only noises were those of skin against skin and fabric and gulps and a man coughing and saliva and hair and —

Rosalita backed out of the office, jamming her shoulder so painfully against the edge of the frame she could see the colors of the bruise that would form stamped against the inside of her eyelids as she blinked back tears. A short cry caught in her chest as her back bowed and she clutched at her arm. Tingles raced electric bolts down to her elbow. Her mind tilted into a spin of double vision that churned her stomach. She had just enough sense to close the door.

Crystal stood from behind the cart, holding a bottle of Windex like a gun. "Are you okay?"

Rosalita's internal organs stampeded for her throat. "We're skipping the corner office tonight."

"Why?" Crystal stared through the door as if she might see what Rosalita had seen.

Rosalita swallowed. Her shoulder hurt. "Someone's in there."

"But you said —"

"Not tonight." Rosalita half expected the door to fling open, but so far, it hadn't. Her face felt feverish. She didn't look at Crystal. "I have to use the restroom," she said. "Go ahead and take care of this line of offices."

Rosalita's ears rang. She stretched her hand out, letting her fingers follow along the wall for balance and direction. It led her to the restroom. The lights beamed on in one click, too bright and demanding. She leaned over the faucet, pushing her weight onto the white porcelain. Sweat glimmered between the dark roots of her hair and beneath the follicles of her eyebrows.

She stood, almost panting. Her brown eyes were pools of mud reflected back to her. She splashed her face with cool water and let the rivulets run down to drip from the tip of her nose and her chin. Then she squeezed her eyes shut against her own reflection and wiped the beads from her eyelashes. Her body, she knew, had always had the better memory.

CHAPTER EIGHTEEN

31-Mar

Sloane had returned home from Target, where she'd purchased a birthday present for Ardie's son, Michael, an hour ago. The party was tomorrow. Saturday. It had snuck up on her, all tucked innocently as it was on her calendar right after a hellish Friday and, well, here it was. Now, the night before the birthday party hardly seemed the appropriate time to *tell* Ardie. She tried to draft the text message in her head as if it were a work email: *Ardie, I have something to tell you, could we have a quick word?*

She could pick up the phone. She wasn't a teenager. But she wasn't exactly sure that was a good idea, either. Sloane really was the worst for procrastinating, wasn't she?

She had a Dilemma on her hands and, to cope, she'd been standing barefoot in the kitchen, eating her feelings, when the second moral quandary presented itself.

Abigail's phone buzzed. That was how it began, anyway. And now, well — Sloane wasn't being *nosy,* was she? She was being a *good* mother. Poking around was just as much a requirement as helping with homework. Anyone would agree with that. In fact, as Sloane thought about it she was sure she'd read it in an article somewhere. Snooping was Sloane's love language.

Maybe it did deserve some rebranding, though. Curiosity. There, that sounded better. Just in case Derek ever asked how she came to be scrolling through Abigail's cell phone. She would shrug and say, Oh, I don't know, I was *curious.*

Derek was in their bedroom doing pull-ups from a bar he'd wedged into the doorframe. She could hear his big, manly breaths from her spot perched in the kitchen where last week he'd installed two light fixtures — French country chandeliers custom-made in the Luberon — that now hung ostentatiously over the island, taunting Sloane with the knowledge of the accompanying credit card statement that would soon arrive in the mailbox. Not that she could talk, having just "invested" in a pair of Clizia Mesh Manolo Blahniks, the sight of which nearly brought her straight to climax. But still. Before she'd gotten married, her mother had told her that for any marriage to work, both partners needed to share similar attitudes toward money. Consequently, Sloane had taken her and Derek's mutually expensive tastes as a sign of their compatibility. Years later, her parents were divorced and she'd discovered that what mutually expensive tastes amounted to was *two* people spending her paychecks at an alarmingly fast clip instead of just the one.

Abigail's phone vibrated facedown on the countertop again, spinning a quarter inch. It was ten-thirty at night. *Who* was texting Abigail?

Then it occurred to her: She was Abigail's *mom,* not some jealous girlfriend. She didn't have to *wonder,* she could just check. One moral quandary solved and just like that her concern over speaking to Ardie before tomorrow's party faded to background stress.

She punched Abigail's passcode into the phone and navigated to the green-and-white messaging icon. There they were. Three new messages neatly lined up on the left side of the screen.

Sloane devoured them whole:

Grady Reed
Everyone knows you ran and told your

mom on us. We didn't even do anything. Not cool. We wouldn't have talked to you if we knew you were a tattletale.

Steve Lightner
Yeah. My dad says that we can't have you at the boy-girl party at my place now because you tattle and are too sensitive.

Grady Reed
Sorry BLABIGAIL.

Sloane slammed the phone down on the granite with a grunt of carnal anger. "You all right in there?" Derek called from the other room.

"Fine. I'm fine. Sorry." The decision not to respond with what she'd found on Abigail's phone was swift and instinctive. Unfair, probably. Immoral? Maybe. Abigail was his child, too. Equal parts. Though she did feel that, in the event of a tiebreaker, surely Abigail was just a tiny bit more hers, what with the gestating inside of her for nine months and what have you. Derek certainly didn't have a flabby kangaroo pouch underneath *his* belly button. Still, in a perfect world, she ought to be able to invite him along in her parental fury.

But no. She couldn't risk her husband's

propensity towards reasonableness. Her daughter was being *harassed.* Obviously. And Grady Reed had brought Sloane Glover's name into it. He'd said *"mom"* and *"mom"* meant Sloane. Not Derek. No, she absolutely couldn't risk being talked down from a ledge. She was angry. She should be angry. Anger was actually the only reasonable way to feel at the moment.

Her daughter's social status was teetering precariously. Isla Lombardi wouldn't even talk to Abigail anymore and apparently that was important because Isla Lombardi had divided the girls in the class into Cool and Not and Abigail hadn't made the cut. Hence those first nasty text messages — *bitch, cunt, slut.* Only the Nots received them. Isla's mother — a marketing director in Irving — had been trying to sell the school on the idea that Isla and her friends were exhibiting some form of new-generation feminism — girls being opinionated, forceful, and outspoken. They simply weren't fitting into the likable female character narrative and therefore shouldn't be punished. Sloane hoped Isla's mother got her hand caught in a garbage disposal, so maybe Sloane was exhibiting some new-generation feminism, too.

When Sloane turned the phone over, a

hairline crack snaked across the glass screen. She closed her eyes, breathing heavily, until she felt the color in her cheeks fade.

"Derek." She padded into their bedroom, where her husband was crunching, shirtless, on the Persian rug, God bless him. "I got an email." Like anything else, lying was a skill that improved with practice and Sloane had some experience in deceiving her husband. She wasn't proud of it. But *this* was for Derek's own protection. Saving him from how the sausage got made, so to speak, and so, if anything, Sloane should be applauded for bearing the burden of their shared lives. Some might say that she was even a little heroic. "I have a bit more work to do tonight. I'll be upstairs in the office." He bared his teeth as he hissed air out on an upward crunch. It looked painful. Sloane wondered if the two of them — Sloane and Derek — were in a game of chicken to see who would let themselves go first. She prayed that he would.

"Okay. I'm going to bed soon. Can you check that the doors are locked on your way up?" She nodded. "Sure you don't want to . . ." He made eyes in the direction of their California King–sized mattress. ". . . first?"

"Quite," she said. Given that Derek had

the body of a twenty-five-year-old, Sloane should probably worry about her husband's fidelity, but for whatever reason, she didn't. *How would you feel, honestly, if you found out Derek had been prowling around?* Grace once asked her. *Like shit,* she'd responded. *But then I'd get over it.* And in her core, she believed that to be true.

In any event, she couldn't fake heavy sex breathing and maintain her current level of rage at the same time. So she escaped upstairs, her indignation set to boil.

At her computer, she used the built-in mouse to navigate to her remote desktop, where she pulled up a template on Truviv letterhead and dashed out the school board superintendent's name in the address line. Sloane had been circling around an idea ever since Abigail had received the first text messages calling her *those* names.

It had been a year or so ago that Sloane had seen a news story about a girl who'd hung herself in her bathroom because her classmates were cyberbullying her over a boy. It had been a salacious news story. The kind designed to make parents everywhere collectively freak out. Pictures of this sweet, smiling girl with braces and fuzzy pillows on her bed went viral and Sloane had thought, along with everyone else, *Oh, please let that never be my child.* That was the point.

But hidden in all of the human interest, heart-strings-pulling *meat* of the story, there had been an actual legal theory that had snagged Sloane's attention. The students who'd bullied the girl faced both criminal and civil responsibility for the girl's death. They faced *jail* time. And it had opened up a conversation, too, about how much responsibility the school should bear for the suicide. *Real* consequences, *real* case law.

See! Sloane wanted to wave her laptop over her head at a PTA meeting: *I am not crazy!*

Because enough was enough. That was how Sloane saw it.

On screen, the cases multiplied. Laney Presper, twelve years old, jumped to her death after complaining about online bullying months earlier. The conclusion: purported bullies could be charged with criminal offenses when their victims committed suicide.

Jackson Worrall, eighteen, killed himself via carbon monoxide poisoning following a series of text messages from his girlfriend, who was later convicted of involuntary manslaughter.

Matt Renard, fifteen, hung himself to

escape cyberbullying. The result: legislation passed that allowed law enforcement to press traditional charges against harassers whose behavior contributed to another person taking his or her own life.

She ran search after search, summarizing and piecing together an argument that might finally encourage the school to do something about the way her daughter was being treated. So what if she was exploiting the fact that she was an attorney. This was her daughter!

Sloane was an excellent typist. Fast and deadly accurate. She lost track of time as she banged words into her keyboard deep into the night until she resurfaced to a world lit only by the red, green, and yellow stars of modem, alarm, and DVR receiver lights.

She stared at the final product, a legal memorandum to the school board. Her case citations, she knew, were impeccable. Her argument, which centered around the idea that bullies and those who allowed their bullying could be held liable for the physical and psychological pain of their victims, felt reasonably solid. There was just one thing that was bothering her: she was Abigail's mother.

It was just that, well, wouldn't it feel a bit more *weighty* if it came from an attorney who was *not* related to Abigail? An outside source. Someone else. Someone like . . . Ardie.

Her fingers hovered over the keyboard. It was only a bit of artistic license. A white lie, really. Sloane was sure that Ardie would have agreed if she'd asked her, but time was of the essence and tomorrow was Michael's birthday party. Ardie didn't have time to be bothered and, really, what she was proposing wasn't wrong, exactly. Plagiarism was wrong. This was the opposite. Sloane was giving Ardie credit for a memo that she'd written herself. It was actually fairly nice of her, wasn't it? No harm, no foul, and whatnot.

Sloane made the decision. She signed the legal memorandum: *Adriana Valdez, Attorney-at-Law.* And before she stood — knees aching from sitting crossed-legged in her ergonomic chair — she searched the web for the email address and copied it into the "To" line. *I'm copying our attorney, Adriana Valdez,* she typed, *to assist in this matter, as needed.* Please find attached a legal memorandum she's written on the subject for your review and consideration. *Kind regards.*

DEPOSITION TRANSCRIPT

26-Apr

Ms. Yeh: Mrs. Garrett, allow me to introduce myself. My name is Helen Yeh and I'm acting as counsel for the respondents. I'll be conducting your formal interview. In your deposition, I will ask you questions and you are going to answer them under oath. The court reporter is attempting to transcribe everything we say. It's important that we don't interrupt one another and that you answer each question verbally. Let's begin.

Ms. Yeh: How long have you been married to Ames Garrett?

Witness: Twenty-seven years this May.

Ms. Yeh: How would you describe your marriage?

Witness: Well, after that many years, it's not exactly fireworks and rose petals every day, but I'd describe it as happy. He still always planned a weekend trip for my birthday.

He never forgot our anniver-
sary. We had family dinners. We
talked. Not just small talk
about the kids. We really
talked. He told me about work
and he took my career advice
seriously even though I haven't
had a job in years. I have
always appreciated that. Of
course, over the last few weeks,
his demeanor completely
changed. Depressed, moody,
stressed.

Ms. Yeh: Was there a reason?

Witness: I'm sure it's because
of the BAD Men List. All those
lies.

Ms. Yeh: Okay, so you saw the
list and you are telling us that
Mr. Garrett's name appeared on
it?

Witness: Yes.

Ms. Yeh: And you felt that his
name didn't deserve to be included?

Witness: I knew he didn't belong
on that list from the start,
but once I figured out Sloane
Glover was the one who added
him, well, that told me every-

thing I needed to know.

Ms. Yeh: Stepping back from Ms. Glover specifically, what motive would a woman have to lie in making sexual harassment and other allegations that were found on the spreadsheet?

Witness: Attention. Career advancement. Financial gain.

Ms. Yeh: The list was anonymous.

Witness: It's not very anonymous now, is it? If it was meant to be so anonymous, then why did Sloane sue my husband and his company with her name on the docket?

Ms. Yeh: That's a valid question. Let's see. Mrs. Garrett, do you know who Clarence Thomas is?

Witness: A Supreme Court Justice.

Ms. Yeh: Do you know the name of the woman that accused Justice Thomas of sexual harassment?

Witness: I think I might have known once but I can't recall at the moment.

Ms. Yeh: How about any of the women involved in the sexual harassment allegations of David

Letterman? Bill Cosby? Do you recall their names?

Witness: No, I don't.

Ms. Yeh: I could go on, but is it fair of me to assume that these men, Bill Cosby, David Letterman, and Justice Clarence Thomas, are better known than your husband, Ames Garrett?

Witness: Yes.

Ms. Yeh: So it doesn't appear that these women achieved any sort of widespread notoriety as a result of their sexual harassment claims. Do you know who Tyson Grange is?

Witness: He's a basketball player. He plays for the Lakers, I believe. One of my husband's friends, actually.

Ms. Yeh: That's right. He plays for the Lakers and he is sponsored by Truviv. You may also know the name, Ariel Lopez, silver-medal Olympic gymnast. She was also sponsored by Truviv. Six months ago, Miss Lopez accused Tyson Grange of sexual assault. Do you know what happened next?

Witness: No.

Ms. Yeh: I'll tell you. Nothing happened to Tyson Grange. Miss Lopez, however, lost her sponsorship with the very company your husband worked for. Not a lot by way of financial gain, you might say. And Tyson was, as you mentioned, Ames's friend.

Witness: Those are different cases. Apples and oranges. I never said all women make sexual harassment allegations for financial gain or notoriety. I believe women. Most women, anyway. But there's an exception to every rule. We can't just give *every* female accuser carte blanche, can we? Look, I'm a woman and I'm saying that. This "believe all women no matter what," come on, that's ludicrous. Sorry for the strong words, I know it's an unpopular opinion, but that's the truth.

Ms. Yeh: And so if Sloane Glover, as you said, added your husband's name to the list, claiming that he had a history of

sexual harassment, you're saying that you do not believe her.
Is that right?
Witness: Listen. There are some
people that have to give *everything* a label just to make
themselves feel better, to feel
like the victim. I'm telling
you, that's Sloane. You should
hear what's been going on at
Abigail's school just because
her little ten-year-old daughter wasn't *popular* enough! Kids
just being silly kids and Sloane
has to go on the warpath, telling everyone who will listen
that it's *bullying*. I know what
happened and it wasn't bullying. And now she does the same
thing here. All of a sudden it's
"sexual harassment." Unfortunately, my husband — my family
— actually has fallen victim to
malicious bullying and who do
we have to thank for that?
Sloane.

CHAPTER NINETEEN

Michael still slept in pull-ups. Ardie cherished few things as much as her sleep and getting up for frequent potty breaks in the middle of the night would have been sacrificing a piece of herself that she wasn't prepared to give up. *Cars 3* roared in the background, the remote a few inches too far for her to bother turning down the volume. She'd made a compelling case for *Tangled,* but lost out and found herself looking up from the strewn carcasses of cardboard boxes, from which she was fashioning buildings for tomorrow's superhero party, to see what the talking cars were going to get up to next. Michael darted in and out of the living room in his pull-ups and a Spider-Man T-shirt, waving orange-and-white pom-poms around and calling them "fire."

Ardie's legs splayed out into a floppy "V"

on the floor, another sheet of white butcher paper laid between them. Her back ached as she colored tiny black windows with magic marker onto it. She wouldn't get the ink off her hands for weeks. But it was worth it. Trays of peanut butter and jelly sandwiches cut into shields cooled in the refrigerator. Superhero masks had been laid out on the party table. And soon Ardie would be finished with the life-sized — or at least child-life-sized — city, which her son's tiny guests would plow through and save. So Ardie felt a little like a superhero herself.

Ardie, like many of us, had caught perfectionism, an illness that we heard was more common in women by a factor of roughly twenty to one. To the best of our understanding, it was transferred through social media and the pages of glossy magazines that were displayed face-out in the checkout line and, once contracted at the age of twelve or thirteen, could be cured by no number of Jezebel think pieces or edgy rom-coms in which the leading lady boldly portrayed a train wreck or a bad mommy. For our children, we chased the gold standard of suburban contentment set by our own stay-at-home mothers, while simultaneously stepping into the shoes of our bread-winning fathers. And we made sure that everyone knew we were handling it all swimmingly by the way we wrote notes on napkins dutifully folded into our children's lunch boxes and threw Halloween parties with Swiss cheese cut into the shapes of ghosts.

Because honestly, if that wasn't success, what was?

As for Ardie, she saw no need to psychoanalyze exactly *what* she was trying to prove or to *whom* by this uncharacteristic display of domestic prowess. She was taking a long swig of Diet Coke when the doorbell rang.

Ardie glanced toward the front door, bristling. How many times had she told Tony *not* to ring the doorbell when Michael might be sleeping? Whether or not Michael *was* sleeping was hardly a prerequisite to her annoyance.

"Michael, your father's here," she called in the direction of her son's bedroom, hating herself for saying "your father" instead of something more inclusive, like "Dad" or "Daddy."

She was terrible at being divorced. But then it wasn't exactly a life skill she'd planned to need. Like building a fire. Or sewing.

Her joints felt a hundred years older as

she crawled from the floor to her feet.

"Coming, coming," she shouted as Michael zoomed past and beat her to the door.

"Hiya, champ." Tony ruffled Michael's hair. Unsurprisingly, Michael looked nothing like either Ardie or Tony. Michael had sunburnt hair and freckles, big, adorable ears, and legs as thin as Ardie's wrist all the way up to his waist. When Tony left, she worried that he'd abandon Michael. That he and Braylee would start a nice biological family. And that the son they'd shared between them wouldn't be enough to hold her ex-husband without the pull of DNA. But she'd been wrong. So wrong, in fact, that she almost felt guilty. If anything, Tony had dedicated himself twice over to Michael and apparently he and Braylee didn't intend to have children at all.

She'd have thought that having an adopted child amid a divorce would spare her from the frequent exasperating reminders of *You're-acting-like-your-father,* but also no. Michael was Tony in so many ways and it did something to her heart for which she'd never have the right words.

"Where's Braylee?" Ardie asked, because she didn't want to feel the familiar spike of jealousy when Michael asked Tony first.

"Hanging at home." Tony wore his plaid

pajama bottoms. He'd driven ten minutes and showed up at her door in *pajamas* and Ardie was supposed to accept that she and her ex-husband weren't a perfect match. "The balloons are in the truck. I'll grab them."

"Let me help! Let me help!" Michael's little-boy hair flopped atop his head as he bounced around his father's legs.

"You don't have shoes on," Tony said.

"Or pants," Ardie pointed out.

But the mission was already lost. Tony smiled apologetically and the pair came back with three cellophane bags bursting with red and white balloons.

"Thanks, you can tie them on the kitchen chairs."

"Wow, you've really gone all out. He's going to love this." She was so tired of Tony being generous with his words just because he'd been the one to leave. It left her no choice but to be civil.

"Yes, he will," she said.

"Four years old, how did *that* happen?"

"Change is inevitable." What she wanted to say was that yesterday Michael had sung the entire rap verse of "You're Welcome" from *Moana* and didn't that mean that their child was a genius? They used to collect these little Michael anecdotes and share them with each other excitedly as they brushed their teeth and washed their faces, still talking about Michael as they climbed into bed side by side. Had that been part of the problem? Or did he now do this with Braylee?

Ardie did nothing to ease the silence, though this was a characteristic that had existed long before the divorce. They watched the little boy between them until at last Tony pushed his hands on his thighs and his knees gave a familiar *snap-crackle-pop* as he stood. "Well," he said, which meant that he was leaving. She was still trying to get used to this quiet revelation. Tony was a person who left. Ardie, meanwhile, was a person who stayed.

DEPOSITION TRANSCRIPT

27-Apr

Ms. Sharpe: Ms. Valdez, you mentioned a party earlier. What party were you referring to?

Respondent 2: A birthday party. For my son. He just turned four.

Ms. Sharpe: And some of your co-workers attended, is that correct?

Respondent 2: That's correct.

Ms. Sharpe: May I ask which ones?

Respondent 2: Sloane Glover, Grace Stanton, and Katherine Bell, though I think, in retrospect, that perhaps inviting Katherine wasn't such a great idea.

Ms. Sharpe: Why do you say that?

Respondent 2: Well, because of what happened after.

CHAPTER TWENTY

1-Apr

We will say this: none of us thought that motherhood and work could exist harmoniously. If anything, they were two forces, diametrically opposed. We were the prisoners, strapped to the medieval stretching device, having enjoyed the rare privilege of both loving and having chosen our torturers. There was only the small matter of our joints being pulled apart and our hearts spilling out from our rib cages.

We woke in the night to the sound of small voices and trudged half-asleep down halls to faces that didn't care whether we had a draft due by lunch tomorrow. We held our breath as we checked for fevers, rifling through the earthquake a sick kid would wreak on our schedule, and then making urgent calls to friends and family in a last ditch effort to piece together childcare or whatever the minimum requirements were to keep someone from calling protective services. We told our kids to "pretend not to be sick" so that we could send them to daycare to get everyone else's kids sick. We figured the favor had often been returned. We told ourselves, as our noses ran and our heads ached and our stomachs refused food, that we were *fine.* Because, whatever happened, we were the defaults, the ones stuck with the task of figuring out what to do about, well, everything.

Was it any wonder, then, that one of us snapped? Was that not precisely what the system was designed to accomplish?

Rosalita walked with her son to a house that represented the two directions in which their lives were already pulling and she worried how her heart would take it if one day he looked back at her not with pride, but pity. She supposed, in the end, that was motherhood.

"It looks empty." Salomon peered up at the house on Morningside Avenue as he walked the brick path with his mother. Rosalita had been expecting an impersonally large mansion, but Ardie's house had the style of a cottage — a very nice, large cottage — with blue trim and ivy growing up the white wall. The oak in the front yard was as thick as a bear and shaded the lawn where an iron bench waited to be sat upon. Rosalita couldn't see how anyone's life could be stressful if they came home to a place this lovely. *Good for Ardie.*

"You are working, Salomon. When you are working, you arrive at least ten minutes early."

As they walked up to the front door, Salomon toyed nervously with the brim of his baseball cap. "*Why,* though?"

"Because you're here to be useful. Not to *party.*" She gave a small wiggle of a dance to tease him and then pushed Salomon gently toward the doorbell. "Remember to keep your hat on, *pajarito,*" she added quickly as he pushed the button.

"Do you think there will be candy?" he turned to ask, smashing his hand over his cap.

The sound of footsteps approached from the other side of the door. "I brought you snacks. You are *working,*" she repeated. "Ms. Valdez is paying you. She's not paying you because she needs a food-eater." She pinched the back of his neck.

"She might," he grumbled, swatting her hand away.

Rosalita had only a spare second to rethink the entire idea, to consider leaving before she allowed her son to step foot inside this beautiful home. And then it was too late.

Ardie appeared and she was ushering them across the threshold and Rosalita told herself she was being ridiculous. It was $125. On a Saturday. All was well. Better than well, even.

Once inside, Rosalita was met with more immediate concerns. Such as whether or not to take off her shoes. She seemed to recall vaguely that this was a thing white people did. Her uncle worked as an air-conditioner repairman and he said that he had to wear foamy foot-covers over his boots before he entered a customer's home. This felt like an opportunity for immense embarrassment should she choose incorrectly.

She glanced at Ardie's feet. She was wearing a pair of slip-on flats — loafers, Rosalita thought they were called — and did not seem to be worrying about Rosalita's feet in the slightest. So she kept them on and when Ardie beckoned her further into the house without mentioning the footwear, she relaxed. A little.

"I have your costume all laid out for you. You can change in the guest room," Ardie said to Salomon, pointing him down the hall. "You're going to make a tremendous Spider-Man." Salomon grinned. He adored

Spider-Man.

"Rosalita, what can I get for you? Mimosa? Coke? Sparkling water? Iced tea?"

She followed Ardie into the kitchen. Her house was much cleaner than Rosalita had expected. Compared to the rest of the women on the fifteenth floor, Ardie Valdez was less . . . contained. Like a person with threads popped at the seams. Her hair was never quite brushed in the back. Her blazers were too long in the arms. She wore wide-legged pants that wrinkled when she sat. But Rosalita had noticed that Ardie made certain investments. A pretty handbag. Beautiful leather shoes, though not the pointy-toed, dangerous-looking ones the other women wore.

Rosalita clasped her hands together at her waist. "I'm okay, thank you."

"We're about to have ten children under the age of five in this house, you may need something to take the edge off." Ardie wiped a countertop with a paper towel.

"I'm okay."

Ardie pushed her thin lips together and nodded. "Me too. I'm sticking to iced tea. Help yourself if you change your mind." She tossed the damp paper towel into the garbage. "Salomon is doing great in our lessons, by the way. He'll be ready for the entrance exam, I have no doubt."

Rosalita perked up. Salomon was a subject matter she couldn't resist. That was how the tutoring sessions came to be. *Do you have kids?* Ardie once asked her after they'd been having their small snippets of conversation for many months. And Rosalita had been proud, proud, proud to tell Ardie about how smart her little boy was and Ardie had listened, and then every time she saw Ardie thereafter, she would say: *How's Salomon?* And Rosalita would tell her that he was well, until one day his teacher had sent him home with a note in tricky, unreadable cursive. Timidly, she'd presented it to Ardie, who translated it for her. The gist? Salomon needed to *change* schools. He would not reach his potential at their neighborhood one. He was, his teacher believed, gifted. Gifted!

Rosalita had cried. Not happy tears. Helpless ones. But a few days later, Ardie had left a few printed pages on top of her desk, along with a sticky note that read: *For Rosalita.*

A new school with an entrance exam and scholarships, and Ardie would help Salomon get in.

"Do you think so?" Rosalita asked. "Is he understanding the mathematics or just memorizing it?" She touched her finger lightly to her temple.

For most of their sessions, Rosalita took Salomon to meet Ardie at the Barnes & Noble where Ardie ordered cold "coffee" slush that came with a swirl of whipped cream. Rosalita wandered the aisles, pulling out travel books and imagining trips to locations she wouldn't visit. Many times since, Rosalita had wanted to ask why Ardie was helping her, but she guessed it had something to do with not wanting to be home alone when her own son was at his father's house. Rosalita wasn't a lucky person, but she was lucky that she didn't have to share.

"Oh, he understands it. He just gets lazy about applying all the steps occasionally. I keep telling him: math is a subject for which you have to show your work."

Rosalita bobbed her head. "I will work with him at home. I will keep telling him." She then checked over her shoulder for Salomon to appear, as though the beautiful house might have gobbled him whole. But he returned, in a full-body Spider-Man suit. He struck a pose and stuck his forearm out, fingers splayed to cast an imaginary web.

Ardie clapped her hands. "Perfect. Salomon, can you please help me carry these trays out to the backyard?"

Rosalita would have liked to ask Ardie more about Salomon's progress. She would have liked to fish for compliments, really. Those for her son were the best kind. If his father was nothing else, he was smart. It was one of Rosalita's sole sources of comfort when it came to Salomon's paternal heritage.

Soon enough, the house was filling. Over the next thirty minutes, kids stampeded into the house, trailing moms and dads in their wake. Rosalita stood patiently in the corner of the kitchen, her purse hooked over her wrist. She tried neither to hide herself nor to mingle with the other guests. She had worn a jean dress from Old Navy with slip-on sandals and was glad to see that she'd chosen well for the party.

Through the windows, she could see Salomon passing out superhero masks and capes to the younger children. He introduced himself to grown-ups. He showed the toddlers how to flex their muscles. He fit in. She wanted this. She did. But it wasn't without discomfort.

Even from her place in the kitchen, there was no missing the Sloane woman's entrance. She wore a fitted blue-and-white striped tee, skinny jeans, and sling-back wedges with a cutesy-checkered pattern.

Her hair was pulled into a shiny, blonde ponytail that bounced against the back of her neck. She was speaking loudly, as if narrating the entrance for her family. Her hands rested on a little girl's shoulders. The man — her husband — closed the door behind them. "Look at *this*!" Sloane exclaimed to the room in general. "Ardie went all out."

Sloane's daughter looked up and whispered something in her mother's ear and then skipped outside. Rosalita's eyes followed and, in moments, the little girl had found Salomon and the two older kids took on the role of chief organizers together.

"Is he yours?" Sloane crossed the kitchen and helped herself to one of the champagne glasses. "Want anything, honey?" she asked over her shoulder. But her husband was already stepping outside to where the kids and other adults were gathered.

"Yes. His name is Salomon."

Sloane poured a mostly full glass of champagne, the foam bubbling up so precariously close to the rim that Rosalita felt certain it would spill over. But it didn't and Sloane topped it with a splash of orange juice. "They look like they're almost the same age, my Abigail and Sal— Salomon." She stumbled over his name.

"I'm Sloane, by the way. I don't think we've formally met. I recognize you from . . . from . . ." She twirled her finger in the air like she was trying to catch the word and then snapped her fingers. "The office!"

"Rosalita." She extended her right hand.

But just then the front door chimed with new guests and Sloane's hand, cool and smooth in her own, slid free as she looked back to the entryway.

"Grace! Katherine! Excuse me." She held up one apologetic finger. "Just one moment." She teetered off in her wedges, champagne glass in hand. "Y'all made it! Did you drive over together? Look at you two."

There was a lot of hugging. That particular lean-from-the-waist, straight-backed, neck-arching hug of women like Sloane. And Rosalita saw that Katherine was a woman with short hair — that woman from the office — and quickly angled her face away.

Rosalita avoided looking down the hall and instead let her eyes travel the room to the cat-shaped cookie jar, to an empty fruit bowl, to a child's backpack hooked onto a miniature table-and-chair set.

And now the women were clomping across the wood floors.

"Wine!" Sloane said to Katherine, who

clasped the neck of a bottle. "To a children's birthday party! I like your style."

Sloane took the bottle as though it were her house and set it on the kitchen counter. "Come in, come in, I was just chatting with Rosalita, here." She pronounced Rosalita's name as though it were a fiesta.

"Grace." Another blonde woman, slightly younger and very pretty, held out her hand for Rosalita.

"Hello," said Rosalita. "My son is helping with the party." She pointed outside to where Salomon was giving a piggyback ride to Ardie's son, Michael. He was a hit.

"I just had a baby. And I'm using this as an excuse to sneak away for a couple teeny tiny hours. I feel guilty, but . . ." She shrugged. She didn't actually seem like she felt all that guilty. Rosalita already knew about the baby from the pumping equipment stowed underneath her desk, but she pretended she didn't.

When Salomon had been born, she hadn't wanted to leave him even for an hour. But she had to. Sometimes she overheard the women in the office complain that they couldn't wait to return to work after having a baby. But Rosalita knew that they could wait. Because they did.

Katherine had seen Rosalita. She was sure

of that much. Katherine had done a similar angling away of her face the moment their eyes had glinted off one another's, like a ricochet. Katherine went straight over to where the beverages were set up. "Want anything, Grace?" she asked, without glancing again in Rosalita's direction. No one else seemed to notice. Katherine skipped the orange juice altogether and when she finished pouring, she suggested they go outside. The suggestion managed not to include Rosalita. But Rosalita saw. Rosalita always saw everything. The question in this case had been: in Ames's office that night, what exactly *had* she seen?

CHAPTER TWENTY-ONE

1-Apr

The champagne bubbles had gone straight to Sloane's head. She was considering asking Rosalita to arrange a playdate with her son — what was his name? Sal— Sal— Sal-something. Yes, she should *do* that. She put the glass to her lips again, one hand on her hip, thinking. But . . . would that be open-minded or condescending? Asking Rosalita's son to play with Abigail, she meant.

And, actually, was *wondering* whether it was open-minded in itself evidence of a lack of open-mindedness? This was a conundrum. Sloane hated these ethical jigsaw puzzles. Wasn't it enough that she *liked* everyone? She'd never met a person that she couldn't talk to properly. But no, that was apparently naïve of her. Or, an uglier word she'd learned — *privileged.*

In Ardie's backyard, the sun shined with just the right fervor. Branches swayed overhead and the shrieks of children knocking over cardboard buildings felt like a snapshot out of a Pottery Barn Kids catalogue. She would worry about the politics of a playdate later.

She really did enjoy the sensation of bubbles swimming up to her head.

For another moment, she stood atypically off to the side of the party, watching her daughter play superhero with Rosalita's son. Two small children whose relative ages made them relatively important in this one particular context.

She'd deleted the text messages on Abigail's phone. *Poof! Gone!* And now look! Her daughter was playing happily outside and Sloane had made that happen. Abigail's meddling mother.

Maybe the emailed memorandum was a bit much in the light of day, but the school needed to be taught a lesson and who could blame her? She was a *mother.*

She smiled the easy smile of someone one-and-a-half drinks in, then returned to the patio, where Grace, Ardie, and Katherine stood around her husband.

"Are you swimming in estrogen yet?" She looped her arm through his elbow. His soft, worn-in polo brushed against her cheek. He was a dad who looked great in backyards.

Tailor-made for tossing a football and carrying children on his shoulders. She was still debating whether to tell him about her missive to the school board. She was leaning toward no. It was, after all, a formal complaint to his employer, but that was precisely *why* she'd had to take matters so firmly into her own hands. It was better for him to be kept in the dark. Innocent. And anyway, a legal memorandum wasn't his purview.

He bowed his head, his stubble catching her hair. "I remembered to hold my breath before I dove in."

She grinned at the group. "Excellent, then what'd I miss?"

Grace held a bottle of champagne by the neck. She wore a chambray shirt tucked into an A-line floral skirt. Sloane had never looked that put-together after Abigail had been born. She'd lost the baby weight relatively quickly despite having gained a full forty-five pounds, but her shape was another story. It had been like her body had shifted half an inch to the left and didn't settle back in until almost a year postpartum. "I was just topping off Katherine's glass, here." She gave a small curtsy. "It *appears* her roots are beginning to show." Grace waggled her eyebrows mischievously.

Katherine took an aggressively long swig of champagne and Sloane squinted at her. She was too young to be showing gray.

"She was just complimenting me on my *potty platta.*" Ardie held up a fruit and cheese tray stabbed through with toothpicks. Sloane hesitated and then her eyes widened, which was probably overdoing it, but she didn't care. "Have you been *hiding* a Boston accent?"

The thought tickled her right along with the champagne bubbles. Perfectly proper Katherine Bell. Master enunciator. Sloane helped herself to one of the toothpicks with watermelon attached and popped it into her mouth. "I thought you were a boarding school girl or some such?" Sloane munched.

"Not exactly," she said, taking another sip. "South Boston. Public school."

"You've come a long way from home, Dorothy," Grace said.

"Dah-thy," Katherine quipped.

"Oh! Oh! Say something else!" Sloane clapped her hands. And she only rolled her eyes slightly when, after that, Derek whisked her glass away. Such a teacher. But she could always locate another.

Katherine held out her glass to Grace, who obliged with a soft, complicit laugh. "I guess I'm driving now."

Katherine pointed a finger at Sloane. Her nails were childishly short. Chewed nearly to the quick. "Sloane Glovah, you ah wicked smaht."

Maybe it was the lovely weather or the smell of fresh cut grass, but Sloane made an impulsive and irreversible decision to like Katherine. Katherine wasn't an *ingénue*. She was a woman who'd fashioned herself out of scraps into a mosaic of a Harvard Law graduate and Big Law associate. She had gumption.

I want to be like you. The words that Katherine had said — maybe said — bubbled to the surface along with the bubbles. Or — wait — did she say, *I want to be you?* Did it matter? Sloane felt the slurpy, slushy feeling of guilt mucking about, weighing her down somewhere in her conscience. Goodness, she hoped she wouldn't have a hangover.

"Okay," Derek said, setting Sloane's half-full glass on the outdoor dining table. "Better question: Who's more of an A-hole, Jerry Jones or Bill Belichick?"

"Well, I know who's more of a winner." Katherine lifted one eyebrow.

"Ohhh, burn." Derek shook his hand out, laughing. Though he really did love the Cowboys. Every year for his birthday, Sloane scored two of Truviv's field-level seats. "So, what brought you here from Beantown?" he asked.

Sloane sighed and slyly retrieved her glass from the table. "Look at my husband trying to be cool," she teased.

Katherine tipped her own glass back and drained it. "Oh, I was fired from my job."

Grace wiped her mouth with a folded napkin.

Ardie's forehead creased. "You were fired? From Frost Klein?"

"Yep."

As Katherine's boss, Sloane wasn't sure she should be hearing this. But as an incorrigibly nosy person, she couldn't resist.

"It was a nightmare, actually," Katherine said, staring into the bottom of her glass. "What's in these things?"

Ardie cocked her head. "Champagne," she answered, slowly.

"That explains it." Katherine nodded, solemnly.

"So, what happened?" Grace asked.

Sloane remembered vaguely where they were, which was a children's birthday party, sometime just after noon. Derek excused himself to check on Abigail. The good parent, Sloane registered with *mild* annoyance. More with herself than him.

Ardie slipped her shoes off and stretched

her feet on the patio tiles for a moment as she listened.

"The year before I was fired," Katherine said, "the firm had done some statistical analysis for this public company on equal employment that made it look like the client was much better off than it was because the partner, who was the section head, by the way" — she moved the stem of her glass in a spiral — "had used the wrong statistics. The opinion letter with that analysis had been used, disclosed, and relied upon to complete a high-profile merger, which our firm helmed."

Ardie covered her mouth with her hand and Grace smoothed her lips together.

Katherine looked down at her shoes, and then back up. Something unreadable played on her features. "I'd done work for the company in other capacities, but was brought on that year to help put together the new financials of the combined entity. I noticed a discrepancy in the statistical analysis and brought it to the partner's attention."

Sloane had lost her own shoes and she crossed her legs, bare toes bobbing from the leg on which her elbow dug a crater. "Sure, of course."

She felt the vicarious sense of dread swell-

266

ing under the narrative of a properly terrifying ghost story. At Jaxon Brockwell, a second-year associate had once left the word "not" out of a crucial sentence in a company's retirement plan and the mistake had resulted in millions of dollars of additional payouts. Sloane had absolutely nothing to do with it and still hadn't been able to sleep for weeks.

"He said to run the analysis this year on the right statistics," Katherine continued. "No one would read them, and if they did, they'd tell them about the error at that point. I wasn't comfortable with the arrangement." She punctuated these words. "But it was the section head. At *Frost Klein*. And, the partner said that if the company asked, we'd disclose the mistake." Katherine ran her hand through her hair. "But the surviving company with which the original one had merged did read the new report, they did notice the discrepancy, and they sued for fraud. I thought, fine, the partner is going to take responsibility. It made me sick, but the buck stopped with him."

Grace's expression had dropped. She lightly held her hands cupped over her ears. It was disaster porn, titillating and horrifying, for the attorney set.

"He had a meeting with the company, to

which I wasn't invited. I went to lunch. When I came back, the managing partner, the section head, and the head of HR were gathered in a conference room waiting for me. I was terminated immediately. The client had demanded the firm take action against me, though I'm sure the partner suggested it. I was confused." She blinked now, reliving the moment. It made Sloane's own stomach churn. "I was prepared to argue my case." Her eyes stayed unfocused. "But the partner looked me straight in the eye and pushed documents across the table, documents they said they'd found in *my* office regarding the analysis from the year before, which I hadn't even worked on, I swear. They were those statistics. The partner said I was the one responsible. He said he'd press criminal charges for my fraudulence on work for a public company under securities law. And the other attorneys there, I could tell that this was what they wanted. So I left. There was nothing I could do. They were threatening to disbar me." Her voice became husky. "It was scary. I almost can't believe I got out of there alive."

"Christ," Ardie said, finally setting down the party platter and dusting off her hands. "You could have made, what, seven hundred and fifty thousand dollars a year if you'd stayed and made partner at Frost Klein."

That was miles from what an attorney working in-house could typically make. Hundreds of thousands of miles, to be precise.

"Yep." Katherine's skin looked dewy, from sweat or alcohol or sun, Sloane wasn't sure. But Katherine didn't try to couch the issue by saying that it wasn't about the money. (We had stopped buying the success-isn't-synonymous-with-money line years ago when we realized how much less money we were making and, by extension, how much less success. We'd learned the hard way that money predicated success, not the other way around. Money was options. Money was the ability to take risks. To jump to the next level. *Money can't buy everything,* we'd always been told. *Money can't buy time.* To which we called B.S. We had the Care.com and Instacart accounts to prove it. *Money* was what we were after.)

Grace pulled her chin back in disgust. "Who was the partner?"

"Jonathan Fielding," Katherine answered, without hesitation.

"Wow." Sloane smacked her lips. "You must have wanted to kill him."

"Sloane," Ardie warned.

Katherine's eyes, though, flashed in recognition. "If I'd had the chance, I think I would have."

"*Shoot.*" Ardie looked out at the backyard, where the child half of the party was devolving into riot territory as little hands and feet pulled and stomped over the cardboard city. Scraps had begun to litter the fenced area. "I have to get the cake."

"I'll help!" Sloane raised her glass and followed Ardie into the kitchen. The screen door clanged shut behind them.

Ardie opened the refrigerator door and Sloane, who wasn't actually particularly helpful at social gatherings, leaned her torso onto the kitchen island.

"Katherine seems a little unglued today, doesn't she?" Sloane whispered, peering back over her shoulder through the window. "Do you think that's really what happened?"

"Yes." Ardie slid a red, white, and blue cake from the middle shelf. She cradled it in her arms, placing it down carefully beside where Sloane stood.

"She who is always so skeptical. That's it?"

Ardie opened the drawer and began sinking candles through the icing around the cake's perimeter. "That's it."

"What's it called when men fail? Failing

270

up?" Sloane eyed the frosting and debated a quick swipe of her finger through the blue swirls.

She struck a match on the side of the box. An orange flame jumped from its head. Sloane tipped it to meet the wicks and watched wax begin to drip onto the cake, until the flame burned just a second away from the tips of her fingers and she puffed it out. A breath of gray smoke curled and dissolved.

"I'll say one thing," Sloane said. "This is the booziest kid's birthday I've ever attended. Well, except for Abigail's first," she mused.

She held the door for Ardie, who balanced the cake. The guests erupted into "Happy Birthday," which Sloane sang with conviction. She noticed Rosalita missing from the ring of faces, but only in passing.

When the singing finished, slices of cake were cut and served. The sun had just begun to tip the day's scales over into uncomfortably warm. Though that could have been due to the fact that she'd misplaced her champagne flute in the kitchen. The adults mingled, restless milling as everyone tried to extract themselves from the party in time to run errands, or get ready for a sitter that night, or to take naps.

It was with her mind on her own home and a pair of sweatpants that Sloane located Derek and then started guiding him toward Ardie to say their goodbyes. Grace was already collecting paper plates and shoving them into an open trash bag. And Sloane was considering how maybe it'd be easier if they all just chipped in for a cleaning service. Wouldn't that be equally nice? If not nicer, she added.

Abigail came to show her a dandelion she'd found in the grass before she made a wish. And it was all such a blur that she hardly noticed who it was that had said to Ardie, "This was such a wonderful party. Thank you," until Braylee and Tony appeared in front of them and Tony was saying to Derek, "There's a scotch and chocolate tasting next month at our club, if you're interested in making it a foursome. Braylee can get with Sloane for the details."

And, well, Sloane had happened to be craving chocolate that very moment and so nodded enthusiastically and promised to speak soon.

When she turned it was to find Ardie's face at point-blank range, the expression washed clean off it. "You're going to get with *Braylee* for the *details*." No question asked.

Sloane was about to press her hand to her forehead and decry the effects of too much bloody champagne. But she would have to do that at home with Derek. Because Ardie Valdez, she could see, wanted to hear none of it.

"It was just one or two times." Or three or four, Sloane thought. Or five. "Derek ran into Tony at the grocery store one time." She tried to imbue her tone with a sense of wonder, a what-are-the-odds type story. "And Tony asked him to play tennis at the club. Derek is always wanting to play tennis and you know I'm never letting him join a club." Actually, there was a membership packet on the counter and Sloane had been very seriously considering it.

Ardie listened, passing out party favor bags without a word.

Sloane had begun to talk with her hands. "One thing led to another and — I've been meaning to mention it."

Ardie's mouth was a needle-sharp line. "But you ran out of time in the ten-odd hours that we work together, five days a week."

Do you know what is worse than a text message? This. This is worse!

Sloane sighed, her posture wilting instantly. "Don't be like that. I know you hate

273

Tony." Ardie glanced sharply at Sloane. "But Derek hardly has any guy friends. He works with a bunch of *women.* And he was a little bit thrilled to be invited, I think." Derek stood at the fence gate, his hand resting on the back of Abigail's neck. She swung a party favor bag at knee-level. *Come on,* he beckoned. "I was just trying to be — I don't know — *supportive.*"

"Of whom?"

Sloane held up her finger to Derek. *One second.*

"Ardie, please don't be mad." Sloane had been under the impression that middle-aged people were no longer *allowed* to get mad at each other. So the slight chill in the air came as an unpleasant surprise.

"I'm not mad."

"I didn't intend for it to be some secret." After that, Sloane wasn't quite sure what else could be said. Because they were too old for petty grudges — weren't they? And they'd been friends and colleagues for too long. And they were, most importantly, career women. They weren't supposed to have time for *drama.*

"Sloane!" Derek barked.

"I have to go. We'll talk about it on Monday. Or before Monday. Whenever you want." Sloane followed Derek and Abigail out of the gate, assuring herself that the interaction had been nothing, that all was well, that Ardie didn't blame her for what she'd done, but Sloane couldn't swallow her own lie. Ardie *was* angry with her. She felt rotten, and in pretty shoes, no less. Her buzz flattened. She climbed into the seat of Derek's SUV, the idea of a headache beginning to play in the center of her forehead. She stared out the window — the weather suddenly too hot, the birds too loud, the chugging sprinklers wasteful. She had other secrets. Lying dormant beneath the surface, safe from the ones she loved. She always believed that she kept them secret to avoid hurting anyone. But maybe, just maybe, that was another lie that would someday blow up in her face.

Chapter Twenty-Two

3-Apr

Mondays arrived for us bearing mixed feelings — guilt, dread, stress, fatigue, and relief. By the end of the weekend, we jonesed for the Internet. Salivated over a chance to peruse online shopping websites and sip company-sponsored coffee without interruption. We knew we should have run more errands on Sunday. That we should have changed the bathroom light bulbs and paid the doctor bill that had been sitting on the kitchen counter since last month. On Mondays, we were bitterly aware that we had long since outgrown summer vacation, that the monotony of work flowed straight through the four seasons without stopping, that a weekend was, at its core, only one real day off followed by a day of steeling ourselves for the coming onslaught of the week ahead, because we hadn't used our free hours to catch up on expense briefs like we'd planned. We had accidentally marathoned episodes of *Jane the Virgin* instead. Mondays arrived with the same promise of New Year's Resolutions — we would eat healthier, exercise more, procrastinate less, not let our children watch so much television. They arrived with the gut-level, self-effacing instinct that by Friday we would have failed on at least half those counts.

On this particular Monday, we pressed the buttons on our monitors, listened to our voicemails, checked our emails, filled our staplers, scribbled over Post-its, numb to the cracks fanning out in the glass beneath our feet. This Monday arrived with no more fanfare than usual, nothing to indicate that it was the last Monday on which everything would be normal.

Grace Stanton had excellent penmanship. She'd made her high school varsity teams in both soccer and tennis. She cooked well enough. She had attended the University of Texas School of Law and graduated not top of her class, but top 25 percent, for sure. She cleaned out her refrigerator on time. She read a book a week. She spoke French.

The point was that Grace Stanton was good at nearly everything.

So why did she arrive to her desk on

Monday morning feeling like a failure?

She simply couldn't explain it. She tried talking to herself as she would to a friend: *You're being too hard on yourself. You are wonderful. Stop beating yourself up over tiny things. No one even notices.*

The problem was that, when she said those things to a girlfriend, she actually meant them.

Grace clicked out of The Skimm, a female-centric newsletter that explained the day's most important news stories, then popped over to an interior design blog she followed before she could avoid her day no longer.

A contraband space heater hummed by her feet as she turned to a summary of recent regulatory updates and began scanning the files for any proposed changes that might impact Truviv. She added notes to a Word document of issues to raise with outside counsel who would run the proper Westlaw searches for her.

She was finally sinking into her workflow when there was a loud *thwack* on her door. She looked up to see Ames's hand gripping the inside of the doorframe, as though he'd been walking by and caught himself before he missed his exit.

He reeled himself back into view. "Oh, hey." He snapped his fingers in rhythm before punching his fist into his hand, a *one-two-three* rhythm. Her father often did the same thing. "Did you happen to have a chance to take care of that thing we talked about last week?" He scratched his cheek where silver speckled the weekend stubble still lingering there.

Grace was used to men popping in and knew that it happened more frequently to her than it did to, say, Ardie. And if that had caused her more than mild annoyance, she might have considered changing her look. But she came from a family of Southern women who wore high heels to the grocery store. Old habits didn't die hard. They didn't die at all.

"Actually, not yet." She strived to match Ames's offhanded tone.

He ran his hand through his hair, causing the white streak at his forelock to disappear for a moment. "I see."

Grace's fingers still hovered on the keyboard. "But it's on my to-do list." It wasn't as though she'd forgotten about Ames's favor. And it wasn't as though she didn't want to do it.

Why shouldn't she? Such a small thing. She liked Ames and he saw something in her. She was allowed to like Ames. Wasn't she?

She smiled back at her boss, allowing herself to remember how to put a man at ease. It was simple, really. A warm smile and an easy laugh and — boom — whatever man she was speaking to instantly felt happier. Look, it was already working.

He folded his arms and leaned his shoulder on the doorframe. "You know I'd never want to ask you to do anything you were uncomfortable with." He rested a knuckle on his mouth, studying her.

"Right." She removed her hands from the keyboard and pressed them into her lap. "Of course not." And, she thought, he would probably never want her to do anything to make *him* uncomfortable, either.

She could lie. That was an option. But a good one? Not likely.

"Anyway, I have to get going. Comp committee meeting." For a cynical moment she wondered whether his mention of compensation was a coincidence or a suggestion. Then she recalled again how kind he'd been up there on the balcony, about their plan to advance Grace's career inside the company, and she felt sorry. "But hey." He snapped and pointed up. "Maybe after you're finished we could hit the balcony for a quick . . ." He mimed smoking. "I have a few projects coming down the pike that you may want to call dibs on. And I'd love to get your input on a few regulatory concerns."

"Well," she said, "you know how I love . . . regulatory concerns." Inane office talk. She indulged.

"I knew I liked you, Grace." He winked. "I'll touch base later." And on his way out, he tapped the doorframe twice.

Her screen had gone to sleep in front of her. She nudged the mouse to bring it back to life. She considered the interaction, considered it and saw little choice but to do as Ames had asked. But was that wrong? Wasn't the point of business to get as much as you thought you could get away with?

She considered it from another angle and asked herself, if she did have a choice, a choice without consequence, what would she do then?

Perhaps the answer didn't change. And if that were truly the case, then that ought to be a comfort. Ames was a father and a husband, one with a complicated past with Sloane, but that didn't make him a monster.

He *could* be an asshole, she had no doubt. Not to her, but he was, she agreed, capable. But she doubted whether Sloane and Ardie, for instance, had as much experience with men of a certain ilk as she did. Because

281

Grace had grown up in Cotillion, been a debutante, joined a sorority, and at each stop, she'd understood the discreet underpinning at the heart of these men's behavior. It was entitlement.

Anyway, entitlement wasn't such a dirty word, not unless you allowed it to be. It just meant that you thought you deserved something valuable.

Grace thought she deserved more money and more recognition. In fact, she believed she was entitled to it. She wondered if this thing was what she needed to do to get it. In order to be something other than "new mommy" Grace.

She opened up a blank document, typed out the date in the upper left hand corner. She hesitated. Her canines chewed the pink flesh inside her cheek. She checked the time. The cursor blinked.

There was just the one dangling thread that she needed to tie up.

"Katherine?" Grace poked her head into Katherine's office. Inside it were still three blank walls, alabaster white, without a photo or diploma to break up the sterile monotony of the place. Not unlike a mental institution.

"How you feeling?" Grace invited herself in.

"Physically? Fine." Katherine squeezed her eyes shut for a second. "Emotionally? A bit mortified. A four-year-old's birthday party." She pinched the bridge of her nose.

Grace waved her away. "Don't be. I'm counting the days until my breasts are free agents and I can consume all the alcohol I want at will." She stared down at her boobs, which were already beginning to swell with milk. The countdown to the dreaded process of trapping herself inside the tiny cell of a room and strapping her chest back into the laboratory-like equipment started to tick silently in her head. Even though she'd replaced a session with a nap, she was still trying to stay committed to pumping. Committed to everything, really. To perfection. It was one *minor* slip-up. It wasn't as if Grace had given Emma Kate a pacifier or anything.

"Hashtag-Free-Grace's-Breasts," Katherine said. "That should go on a T-shirt."

"Hey." Grace snapped her fingers. She actually snapped. Just like Ames. She clasped her hands together, controlling herself. "I meant to ask: Are you still staying at The Prescott?"

"No." Katherine jostled the mouse and then leaned back in the ergonomic chair.

283

Where Katherine was living somehow hadn't come up this weekend and it seemed strange, now that Grace thought of it. "I just moved into my new place uptown. You . . . you should come over sometime." Grace noticed that Katherine didn't look at her when she said this, not until she finished asking the question and then, Grace could have been mistaken, but she believed Katherine was holding her breath.

"I'd love that," said Grace quickly and meant it. Katherine's smile was quick and fleeting. "Actually, though, I was wondering, who'd you say hooked you up with your room again? At . . . at The Prescott." She was being obvious, wasn't she? She felt obvious. But then, obvious about what? Nothing would be obvious if there was nothing there to hide. Grace relaxed.

Katherine returned her attention to the screen, sliding her chair back closer to the desk. "Just a friend. Why?" A quick flit of her eyes up to Grace and then back to the screen.

"Oh, um, no reason." Grace never liked standing in someone else's office, her back completely exposed to the gaping glass pane behind her. "I was just curious. Looking for a hookup, too, possibly. Nothing free, of course. What was her name?"

Katherine's eyes drifted across the screen. Her mouth moved ever so slightly, silently reading whatever was there. "Alice," she said. Another glance Grace's way. "Alice Baxter."

"Alice," Grace repeated.

"But I don't know if she still has a connection, you know." Katherine stopped Grace as she turned to leave. "I can check for you."

"That'd be great. Thanks."

Grace saw her ghostly outline in the glass as she walked to the door and, moments later, she was back in her office — home base — where she could hide behind her own computer screen.

Alice Baxter. Had Katherine been telling the truth? Should Grace simply have asked Katherine point-blank: Was Ames Garrett paying for your room at The Prescott? No, that would have been rude.

She thought back to her own lie to Liam, how easy it had been to say that she'd had to work all night. Maybe women were just *good* at lying.

Grace sat, thought for a moment. Facebook was a blocked site on the Truviv computers, but she pulled out her phone and navigated to the app. She typed in Katherine's name, searched for the correct listing and sent her a friend request. She was able to return her focus to work until fifteen minutes later, when her phone alerted her to the fact that she was now connected with Katherine Bell. Their friendship was official.

Grace swiped her index finger across the screen and pulled up Katherine's friend list. It was short. Very short, for a woman her age. But there, at the top of it, was the name: Alice Baxter.

Grace set down the phone. *There.* It checked out. She felt better now. Conscience clean. Grace opened up the Word document, entered the date at the top of the screen, and soon began to type.

DEPOSITION TRANSCRIPT

27-Apr

Ms. Sharpe: State your name, please.

Respondent 3: Grace Stanton.

Ms. Sharpe: What's your occupation, Mrs. Stanton?

Respondent 3: I'm an attorney, part of the in-house team at Truviv. I handle regulatory matters, mainly SEC issues.

Ms. Sharpe: How long have you worked at Truviv?

Respondent 3: About six years.

Ms. Sharpe: And to whom do you report?

Respondent 3: I reported to Sloane Glover, SVP of North American Legal.

Ms. Sharpe: What about Ames Garrett?

Respondent 3: Yes, he was in my supervisor chain. The company's General Counsel. Everyone in the legal department technically reported to Mr. Garrett.

Ms. Sharpe: Did you know Mr. Garrett well?

Respondent 3: I knew him professionally.

Ms. Sharpe: Did Mr. Garrett ever sexually harass you, Mrs. Stanton?

Respondent 3: Not me personally, no. My claim was under Title VII, based on an unsafe work environment.

Ms. Sharpe: Yes, I'm aware of the legal basis of your claim. What I'm struggling with is the factual one. Mrs. Stanton, can you please cast your eyes over Exhibit 13, which I've now placed in front of you? I'll wait.

Ms. Sharpe: Did you write this letter?

Respondent 3: I did.

Ms. Sharpe: Can you, for the benefit of the record, describe this letter to us?

Respondent 3: It's a character letter, I guess you could say. A recommendation to the board of directors.

Ms. Sharpe: A recommendation in favor of whom?

Respondent 3: Ames.

Ms. Sharpe: A recommendation —

or character letter — in favor of Ames Garrett for the position of CEO of Truviv, is that accurate?

Respondent 3: Yes, it is.

Ms. Sharpe: You wrote, and I quote, "Ames Garrett has been a mentor. He is bright and ambitious and his door is and always has been open to me each and every time I've had a problem, whether personal or professional. I value my relationship with Ames and look forward to continuing it at Truviv in whatever role he may occupy in the future." Those are rather glowing words for a man you sued not more than — *what?* — two weeks later.

Respondent 3: I don't believe the number of days or weeks matters as much as what happened during them, as well as why I wrote the letter in the first place, do you?

Ms. Sharpe: Why did you write the letter?

Respondent 3: I felt pressured to. I thought it would be good for my career to help him with this favor that he had asked.

Ms. Sharpe: What exactly did he do to pressure you?

Respondent 3: He asked. Because he was my superior, I felt the implication was that I needed to do as he'd asked. He had power over the trajectory of my career and my compensation.

Ms. Sharpe: Are you in the habit of lying when under pressure?

Respondent 3: No.

Ms. Sharpe: How about to help your career?

CHAPTER TWENTY-THREE

3-Apr

Ardie had vowed to focus on work today. This morning, she left her house still looking as though a tornado had blown through it. Michael had spent the night with his father, so she hadn't even had him as an excuse. It had rained and the remains of the cardboard city were dissolving into pulp in her backyard. She'd thought she might save them. She'd been so proud of the party on Saturday morning.

And then it was over. Tony had left, taking Michael with him to "give her time to recuperate." There had been no one with whom to recap the success of the party or to talk about what Michael had done and said, what his favorite parts were, to laugh at the pictures of him shoving chocolate "cake cake" into his mouth, because he still called it that; had since he was a toddler. Saturday night she'd curled onto her king-sized mattress (*Sell that bed,* friends had told her after the divorce; she never had) and she hadn't bothered to get dressed until this morning. It was a dreary Monday back at work.

Now there were new IRS opinions to review. There was language to interpret. Solvable problems to sort through. Ardie liked having her mind productively occupied.

A veil of gray hung outside her office window and spat rain onto the glass. When the wind blew, it sounded like bird shot peppering the pane. The office had a different energy when it rained and today it was subdued. Cooped up. Quiet energy. Vibrations shuddered through the floors with each roll of thunder.

At eleven o'clock, the landline rang with a local number and Ardie picked up the hand receiver. "Adriana Valdez speaking."

"Ms. Valdez," came a warm voice on the other end, "this is Tonya Loughlin calling from the Highland Park Independent School District. I'm calling to set up a formal interview with your client, Abigail Glover, regarding the recent harassment complaint you filed." *Fantastic,* just the thing that Ardie was trying *not* to think about. Lovely timing. Ardie sat back and tucked her hand in the crook of her elbow as she held the phone. "You see, school policy requires that we arrange for formal interviews between all parties involved in the alleged misconduct. As the family's attorney, you, of course, have the right to be present. Could you let me know of a few times that might work for your schedule?" The question dangled with expectation as Ardie moved to rifle through her desk for a notepad. She found one and flipped the sheet.

Ardie punctuated her resentment with a punch of the pen top, the inky tip knifing out onto the page. "Thank you, Tonya. I'll speak to Abigail's mother and get back with you on timing. Can I get your contact information, please?"

Tonya obliged and when Ardie had returned the phone to its cradle, she ripped the paper from its sticky seam and folded it with one sharp crease.

Over the weekend, Sloane had filled Ardie's phone with an abundance of texts and voicemails, which Ardie had diligently ignored. It was exactly what Ardie expected from Sloane. Rushing her to get over it, to forget about this platonic fling that Sloane and Derek had apparently been carrying on with her ex-husband. And now, Sloane's impatience to kiss-and-make-up had relegated Ardie to the position of grudge-holder. Sloane wanted to *talk about it.* But really, what did she expect her to *say?* *Sloane, you hurt my feelings.* They weren't in kindergarten. Tony was an adult. Derek and Sloane were adults. They could associate with whomever they liked.

But, what a load of horseshit that was. Sloane should never have hung out with Tony and she knew it. Sloane *should* feel bad. Rotten, preferably.

Though she probably already did.

"Here, this is for you," Ardie said when she had walked herself down to Sloane's end of the hall and handed her the sheet of paper on which she'd neatly transcribed Tonya's callback details. "It's for Abigail. I'm not your secretary, by the way. Or your actual lawyer." Oh yes, in addition to Tony, Sloane apparently also felt entitled to author a legal memorandum . . . In. Ardie's. *Name.*

It wasn't even good.

It was maybe a little good.

That was beside the point. Ardie had not even been given the courtesy of vetting it and Ardie didn't play fast and loose. Sloane knew that.

Sloane stood and gingerly took the contact information. "Oh fuck, Ardie. I'm sorry, you didn't have to —"

"Well, you're the boss." Ardie hadn't actually wanted to say that out loud. It was mean. Damn. She didn't want to sound mean. It made Ardie look small and petty. That was why she'd never said anything awful to Tony. The better she was, the worse he'd feel. "You know I love Abigail," she added, pressing the pads of her thumbs together. It was a true thing, at least. She would have done anything for Abigail. How Sloane and Derek had raised such a beautifully odd kid, Ardie hadn't the slightest idea, but Abigail was absolutely wonderful and Ardie would just as soon flatten any boy — or girl — who messed with her as Sloane would.

"Ardie, I'm sorry." Sloane leaned on her desk, looking perfect in a geometric-patterned silk blouse that was most certainly designer. "I fraternized with the enemy," she said, solemnly.

"I never said he was the enemy. It was that you lied about it."

Sloane held up a finger. "Not technically." Ardie lifted her eyebrows. "No. You're right. I wasn't honest. I kept meaning to find the time to tell you, but . . ."

"You didn't," Ardie completed the sentence.

"I didn't," Sloane agreed. "But I also haven't gotten my car washed in nine months, so." Sloane was a good negotiator. Always had been. She had that "attract more bees with honey" quality that made people *want* to agree with her. Grace had once asked Ardie if it bothered her that Sloane was promoted ahead of her, but it never had. Sloane's position required her to be good with people, while Ardie wanted to avoid them at all costs. Ardie wondered if something was wrong with her. Some actual diagnosis. A personality disorder. Something more concrete than just: natural introvert. But, well, to find out, she'd actually have to talk to someone she hardly knew for an extended time period, which was out of the question.

Sloane pressed her hands to the desk, as though laying out her points. "Braylee is the worst, though."

"No, she's not," Ardie said. No emotion.

Sloane's mouth twisted. "You're right, she's not. Not in the traditional sense. But still."

But still, *what*? Ardie wanted to know. It was a typically irritating Sloane way of finishing a thought. Was it, Sloane wanted to continue seeing Braylee, but still she wasn't going to because of Ardie? Or perhaps, Sloane thought Ardie was being unreasonable, but still she would respect her friend's feelings? Or, Ardie's husband had left her for that woman, but still Ardie loved him.

That one was Ardie's.

Last night, she'd pressed *67 and dialed Tony's number. She had lain in bed with the phone pressed to her ear, listening to him say, "Hello? Hello?" as she held her breath. She'd hung up and called once more, then fallen asleep with the sound of her ex-husband's voice freshly ringing in her ears.

"It's fine." Ardie lifted her fingers. *Fine.*

"It's not."

Okay, so it wasn't, but Ardie couldn't see the point in hashing it all out with Sloane. Ardie could either choose to get over it or not and, logically, she would have to choose the former. She and Sloane *would* be fine. Eventually. Mostly. Though she remembered there'd been a time when she'd thought the same about her relationship with Tony.

Sloane sighed. "Haven't you ever done anything that you regret?"

Yes, Ardie thought at once. *No.* Had she? *Yes. Once.*

In either case, it wasn't something she would — or could — share with Sloane.

On the way back to her office, she saw Katherine working behind the glass, head bowed over her keyboard. She almost walked by, but at the last moment, paused, remembering something in one big swallow. She rapped her knuckles softly on the open door and Katherine smiled up at her. A pair of reading glasses that Ardie hadn't known Katherine wore reflected twin glowing screens.

"Katherine." She tried to sound nonchalant. Not exactly Ardie's strong suit. "I was just thinking." She shoved her hands into the copious pockets that her wide-legged trousers provided. Shoot, what all had she *said* to Katherine on Saturday? Grace had gone off to pump and, *god,* Ardie was so mad at Sloane. Blindsided by Braylee and she'd only just seen the email with the memo that she'd *supposedly* written and she'd just sort of *snapped.*

She faltered, awkwardly. "Would you mind keeping what we discussed after Michael's birthday party — you know, about Sloane — to yourself?" Katherine's smile slipped. "It's just that . . . I was only venting."

CHAPTER TWENTY-FOUR

3-Apr

She was flirting. She was trying to sleep her way up the corporate ladder. We had known someone in college who had known her in law school who had said she'd done this sort of thing before. What type of thing was she doing, again?

She was in over her head. She was being preyed upon. She was a lamb in a lion's den. She was a femme fatale. Affairs were a fact of life. We shouldn't be so moralistic. We were being naïve. Plenty of legitimate relationships started at work. Couldn't we have friends of the opposite sex? She was talented. She was compensating for a lack of talent. She was a slut. She was a tease. We liked her. We liked her professionally. Probably wouldn't be friends with her personally. She was one of us.

Through all this, we'd heard that those who lived in glass houses shouldn't throw stones. But no one had told us anything about how to conduct ourselves within the display cases of crystal conference rooms and buildings constructed out of thousands of soulless glass eyes. Poised between our fingertips, not rocks, but the sleek weight of a brick-shaped smartphone. See and be seen. *That* was the nature of our particular glass house. And so accustomed were we to the glass cages that we distrusted anything that happened beyond the scope of our peripheral vision. Perhaps nosiness was a biological adaptation. Survival of the most informed.

Who were we to judge? More like, who were we *not* to?

Sloane judged her appearance in the foggy metal of the elevator doors on her way to her personal training appointment with Oksana. She'd thought to cancel more than once. But Oksana didn't exactly *do* cancellations and there was a chance the workout would help. She felt terrible. Mainly because of the thing with Ardie, but that wasn't all.

The movement of the chamber eased to a stop. The steel mouth opened and in walked Chrissy Ladner, a senior accountant at Truviv, holding a company-issued water bottle. They greeted each other good-naturedly and Chrissy took her spot next to Sloane, shoulder-to-shoulder.

"How are things in Accounting?"

Chrissy, small of stature, large of chutzpah, shrugged. "Same. Legal?"

Sloane shifted her weight. "Same." Which was true only in all the worst ways.

Chrissy gave a soft snort. "I don't know how you work for that guy," she said, glancing up at the red, digital numbers reconfiguring at the top of the elevator.

"Who?" asked Sloane, already knowing. *How do you work for that guy?* It felt more like accusation than commiseration.

"Ames. We were all wondering when you were going to add him to that list."

The corners of Sloane's mouth pulled down. "Who said that I did?"

Chrissy raised her bottle as though in surrender. She'd always been no bullshit and Sloane liked running into her at Truviv events. If they worked in the same section, Sloane imagined, they'd be good friends. "Anyway, I guess we all might be working for him soon enough."

"You believe that?"

Chrissy lifted her penciled eyebrows and sipped. "I wish that I didn't. But haven't you heard? The board met this morning. Apparently he's as good as in."

Chrissy disembarked on the next floor,

leaving Sloane to absorb this news alone.

The reality was that Sloane, who was accustomed to operating at the very edge of chaos, suddenly felt herself starting to lose her balance, to skid over the cliff into real, honest-to-God turmoil. Sure, she'd felt the strings pulling for some time now, but she'd believed she had a hold of them, right there at the ends, where she could reel them back into place if need be. Chrissy's news should hardly have come as a big surprise. But she still found herself unprepared for it.

She believed she was seeing, for the first time, the rickety tower on which her life was constructed. Sloane worried over her cuticle. She felt as though it all — her life — might shatter. Ardie, Abigail, the school board, Ames, her job, her credit card balance, her to-do list, and even Katherine. Katherine, who represented something to Sloane, something uncomfortable: *I want to be like you.*

Press any and — *Jenga!*

On the eighth floor, she swiped her fob on the keypad and the glass door to the gym clicked. Her personal trainer, Oksana, was already waiting at the receptionist's desk and she didn't look pleased. Sloane had completely forgotten that she was running late.

"If it helps," Sloane said, swiping her hair into a ponytail, "I've only had a Lärabar today." Though Sloane had actually had two, one for breakfast and one for lunch, and while they were healthy, they probably weren't intended to sustain an entire human being.

Oksana used to be an MMA fighter. That was when the women fought in a cage and tried to break each other's arms and noses and rolled around on the floor while kicking each other's ribs to death.

"Twenty push-ups." Oksana pointed to the ground in front of her. Sloane hadn't made it into the locker room and was still wearing her narrowly tailored suit and Dolce & Gabbana heels. She hesitated until Oksana snapped her fingers and, dutifully, Sloane let go of her bag and dropped to her knees, where she began huffing and puffing through a series of push-ups, like she was in military school instead of paying Oksana an exorbitant amount per hour to be chastised for tardiness.

For the last three push-ups, Oksana placed a foot on her back, making the exercise exponentially harder. Sloane was chagrined to find she was sweating into wool.

"Twenty," Sloane announced breathlessly. And at last, she was permitted to hurry into the locker room and change into proper workout attire. So long as it took no more than 120 seconds.

Sloane tended to like people who took their jobs too seriously. Like her eyebrow lady, who claimed to be a visual artist. It showed gumption. And so, for their hour-long sessions, Sloane was willing to surrender herself, fully, to the world of Oksana.

When she returned, Oksana informed her it would be a "leg day" and Sloane knew she was in for it. Double pulse jump lunges followed by barbell squats on top of weighted reverse lunges. By the end of the first rotation, lactic acid tore through Sloane's thigh muscles like snake venom.

"For how much it hurts, I really don't understand why my legs don't look like Carrie Underwood's." She panted.

Oksana's bubblegum popped over her lips.

"What?" Sloane looked offended. "You're telling me that Carrie Underwood's legs hurt *more* than mine? I am suffering, Oksana. Do not make light of true suffering. It's very passé."

"You think you're the first client to try to distract me from making you work hard with conversation?"

"No, of course not. I just think I'm the best at it." It was true. Sloane did use her chattiness as a shield against Oksana's sadomasochism. That was probably why she told her personal trainer more than she'd ever told her therapist. That and the fact that she only went to her therapist once, and it was five years ago. She assumed trainers were like hairdressers in that you could tell them anything. But at the moment, Sloane wanted to distract herself as much as anyone else. She was still thinking about Chrissy. About Ames.

"Sumo squats. Go." Oksana set a timer on her watch. Sloane was never privy to how much time was on it and it drove her mad.

"But I did want to ask you one thing."

Oksana took a deep, exasperated breath.

"Sorry, squatting and talking." Sloane widened her legs and tried to block out the burn as she imitated ballerina pliés. Oksana studied her watch. "Okay." Sloane's voice was strained. "So my question for you is this." She lowered her voice, conscious of the sweaty men pulling cables and giving themselves hernias nearby. "Do any of the men here ever, you know, *try* anything?"

Oksana snorted.

Sloane wrapped her hands around her waist as she squatted. She was beginning to get a stitch in her side. "Is that a 'yes' snort or a 'no' snort?"

"What do *you* think?"

"Yes."

Oksana took mercy on her and allowed her to quit sumo squatting, but then she had to transition instead to walking lunges. Oksana kept pace alongside her.

"There are the relatively harmless ones," she began. "The ones that walk by and shill out advice while I'm working out, like I'm supposed to care about some guy's opinion who went to CrossFit one time." That was the number of times Sloane had been to CrossFit too. She wheezed her appreciation. "But then there are the other ones." She glanced sidelong at Sloane. "They hear 'no' and reframe it as an opportunity for 'persistence' or 'relentlessness' or whatever other corporate buzzword they've just learned from the most recent Ted Talk they watched on YouTube. Those are the types you have to watch out for. So buttoned up. *Established.* And don't even get me started on my Instagram DMs."

"Dirty?" Sloane asked, legs trembling.

"Filthier than the inside of a port-o-potty at Coachella."

"Okay, then," Sloane said. "Do you just put up with it?"

Oksana laughed. "No. It's all fairly orga-nized, really. The female trainers here, we have this system. First, we hire female receptionists. Only female receptionists. That's key." Sloane glanced at the young, red-headed woman standing behind the front desk. "If a client becomes a problem," Oksana continued, "we ask the receptionist to highlight his name with yellow in the computer file. If that client requests evening or early morning training, the receptionist tells him that the female trainers are booked up or have off. If a problem client gets too out of hand, we code him red. And if that's the case, all the female trainers become too busy to work with him at all."

"That's kind of brilliant."

"Why, is someone giving you trouble?"

"No more than the standard fare. Code yellow, I guess you could say." She hoped that was true. She felt she'd committed to it being true. She had tried to put the office conversation with Ames, during which she'd ostensibly agreed to ignore whatever it was that was or was not happening with Katherine, behind her. And whatever definitely had happened in the years before Katherine. But it was like the laundry hampers at home: no matter how many times she shoved the clothes down, eventually they overflowed the top again. She was better, however, at ignoring the laundry.

Bigger office. More pay. Better benefits.

She tried to look at it the way Ardie would. Dollars and cents. Or was the phrase actually dollars and sense? She didn't know. She thought it might make a difference.

"Right. Well, just remember, hands on the shoulders. Front foot planted. Aim higher than you think is right." Oksana demonstrated in the air: knee to testicles.

"Still looking for something a bit more subtle, I think, but thanks." And she meant it.

After she had rinsed her body and changed back into her office attire, Sloane returned to her office. The phones were ringing. The printers were chugging. Secretaries were typing. Everything was normal. Except for one thing: Ames Garrett was about to become the company's next CEO.

EMPLOYEE STATEMENTS

13-Apr

Marvin Jefferson: Ames was a stand-up guy. Anyone who had ever met him knew that. He had a beautiful family. He worked his rear end off for this company. Every single employee in this company with stock options should be bowing down to that man in gratitude. That's the truth. When I heard his name had been added to that stupid list circulating then, well, that was immediate proof to me that the whole darn thing was a load of crap. No good deed goes unpunished, I'll tell you that for sure. Ames learned that the hard way.

Bob Rogers: What I want to know is, where's the list of women? Some woman from accounting asked me to go get a drink and I didn't call the police on her. She's seven years older than me. You think that was *wanted* attention? I don't think so.

Zane Spivey: I think you'd have

309

to be pretty naïve not to know
that the types of things detailed on the BAD list were going on. I mean, I've found a
condom and lady's underwear in
the men's room. Did I know about
Ames's behavior in particular?
I'd rather not say.

Josiah Swift: You know what I
think? I think someone — someone
high up who didn't want Ames to
be CEO — paid those women to
add his name to the list. That
list is a life-ruiner. I bet
that sort of thing happens more
than we think. Corporate espio-
nage and backstabbing and all
that. These are high-dollar
positions. Is it really so
crazy to think that the very
purpose for the list's creation
was to bring people down professionally? I think it's worth
looking into. Are you writing
that down?

CHAPTER TWENTY-FIVE

3-Apr

The thing we would articulate, far too late, as it turned out, was that when a building's burning, no one just whispers, "Fire!" No one sits quietly at their desk, diligently completing their work and checking for typos while the smoke pours in overhead. No one cries for "help" softly, under their breath, so as not to disturb their neighbors.

So why did we?

Shhh, don't tell anyone but . . . Keep this quiet, please, but . . . We haven't told anyone else, but . . . This stays between us, but . . .

Perhaps the people closest to us would manage to evacuate and the people closest to them and to them and to them, but whispers could only carry so far. Such was the purpose of whispering — to ensure that not everyone heard.

Hush, but the building is in flames.

Rosalita had never understood why her

son couldn't hear out of one of his ears. She often thought about it as she pushed a vacuum down the carpeted floors, trying to imagine what it must be like inside her little boy's head. Quiet-loud, he'd once told her.

She hated vacuuming days where she had to be at work a full two hours early, even though she was only working third shift. The pay, however, was better.

The clock on her phone read: 7:01 PM when she finished going over the lobby. She flipped the switch and the roar of the vacuum died. She wrapped the cord around the crook of her thumb and elbow, pleased at the tight wad of muscle bulging from her biceps. She had been following exercise videos on YouTube.

She pushed the vacuum over to the next outlet, plugged it in. Crystal hadn't showed up to work today. It was a fact that Rosalita found bothersome, mostly because Rosalita wouldn't get paid double for doing Crystal's half of the work. If she was supposed to worry about Crystal, young, pregnant, and expected to be at work right now, she was deliberately trying not to. She wasn't the girl's mother.

The halls were mostly empty, the secretaries and runners having already left for the evening. Rosalita hummed a tuneless song as she worked, not because she was feeling happy, but because she was bored and frustrated. The happy, sitcom version of her would be grateful for this job. Rosalita didn't know how to be thankful for a job that required her to turn off her brain for eight to ten hours at a time, to be a machine. Not even a machine, because all she had to do was push one, back and forth, back and forth, until she'd lulled herself into a stupor finally broken by the sound of a man's voice, clipped, talking into a phone.

When she heard him coming — the seal of the lobby doors slicing apart, slacks brushing together at the inseam — Rosalita had dueling urges: bend down and pretend to fiddle with the cord or don't. The result landed somewhere in between.

She stood in the crosshairs. The voice, something faintly West Texas in the way that he pronounced his "e"s as "a"s, a quirk she recognized from her uncle's wife, who was born in Rule, cut in and out with the rhythm of the conversation, surfacing closer each time.

Ames Garrett. She committed his full name to memory only after.

He snatched the phone from his ear, transitioned immediately to tapping at his screen. The wave of white snaked through his dark hair. There were patches of razor burn, dried pricks of blood left behind on his neck.

People on the upper floors walked with speed in direct proportion to how important they believed themselves to be. When Ames walked, loose papers fluttered on the secretarial stations as he passed.

He would go by without noticing, she hoped. But then there was a chance glance up, instinctive so as not to collide with whatever — whoever — was in his way. She sidestepped and shrank into the wall, which had the texture of cool fingerprints pressed to the backs of her arms.

Ames stopped directly in front of her. The cuffs of his suit pants broke at the ankle. "Oh, um," he snapped. Twice. It reminded her of a thumb pressed over the spark wheel of a lighter. "Glad I caught you. You mind coming in to empty my bin now?" He made a "follow me" gesture with his whole arm. "UberEats for lunch. Tired of smelling like Korean barbecue."

Do you mind?

It was a formality. It created the illusion of choice and decency. She had been surprised when he'd spoken to her that day in Ardie's office. Had it only been a warmup for this, whatever this was?

She followed without comment and went straight to the corner behind the desk, where Ames's trash bin was located. Her body listened for the click of the door shutting behind her.

But Ames had moved beyond it without bothering to close her in. He pulled a can of Coca-Cola from a coaster on his desk and popped the tab. He tipped his head back and let out a smack of satisfaction when he'd taken a large gulp. He was in a good mood.

"How long have you been cleaning here?" he asked, as though they were old friends who'd bumped into one another after a long while.

She stood, feet hip-width apart, the full pail held at her waist. The power differential loomed massive. She didn't know enough about Korean food to know whether there was any left inside.

"Nine years, give or take." She'd always liked that phrase, as she did most idioms she learned. *Get the hang of it. Before you know it. Blow off steam.*

The corners of his mouth turned down, as though he were impressed. He lifted the Coke can to his mouth again. "You may have heard that I'm poised to be promoted to CEO of the company. Chief Executive

Officer," he explained.

She was careful not to let her face move. "The walls are thick," she said. She hadn't heard. For all she knew, the jobs of the men and women who worked on these floors were to tap nonsense into their keyboards, yell into speakerphones, and shuffle papers. In substance, it was a black hole to Rosalita, as she assumed her world was to them.

"Desmond was a loss, no doubt." Ames shoved a hand in his pocket. "Truly saddened me. We'd been through a lot together." He watched Rosalita, who at once understood that there was a script to this meeting that she hadn't been provided. She said nothing. "I don't expect any problems from the cleaning staff. Is that right?"

She shifted the waste bin to the other hand. "I can't imagine why there would be any more than there would be problems from management," she said, pleased by the steadiness in her voice.

And with this, she knew she was permitted to take her leave. The dismissal was implied. He'd said what he needed to say. But she hadn't.

She looked to his desk, where sterling frames held pictures of two small children. "Yours?" she asked, picking up one of the photographs. One of the boys looked more like Ames, but without the odd streak in his hair.

The chug of a printer spitting out paper sounded from down the hall. He lowered the can from his lips, this time without taking a sip.

"Yes."

"Still married?"

His eyes sharpened. "Yes. I am."

She nodded. They stood across from one another. Rosalita and Ames. He still wore the same watch — silver and gold link — the one that had once left a scratch on her arm the length of her hand.

"Good," she said. "That's very good."

18-Apr

APPEARANCES:
Detective Malika Martin
Detective Oscar Diaz

PROCEEDINGS

DET. DIAZ: This interview is in reference to a fatality referenced under Dallas County Police Report Number 14-83584. The person being interviewed is Adriana Valdez. Okay, um, Ms. Valdez, we spoke prior to this recording about the events of April 12th. Can you tell us in your own words what you remember?

MS. VALDEZ: It was a normal day. I arrived at work around eight-thirty AM after dropping off my son at daycare.

DET. DIAZ: Where does your son attend daycare?

MS. VALDEZ: Children's Courtyard of Preston Center.

DET. DIAZ: Continue, please.

MS. VALDEZ: I sat down at my desk and worked on some ongoing property tax protests, which took up nearly the entire morning. I picked up a salad and a croissant from the coffee shop downstairs — Al's — and brought it back to my desk to eat.

DET. DIAZ: And what time was that?

MS. VALDEZ: I don't know, probably around eleven-thirty or eleven-forty-five AM. That's when I normally eat.

DET. DIAZ: And do you have the receipt for that lunch if required?

MS. VALDEZ: I'm sure it can be obtained. I swiped my card into one of those iPad things, the ones that prompt you to tip for every little over-the-counter thing.

DET. DIAZ: Thank you, we'll follow up on that. Go ahead.

MS. VALDEZ: I worked through lunch. This time of year is busy for us. Just enough time before the summer lull to really make some headway.

DET. DIAZ: Where were you around one-thirty P.M. on that day?

MS. VALDEZ: Around that time, I had gone to go get a payroll form signed.

DET. DIAZ: Anyone that saw you there?

MS. VALDEZ: The payroll officer. After that, I came back to my desk.

DET. DIAZ: At what time?

MS. VALDEZ: I don't remember exactly.

DET. DIAZ: Anyone that could verify?

MS. VALDEZ: Grace Stanton or Sloane Glover, maybe.

DET. MARTIN: Anyone else?

MS. VALDEZ: I don't know. Maybe my secretary, Anna Corlione.

DET. DIAZ: Ms. Valdez, when was the last time you saw the victim?

MS. VALDEZ: Detective Diaz, who exactly are you referring to as the victim here?

CHAPTER TWENTY-SIX

3-Apr

Ardie used to think it was a phase. This desire to retreat into herself, to claw inside her own skin like a hermit crab. It had always been this way. Back in high school, she would arrive early to her classroom and wait outside the door for her teacher to invite her in. When her classmates began to arrive, she'd pretend to read a book or, worse, make her eyes go strangely unfocused like she was daydreaming just to avoid conversation. Not all the time, but the mood and desire struck her unexpectedly, like a gastrointestinal virus, and she was forced to heed its call. By college, she'd discovered that this particular affliction wasn't a phase, but had instead decided it must be a disease passed down by her father. Something only semi-debilitating, but with no cure or hope for marked improvement.

So when Ardie boarded an empty elevator

and moments later heard footsteps before a hand shot out to catch the split doors, frustration jolted through her. She'd long since given up on the "close" button doing anything more than offering a psychological comfort.

Ames shouldered his way through the opening and saw her standing there. Their twin looks of disappointment had to be the only thing the two of them had in common. He did this sort of half-opening of his mouth and half-hard sigh by way of greeting and then nearly imperceptibly shook his head as he turned to face the closing doors. Ardie pictured one of those police black lights that showed blood splatter and thought that if there were one that showed mutual disdain, the elevator would light up with it.

Ardie stared at the back of Ames Garrett's head. He removed his hand from his right pocket. For a moment, his pointer finger hovered over the emergency "stop" button. Then traced up to a lower number. Hesitation. Then hand back into his pocket. Another sigh.

Agitation rolled off him in waves. Hands out of pockets now. Bowed head, clutching his left wrist. Shifting weight from one foot to the other. He waited in the center, so close to the doors that the tips of his shoes almost touched them. Ardie glanced at the upper corner of the elevator. Cameras watching.

Small testament to Ames: He was better at masking his temper now. Back before either Grace or Sloane started at Truviv, she'd witnessed him throwing a stapler at a wall after a purchase agreement call and later heard a younger associate relate the story in reverent, impressed tones, the takeaway having morphed into something about how seriously Ames took his job.

But these days, she could detect that below-surface aggression, like holding her palm to the surface of water on the verge of a boil. The elevator moved, rushed down, and neither of them said anything to the other. Last-minute decision, he punched the button for the eighth floor and waited for the doors to open.

"You're all fucking crazy. You know that?" he said just before the doors shuddered back into place.

Fifteen minutes later, Ardie returned to the office kitchen with a gyro to find Katherine scavenging for La Croix. Katherine stutter-stepped at the sound of the door behind her.

"Whoa, sorry." Ardie slowed her steps. "Didn't mean to scare you."

Katherine released her breath, her hand pressed hard to her chest.

"Are you okay?" Ardie squinted, examining.

Katherine pressed one of the cold cans to the back of her neck and then her cheeks, looking rueful, but not completely recovered. "I'm fine." Her voice had a husky quality to it. "I just thought maybe you were —"

CHAPTER TWENTY-SEVEN

3-Apr

"— Ames."

The forces by which four women gathered in a pumping room to discuss a man whose marked presence seemed to fester and flare among them like an unmedicated case of herpes were beyond Ardie's comprehension. She knew only that, a few short weeks ago, she'd been seated in nearly the exact same position, talking about the exact same man, and she thought it must be some sort of gravitational pull. Even black holes had them.

Sloane closed her eyes as she paced and pinched her forefinger to her thumb. "Wait, wait, tell me exactly what happened," she said.

Breathe, Ardie wanted to tell Katherine. *You can't forget to breathe.*

Ardie had needed a safe place to bring Katherine and she'd needed safe second opinions. The pumping room now felt like a nuclear fallout shelter, dark and dank and secluded from whatever calamities went on outside. ("Is that an Anthropologie candle?" Sloane had asked Grace when she'd arrived.) For the time being at least, Grace kept her breasts stored away. Easier to listen that way, probably. And Ardie had stored away her own hurt feelings long enough to let Sloane in, having recognized her shortcomings in this department — the comforting of Katherine — instantly.

And so the four women convened to discuss how to solve an unsolvable problem.

"I . . . upset him." An unmistakable note of bitterness saturated Katherine's words. But they'd already heard this part. "I think we had different ideas about the nature of our relationship and where it was going." There was an automated quality to what she was telling them, as if she'd explained the whole thing to herself multiple times.

"Well, looks like no one in here is going to be passing the Bechdel test anytime soon." Grace had removed her heels and was ballerina-stretching her bare toes on the tiles.

"I saw him in the elevator earlier," Ardie confessed. "He said, 'You're all crazy, you know that?'" She turned her voice low and gruff to mimic him.

Of course, Ardie should have known right then and there that the comment was a preemptive strike. The temptation, nurtured by people like Ames, had always been to conjure up an image of bored housewives in business formal attire, playing a game of telephone on the office lines. We had to have been overreacting, behaving hysterically, a word which was quite literally derived from the Latin *"hystericus"* — or — "from the womb." Actually, a great deal of time and words had gone into the art of not quite believing us. Adjectives like "bossy" and "feisty" and "pushy" and "intense" became subtle excuses meant to help justify selective hearing loss.

When Ardie had found Katherine in the kitchen, she had seen the same expression she'd found on Sloane's face so many years ago. *What the hell am I going to do now?* it had said. And now it was starting all over again. It was like suddenly realizing that, though you *believed* you'd been running in a race, you'd just been on a treadmill the whole time.

"But . . . didn't you read the list?" Sloane ventured.

They'd all been clinging to the promise of the BAD Men List as a little life raft bob-

327

bing on the seas of the Internet. It had been the disclaimer written on the sign nailed to the amusement park ride. *Enter at your own risk.* Once the warning had been issued, they'd fulfilled their legal liability. But not until now did they suddenly realize how untrue that was.

"I read it." Katherine's cheeks puffed out from where she sat on the couch. She tucked her feet underneath her. "When you sent it. I didn't know what I was supposed to *do* with it, though. Ames got me this job. I'm not an idiot." She glanced around the room, daring each of the women to disagree with her. "You weren't telling me anything I didn't sort of know on some level. I knew I was already walking a fine line. Yeah, I'm qualified." As if the facts that she'd gone to Harvard and worked on Law Review were less important data points about her. "But I came without any recommendations. Worse, my past employer actively hated me. I met Ames in a *bar* in Boston. I sorted out that he was, you know, attracted to me, probably. But I worked really hard to get where I am. And, I needed a fresh start. Somewhere that didn't feel like taking a step backward. That sounds bad." She pushed her shoulders into the sofa cushions. "But what woman doesn't do that a little? You run out of gas on the side of a road and, okay, well suddenly it's not so bad to play a little . . . you know, *cute,* to get some help. Don't look at me that way," she said to all of them. "We all do it."

Sloane nodded. "This is a judgment-free zone. You're one of us."

"Anyway." Katherine sighed. "I reasoned that, once I got my foot in the door, I could gradually create some distance and it would become a non-issue. He was taking an interest, but, honestly, it had seemed in a good way. He was helping me and he hadn't asked for anything in return. It was under control."

Grace dropped her heels to the floor and stared. "And The Prescott?" she asked.

Katherine looked up at Grace, who stood near the TV. The black screen held a miniature picture of Sloane and Katherine inside it. "Ames paid for it," she answered slowly. "He asked me not to mention it to anyone. I'm sorry. He said that the company didn't usually cover moving expenses, but that I should consider his help part of my hiring package. He was using a company credit card and everything. I told him I ran into you and that was the first time he seemed a little, I don't know, dodgy about it." The skin around Grace's eyes tightened. She crossed her arms protectively over her chest. "But I swear nothing *happened* at The Prescott."

"Okay, so nothing happened at The Prescott." Sloane rolled her hands in midair: *go on.* "So what did happen?"

Katherine's throat tightened in a swallow. "He asked me to stay late to help with — I don't even remember, honestly — and I went to his office and we started talking and he got kind of . . ." She tilted her head sideways as if examining it in her mind's eye. ". . . closer, I guess, and . . . This is going to sound weird, but it was dark because he said that it was easier on his eyes with the computer screen at night. And then it just kept — I thought something else — but he was . . . He *kissed* me. And then." Her mouth flickered with an unpleasant memory. "And, initially, I was just kind of *surprised.* Not in a nice way. But. I was trying to remove myself, you know, gracefully. He's persistent, though. He tried — he kept, you know — so I tried — anyway, he took my hand and he placed it on his . . ." She made eyes so that they all understood. There were so many words missing from Katherine's sentences and yet Ardie understood the meaning perfectly. "Someone walked in on us, actually. The cleaning lady."

Ardie blinked. "Rosalita?"

"I'm not sure. I think so. I don't know." Katherine bent over her knees, cupping her forehead. "I said something relatively innocuous to him, I thought. Something like, 'Oh, I'm so sorry, I don't want to get involved with anyone at the office.' He threw a pen on the ground and said I had to be fucking kidding him. I left. I figured we could smooth things over later when cooler heads prevailed."

"Maybe you were giving off signals? Could he have misinterpreted —" To her credit, Grace didn't sound judgmental, exactly. Though she didn't sound supportive, either. "Office affairs are a thing, aren't they?" She didn't look to Sloane, but she might as well have.

"Grace." Sloane wheeled. "She is — I don't know, how old are you, Katherine? It doesn't matter — don't you think she *knows*?"

Grace gave no response.

Because Sloane was voicing something we all believed, which was that we *knew* the difference. How did we know when behavior was inappropriate? We just *did*. Any woman over the age of fourteen probably did. Believe it or not, we didn't *want* to be offended. We weren't sitting around twiddling our thumbs waiting for someone to show up and offend us so that we would have something to do that day. In fact, we made dozens of excuses not to be. We gave the benefit of the doubt. We took a man's comment about the way our high heels made our calves look as *well intentioned.* We understood the desire for us to draw a line in the sand — this was okay, this was not okay. No such line existed, or at least not one that we could paint. But trust that by the time we were working, our meters had been tested dozens of times over. We were experts in our field.

"That's what I thought."

"I'm sorry, Katherine," Grace said, softly. "I'm just trying to fully understand. I just — I don't *know* that side of Ames, that's all."

"So?" Ardie asked.

"So Ames isn't taking the rejection well," Sloane jumped in.

"At first, I thought he was. It seemed like . . . okay, this happened. That was unfortunate, but you know, maybe I was giving off signals." She cast a look to Grace. "Or something, and we could all be reasonable adults. Then he found out about the list."

"Wait, what?" Sloane's eyes bugged.

Hello, lede, thought Ardie. *Glad you've finally been dug up.*

"Today, actually. And he thinks I added him," said Katherine.

Sloane pinched her waist, sucking the bottom of her rib cage concave as she paced the room. "Oh, fuck," she said. "Fuckity-fuck-fuck-fuck." She walked in circles now. Little, tiny, sad circles. Ardie wondered exactly what percentage of this might be considered her fault.

"*You* didn't add him," Sloane said. "Did you tell him that? Did you tell him that you didn't add him?"

"Of course I told him that."

"And he said what?" Ardie asked, her tone smooth. They were gathering the facts. That was all. They were on a fact-finding mission. Research. This was a room full of lawyers. They had thirty-two years of advanced schooling between them. The objective: to sort out what was what and to help their peer navigate through a sticky situation with her job intact.

Perhaps "sticky" wasn't the best word choice.

Katherine folded her arms and crossed her legs. It gave her terrible posture. Ardie had never seen her with anything less than perfect physical deportment and it felt like a particularly obvious, alarming symptom to observe.

"He didn't believe me," she said, speaking more to her knees than to them. "He told me I was full of it. He said that he had worked with all of the people in this office for years and years and that I'd started and I'd, I don't know, yeah, sent him mixed messages." She used air quotes here. "And then, all of a sudden, it's supposed to be his fault and there's this list going around with his name on it and that it's clearly no coincidence. His words not mine."

Sloane's and Ardie's looks found each other. Cut right in line to one another. Yesterday, Sloane had showed up to her office declaring, *I don't have an olive branch so I brought Olive Garden.* And though it would have happened anyway, the breadsticks certainly expedited the healing process. They were, of course, allies again. And they were old ones. Practiced. Which were the absolute best kind. And Sloane was her best friend. She felt around in her heart for whether that was still true and hoped very much that it was.

Ames's reasoning was actually fairly sound. Sloane and Ardie had worked with Ames for over a decade. Why would they, all at once, decide to up and out him, especially when Sloane's own promotion in the company was on the line?

He underestimated them.

"Well," Grace said. "That's definitely a pickle."

"God. I should have warned you more directly, Katherine," Sloane said, stopping in her tracks. "I'm sorry. I just thought . . ." She shook her head. "I don't know what I thought. I should have told you about Ames myself."

Katherine lifted her chin. "Did *you* add Ames's name to the list?" The room stilled for a beat. A ripple of anger passed over Katherine's face.

"Yes," Sloane said. She didn't implicate Ardie at all. Ardie had *been* there. Ardie hadn't stopped Sloane from adding Ames's name. More than that, she'd agreed to it.

"I've been there," Sloane said. Katherine sized Sloane up, or at least that was how Ardie interpreted it. Taking in the age difference and the disparities in aesthetic. One did not look like the other. But, were these things ever about looks? "Oh god, years ago. Eons, really." Sloane waved her hand. "We were *involved* once, as a matter of fact." Sloane Glover's worst-kept secrets tended to be her own. "But we still have our . . . misunderstandings."

"It wasn't *exactly* the same," Grace pointed out, but the other three ignored her.

Katherine tilted her head back and stared at the ceiling. "Then, what now?" she asked. "I'm pretty sure my career doesn't have nine lives. It might not even have two."

What must it be like to build yourself from South Boston to Harvard and then find that wasn't even the hard part?

"Do you want to file a complaint?" Sloane asked. "Because we'll support you. No question there."

Katherine sat up, startled. "What? *No.* No. You can't tell *anyone.* You have to swear to me. I've already lost one job."

There was something weighty sitting in the pit of Ardie's stomach.

"That was different." Sloane spoke to Katherine like Ardie had sometimes heard her speak to Abigail.

Grace watched on. "A complaint sounds like a good option. I think there's even a hotline."

"It's my word against his. Doesn't seem that different to me."

"Okay . . ." Ardie watched Sloane's head, the neatly cut line of blonde hair. "Ardie?" Sloane turned to her for ideas.

"I don't know what now. What ever?" Ardie said. "Do you remember when Debra

336

was with the company? Y'all probably weren't even here yet. Maybe you were, Sloane. Different floor. She filed a harassment complaint with HR about one of her supervisors. There was a random round of downsizing a few months later, which was small. Laughably small. She was out. Flat on her ass. Just like that."

There were other examples she was leaving out.

"That could have been a coincidence," Grace said. "We shouldn't jump —"

"He's going to be CEO," Sloane said, cutting her short. "The board met. I heard it's as good as done. Once it's announced, there will be even fewer options. Maybe none."

"You should have seen his face." Katherine pushed her hair from her forehead. "I'm so dumb." She had moved on to the stage in which she scolded herself. Sloane had followed the same trajectory. "This didn't exactly come out of the blue."

No one asked what that meant. If someone were to, it should have been Sloane, but she let it hang. How much information did they really need, anyway? They either believed Katherine or they didn't. Should Katherine have to detail every interaction just so they could decide for themselves how problematic certain behavior truly was? Or maybe even: whose problem was it?

Ardie and Sloane looked at each other. *The more things changed, the more they stayed the same* — where did that come from? A song? Ardie thought the lyrics were wrong. More accurately: *the more things didn't change, the more they stayed the same.*

Sloane cupped her hand to the back of her neck, her fingers kneading there. "Well." In the pause, Ardie could feel that in a moment they'd have to disperse, to reenter the world where all of this was happening and mattered. It was going on, Ames existed, just on the other side of that locked door. "I don't think we can keep sitting around and praying he gets hit by a bus," she said.

But, *God,* thought Ardie, *wouldn't* that *be a nice coincidence?*

CHAPTER TWENTY-EIGHT

3-Apr

"You want to sue your boss." Derek ignored the two fingers of Scotch Sloane had poured for him prior to starting this conversation. They sat on their California King bed. For some reason, all of their important conversations took place on this bed. It was multipurpose. As advertised.

"And Truviv," she reiterated. She was toeing the line between properly explaining, because Derek had no legal background, and needing to remain this side of condescension.

He tipped his head back onto a Euro sham. "Oh, that makes it so much better."

"Sarcasm isn't a good look on you." Sloane hugged a pillow. She balanced on her hip, legs curled to one side. Derek wore his undershirt and boxers. An hour earlier, she had requested a "family meeting," even though Abigail had already gone to sleep, because Derek liked that term. He'd heard it in a parenting audiobook, which was a thing she would have listened to in order to *seem* like a better parent, but that he would listen to in order to actually be one.

He lifted his head. He had great hair for a man over forty. She could only imagine what the middle-school girls said about him. "Look at this house, Sloane." He held out his arms. Truthfully, this house she was supposed to be looking at wasn't particularly massive, but "location, location, location," as they said. "How much money do you think I make?"

Sloane smelled a trap. She had married a man who didn't mind if his wife made more than triple what he did, so long as no one mentioned it.

"I'm serious, Sloane. What do you think happens, exactly, if this goes south? If you, I don't know, lose your job over Ames? In case you haven't noticed, money isn't growing on trees around here." He pinched the back of his neck and rubbed.

"Only because we spend it like it does," she said. "We don't *need* to have the bathroom remodeled with Ann Sacks tiles." She would never have guessed that her husband's most expensive habit would be his closeted love for interior design, but here

340

they were.

"And we don't need to have five pairs of Louboutins." Which wasn't exactly fair, in her opinion, because *she* made the money to pay for those Louboutins and *she* didn't care if their bathroom was tiled from Home Depot. She wouldn't say this, because she knew that if it were a working *man* who told his wife that, she would have thought it was a hideous indecency, and so she held herself to the same standard. The money was theirs. And Derek was right, if she lost her job, there'd be a domino effect — a car first, then maybe a vacation, then eventually, the house. Unless she found a way to staunch the bleeding.

Still, a job was supposed to pay an employee, not cost her. The reality of her situation was that, if she wanted to do something about Ames, it was now or never.

She hugged the pillow more tightly. "What kind of example are we setting for Abigail?"

He tossed the nearest two-hundred-dollar, hand-painted throw pillow off the bed thoughtlessly. "None. Because she doesn't know this is going on. You're the one thrusting it into the limelight." She stared at him. "Settle it out of court," he said.

"I might. But the only way for that to happen is if I *file* the lawsuit first. No suit, no settlement." It felt good being the calm, reasonable one. She should try it more often. His head hung limply on his shoulders. "If I file a lawsuit for sexual harassment, they actually can't fire me." Fire her, no. Reduce her responsibilities? Fail to promote her? Saddle her with poor reviews? Make her life miserable? Drive her to want to quit? Yes, but it didn't seem prudent to get into detail. "That's why it's better than simply complaining. Did I ever tell you about the time Ames told opposing counsel that I was too emotional to be a good negotiator? 'Move over, we can handle closing the deal.' " Sloane performed some old-fashioned Mid-Atlantic accent, the sort of thing that usually got a smile from her husband. "*My* deal, Derek," she said, more earnestly.

"You . . . have mentioned it, as a matter of fact."

"We might actually *make* money off of this." She didn't know at what point the idea had transformed from being an idea to being an idea that she actually wanted to materialize. Probably during the course of convincing Derek. She was that persuasive, honestly. "I was going along with Ames becoming CEO because I thought — okay — Ames becomes CEO, I become General

Counsel, I suck it up, I get a big raise, hopefully everything is fine. But . . . but . . . what if it isn't? This way, Ames doesn't become CEO. There is still a vacancy for me to negotiate. There are anti–employment retaliation laws. But mainly I stop watching that man have the same power over other women that he has tried to have over me. We can control this situation if we take control over it. Right now, he has the control. All of it. You understand that, right? That will increase tenfold if he becomes CEO, which he will unless I — unless *we* — do something about it before it's announced." She scooted across the mattress, closer to her husband. "You think that I'm a good lawyer, right, that I deserve this?"

"You're in my top five, for sure."

Her shoulders relaxed by half an inch. "You have a top five?"

He scoffed. "Of course I have a top five. Are you kidding me? Let's see." He counted off. "Johnnie Cochran. John Adams. Robert Kardashian. Sloane Glover. Ruth Bader Ginsburg."

She cracked a smile. "Huh. So I come before RBG but after Robert Kardashian." Things could still be funny. Her husband was one of them. She needed that. Needed him, really.

"Hey, it's my list." Derek was picking feathers out of the down comforter, extracting them by the stem. It was never a fair fight. Sloane got her way in nearly every relationship she was a part of. It wasn't that Derek didn't have opinions; it was just that Derek loved her. He was the better person and she was fine conceding that ground to him as long as it was *only* that ground.

He dimpled the corners of his mouth into deep parentheses. "Okay," he said. "Okay. If this is what we need to do to move forward, then this is what we need to do to move forward. You're the boss."

And she tried very hard not to take that as a dig.

"Thank you, Derek." Sloane slid from the bed. It was late and she was still wearing her work clothes, rumpled and partially unzipped. She felt mostly relieved. If a part of her worried that she was following a pattern of impulsivity, she reasoned that a case against Ames was years and years in the making. She knew that she was in the right and Sloane loved being in the right almost more than anything else. It was one of the reasons she'd decided to become a lawyer.

She pulled open her drawer and selected a pair of Thai silk pajamas. Derek read on his phone as she undressed.

She took a deep breath. "There is just this one thing that I feel like I need to tell you, in case it comes out," she said as she put a blue line of toothpaste onto her brush. Five years ago, she wouldn't have even considered telling him because it would have been too soon. But now, with double digits, it felt like a lifetime ago. She'd found herself wondering things like, when did Derek propose, March, or was it November?

"Hm?" He didn't look up from his phone.

This was her moment to turn back. But she watched her husband, his familiar bare feet, his long, crooked toes. They'd so often watched crime dramas in which a child had been abducted and one of the parents was busy hiding their affair and they'd said to each other, *For fuck's sake, if you're having an affair, when something more important is going on, just say so!*

Sloane was a modern woman with a modern husband. She negotiated at car dealerships. She made money and decisions. She pushed off half her household duties. She didn't cook. She'd had *sex*. Her affair wasn't a reason to let other women be taken advantage of, to be assaulted for, was it?

"Ames and I were involved once." He jerked to attention. She held up her hand. "*Before* we were married."

345

He eased by a degree. "*When* before we were married?" It was almost as if he'd been married to a lawyer.

She stuck the toothbrush in her mouth. "A few months before."

"So we were dating." He set down his phone so that she had his full attention. She could have lived without it. Just this once.

"Engaged. Technically. I think," she said.

"Engaged," he repeated. She spat into the sink, rinsed her mouth out with water. "And he was married?"

"He was definitely married.

"It was right after you proposed. I wasn't sure what I wanted. I was going through a crisis of conscience." She thought it was good to put a label on it. It was like a diagnosis. Everyone had to support you once you got one of those or else risk being a ghastly, selfish person with a bias against mental health issues. And Derek definitely wasn't that.

"Well, that's comforting to hear." Derek finally lifted the Scotch from the nightstand, sniffed it, and took a swig. It was very good Scotch. She thought that should matter.

"I'm sorry, what exactly do you want me to say?" And there was a definite snarl to his tone.

Okay, then, she thought, *let him.* She

deserved that.

Sloane holstered her toothbrush. She started to answer and then creased her brow, only of course her brow didn't crease at all. "I'm thinking," she said. "You just can't tell because I've chosen to poison my face due to unfair societal beauty standards." She fingered her forehead gingerly. "This is what it must feel like to be paralyzed."

Sloane was talking too much. It was her primary stalling tactic and Derek knew this. It turned out that, in her mind, she hadn't exactly articulated *what* she thought Derek would say to her confession. She had vaguely imagined her husband expressing the disappointment of a strict parent having heard that his forty-year-old daughter used to sneak out and drink beer back when she was in high school. Derek's face told a different story, hurt and anger locked in a neck-and-neck battle for dominance.

"Does it really count before we were married? Think about it. That's the entire point of saying 'I do.' " She was afraid to say so now but she'd always felt that anything before marriage was sort of, she didn't know, fair game? Practice? Or maybe she had only been telling herself that because that was how she'd treated her relationships

347

pre-Derek. "Nothing ever happened after I said those vows."

"How fucking honorable, Sloane."

They both cursed. Never *at* each other, though. And it took a feat of self-restraint not to allow herself to assume the role of the offended. She was so much better at that.

"Derek." She returned from their shared bathroom, a dollop of night cream poised on her fingertip. "It was twelve years ago. I get it. I was young and horrible and stupid. But." The mattress springs squeaked. Derek gathered up his two pillows and tore one of the throw blankets off the bed. He had to twist it around his forearm to carry it all. "Derek? Derek, where are you going?" She followed him into the living room as he headed up the stairs in the direction of the guest room. "I thought you agreed we were going to be on the same team here." She smeared the night cream on her leg. An ounce of it cost forty-three dollars and she couldn't believe she'd just wasted it. Her feet pounded too loudly on the steps. She'd wake Abigail if she weren't careful.

Derek looked down at her from the top of the stairs. "Yeah, I think *that* is actually the point of saying 'I do.' " And he disappeared into the guest room, where she heard the lock snap into place.

Sloane's footsteps were softer on the way down. She curled onto Derek's side of the bed and picked up his mostly full glass of Scotch. It was going to be fine, she told herself. In their early thirties, a similar fight would have elicited slamming doors, long text messages sent rapid-fire, one of them driving off — probably her — then returning to ignore the other person before yelling again.

Now the house buzzed with silence. She tipped the remainder of the Scotch into her mouth. The earthy flavor of peat filled her nose. *You have certainly made your bed,* she thought.

She and Derek were supposed to watch the series finale of *Orphan Black* tonight. Instead, she went to the kitchen to refill her glass.

Deposition Transcript

27-Apr

Ms. Sharpe: How much do you make at Truviv per year?

Respondent 1: Why is that relevant?

Ms. Sharpe: If an objection stands, your attorney can argue it before the court. How much do you make at Truviv per year?

Respondent 1: My base salary is $310,000 annually, plus a discretionary bonus.

Ms. Sharpe: Are you aware that this salary is within the top one percent of salaries in the country?

Respondent 1: Again, I don't see how that's relevant. It is by no means an exorbitant amount for a person at my level of experience to make.

Ms. Sharpe: Were you able to live comfortably on this income, Ms. Glover?

Respondent 1: I'm sure that's relative. For instance, compared to you, Cosette? Probably not. But, more broadly speaking, yes, we do just fine.

Ms. Sharpe: So, the sole consideration when filing suit against Truviv and Mr. Garrett was to take up the cause against sexual harassment. Is that right? This was in no way a moneymaking scheme?

Respondent 1: Of course not. By which I mean, of course it was not intended as a means to make money except insofar as forcing a corporation to pay money is one of the most surefire ways to encourage a corporation, and people, for that matter, to change behavior.

Ms. Sharpe: Were you facing any undue financial pressure that may have altered your own behavior at the time of the suit, Ms. Glover?

Respondent 1: Nothing out of the ordinary.

Ms. Sharpe: Interesting. You see, I have a credit report here. It tells me that you are pretty heavily leveraged.

Respondent 1: I think that's fairly natural. Seven years'

worth of school loans. A mortgage. Credit cards. Two cars. It adds up.

Ms. Sharpe: So you didn't want any more money? More money wouldn't have been helpful to you?

Respondent 1: I'm sorry, Cosette, Truviv is paying you how much to ask hard-hitting questions like: Would more money be helpful? Cosette, I want to keep working at Truviv. As you said, I make $310,000 per year and my family and I, we enjoy a certain quality of life. I didn't exactly think I'd be retiring early to the French Riviera on whatever payout I got from a lawsuit here. But, please, write me a postcard from whichever vacation home this proceeding helps *you* to pay the down payment on, won't you?

CHAPTER TWENTY-NINE

3-Apr

Grace returned early that night and dropped her purse on the kitchen table. Liam was already home, loading the dishwasher. The microwave hummed, the sterilizer turning inside it. Bottles — beaded water stuck to the insides — stood at attention in the plastic grass mats that sat next to the sink. Grace had a theory that the main reason Liam was so helpful around the house was actually because he made so much money. All these career women she knew griping about how *they* were the breadwinners but their husbands still didn't do the grocery shopping and she thought: *That's because they're threatened!* It had been, and still was, a working theory.

Grace greeted Liam and went to the living room where she knelt down beside Emma Kate. She was playing on her back in her activity gym, staring up at the assortment of elephants, lions, and toucans that had been hung above her head to keep her attention. She held her daughter's foot in her hand and Emma Kate kicked. She couldn't think of much to say, so Grace returned to the kitchen and grabbed a sleeve of Ritz crackers from the pantry.

She leaned over the granite countertop, her heels still on. "Liam, why do you think I've never been, you know, sexually *harassed*?" She wondered whether the premise of her question was even true. She had been whistled at on the street, asked to smile in the line for lunch, had men in meetings stare at her breasts. Her high school tennis instructor had once even asked her to sit on his lap on a crowded car ride (she'd declined, choosing one of her teammates' laps instead). But she wasn't *traumatized* by any of it.

Liam slung a dish towel over his shoulder and pushed up the door of the dishwasher. He was tall and well-built, a former lacrosse player at Vanderbilt. "You've never had chicken pox, either."

Emma Kate cooed from the other room.

"I don't think it's that random. I mean, I'm not immune, am I? At the risk of sounding like a huge bitch." Grace probably *was* a huge bitch. "I'm, you know, pretty. Prettier than some of the women I know that have had negative experiences."

He held out his hand. She passed him a cracker. "You're feeling left out of sexual harassment?"

"Of course not." Maybe she was. "I'm trying to understand."

"I don't know." The timer on the microwave went off and it was Liam who moved to take out the sterilizer and who began unloading it. Grace slipped off her shoes. The tile cooled the soles of her feet. "You're asking me to get in the heads of people with whom I don't have a whole lot in common."

She hoped that was true. She believed it was. It bothered her that she didn't know whether Ames's wife, Bobbi, felt the same way.

Liam considered. "But probably something like animal instinct. They're preying on the weakest in the herd. The young. The vulnerable."

Grace snorted. Cracker crumbs flew from her mouth and she cupped her hand over her mouth. "Sorry. Sloane isn't what I'd call vulnerable."

She quickly tiptoed around the corner — such a good mommy, as Liam would say! — to check on Emma Kate, who was now quiet, mouthing her own wrist.

"Yes." Liam held up a finger. "But she made herself vulnerable with the affair, didn't she? He had something on her." Grace didn't know the rules on whether she'd been allowed to tell Liam about Sloane's affair. As an adult, she believed the understanding was that if a friend told you a secret, you could tell your spouse. But she'd never confirmed this with any of her friends in case she was wrong, and that alone probably meant that she was.

"So, it's their fault, then? I haven't been harassed because I'm not harass-able?"

"No." Liam twitched. "It's just like a crime of opportunity, I suppose. You wouldn't blame a murder victim. The murderer's just trying to commit a murder he thinks he can get away with."

"That's dark."

"Are we ordering dinner or were you going to cook?"

The message from Sloane came sometime just before ten, after Liam had gone to bed. Grace was waiting to perform something called a "dream feed," which she planned to do at approximately ten-thirty. A dream feed involved picking up Emma Kate and, without fully waking her, holding her to Grace's breast and encouraging her to nurse for a full meal so that she would sleep through the rest of the night. That was the concept. The reality was usually that Emma Kate woke up angry at having been roused, tiny fists balled, eyes pinched into her face. But Grace couldn't give up the promise of six hours of uninterrupted rest. The fact that it hadn't happened yet didn't matter.

She'd been scrolling through her Netflix watch list, which was dwindling with all the added TV time since Emma Kate's birth, when her phone buzzed.

Sloane Glover
Going to file lawsuit. Public = only way to have protection + prevent Ames from taking over the company. Talked to Katherine. She's scared re: what happened at Frost + I feel a little responsible. Tired of ignoring it all! Kisses.

Grace waited for Ardie, who was included on the chain, to respond, but when she didn't, she realized that Ardie must have already gone to sleep. Grace decided to pretend she'd done the same. What, exactly, did Sloane want them to say, anyway?
You go, girl!
If anything, Grace was thinking about how disruptive a lawsuit from Sloane would be

to their jobs. Was anyone worried about *that*?

Twenty minutes later, she'd positioned herself inside the crater now permanently embedded within their sofa from incessantly sitting cross-legged there, the "U"-shaped pillow balanced around her hips. Emma Kate had switched from screaming to sucking, at which point Grace realized that she'd forgotten to place the cup of water on the side table next to her. A desperate thirst overtook her every time Emma Kate latched. She needed to distract herself. The TV was on a low volume, the remote inches out of reach. She clasped her phone. The text from Sloane was still on screen and she got the same snag of annoyance she had when her mother was texting too often.

She wanted to talk to someone who agreed with her. It was late, but she scrolled through her contacts and dialed Emery Bishop, one of her closest sorority sisters. The two of them still took a girls' trip to Fredericksburg every year. Emery lived in Houston. She didn't work "outside of the home" and sat on the board of both an AIDS foundation and a local theater. She picked up on the second ring. "Is everything okay?" Emery had a chronic raspy voice caused by vocal cord nodules and a slight Southern accent.

"Yes, yes," Grace said quietly so as not to disturb Emma Kate. "Sorry, were you asleep?"

"God, no." Emery had always been nocturnal. In college, she ate a second dinner at midnight. "Emma Kate?"

"Also fine. Feeding her right now." The blue light of the television played off her baby's head.

"Christ." Emery made the word two syllables. Grace pictured her friend. Hair drained of color by way of bleach, a lasting affinity for turquoise jewelry. "I remember those days. Don't have four kids, Gracie." Grace smiled into the phone. There were few friends made after high school that you could call just to talk. Emery was one of Grace's last.

"Do you think women are too sensitive?" Grace asked after a short pause.

Emery hummed. Grace heard rustling on the other end and then the crack of a refrigerator door opening. "It depends who's saying it. Like, if Clark calls me too sensitive, I will cut off his testicles and feed them to Willie."

Grace laughed, then stopped herself when she felt Emma Kate almost lose her suction. "At work, there are women complaining that they've been, I guess, sexually harassed. Not in those words, but that's the gist of it."

"Oh." A drawer opening. Silverware. "I don't know. Not all women are like us, you know? My mom always says: nothing really changes after high school."

"That's depressing."

"Certain girls need to get attention one way or another. I'm not saying that they're doing it *intentionally* for that reason. They probably believe, on some level, that's what's happening. You know?" Grace didn't say anything. "I'm always worried that Clark is going to be accused of something he didn't do. Or Tyler or Mason when they get older. Scares me to death. What am I going to tell Tyler or Mason? *Never* be alone in a room with a girl you don't know *extremely* well? Is that even enough?"

Grace pinched the phone to her ear, used her pinky finger to unlatch Emma Kate, like the lactation nurse had taught her, and moved her to her left breast. "Um, I don't know," she said, absently, trying to imagine Ardie having the same conversation about her son, Michael.

"When Clark was at Air Force Academy, he told me stories of cadets getting kicked out just because a woman *claimed* misconduct. Those women had the power to ruin

360

those young men's lives and they chose to use it." It sounded as though Emery were now eating ice cream, the clink of a spoon on her teeth.

Grace listened, imagining Ames's wife, Bobbi, saying that. And it did make Grace think: What if someone came to her and said that Liam had been harassing women? What then?

She listened to Emery talk about Tyler's tackle football team — he was eleven — and Mason's soccer and Annabelle's ballet and Finley's physical therapy until Emma Kate had finished feeding. Then she could no longer keep her eyes open and she said good night to Emery and swaddled Emma Kate and patted her until she agreed to go willingly into her Rock 'n Play, which was still stationed in the first-floor office, not in the nursery upstairs, which had never actually been used.

Grace woke up to the sound of her daughter's crying. She had read somewhere that a baby's cry was physically louder to its mother. Liam slept. She felt like she'd been asleep only twenty minutes, but it had been three hours. Small consolation. Soon she was wide awake, having nursed and now rocking. Rocking and rocking and rocking even after Emma Kate's eyes had closed and her cheeks had gone slack.

Grace tugged her cell phone from where it stuck to the skin on the back of her leg. She swiped the phone screen open and typed a message to Sloane.

DEPOSITION TRANSCRIPT

26-Apr

Ms. Sharpe: I'm not saying necessarily that you set out to ruin Ames Garrett's life. I'm not saying that was your intent, your primary objective.

Respondent 1: Is a failure to become the head of a public, Fortune 500 company life-ruining? I hope not or else a lot of us have pretty sorry excuses for lives.

Ms. Sharpe: What I'm saying is that I know these issues are hard to discuss objectively. I know there are sensitive issues buried in the salacious details of this complaint. I am not trying to make light of the seriousness of the allegations. I'm a woman, too. But I'm also a lawyer and, as a lawyer, I search for facts. For evidence. Truviv has actually undertaken its own independent investigation and I will say this: no other women have come forward to complain of Ames Garrett's behavior.

Respondent 1: You mean other than the three that already have. How many would be enough?

Ms. Sharpe: Yes, we have three women with complicated motives. Walk me through your reasoning the day you decided to take legal action.

Respondent 1: Katherine had told us that Ames had become aggressive, sexually, with her and he seemed ready to retaliate professionally based off her rejection. At the same time, he told Ardie that all women were crazy. Something finally clicked. I realized that I couldn't keep doing what I'd been doing for so many years. Nothing was going to change the way Ames acted unless I changed it myself.

Ms. Sharpe: So, you filed a lawsuit and we all know what happens next.

Respondent 1: Do we?

Ms. Sharpe: Tragedy.

CHAPTER THIRTY

6-Apr

We wanted to do our jobs — was that too much to ask? We were tired of planned server outages and mandatory training sessions to learn the latest updates to Adobe Acrobat Pro. We a little bit hated cake day and whoever came around to force us to attend, despite the fact that we'd already announced quite publicly that we were trying to eat Paleo this month. We couldn't understand *who* was still clicking on those virus emails that prompted the proliferation of so many *more* emails aimed at encouraging us to stop clicking, but without fail, one of them popped up in the right-hand corner of our screens the precise moment we were trying to close out of Outlook to do actual work. (Wait, was email actual work?)

We were always signing last year's, this year's, or next year's beneficiary forms with a frequency that defied the calendar and our ability to recall our dependents' Social Security numbers. We had an inkling that face time requirements were an instrument of the oppression. We would prefer 65 percent less networking, but likely needed to do at least 50 percent more of it. There were a hundred things small and large that stood between us and our jobs every day, ranging from the incidental to the nefarious. So when we said that we would prefer not to have to be asked to *smile* on top of working, we meant that: we would like to do our jobs, please. When we said that we would like not to hear a comment about the length of our skirt, we meant that: we would like to do our jobs, please. When we said that we would like not to have someone try to touch us in our office, we meant that: we would like to do our jobs. Please.

We wanted to be treated like men at work for the same reason that people bought smartphones: it made life easier.

Ardie had been trying to do her job while battling a slow computer connection this morning when the two men in suits had passed by her office window on their way to Ames Garrett. It had been one day since Sloane hired Helen Yeh to file suit against Truviv and Ames, a lawsuit to which Ardie had made the decision to become a party.

With the looming possibility of Ames being announced as the successor CEO any day now, time had been of the essence.

Two hours after the men in suits had passed her office, a meeting invitation appeared on her screen to request her presence in HR in twenty minutes. She chose "accept" and the meeting appeared on her calendar.

Ardie was a single mother — did that mean she had the least to lose or the most?

The two men in suits had stayed in Ames's office for approximately forty-five minutes before leaving. Whether this was a long period of time or a short period of time, Ardie wasn't sure. She watched the clock. Her own twenty minutes managed to be both long and short, too.

She got up, pulled her blazer off the back of the door, and stuffed her arms through the sleeves. Sloane waited for her at the elevator banks.

"And so it begins," Sloane said. "You ready for this?" Ardie had never understood the strategy of focusing all one's energy on appearance when something important was going on, but that was clearly Sloane's MO today. She wore a crisp, royal blue skirt suit with a white blouse, her hair tied into a sleek, low ponytail, not a hair out of place.

It was like she was Corporate Wonder Woman and this was her superhero costume of choice.

"I'm sure as hell not letting you do it alone." Partially true. Or, perhaps something could be wholly true without being the entire truth, in which case that was what she meant.

Sloane pushed the button. Moments later, from out of the restroom, Grace appeared.

"Well," she said, "if we need someone to wield the bloody tampon at them, I just started my period for the first time in fifteen months." The three of them stepped onto an empty elevator. "I thought I wasn't supposed to get my period while I was breast-feeding. What the hell?"

You're going to need me.

That was the text message Grace had sent late the night Sloane had decided to sue. She wondered if Grace could tell how much Ardie had misjudged her, whether it was broadcast on her face.

A short ride upstairs, and a bald man, who had neither mustard stains on his shirt nor glasses but seemed like the type of person to have both, stood in the foyer waiting to greet them. "Al Runkin." He clasped each of their hands with both of his. "Come on

368

down, ladies, let's see what we can do you for."

Sloane and Ardie exchanged a look. There was a physical difference in the landscape between the ninth, where HR resided, and fifteenth floors. Like taking the train from the Upper West Side into an only partially gentrified neighborhood in Queens. The employees here mostly occupied cubicles instead of individual offices. The staff trended younger, except for the exceptions, who, because of their juxtaposition against their colleagues, seemed stuck.

Al Runkin ushered the women into a conference room. He took a seat in a cracked leather ergonomic chair opposite them and laced his fingers behind his head. The salty remnants of underarm sweat haunted his dress shirt. "So." He looked down his nose at the stack of papers on the table in front of him. "You're aware of this." He squeezed his chin down his neck, the skin folding.

Sloane folded her hands on the desk. "It's probably best we get the obvious parts out of the way. Yes. We've filed a suit as co-plaintiffs against Ames Garrett, as General Counsel, and against Truviv, Inc., more generally, under Title VII. While I've experienced direct harassment under Ames Garrett's tenure at this company, my colleagues Ardie and Grace have brought their claims under the same act beneath the unsafe work environment umbrella, which permits claims where employees have been indirectly but negatively impacted by the harasser's behavior. There. That should save us both some time, don't you think?"

"Lawyers." His thin lips drew thinner. "How refreshing." He sat up abruptly. The hinges on the chair squealed. "Here's the thing: We have procedures in place for this sort of thing. A lawsuit? Well, I understand that you all are lawyers, so this is your — how do you say it? — *milieu,* but it's not necessary." He made a face as though he had smelled something bad. "In fact, an investigation is already underway. In the future, we have a hotline that allows you to call in these types of complaints. Helps to avoid the expense of lawyers and filings and such for everyone."

Ardie wrapped her hands around her knee. She didn't know how she would feel about being in this room. The sickly over-head lights. The coffee mugs filled with pencils. "A hotline," she said, "that's often routed directly back to the person about whom you're making the complaint. It doesn't exactly require a doctorate to determine who then is making said complaint." There, Ardie sounded like herself there. Her heart started beating. Presumably it had been beating all along.

"We have a policy that allows employees making a complaint to skip the usual steps and go directly to senior management."

Grace — "The person about whom we're complaining *is* senior management."

He threw up his hands. His forehead was a shiny ball of wax; the reflection of light kept moving across its surface. "What do you want us to do?"

Sloane, who sat in the center, put a hand on each of their chair arms. "We think Ames Garrett's employment needs to be terminated, for starters."

"Like I said, it's under investigation."

"How long do you expect this investigation to take?" Ardie worried that "investigation" was a stage that had an ability to last until anyone who'd previously cared had lost the will to. It came with an image of endless accordion folders stacked on storage room floors, replete with meaningless papers. Maybe this was offensive to the hard work Human Resource workers otherwise performed, but it was Ardie's particular bias and she allowed herself to carry it.

"It's hard to say. I would expect three

days, a week at most." Al shrugged.

"Great," Sloane said in a voice that said she didn't think it was particularly great. "Then we'll expect to hear a follow-up at that point. In the meantime, I'm sure you'll be hearing from our attorney."

Our attorney. Ardie could imagine a person who was not an attorney feeling more powerful at the chance to use that phrase, but Ardie had peeked behind the curtain to the Wizard of Oz.

They stood as one. Southern etiquette dictated that Al jump to his feet, too, but his lap got hooked between the chair and the table, so he hunkered awkwardly while trying to stand and wave.

"Ardie." He pushed the wheeled chair free and it clacked against the back wall. She paused in the doorway. "It's nice to see you again. It's been a while," he said, voice lowered.

She hesitated. "Yeah. I think you had hair back then."

Ardie Valdez hated Al Runkin.

Employee Statements

14-Apr

Kimberley Lyons: No, I wasn't there when it happened. You see, I take care of the secretarial coverage during the lunch hour, which means that my lunch hour is late and so I had just left about fifteen minutes earlier. I'm sorry. It's difficult for me to talk about. I've never known anyone who has died before, other than my grandparents, and that was when I was too young to even remember. It's a shock to everyone on the fifteenth floor. We're like family.

Kunal Anand: The women went crazy. If anyone says that isn't the case, they're lying or trying to be P.C. or something. They were like rabid dogs, thirsty for male tears. Rabies makes you thirsty, in case you didn't know. I saw it on *Viceland*.

Katherine Bell: I just started here. In fact, I moved from

Boston, so I'm new to the Dallas area as well. This is a difficult first impression, I guess you could say. I really wasn't involved in office politics.

Al Runkin: I'm not aware of anyone exhibiting any violent behaviors, no. Our department takes personnel and, particularly, mental health issues very seriously. Think of us as guidance counselors for grownups. Homicide? I doubt that.

CHAPTER THIRTY-ONE

7-Apr

The bar where Sloane sat nursing a thirteen-dollar glass of Merlot traded in black leather and copper metals. The atmosphere was luxe and inviting, though she'd chosen it primarily for proximity — it sat on the same block as the Truviv office building — and for the fact that the dim lighting managed to make her look at least ten years younger. She could see her reflection in the mirror behind the bar, between the half-full bottles corked with plastic nozzles promising intricate drinks mixed by bearded men with tattoo sleeves and plugs in their earlobes.

She should go home. Her phone had been silent all day. Derek had been gone by the time she'd gotten up and he hadn't responded to any of her text messages. It made her feel like a high school girl, all insecurity, chin acne, and a vicious internal monologue that had come out of thin air.

He could get someone younger, Sloane. Men could do that. Prettier, too. There was always prettier. And now you've handed him permission to do it with a clear conscience. Bravo.

Yeah, but he couldn't get Abigail's mother, she shot back. *He couldn't get* me.

"Can I buy you another glass?" She probably had that startled look, cords in her neck flaring like a reptile. The man who had taken the seat beside her could only be in his twenties. He was boyishly handsome, freshly shaven, a thin build, with enough dark hair to sweep to the side. He wore a pink, short-sleeved, collared shirt that was trendy without trying too hard.

She noticed with mild surprise that there were only a couple sips left in her glass.

"I'm married," she said. *And nearly twice your age,* though she didn't feel the need to add this part.

"Then it's a good thing my question wasn't: Will you marry me?" He drummed the bar top. "Because then I'd have to be properly embarrassed." He had dimples in his cheeks, because, of course he did.

She turned her attention away. She hated when men did this, pretended that she was being presumptuous — worse, full of herself — for assuming that buying a drink was short for, would you be interested in me?

They sat in unamiable silence.

"Sloane Glover, right?" Out of the corner of her eye, she saw that he was holding out his right hand.

She turned slowly, eyed the bartender who was drying highball glasses on the other end of the bar. "Yes," she said, taking his hand.

"Cliff Colgate. *Dallas Morning News.*" He slid a business card across the slick wood to her. The word "Reporter" appeared underneath his name. "Do you have a minute?"

Sloane didn't move to leave.

"I've been working on a story about a spreadsheet that has been cycling around a group of professional women in the Dallas area. The BAD Men List — I'm sure I'm telling you what you already know — details the sexually predatory behavior of men in power here in town."

"Interesting." She pushed the base of her wineglass in a circle, the remaining liquid swirled around its edges.

A pocket-sized notebook appeared, along with one of those pencils people used to write down miniature golf scores. "Would you like to comment?"

"On what?" Sloane's mind was calculating.

"On the BAD Men List — its contents, its usefulness, its ethics, anything." His elbow rested easily on the bar, the pencil pinched between his fingers. She had a vague thought about what it would be like to fuck him, but it was only a passing one. Sloane had moved past the age at which she could have a one-night stand never having gotten around to having one. She didn't know whether to mourn this or be grateful.

She took a short swig of the wine. Almost gone and she hadn't decided whether or not to order another, now that she had company. "What makes you think I would have any commentary to add?"

"The name Ames Garrett showed up on that list." He had the air of a schoolboy, perhaps a bit of a teacher's pet. "Not long after, you and your colleagues, Adriana Valdez and Grace Stanton, filed a sexual harassment lawsuit against him." He tapped the butt of the pencil against his temple. "The power of deduction." He was joking, of course.

"You've been following it." She took another sip of the wine. The drops of red that settled at the bottom when she returned the glass were so few that she would look desperate if she tried to reach them with another drink. "Sorry, but you don't strike me as a 'professional woman,' as you put it." She twisted in her seat; her skirt rode an inch or two higher up her thigh, but purely by accident.

Ames had found out about the list — she didn't know how, exactly — and so she should have assumed that anyone might have seen it and, still, she hadn't expected a reporter. She suddenly felt that she was at the starting line of a race; the gun had just fired and she had no clue how far she was going to have to run.

"Over three thousand people have access to that list, Sloane." Her first name. Her hackles rose ever so slightly. "You really think that three thousand people can keep a secret?"

CHAPTER THIRTY-TWO

11-Apr

Wet pavement stretched out like a tongue from the open loading station on the basement level. The cavernous cement block smelled like gasoline and old compost. Men trucked crates of soda cans using dollies.

"I need the supply-room keys," Rosalita said to the foreman. Crystal waited by the elevator, keeping watch over their cleaning caddie. She was back.

The foreman sat on a stack of cardboard boxes, slouched over a clipboard. His stomach pooched under his yellow polo. A hollow dimple marked his belly button. "If you're asking something, mina, you best be doing it from your knees," he said without looking up. He signed her paychecks.

"No problem, but I warn you, I bite."

"Fuck you." He spat on the cement floor. But he undid the key ring hooked to his belt loop and tossed her two keys. "Don't steal shit. I'll check."

Crystal and Rosalita dragged the cleaning cart over the elevator ridges on the upper floors — *thud, thud, thud.*

"He asked me to blow him." Crystal pulled on rubber gloves.

"He asks everyone to blow him. Just don't do it."

Crystal didn't reply. She studied the fingertips of her gloves, pinching them — too big.

Well.

Sometimes Rosalita thought how the foreman was a kid once, who probably liked Batman and toy cars and Legos and stuff. She pushed the cart. Her calves sprung to life. She parked it midway down the hall. "I'll be back," she told Crystal.

"You know I don't like being left alone."

"Says the bitch that didn't show up to work," Rosalita said, with a laugh, over her shoulder. "Who do you think I was with then?"

At the supply and copy room around the corner, Rosalita slipped the key into the lock and pushed down on the lever. The room smelled like warm paper — chemical and woodsy. The copiers emitted blue lights as they slept. The automatic overhead bulbs flickered on as she crossed the room to the dual-level cabinets. She knelt, read the laminated labels that appeared on each of the cabinet doors. She selected three pens, four different color highlighters, a package of notecards, three envelopes, and a notebook for Salomon. Rosalita was stealing, but only in the same way that the men and women who worked on these floors did for their children's school projects. And they didn't feel guilty, so why should she?

Two days until Salomon's entrance exam.

She returned and placed the supplies on the bottom shelf of the caddie. "What are those for?" Crystal asked.

"None of your business." Rosalita checked the dangling clipboard.

"I didn't go to college." Crystal peeked at the school supplies.

"Maybe you should have."

They cleaned the darkened office floors. The city lights pierced through the slats of closed blinds. Their ghostly silhouettes passed over glass partitions. Occasionally, inside the conference rooms, she would look through the windows and notice a building engulfed in black save for one or two golden cubes of light and see a person inside vacuuming the floors and dusting the bookcases.

She passed through the fifteenth-floor offices, observing only secondary signs of life — a change in scent, a granola bar wrapper left on a desk, an open gym bag — and, pooled in the bottom of a waste basket inside Ames Garrett's office: a puddle of soupy brown vomit.

THE DALLAS MORNING NEWS —
APRIL 11 — ARTICLE:
DISGRACED CEO HOPEFUL FACES
SEXUAL HARASSMENT CHARGES

VIEW COMMENTS

Anonymous Former Truviv Employee
04/11 at 6:26 AM

This is not the only offender at Truviv.

Anon Current Truviv Employee
04/11 at 6:31 AM

I have worked for years with Ames Garrett. He is a good man with a proven legacy. He has never demanded accolades, but has quietly steered the company through choppy waters and numerous potential legal hazards and into the prosperous age of recent history. These claims are unfounded and it is embarrassing that this is what passes for reporting these days.

Ruth McNary
04/11 at 6:36 AM

Stop. Believe women. There is no

384

value in a "He's a good guy who did good things for the company" defense. This comeuppance is long overdue.

Anonymous & Fed UP
04/11 at 6:45 AM
There is no evidence of any-thing. Every false complaint makes it harder to believe women and somehow wanting actual facts makes us the bad guys. Yes, guys. Was anyone raped? Was anyone assaulted? No. And no one is alleging otherwise.

Truviv Employee
04/11 at 7:01 AM
Seriously, Anonymous & Fed Up? Yes, someone, someones actually, were assaulted. That is exactly what is being alleged. And by the way, no one has to be raped for an assault to take place. This isn't the 1950s.

Anonymous & Fed Up
04/11 at 7:02 AM
Were you there, Truviv Employee? Do you know what happened?

Great, then you don't know.

Anon Victim
04/11 at 7:16 AM

I'd like to thank the women that came forward to accuse Ames Garrett. It's inspired me to name my own abuser at Truviv. His name is Lamar O'Neill.

Lamar O'Neill
04/20 at 2:11 PM

I have been made aware of this commenter and also know who has made these false allegations against me. Out of respect and kindness, I am choosing not to name this person publicly, but will be taking immediate legal action against this person.

Ruth McNary
04/11 at 7:35 AM

@AnonVictim I believe you. I am so sorry you went through this.

Anonymous & Fed Up
04/11 at 8:12 AM

Really, @RuthMcNary? On what basis? Is this where we're at as a country? We don't care about due process or evidence anymore? Why are we okay with slander in its most obvious form? You are ruining people's lives and careers. Let's see the proof. Texts, emails, this is a digital age, so if the women's and your allegations are true, show us. Everyone is innocent until proven guilty. I for one still have some respect for our founding fathers.

Anonymous
04/11 at 8:45 AM
You don't know what went on there. No one knows.

CHAPTER THIRTY-THREE

12-Apr

Since filing the lawsuit, Sloane had taken to
working with her office door shut more
often than not. She was cloistered in her office when the commotion began. It was a
buildup of noise, really. Voices. This happened sometimes. A senior attorney reamed
out an IT person, someone got engaged or
brought a new baby around to show their
colleagues and, for a moment, a small flurry
of activity would break out on the office
floor.

Sloane finished typing up the email that
was sitting on her desktop. Then, curious,
she poked her head out. A clump of secretaries gathered at Beatrice's station.

"What's going on?" Sloane asked.

Anna, Ardie's secretary, turned. "They're
saying someone jumped off the building."

Sloane stepped out into the hall to join
them. "Jumped off the building. This build-

ing?" She pointed at the floor. "Who's saying?"

Corey, the fifteenth-floor receptionist, answered. "I was just covering for lunch on Nineteen. That's what the receptionist there told me."

A phone rang. Beatrice glanced down at the blinking handset and ignored it. Two more lines lit up. Then three. Beatrice sent them all to voicemail. But within seconds, the lines were flickering red again. She picked up. "Hello?"

Anna tapped her hand on Beatrice's desk. "I just got a text." She held up one finger. Lowered it. Anna pressed her fist to her mouth. "I just got a text from my friend Kristen on Nineteen. She said that she heard . . . that she heard it might have been Ames."

Sloane's mouth curled around words, most of which got away. "Who? Wait. What?"

Sirens. Definitely sirens now. The sound spiraling into the foreground. Rising up the stories like hot air.

Corey separated from the group and let herself into an unoccupied office. She pressed her nose to the window. "There's a fire truck down there," she reported. Her hands left smudges on the glass. "A couple police cars. And an ambulance."

Beatrice had hung up. Deep parentheses burrowed into either side of her mouth. The line chirruped. "Bobbi's calling." She shoved her fingernails in between her teeth. Her cheek twitched. "Should I answer?" She looked across the desk to Sloane. Sloane pressed her hair back from her forehead. Her blazer hiked awkwardly.

"Anna, check Ames's office." Sloane was already hustling down the east half of the hall. "Hold on, Beatrice," she called. "Grace? Ardie?" She stuck her head in each of their offices. Both empty. She returned.

"He's not in there," Anna informed them, grimly.

Corey — "I said that there's an ambulance down there. You don't think he's *alive,* do you? Do you think he's alive?" She turned her face from the window, seeking opinions from the group.

"We don't know that it's him." Sloane's heartbeat had picked up speed.

"Bobbi's calling still." Beatrice's hand clutched the cradled receiver. "What do I do?" She looked stricken.

Sloane took a deep breath, thought, then swiped her cell phone off her desk and tucked it into her jacket pocket. "Give me ten minutes," she told Beatrice. "I'll go down there and see what's going on. Hold tight. Don't do anything yet. I'll be right back, okay?"

Red and white lights flashed outside the revolving door. She pushed her way through to where people milled outside the front of the building. Two cops in dark blue uniforms were waving their hands at onlookers and yelling at them to back up.

Sloane stood on her tippy-toes and shifted a few people to the left for a better view. A white sheet draped over a human-shaped mound on the sidewalk a few feet from the seam of the Truviv building. Sloane glanced around. Was it him? Was it Ames?

Shit.

Sloane skirted the crowd to the far side, where fewer people hovered. She was surprised at how orderly everything was, as though the street and those who occupied it had agreed to operate at half-volume. The sirens had been cut. The biggest source of noise seemed to be road traffic and the crackle of walkie-talkies pinned to the hips of policemen.

She edged around the side, her eyes on the shrouded figure, her heart lodged in her throat. Sloane squatted down to one knee. She pulled out her cell phone and scrolled to Ames's number. There, she inched as close as she could, and dialed.

Her breath stilled. A beat. And then the trill of the marimba ringtone floated out from beneath the still, white sheet.

From a phone that Sloane knew all too well was entombed in a bullet-colored, OtterBox protective case. The cell, intact; the man, not.

Off, off. She rushed to press the red icon on her screen. The ringing — *fuck, the ringing* — stopped. Her stomach pruned.

Ames was dead.

Ames Garrett had jumped.

The man had killed himself. Here.

She had worked for him; she had endured him. She had been angry with him. She had sued him. She'd even kissed him, back in the day. But it was the thought of Ames's two small children that choked her with a surge of pity.

Jesus Christ, Ames.

Why?

CHAPTER THIRTY-FOUR

13-Apr

The strangest part was how little happened right at the outset. Events came in snapshots those first few hours. Moments of darkness, then focus as the shutter twisted into a pinhole and then reopened. The first tent-pole event, which was to say the first notice-able climate change that happened when the General Counsel of one of the world's largest sports brands jumped off an office building, was that everyone who worked on his floor left, scattering like ants from a flood.

"*That* was a mistake," Sloane was being told. In her mind's eye, the lens had just opened again, bringing into focus the sec-ond tent-pole event: detectives. "To let everyone go. Who made that decision?" Detective Diaz was short with thinning, slicked-back hair and a stumpy mustache. His holster tipped down below the curve of his stomach. Beside him, Detective Martin had a shelf of bosom and thick, natural hair that sprung out of a ponytail positioned at the nape of her neck.

Today the office was operating under only a thin guise of functionality, with staff walking back and forth carrying redlined documents from the printer while ostensibly attempting to eavesdrop. Beatrice glanced over the top of her vestibule every three or four seconds to where Sloane greeted the officers in the hall.

"Please, come into my office and have a seat." Sloane gestured for the pair to join her and at once became hyperaware of the mess of papers piled on top of her desk. She took her chair behind the desk and pushed her keyboard closer to the monitor to have more space. "To answer your question, I don't think that anyone made the decision. I think everyone was just trying to get out of the way."

Detective Diaz had thick arms that took some maneuvering to fold across his chest. Wrap-around Oakley sunglasses with mirrored lenses perched on his head. "But you could have insisted everyone stay?"

"Me, personally?" Sloane considered. "I suppose I could have tried. I'm sorry. I'm sure I wasn't thinking clearly."

Grace had been ashen. Sobbing. Katherine was shaky as she tried to help Grace. Sloane's emotions had been whipping between shock that Ames would jump and fury that he had and horror that she'd maybe had a hand in his decision. Ardie hadn't pretended to be sad, but she'd noted, almost immediately, that this would change everything.

"How did you learn about Ames Garrett's death?" Detective Martin's hips pushed out from below the armrests. She extracted a notepad from her pocket.

"I'm sorry, is this —" Sloane rested her elbows, clad in black silk, on the desk. She placed her chin on the backs of her hands. "Do you mind if I ask — is this normal for a suicide?" She pointed to Detective Martin's notepad. The word — "suicide" — was hard to say out loud. It felt in poor taste. Sloane wondered if there was some other, nicer word she ought to be using instead.

"We're investigating all angles, ma'am," answered Detective Diaz. The grease beads on his forehead reminded her of old cheese.

"Which means . . . sorry, I'm not down with the lingo." She reached into her desk drawer and extracted a legal pad and blue-inked pen. She clicked the pen top with her thumb. "I've watched shockingly little *Law*

& Order in my life, considering I'm an attorney." Nervous laughter bubbled out, a tic that had gone dormant after Derek had told her, in their early years of togetherness, that it made her sound *unhinged.*

"That won't be necessary." Detective Martin peered down her nose.

"Hm?" Sloane had just rested the tip of her pen onto the page and glanced up. "Oh." She dutifully set down the pen, but now didn't know what to do with her hands.

"Suicide is one possibility, yes, ma'am." As she talked, Detective Martin was scribbling down the date at the top of her notepad, followed by Sloane's name, which she underlined. Twice. "Another was that Mr. Garrett's death wasn't voluntary."

Sloane's eyes darted between the two detectives in front of her. "But he jumped off the side of a building."

"Like I said, that's one likely scenario." Detective Martin had a pretty smile.

At this point, Detective Diaz leaned forward, elbows to knees, and rubbed his hands together. "Mrs. Glover, there was no note and Mr. Garrett was carrying a surprisingly small amount of life insurance for a man of his position. It's our job to rule out foul play."

Why on earth didn't Detective Martin

want to allow her to write things *down*? "So then that would indicate — what — a lack of planning?"

"Maybe." Detective Martin continued writing. "That does happen."

"Mrs. Glover." Detective Diaz reached into his shirt pocket and withdrew a toothpick, which he stuck between his teeth. "There was a scuff on the back of his shoe, a fresh scratch on his hand, and a cut above his right eye. A trace amount of blood —"

"Still waiting on lab analysis." Detective Martin didn't look up at them.

"— was found on the balcony near where he must have jumped or fallen from. Were any of those injuries that you'd noticed prior?"

Sloane interlaced her fingers. "No. Not that I noticed, but we hadn't . . . we hadn't spoken in a few days at least."

He nodded and took a deep breath that fluttered several of the coarse hairs on his mustache.

Sloane roosted at the edge of her chair, mouth pursed. And fine, she might as well just say it out loud: "Are you trying to tell me that you think Ames could have been pushed? That's insane." Except, even as she said it, she felt that inch of doubt announce itself in the back of her mind. That one percent chance.

"Usually this is all sorted out in a few days, a couple weeks at most. It's just with this high profile stuff."

"Like we said" — Martin rested the pencil on the pad — "we need to be thorough. Standard procedure."

"Of course." Sloane moved her hands beneath the desk and folded them there while her mind already raced through the questions, anticipating, the way any good lawyer would. Any good lawyer — any lawyer at all, actually — had a duty to tell the truth. But no such requirement existed to volunteer all of it. So how much of it would she tell? How much of it did she even know?

The lens had already begun to refocus and a new filter colored everything that had happened yesterday. Those hours leading up to Ames's ending. If there was one thing that Ames Garrett loved, it was Ames Garrett. What had changed? Had anything?

Detective Martin settled her attention on her. "So, Sloane," she said. "Let's start from the very beginning."

The feminist witch hunt has claimed its first casualty and, excuse me, but where is the public outcry? In this search for the bogiemen who are supposedly haunting Dallas unchecked, it seems that, just like in Salem, those leading the charge have been allergic to cold, hard facts (likely because there are none or they are too inconvenient to bear repeating), and have instead focused on how those accused are making them *feel*. It started with an unverified list, moved into lawsuit territory, and has now resulted in a man plummeting eighteen stories to his death. Are we surprised? This country is supposed to protect its citizens from the taking of life, liberty, and property without due process, but what's transpired in this town is an assault on men's reputations and

I, for one, would like to see
justice served against the bullies masquerading as the bullied.

CHAPTER THIRTY-FIVE

13-Apr

The night Ames died, Grace had sex with Liam for the first time since the baby. She wore a black lace slip to avoid any confusion about exactly what she had on the menu for the evening's entertainment. *No Lester Holt for you tonight, Liam-baby!*

At no point did Liam think it odd that his wife felt frisky — *finally!* — on the day that her boss had died. On the contrary, he was happy to dive right in.

Under normal circumstances, Grace would have said that she and her husband had good sex. She'd never understood her girlfriends who, in their twenties, prattled on about how you could never-ever marry a man with whom you didn't have *great* sex. Grace didn't think she'd ever had great sex. She liked sex. Very much. But *great*? She figured that if you loved someone, then surely you could sort out the details of mutual satisfaction in the first couple of years. And it wasn't as if she'd ever had bad sex, either. At least, that *had* been true. Until that very moment. That moment when she had listened to Liam's ragged breaths, feeling as though someone were stuffing her insides like a Thanksgiving turkey.

Want to know what I did today, honey? she thought to ask him as she stared up at his bare chest.

The sex hurt. There was no way around that. She winced silently. But then again, that was the point. She deserved a bit of suffering. Craved holy penance.

Afterward, when the parts between her legs felt as if they'd been sandpapered, she slid from the bed and ran a damp towel over her body.

Liam lounged on the pillow. Tufts of hair stood up from underneath each arm. "Are you okay?" he asked, watching her wet her face in the sink. She pulled a pair of matching J.Crew pajamas from her drawer and tugged them on. "With . . . everything?"

Honestly, what was she supposed to think he meant by that?

"You seem a bit, I don't know, off." He tucked the wrinkled sheets around his waist. *Really, Liam, do I seem a little off? My, my, aren't you observant.*

She was being mean. If only in her head.

"I'm fine," she said. "You know me."

He was a good husband. Dressed impeccably, bought jewelry, cooked dinners, called on his way home from the office each day, took shopping lists to Target. Here she was, defending her own husband to herself.

He retrieved his cell phone and rested it on his stomach. They both did this: checked their work email up until the moment they went to sleep. "You're amazing, you know that?" he said.

She turned from the mirror. "I'm going to go get a glass of water. You want anything?" She sounded the same as always, so the fact that Liam — her dearly beloved — didn't press her any further was almost entirely her fault. Just like everything else.

For a moment, before she left, she watched the groove of his shoulder muscle deepen as he stretched across to turn off the lamp on his nightstand. And then it was dark in their bedroom.

She padded out into the living room. The house at night was artificially cold — their electric bill another luxury in her life, proof that she had no right to complain — and her arms pricked with goose bumps. She found her purse slouched beside the front door. She reached into the middle compartment and pulled out a pack of Marlboros and a lighter. Quietly, she opened the front door and sat down on the porch. The paper tube stuck to the moist insides of her lips. She lit the end and breathed.

As she puffed, she stared out into the night, out at her neighbors' houses, with their attractive floodlights shining up the trunks of old trees. She wondered what would have happened if she hadn't seen Ames's message on her computer screen: *I thought we were friends.*

Anything? The same thing?

Friends.

There were no answers out here on her porch. She walked to the road and rubbed the butt of her cigarette into the brick mailbox and then flicked it sideways into the bushes. Back inside, she washed her face again and swished mouthwash over her tongue and her teeth. Liam's breaths were slow and even beneath the covers. She shook him awake. "Liam. Liam," she whispered. "Emma Kate's crying."

He turned over, his eyes adjusting in the dark. "Huh?"

She listened.

"Emma Kate's *crying*." Grace yawned. "Can you go give her a bottle?"

Liam rubbed the heel of his hand into his eye sockets and propped his torso up with his elbow. "Bottle? Yeah. I can do a bottle."

"Thanks," she whispered. "I stored a couple new bags of breast milk in the fridge."

A lie. Grace had stopped breastfeeding three days ago and had hidden a box of premixed formula underneath a tarp in the garage. *What other people don't know can't hurt them,* she thought, almost as a reminder to herself. And then, she went to bed.

That was two days ago and, since then, she had hardly left.

CHAPTER THIRTY-SIX

14-Apr

The tide had changed the moment Ames's body hit the concrete. A high-powered PR firm couldn't have orchestrated a more effective campaign to rehabilitate Ames Garrett's image than the man's own death. Ardie got an inkling of the aftereffects as early as the next afternoon when she came upon a knot of young associates — all male with pressed khakis and Ivy League rowing haircuts — as they leaned over the candy dish at reception, pinching out Skittles as they talked. "They should be sick," she heard one of them say; she still didn't know which one.

She stopped behind them so that they had to turn and take notice. "Why?" she asked. She would have pretended not to have heard if they'd been older and more influential. "Why should *I* feel sick?"

They didn't try to deny they'd been talking about her. Not just her, but that made it no less personal. Their postures turned unconvincingly unapologetic, chests puffed out as though they would have said the exact same thing to her face. The third man-boy glanced at his friend, Adam's apple bobbing, more expressive than a penis. "Sorry," he muttered.

Ardie gave them a look that would shrivel testicles into raisins, but thought that, when she'd passed, she caught a few nasally notes of stifled laughter.

Later, she would return to her office and find a blank sheet of paper with the words "bitch" typed neatly across it and wonder if it had been left by the same young associates or if there were that many people in the office who hated her. She didn't mention the note to anyone.

It was as though someone had tapped the terrarium display case in which they were living and the glass walls had cracked. What Ames's death had done was give everyone permission to come to his defense.

It was dumb luck when she found Katherine alone. The usual influx of group text messages and instant messenger boxes had dried up and so had the ebb and flow of normal office conversation. Ardie believed it was instinct, that they all felt the loaded-gun quality of anything written down between them and thought: *Don't point the barrel at me.* The word "liability" screamed in their lawyerly brains. So they'd stopped messaging.

She and Katherine both came out of their separate stalls at the same time, their eyes meeting in the mirror as they washed their hands.

"Did the police come talk to you?" Ardie asked her.

Katherine lowered her eyes and scrubbed her hands hard under the hot water. Red bloomed on the skin around her thumb. "They did."

"How'd it go?"

Ardie turned from the sink, her hands dripping onto the tile floor. She ducked her head to check underneath the stalls.

"I was honest." Each word given equal weight. "I told them I hadn't worked here very long and that I was upset this had happened." She shut off the faucet and reached for a paper towel. Ardie wondered how she would have described Katherine to a friend, if she'd been the sort of person to describe people to friends. If she had friends other than Sloane and Grace. This woman who'd occupied so much of their collective mental space, it suddenly felt to Ardie like she was seeing her for the first time without a filter. She was not, as Ardie previously thought, ripe and womanly. She was bony, with a white scar on her dry, flaky elbow. She was like a bunny sighted in a neighbor's yard, twitchy and alert. Ardie wanted to stretch her hand out, to coax her. But Ardie could still see the smolder of stubbornness and intensity and mettle that had gotten her this far haunting her eyes. It hadn't gone out and that was a good thing.

"And?"

"They asked a few more questions and left." Her tongue worked unseen against her teeth, visible in the way it bulged beneath her cheek.

It seemed there was not a time in a woman's life in which intense conversations didn't frequently take place in ladies' rooms. Ardie remembered her brother's obsessions with women's restrooms when they were younger. *What are they like?* he'd ask and she would dutifully describe different ones she visited as if they were each foreign countries — chaise lounges, tampon dispensers, purse hooks, and, sometimes, if particularly exotic, hair spray and aerosol deodorant cans.

"Ames asked to meet with me. Before." There was a hidden urgency in the statement that stopped Ardie's hand as she pumped the paper towel dispenser. "Someone may have seen me looking for him. What if they tell the police?"

By necessity, "before" had also been on Ardie's mind. She'd gone upstairs to get tax documents signed by a payroll officer. She had repeated this to Detectives Martin and Diaz. By the time she returned to the fifteenth floor, Ames was dead.

"Looking for your boss isn't a crime." She ripped through the roll. "Who else knows?" Ardie asked, placid. Seismic activity underground.

In the background, water rushed through pipes like blood through veins, pumping through the living organism of the office building.

"Grace," she said, voice thin as paper. "I saw Grace that morning. I told her that Ames wanted to talk to me and she asked what I was going to do."

"Okay," Ardie said. Since the incident, Grace had twice called in sick. The Incident. That was how Ardie had begun to frame it in her mind. A word that, as a noun, meant event or occurrence, but, as an adjective, meant falling on or striking something.

"Are you going to drop the lawsuit?" Katherine returned her attention to her reflection.

"I don't know," she answered, truthfully. "I think we'll press 'pause' on it." Their lawyer, Helen, had filed the formal complaint and pressed the causes of action. She'd reached out to HR to set a time for discussion and mediation. And then Ames had gone and fallen off an eighteenth-story balcony and that changed things. How much, Ardie couldn't say. "Until the investigation wraps and then figure out how best to proceed."

We're checking out all angles, the female detective had told her when she and her partner showed up in Ardie's office, guns fastened to their hips. Truviv was a big, high-profile company. People in Dallas were going to pay attention. So Ardie understood why the police had to ask questions, to cover their bases.

"Sometimes I think I'm cursed," Katherine was saying to the version of herself — whatever that was — that she saw in the mirror. "It's like the universe can sense I'm supposed to be working in some factory or flipping hamburgers back in Boston and wants to set the balance right." Her voice was too high. She dropped her hands and breathed deeply. "I'm just kidding," she said, to Ardie now. "If I really thought things

worked that way, I wouldn't be here. Would
I?" Her face transformed and, like magic,
Katherine was pretty again.

"I'm sure you have nothing to worry
about." It was such a comforting idea that
she decided she, too, would believe it.

13-Apr

APPEARANCES:
Detective Malika Martin
Detective Oscar Diaz

PROCEEDINGS

DET. DIAZ: Mrs. Glover, is it true that you at one point said: "It would be easier just to kill him" in reference to Ames Garrett?

MRS. GLOVER: I'm not sure I said that exactly and if I did I was joking. When we were considering how to proceed — whether to file a sexual harassment lawsuit, I mean — I may have pointed out that, logistically, one would be simpler than the other. Again, in jest.

DET. DIAZ: Is that your usual brand of humor, joking about murdering someone, someone who — I'll point out — happens to be dead, Mrs. Glover?

MRS. GLOVER: Obviously, Detective Diaz, we chose to sue him not to kill him. To do both would have been a bit of overkill, don't you think? Sorry, poor choice of words, but you grasp my meaning.

DET. DIAZ: The elevators have security cameras inside them.

DET. MARTIN: You were on the elevators shortly after Ames Garrett died. In fact, you, and Grace Stanton, and Adriana Valdez, and Katherine Bell were all on the elevators around the time of Mr. Garrett's death.

MRS. GLOVER: I'm sure that's right. It's an office building.

CHAPTER THIRTY-SEVEN

17-Apr

The woman standing in the lobby of the Truviv building held herself like someone who was starting to get used to getting what she wanted. She was tall and trim, not exactly a model, but certainly further along the scale than Sloane, who had only ever been referred to as a "spitfire" or "spunky" (inexplicably, not words typically used for taller women). The woman's auburn hair — no way was it natural — was pinned into a French twist and she had a straight nose suitable for a Greek statue. A younger woman, perhaps thirty, and a graying but handsome man flanked her, like well-paid accessories.

"Cosette?" Sloane clipped over to the woman, who was utilizing both thumbs to tap a message into her device. Sloane gently touched her elbow. "Hi, I'm so sorry, was I expecting you?" Sloane was already cataloguing the week's commitments, but no memory of a Cosette meeting surfaced.

Cosette Sharpe sheathed her phone in the pocket of her blazer. She smiled at Sloane and bent down to kiss both of her cheeks. "No, no, I just flew in." As if someone *just* flew in from New York. A diamond-encrusted Rolex peeked out from Cosette's sleeve, easily forty grand, by Sloane's count. Cosette gestured to her two colleagues to excuse her and a chill, as icy as the carats on Cosette's wrist, passed through Sloane.

Cosette was a former college classmate, a close friend of her college best friend, Jenny, and seven years ago, Jenny had arranged a coffee date for the two of them while Cosette was "in town." She'd made a pitch for a large portion of Truviv's external mergers and acquisitions work and Sloane had personally gone to Ames to make the case because she believed in doing that sort of thing for other women when it was in her power. Now Cosette was the relationship partner for a Fortune 500 company, and Sloane had excellent outside counsel, and she received a full case of Veuve Clicquot each Christmas. It had been a win-win.

Sloane stared up at Cosette, trying to detect whether or not she'd had work done. "Sloane. The board called me in to handle the harassment suit."

Of all the times for a woman not to lead with an apology!

"You're not a litigator," Sloane said.

"I know. Believe me. I told them that. But we're a big firm. I brought other members of our team." She nodded her head back to the two lawyers staring at their phones. "Truviv feels safe with us. And as the relationship partner, I'll be here to consult for the company."

"Come on. You have got to be kidding me." It really took a lot of self-control for Sloane not to swear.

"Look." Cosette leaned in. "Privately, you know I'm inclined to believe you. But this is an important client for our firm and for me in particular. It's nothing personal."

"I got you this job, Cosette." Heat crept up Sloane's bra. "You reached out to me for help. Women in law have to stick together." She put on a falsely sweet voice. "I think that was the exact quote." She tilted her head and waited for Cosette's response while wondering how long it would take the security guards loitering in the booth at the opposite end of the lobby to reach Sloane if she wrung Cosette's neck. (Only a thought.)

Cosette squeezed Sloane's shoulder. "I remember and, trust me, I will do whatever

I can for you on this side of the table, okay?"

There went the exaggerated blinking thing again. Derek was probably right, it wasn't her best look but — "Um, no, Cosette. Not okay." She pinched the hand resting on her shoulder and removed it from her person.

Cosette sighed. Her lower teeth were beginning to jut. "I'm furthering the cause in my own way, you realize. I stand to be the youngest partner on the executive committee and a woman. That's not such a bad message for young women, either, is it? And I can do my part from the inside. More power, more influence." Cosette smoothed the front of her blouse, pulling herself up to her full height.

"I hope you warmed up before performing that level of mental gymnastics."

"What I hope is that we can resume our business relationship when all this blows over." She smiled. "I can even help you find a job somewhere that pays better than this place, if that's the route you decide to go. Like you helped me. You're a good attorney." Cosette clasped her hands together and instead of shaking hands with Sloane gave a short bow of acknowledgment before turning back to her colleagues, who were waiting at the elevator bank.

Sloane waited for her to walk a couple

steps away. "And you're a bitch."

The words echoed in the lobby and Sloane thought she could see Cosette's spine stiffen.

CHAPTER THIRTY-EIGHT

17-Apr

"Cosette is here." Sloane believed that real friends didn't knock or ring doorbells; they came right in and helped themselves to whatever wine bottle was already open in the fridge. She applied this philosophy liberally throughout her life.

"Where?" Ardie asked from behind her desk. It was almost comical how they were all hanging around, manning their desks, as though everything were perfectly normal. A lawsuit. A dead boss. A — dare she even think it? — murder investigation? And here they all were in Theory suits, saving drafts onto iManage like they *mattered*.

Except for Grace. What the hell was Grace up to?

Sloane paced the narrow space that Ardie had been allotted on the fifteenth floor and, for once, it had absolutely nothing to do with reaching her step count goals. "In the building, Ardie. Cosette Sharpe is in this building right now. Do you feel that?" She tilted her head up to the ceiling. "I think the air actually just got colder."

"Why's she here?"

"I'll tell you why. She's helping with the sexual harassment case. *Our* sexual harassment case, Ardie. Not helping us, mind you. She's helping Truviv." She circled her finger in the air to demonstrate.

"Wow."

Sloane ground her teeth like a pestle to a mortar. "*Et tu,* Cosette?"

"But . . ." Ardie considered and Sloane could tell that Ardie was going to try to be rational. Why did Sloane insist on surrounding herself with such rational people in her life? Big mistake. "Maybe that means they're actually taking it seriously. Our claims."

This stopped Sloane just short of the fiddle leaf fig stationed in the corner. "You think so?" she asked, turning the idea over. Ardie shrugged. The thing about Ardie was that she didn't consider the other person's *feelings* when choosing whether to deliver good news or bad news. The news simply was what it was: news. Which meant that Sloane could trust her. She was a compass pointing due north. And she had pointed Sloane in the direction of a previously unseen possibility. "Maybe you're right," she said, cooling by a couple of degrees. "That would be one less thing to worry about." Their eyes met. A small, unintentional admission.

And, honestly, it wasn't even as though Sloane had been *worrying* about the investigation, per se. Or was "honestly" only a thing liars said? She should be mindful of that going forward.

The police had come for Ames's things. The day the crime scene investigators came to box up Ames's office, Sloane wondered what they'd find. The atmosphere in the office had been buzzy, alert with the possibility of a juicy morsel, some scrap to share. It was as if they were all watching the pallbearers at a funeral to which none of them had been invited. Instant messenger applications dinged with the messages of information beggars, hungry for those scraps. *Did they find anything? Was there a note? Were those women blackmailing him? Did he really scratch goodbye into the balcony? Why are they still investigating?*

Many of Sloane's colleagues had made flimsy excuses to visit the secretarial kiosks or make copies or go to the restroom an inordinate number of times to catch a glimpse of the carrying out of Ames's desktop computer or the removal of his gallery of famous photos from the wall. A popular theory had hatched that Ames hid a suicide note behind one of the pictures, but so far, none had surfaced. And not even Beatrice had been able to secure reliable information.

It was the not knowing that was the problem. If he didn't jump, then someone had to know something . . . but who? Sloane had started by considering the possibilities she knew.

Katherine was being awkward, but then she *was* a little awkward. She probably felt that, on some level, she'd set all this in motion. Ames's death followed the lawsuit, which followed Katherine's story. So yes, there was catalyst Katherine. Grace hadn't come to work since the day that Ames had died. Out-of-character, yes, but she'd also been so sensitive since having Emma Kate, so she might simply be in self-preservation mode. Or maybe she was actually sick. At least Ardie seemed to be her usual unflappable self.

Sloane wanted to know what really happened and whether her friends knew anything they weren't saying, but she hadn't yet sorted out how to go about it.

Never be surprised. That was a solid legal

strategy. Never be surprised by what the other side would find. And now she had both Cosette and the police to contend with. So, honestly, wasn't it imperative that she knew what had gone on prior to Ames's death in order to protect herself and her friends?

"Honestly." There it was again. That pesky little word.

Sloane lowered her voice and leaned in. "How do you think that blood got on the balcony?" she whispered.

Ardie: "I honestly don't know."

CHAPTER THIRTY-NINE

18-Apr

When Rosalita arrived on the fifteenth floor, Ardie was on the phone. Ardie saw her and gestured her to stay. *Stay,* she mouthed. *Come, come.* Giant waves of her arm, leaving Rosalita no choice.

"When are you coming back?" she was saying into the handheld receiver. A question: Why did nobody in fancy offices use cell phones instead? A badge of honor to be chained to a desk, loopy cord like a leash yanking the employee back to work? Random thoughts occurred to Rosalita as she waited, like tracing cracks in the wall out of boredom. She tried not to listen, but she wasn't Salomon. She wasn't half deaf. "I don't know what to think." Ardie sighed. She twisted her chair sideways, slacks draped like hanging curtains over her knees. Under different circumstances, Rosalita might have been annoyed at being asked to hold still. She might have read it as an insult, her time less valuable than the lawyer's just because her time was literally less valuable. "No, I don't regret suing him, suing . . . Yes, of course it's unfortunate. But it's — I'm not sure . . . Probably, yes. Ultimately. But, things are still delicate." She smiled at Rosalita. "Are you okay?" Rosalita thought she was speaking to her and only closed her mouth in time for Ardie to say, "I'm worried about you. You sound — okay. I have to run. Have you been sleeping? Try to get some rest. Bye." The phone clattered into its cradle.

"Trouble has a way of multiplying, doesn't it?" she said to Rosalita, who didn't know whether that was true, only that trouble metastasized if it went untreated. Ardie looked at her expectantly and then Rosalita remembered the reason she was here. The something wonderful.

"I brought something for you," she said, holding out a simple, brown paper bag.

Ardie narrowed her eyes, skeptical. In a different life, they might have been sisters. Cousins, at least. "I thought we settled." But she took the bag.

"Tamales. I have a friend that makes them. Good ones."

Ardie's eyes went soft. She opened the

mouth of the bag and breathed in the scent of cooked corn.

"Salomon got into the program."

Ardie crunched the bag closed. "He passed?" Her eyes turned to saucers. A flush rose in her cheeks.

Rosalita nodded, her throat clogged and swollen.

Ardie rushed around the desk to meet her, enveloped Rosalita in a hug, pulled her in tight, and kissed her forehead. Rosalita allowed this to happen because it took the edge off a craving inside of her. When Ardie pulled away, she was scooping a tear out from underneath her lower eyelid and Rosalita wore a silly doll-like frown, painted on, eyes sparkler-happy. "That's the best news I've heard all week," said Ardie. Growing up, the moments in which girls were genuinely happy for one another had been hard to find. Rosalita was grateful. "All month. Maybe even all year."

It had been several days since Ames Garrett had jumped off the side of the building. Two men from the basement had used a jackhammer to claw the block of sidewalk from the ground and then used a spinning silo to pour fresh cement where the body had fallen.

That was the day before Salomon passed

427

the entrance exam into the private school program. Rosalita didn't tell Ardie this: how the two events would always be linked in her mind, how they would matter in some way.

After the two women had said all there was to say, which wasn't very much given the momentous event that had happened between them, Rosalita left to do nothing but wait until dark.

She collected Crystal without any of her usual grumbling. Tonight, she moved through the floors of the office with extra efficiency and even Crystal didn't need prodding. It was payday. The promise of a full — or, at least fuller — bank account awaited.

The evening passed in pleasant monotony. Thin carpet underfoot. Breathless halls blinking awake. The off-key hum of Crystal singing to herself. Or to a baby. Rosalita lost herself in her mind, wandering down happy passageways, most of which led to Salomon.

She spotted a soggy paper in the men's urinal on Nineteen, the last restroom on their shift.

"Look." Crystal had found another, clogged in the drain at the end of the row.

Rosalita felt the outer edges of her nostrils

pull up. She stretched plastic gloves onto her hands and plucked the fingertips to break the suction. She pinched the corner of the first piece of paper. On it, a smiling portrait of Sloane Glover, printed from the company directory, bled piss and printer ink. Rosalita extracted two others: the face of the new mother named Grace and, last, of Ardie. She dredged the photographs out of the urinal basins with the solemnity of one turning over a body found lifeless in shallow water, to find the mouth and eyes and skin bloated and waterlogged.

"What is it?" Crystal asked, moving out of the way as drips of urine trailed the floor on the way to the trash can. Rosalita skinned her hands of the latex. The smell of ammonia thickened.

"Target practice. It looks like." Rosalita wanted to take a shower to rid herself of the ugliness of men — of the things they did when they thought no one was watching and, worse, when they didn't care whether someone was watching or not.

Rosalita and Crystal didn't finish cleaning the nineteenth floor bathroom. Instead they rolled their cart back into the elevator and sank to the basement below ground, their backs throbbing, their hands dry from disinfectant, their feet tired.

Rosalita stood in front of the foreman now. "You hear anything about up there — upstairs — recently?" she asked when he handed her the envelope made out in her name.

"Other than a guy making ten times more money than I do offing himself? Nah. Don't care to." Rosalita thought about the vomit in the trash can in that man's office, wondered if she alone had seen the first sign and whether that meant anything.

Distracted, she took the envelope. Something was going on upstairs. She had caught the short-haired woman and the dead man doing . . . doing *something.* Seen the puke in the plastic bag. Found that the men on the executive floors had been urinating — literally pissing on — the likenesses of the women who worked for them, women she knew. For all three to happen so close in time, Rosalita thought, they had to be connected. But how?

Rosalita ripped the envelope with her pointer finger, a flap of skin opening up like a gill underneath the paper where it cut. She read the numbers once, twice, three times. She had never been good at math. But any way that Rosalita looked at the

check, it was for less than half its usual
amount.

CHAPTER FORTY

18-Apr

We lived with guilt the way other people lived with chronic medical conditions, only arguably, ours was the less treatable. We had guilt of every flavor: We had working-mom guilt, childless guilt, guilt because we'd turned down a social obligation, guilt because we'd accepted an invitation we knew we didn't have time for, guilt for turning away work and for not turning it down when we felt we were already being taken advantage of. We had guilt for asking for more and for not asking for enough, guilt for working from home, guilt for eating a bagel, Catholic guilt and Presbyterian guilt and Jewish guilt, none of which tasted quite the same. We felt guilty if we weren't feeling guilty enough, so much so that we began to take pride in this ability to function under moral conflict. Sometimes we went so far as to volunteer to cut our own pay simply to alleviate the guilt of having a job and being a mother at the same time.

We wondered constantly: Were we doing the right thing? Were we screwing it all up? We wished we could say that, in light of everything, this had changed, that we acquired some fresh perspective. Instead, we would merely slather on another layer of deodorant, open a tube of Tums, prepare our lying faces, and refine our skill set.

Because one of us, we would learn, really was guilty.

"Honk, honk!" Sloane rolled down the window of her Volvo SUV, the newest model. Her fist pushed into the soft spot of the steering wheel, which gave like the spongy point in a baby's head. The car blared. It was her mother who had always put words to noises — *knock, knock, honk, honk, bang, bang* — and Sloane had dutifully rolled her eyes until she'd given birth and had promptly begun to do the same thing for Abigail. It had become second nature and so it went; she was turning into her mother, day by day by day.

She came to a lurching stop in the pebbled drive of Grace and Liam's house. The front door — Farrow & Ball, Hague Blue —

cracked open and Grace appeared on the porch.

A white pashmina draped around her shoulders, giving her the delicate look of a piece of origami, arms tucked around herself. "I told you I wasn't sure that I was feeling well enough to come to work today." She squinted like the sun hurt her eyes.

Sloane had never asked Grace to join the lawsuit against Ames, but recently she'd been struck by the niggling worry that Grace might have felt pressured to, given that Sloane was her superior just as much as Ames had been. Sloane hated worries, especially those that niggled.

Still, it hardly mattered now, Ames being dead, the lawsuit having been filed. Sloane just felt the pressing need to gather her friends up, to collect them, to keep them under her wing. The edge felt so close these last few days. A beam had materialized and all four of them — Sloane, Ardie, Grace, and Katherine — were now balanced on top of it. One foot in front of the other, the concrete spiraling dizzyingly below. A fatal fall, she worried, might be contagious.

As might be a push.

"Grace." She projected over the low purr of the engine. "You know we need you in the office. It looks . . . odd."

Grace, for her part, didn't argue. She wasn't an arguer.

Grace dipped inside the house and returned with her purse. In the passenger seat, Grace drew the buckle across her chest and sat gingerly beside Sloane, her fingernails plucking at the leather stitch seams.

"Do you want to talk about it?" Sloane asked, reversing the car into the street and pushing the gear shift into drive. Sloane eased the SUV down the wide streets of Highland Park, where cops had nothing better to do than pull people over for failing to come to a complete stop at an empty intersection. They had passed Highland Park Village, the neighborhood shopping square, with its unattainable storefronts like Carolina Herrera, Fendi, and Balenciaga, before Grace said anything.

Her gaze pierced through the windshield. "I'm fine, really, I am. I'm sorry. You remember what it was like when you had Abigail." Her eyes flitted for the briefest moment over to Sloane: hope and accusation. "The combination of everything going on — Ames, the company, it's just a lot. It's catching up to me."

"You feel . . . responsible?" Sloane asked, knowing that could mean so many different things.

"No." Grace stilled her hands. "I don't know. Detective Martin called me at home. I feel bad. I didn't have much to tell her."

These angled glances at one another were so tricky.

Sloane twisted her grip around the steering wheel and wetted her lips. "I think it might be time for you to talk to Katherine." She'd been gearing up for this conversation, weighing the best time to have it and with whom. Grace needed a purpose and they needed Grace.

Sloane was fairly certain that Ardie had lied to her now. First about believing the company had brought in Cosette because they were considering bowing to the women and second about something else. It was the way she'd said *"honestly"* that had raised Sloane's antennae. Ardie knew something about someone; Sloane just didn't know what or why Ardie wouldn't tell her. Sloane had done a bit of snooping and Ardie had not been lying about getting the payroll form signed, but then again, why would she lie about payroll forms? So, Sloane wondered, what would Nancy Drew do next?

Nancy Drew wasn't middle-aged, you idiot.

Still, she wanted to be the first to talk to Grace.

"Yes," said Grace, simple and elegant as

the pearls around her neck. "I agree."

They came to a red light and sat for a moment in silence. Then Grace said, "He was trying to manipulate me, you know. That's why I joined, really, in case you were wondering. I just wasn't going to let him go around thinking that he'd pulled one over on me."

Sloane let out a heavy breath. "How?"

Grace laughed quietly and toyed with the tip of one nail. "He asked me to smoke with him up at the balcony a few times. He" — a sort of hiccup or indigestion — "acted like he was genuinely interested in my career."

God, had Grace been smoking? Smoking with Ames? Sloane did a teensy bit want to judge her friend — gloat, more like. She imagined telling Derek: *Can you believe it? Perfectly proper Grace Stanton smoking while nursing. I never did any of that. Now who's the better mom?* But, goodness, it was Grace and, well, Sloane wasn't exactly a saint and Derek and Sloane weren't exactly speaking, so it was all a bit moot, really. And still the news was, undeniably, salacious. Grace and Ames. Cigarettes.

"Where did you smoke?" She thought she sounded casual. Mostly casual, anyhow. There was no delicate way to ask. *Eighteenth floor? The balcony? Oh, see anything unusual*

437

up there? How's the breeze?

"On one of the smoking decks." Grace crooked her finger and pressed it to her lips. "As soon as Katherine told us that she'd mentioned to Ames that she had *seen* me at The Prescott, I thought how stupid I was. I must have seemed like such an easy target to him. Butter me up. Offer to help my career. And then I'd be on his side and the sad part is that I was." The edge of her finger came away with a violent shock of red from her lipstick.

Sloane frowned. "It's not mutually exclusive, you know," said Sloane. "He might have really seen promise and offered to help."

"Maybe. I saw the room key, though. To The Prescott. When he showed me a picture of his kids. Even if nothing happened in that room at The Prescott, he kept a key because he wanted something to happen. I think that's why he doubled down wanting me to write the letter. People try to take advantage of nice people."

"What were you doing at The Prescott?" Sloane asked.

"Sleeping."

They drove past Dealey Plaza, the place where John F. Kennedy had been assassinated. Sloane had never passed by it

438

without sparing at least a fleeting thought: blood and brain.

"Did you ever see Katherine up there? On the smoking decks?" It was a long shot, but Sloane had no choice except to feel around in the dark, hoping to bump into something. She didn't like the idea that the only person with opportunity might be Grace. But, no, that wouldn't make sense at all because she'd never even heard Grace fail to say "please."

"I don't think she'd spend time there. Katherine's terrified of heights."

Nearly to the office, Sloane had another thought: "So now what? Why the disappearing act?" she asked. "You feel guilty? For what? For suing Ames? For believing him? For what?"

Grace tilted her head back on the rest. "I've felt guilty about so many things in the past few months, where would I even begin?"

Sloane reached across the cup holders, still occupied by two empty Diet Coke cans, and squeezed Grace's hand. "Welcome to motherhood," she said, and then: "Hey, where's your wedding ring?"

CHAPTER FORTY-ONE

18-Apr

Grace hesitated before Katherine's office, just out of view, shielding herself from the relentless glass walls. She fingered the bare spot on her left ring finger. *Dropped it off at the cleaner,* she'd told Sloane, which, strictly speaking, had been true.

Grace slipped into Katherine's office and closed the door behind her back so softly it only made the faintest click as it latched into place.

Katherine: "You're back."

"I am." Grace's heart couldn't decide what rhythm it wanted to beat in. She needed two things from Katherine. The question was which to ask for first. "Katherine, we would never want to ask you to do something you weren't comfortable with." This was, of course, the exact wrong way to begin. A version of those words had likely started this whole sordid affair in the first place.

Katherine's face became a question mark.

It was important that Grace not screw this up. Any of it. But despite days' worth of sleep, she struggled to think properly. She swore something had happened to her brain, something anatomical and quantifiable since Emma Kate.

Welcome to motherhood, Sloane had said.

But was this really what everyone meant when they talked about "mom brain"?

"Sorry." Grace began again. "Sloane, Ardie, and I are figuring out next steps. The media, Truviv people, they're all, you know, twisting the story, acting like Ames was a saint," she said. "And now Truviv has called in a big New York law firm and we want to make sure that our side of the story isn't forgotten in the mix. That we're not vilified by the circumstances, I guess. With Ames gone, we thought that you might feel better about coming forward with your story."

Grace stopped herself before she could say anything like "brave" or "strong," heaven help her. She also resisted the even more tenacious urge to say that she had "prayed on" this matter and was now coming to Katherine because she felt "called to," which were popular methods of manipulation in her mother's social circle.

Katherine was doing a weird thing with her jaw and Grace thought she heard faint pops that managed to cause psychological hurt in her own mouth. "I —"

"We think it could really help." Grace started talking again at exactly the same time as Katherine and she generally made a conscious decision, when this happened, to finish her sentences to avoid the polite stop-start of two people trying to converse out-of-sync.

"I understand," Katherine said. "I'll share what happened. It's not a problem."

Ames had manipulated both of them. It was funny how, even if the thing people shared was an unpleasant one, the part that mattered more was that it was a thing shared in common. This was the theory behind hazing, Grace supposed, and she'd traded on it with Katherine, gotten her to agree to the thing the group needed from her.

But there was more. There was what Grace alone needed. And what she needed was to stop dreaming every night that she'd jumped off a building, waking up a blink away from the moment her body crushed into the ground.

"We never got to speak. After," Grace said.

A tag on her Tory Burch shift was making her back itch. Katherine's eyes were big and brown and watchful. "Did you wind up getting to see Ames?"

He wants to talk to me, Katherine had told her. Though Grace had been so exhausted from a week of Babywise sleep training at that point, it was almost possible she'd imagined it. Was Grace . . . was Grace paranoid? "I just wondered if you'd gone, you know, *looking* for him?"

The women held each other's stare for a heartbeat.

"No. I mean, I tried to find him, but I couldn't. We never got to talk." Katherine's smile was wan. "I guess he had . . . well, he must have had other plans in mind in the end."

Was Katherine telling the truth? Had Katherine, in fact, *seen* anything? What did she know?

"Probably for the best," Grace said, the air thick between them.

When Katherine combed her hand through her hair, Grace noticed the watery line of blood, a red ribbon of raw skin spreading at the nail line on her pointer finger.

Sometime later, Sloane and Ardie gathered

with Katherine and Grace to escort Katherine to the Human Resources department. Grace hugged Katherine, her slender shoulder blades poking into Grace's hands. They told her the things friends said in moments in which there was little to be said. They told her it would be okay, that she was doing the right thing, that they were here for her, that she was amazing, and it was nearly impossible to imagine a similar event unfolding with a group of male friends or colleagues in even close to the same fashion. Grace watched Katherine disappear behind frosted glass and the remaining three waited a few extra seconds before it was clear they were no longer needed.

Everything would be okay. She was doing the right thing. Grace's friends were there for her. But when she stepped back on the elevator, her reflection obscured in the gray metal doors, Grace wondered when, if ever, she would stop thinking about the last words that she'd said to Ames Garrett up there on that balcony.

Three hours later, and Grace still hadn't heard anything and neither had Ardie or Sloane, but it was easy enough to tell herself this was normal, however relative that term might be under the circumstances. She could assign reasons. The company was considering a settlement in light of Katherine coming forward. Perhaps even other women would share their accounts, too. Grace had heard of that happening at a national news station. A landslide effect. Maybe the board was waiting to announce the next CEO prior to finishing this harassment suit business — good news to buffer the bad.

But then she saw the two building employees carting boxes from Katherine's office and her heart began pounding in her chest — *Knock, knock, knock, who's there, Grace?*

Grace bustled over. "Excuse me." She flagged them down. "What exactly are you doing?"

They had fired Katherine. Grace didn't want to believe it. Katherine had been right not to want to risk going up against the company. She should have joined the lawsuit or kept quiet. *HR is not your friend!* She had read that somewhere but never really suspected it to be true.

The building employees eased a cart off its wheels and onto its flatbed. A man with biceps thick as her thighs looked back at her, at *all* of her, she noted. "We're moving Ms. Bell's belongings to a temporary office upstairs."

"Upstairs?" Grace wore a look of concern that was both honest and put on. Her tension eased. Her spike of guilt fell to its previous elevation, which was high, but at least she'd been bearing it.

"Yes, ma'am."

"Why upstairs?" she asked.

The man cleared his throat. "I assume because that's where Ms. Bell's going to be sitting. This is the right office, isn't it?" He squinted, smudging his finger over the first letter on the nameplate, the rest of which clearly spelled out: KATHERINE BELL.

"That's right," she said and he shrugged and hiked the boxes off the ground again. She didn't try to stop him.

A man in a damp-looking polo shirt stood in front of her office when she returned. "Grace Stanton?" He wore pleated khakis and his forehead was shiny.

"That's me," she said. He held a packet at waist level and she registered it with the surreal panic of someone registering a gun barrel pointed at her head.

"Grace Marie Stanton." He raised the packet and she had a self-preservation impulse to run and never look back. "You've been served."

26-Apr

Ms. Sharpe: State your name, please.

Witness: Katherine Bell.

Ms. Sharpe: What is your occupation, Ms. Bell?

Witness: I work as an attorney at Truviv, Inc. in the corporate and transactional practice, primarily.

Ms. Sharpe: Did you know Ames Garrett?

Witness: Yes, I knew him. Only since I began working at Truviv. He was the General Counsel. I reported to Ames as well as Sloane Glover, who worked directly below him.

Ms. Sharpe: What was your impression of Mr. Garrett? How was your experience working for him?

Witness: I thought he was extremely sharp. He recruited me from a firm in Boston and I was grateful for the opportunity. I hadn't worked in-house prior to this position, so he was willing to mentor me to help get me up to speed. He provided interesting work assignments for the attorneys under his watch. I was really excited to hear that he would possibly be promoted to CEO of the company. I figured this would be viewed as a net positive for the legal department.

Ms. Sharpe: Did he ever make unwanted advances toward you? Did he ever touch you in any way?

Witness: No.

Ms. Sharpe: Did you witness him making such advances to other women in the office? Did you witness any behavior from Mr. Garrett that you might call "sexual harassment"?

Witness: No.

Ms. Sharpe: Were you aware that there were other women in the office who felt differently and who, in fact, planned to sue Mr. Garrett and Truviv, Inc.?

Witness: I was.

Ms. Sharpe: How did you become aware of this?

Witness: Since I started there, it was pretty clear that Sloane and Ardie hated Ames. I wasn't sure how Grace felt about him, but Sloane was definitely the ringleader, so we all had to kind of go along. It felt like, you were either in or you were out. You were with them or against them. I felt like, to be part of the group I had to be willing to listen to them complain about Ames. It was very much a groupthink mentality. Sloane was my direct superior so I wanted to be on her good side. I went to lunches and hung out with Sloane, Ardie, and Grace — I was new to the office — and it became clear to me that they had fashioned a sort of personal vendetta against Ames. It was like a pastime for them. Practically all they could talk about. I want to believe women. I do. But when Sloane added Ames's name to that BAD Men List, she was so gleeful about it. It was like she was bragging.

CHAPTER FORTY-TWO

We never understood the tendency to underestimate us, we who had been baptized and delivered through pain, who grinned and bore agonies while managing to draw on wing-tipped eyeliner with a surgically steady hand. We plucked our eyebrows, waxed our upper lips, got razor burn on our crotches, held blades to the cups of our armpits. Shoes tore holes in the skin of our heels and crippled the balls of our feet. We endured labor and childbirth and C-sections, during which doctors literally set our intestines on a table next to our bodies while we were *awake.* We got acid facials. We punctured our foreheads with Botox and filled our lips and our breasts. We pierced our ears and wore pants that were too tight. We got too much sun. We punished our bodies in spin class. All these tiny sacrifices to make us appear more lithe and ladylike — the female of the species. The weaker sex. Secretly, they toughened our hides, sharpened our edges. We were tougher than we looked. The only difference was that now we were finally letting on.

Ardie fully expected the meeting ahead to be painful. Cosette Sharpe sat across the table from them, her pointed elbows jutted out to either side as she folded her hands in front of her. With eight people in the room, Ardie thought she could actually feel the oxygen dwindling.

"Wrongful death, Cosette." Sloane slapped her hand over the stack of documents. She had a tendency to overenunciate when she got heated, as though the whole room suddenly spoke English only as a second language. "You're suing us for *wrongful death.*"

For the record — and, as a matter of fact, Ardie would have liked some credit on this point — she'd never liked Cosette Sharpe. New York lawyers, as a rule, thought everyone who was not a New York lawyer was an inbred idiot. They ended calls with "Sorry, but I have to jump off." Cosette Sharpe was guilty on both counts and yet she wasn't the one on trial here.

"I'm glad we all have an opportunity to

gather and talk." Cosette's eyes were too close together for her to be pretty. Ardie wasn't in the habit of picking apart other women's appearances, especially when it wasn't relevant, but she could indulge from time to time when the occasion and the person warranted it.

"Why sue us? What's the point?" Grace asked, softly.

A countersuit meant not only that Truviv wasn't considering a settlement payout on their sexual harassment claim, but that they were, in fact, prepared to *demand* money from Grace, Ardie, and Sloane on behalf of themselves and the Garrett family for Ames's death. The amount owed if found responsible in a wrongful death was based off the literal value of the life lost. And Ames Garrett, to put it mildly, was very valuable.

Damages could include the cost of his education and training, plus the salary he would have made over the course of his career (raises and promotions included), then add on stock options and bonuses, pain and suffering, and whatever else Truviv might decide it had cost them to lose their next CEO and, in short, they would be asking for millions of dollars.

"At companies like Truviv, while we take sexual harassment claims very seriously, we're not going to kowtow to women who think that making a false allegation is a path to a quick paycheck. It sets a poor precedent."

Ardie pushed her sleeves up her arms. "There's no 'we' that you're a part of, Cosette. Truviv is your client. *We* are part of Truviv — Sloane, Grace, and me. *We* are taking this very seriously. Right now, it feels like you're attempting to turn this case into a journal article that you can add to your byline." Ardie hated outside counsel that inserted themselves into the clients as if they were all part of the same big, happy family, when, in reality, those same attorneys billed their clients up the nose for every six minutes spent typing out an email. "Ames jumped off of an eighteenth-story balcony, leaving behind a wife and two children, and you're suing *us* for wrongful death?"

A woman to her left, round-faced and probably one all-nighter away from dying of exhaustion in her office, pushed a notepad with something scribbled on it to Cosette's attention. She glanced down her straight nose and nodded. "Allegedly. But yes, that's the theory we're working under."

"What on God's green earth." Sloane pushed her back into the chair. It wasn't a great sign that this early in the game she was already reverting to Southern grandmother sayings.

"And, I'm sorry, but how do you plan to argue that three women are responsible for a grown man killing himself?" A note of exasperation ran under Grace's question. If one of them was most upset by Katherine's betrayal, it was Grace. She'd been steely ever since learning that Katherine would be a witness for Truviv.

Why would she do this? I talked to her. She said she would tell what happened. Why? Grace. Spinning. Disbelieving.

So why, then? Ardie could invent reasons. Truviv had promised her something. She was scared. She was a fair weather fan and had chosen who she believed would be the winning team (she was a Red Sox fan, after all). Or maybe there was something else.

Ardie should have talked to her before. Or else they never should have let Katherine get involved. But that was hindsight talking.

"Actually" — Cosette wielded the word like a knife — "we have Ardie and Sloane to thank for that." Sloane's eyes flitted to Ardie's. And Ardie's back straightened infinitesimally. "We were able to pull the complaint that Ardie penned regarding the treatment of Sloane's daughter at school, which was actually *very* well done." Cosette

454

pushed three copies of another document across the table to them, a letter on official Truviv letterhead, the signature block on the third page from Adriana Valdez, Attorney-at-Law. Of course, Sloane had written that. Not Ardie, but they must have known about it from . . . It had to be from Katherine. Her heart skipped as she started to draw an uneasy line from here to there. "The Laney Presper case, Jackson Worrall, and even now, the Matt Renard law. These all relate to incidents in which people were held criminally and civilly responsible for the deaths of suicide victims as a result of systematic harassment that pushed the victim over the edge, so to speak."

Sloane scoffed. "Come on, Cosette. These aren't fair comparisons."

It had seemed like such an inconsequential thing to vent to Katherine, and Katherine had seemed just enough outside of their inner circle to feel safe. Ardie hadn't meant to sound so bitchy. She recalled now, with a flush, that she had.

"The harassers in your complaint were mostly teenagers. They hardly knew the seriousness of their actions; they were only beginning to understand consequences. But you?"

Ardie felt the sizzle of rage in her veins.

"We weren't *harassing* Ames." Her voice was reserved, not quiet, but those at the table had to lean toward her to hear.

Cosette lifted her eyebrows. "The BAD Men List to which Sloane added the name of Ames Garrett is a form of online harassment in our view. As of today, it's been shared on social media over three thousand times. Given the unsubstantiated nature of the spreadsheet, it serves little purpose other than to publicly shame those included on an online forum." Cosette had put on her *I'm-from-the-most-prestigious-law-firm-so-I-am-obviously-correct* tone. Truviv had already put some money into this. Cosette and her team had been paid. They were beyond the fact-finding expedition. They were formulating arguments. Ardie, Sloane, and Grace were in trouble.

"The parallels don't even stop there," Cosette continued now with the inflection of a Realtor showing off an impressive listing. "As with the Sedwick case, the bullying started when the bullied girl began dating the bully's ex-boyfriend."

"We're not in middle school, Cosette," Sloane said, evenly.

"But isn't that more or less what happened, Sloane? Didn't you get upset when you thought that Ames, someone with whom you'd had a relationship, became interested in a younger woman — Katherine?"

It was as though Ardie had stepped into an alternate universe. If there was an opportunity for Ardie to have handled matters differently, to speak up, she'd missed it. She had never wanted to end up here, and now she had.

"How's your daughter doing, though, Sloane? I think we're all sorry to be here under these circumstances." She gave sympathetic looks to her team and Ardie saw Grace press her hand into Sloane's thigh to hold her. "Still, I'm afraid we can't ignore that asking Ardie to provide legal representation to you is a material breach of company policy. I've asked Truviv to table that issue for now until the matters at hand are resolved, but I'm sure you appreciate that this is a serious matter. A fireable offense, actually, and Truviv's agreement not to take immediate action is extremely generous, under the circumstances." Sloane pressed her lips together and gave nothing while Cosette blinked, waiting, as though for a thank-you. "Right. Well. Let's all take out our calendars and start penciling in depositions," suggested Cosette at last.

The meeting ended with all the warmth

of a hostage negotiation. Grace, Ardie, and Sloane slipped into the elevator. The doors closed and no one moved to press the button.

"So you told Katherine about Abigail," Sloane said. "About the memo?" Sloane asked, a false lightness to her voice.

"Yes." Ardie stared straight ahead.

"When?"

"After Michael's party, I guess."

Sloane nodded, pushing her jaw into an underbite. "So, what, you were complaining about me to Katherine, then? Your annoying boss, Sloane? Your horrible friend, Sloane?" She dropped any hint of levity. "I don't know why you would have brought Abigail into it. Client confidentiality. Didn't you tell her that, Ardie? Didn't you *say* to my daughter's *face* that you wouldn't tell anyone anything? And this will be public record now, you know. They're going to admit that memo into evidence. People will think that . . . people will say that Abigail was actually suicidal." Sloane breathed heavily. "The whole school will know how mean those kids were to her, the things they called her. As if things haven't been hard enough for her this year. She trusted you, Ardie. Not to say anything of the fact that I may not have a *job* now."

Ardie knew she shouldn't feel defensive, and yet . . . "I didn't write that memo, Sloane. *You* wrote it. And you didn't even ask me. You know that's not how I operate. If they didn't have that memo, we wouldn't be here."

"That's not the point right now," Sloane said, with actual volume control. "You had no right."

"Well, you had no right to hang out with Tony. *And* Braylee."

"I wasn't *hanging* out with Tony and Braylee *complaining* about you, Ardie. I wasn't talking shit about you," she snapped. "*I* actually like you."

A smudge of mascara smeared a light black line along the top of Grace's cheek. A few overprocessed strands of hair fell from behind her ears. "And it seems they know about the affair." Grace gently held up her finger to interject.

"Don't look at me like that. You can't blame *that* one on me," Ardie said.

She was just now registering that the speakers in the elevator were piping through a peppy radio edit of "Cheerleader."

The elevator began to descend, the electronic red lines reconfiguring themselves into smaller and smaller numbers until they vanished and were replaced by an arrow.

459

Sloane tapped her ridiculous red pump on the floor. "I never would have complained about you, Ardie. And I definitely wouldn't have brought Michael into it if I did. And I *never* would have jeopardized your job. You really went for the trifecta, there."

"And I never would have cheated on my husband."

"Ha! Glad you finally got that off your chest," Sloane said, without malice, which was why, at the very core, despite all indications to the contrary, Sloane really was the better person between the two of them.

Sloane fished out her jangly keys — with at least six key chains acquired for her by Abigail and Derek from family vacations to places like Atlantis and Jackson Hole and Big Sur. "I guess we're even now?" She stepped out of the elevator without giving Ardie the opportunity to respond.

The lobby was big and airy and disconcerting. When Grace made an excuse about needing a salad — or maybe it was a hamburger — Ardie made no effort to go with her. A message had buzzed in Ardie's pocket and, when she retrieved it, the fire emoji blazed on her screen. Without any ceremony, Ardie swiped her thumb to open it.

SMUalmn75: Hi, I like your profile, do you want to meet up?

CHAPTER FORTY-THREE

26-Apr

After that, they didn't see Katherine. But that didn't mean she wasn't there. She became like a ghost, haunting them. She loomed all the larger in their imaginations because she had all at once become so intangible. Incorporeal. Ferreted away. A blank space to fill with perceived motivations, backstory, and cunning. In the absence of her, they questioned their judgment. They questioned themselves.

The depositions began, it having been several days since Sloane last heard from the detectives without any hint as to where the investigation stood.

Sloane, Grace, and Ardie had hired Helen Yeh from Scott, Wasserstein, and McKenna. Really, Sloane had called in a favor. Sloane had hooked Helen's son up with an internship at Jaxon Brockwell a year ago and he was now starting his first year at the University of Pennsylvania School of Law. From the start, Helen had agreed to take the case on contingency, which meant that if they'd won anything, she would take home 40 percent. They didn't have to pay a dime up front, though it was quickly starting to look like there wouldn't be a dime to take home, either, and Helen was probably starting to wonder how much her son's legal education was really worth to her.

Truviv's strategy, it appeared, was to methodically chip away at the women's credibility — mostly Sloane's. To make their claims sound hypersensitive. To draw as clear a line as possible from the spreadsheet, to the lawsuit, to Ames's death. Hours passed, punctuated by lukewarm coffee drawn from a stationed carafe, during which Sloane had to watch every word that came out of her mouth. In the late afternoon, they broke for the day and Sloane, Ardie, and Grace reconvened at one of the many salad shops that populated downtown Dallas. During those meetings, Sloane attempted to fortify morale. She went over the line of questioning — the affair was irrelevant, Grace's note was written under pressure, which could actually be read as a point for them. They'd been responsible, long-standing employees with a knockout record of loyalty to the company.

But there was no easiness to this time spent together and anyway, Sloane's tone gave her away. A dull edge of hurt still pressed on her that Ardie would *complain* about her. Was Sloane someone about whom people complained? She worried. She worried Derek was preparing to leave her. (What was he doing all those hours up in the guest bedroom alone?) She worried she would lose her job.

Still. "How can they say that something we did made Ames kill himself?" Sloane would say over an unappreciated mix of purple lettuce and goat cheese.

But then the conversation always returned to Katherine.

CHAPTER FORTY-FOUR

27-Apr

Grace wrote the nanny a check when she returned home from the third day of depositions. She had found her nanny, Julieta, through a volunteer-run shelter that helped immigrant women find work. Julieta was close to the same age as Grace, with two children of her own and a moderate grasp on the English language — not that Grace could judge, seeing as how she spoke no Spanish at all. Grace felt her usual twinge of guilt when she wrote out the sum she owed for the week. Women like Grace were supposed to want more time to mother, and women like Julieta wanted more money, also to mother. The relationship should have felt more symbiotic than it did.

With Julieta gone and Liam not back from work, the house was quiet. Emma Kate lay on her back, staring up at the ceiling fan, while she kicked her legs. The television was off because Grace had made sure Julieta signed something Grace's friends referred to as a "nanny contract." Apparently it was an absolute necessity unless you wanted your nanny to melt your baby's formative brain with television waves or shove Oreos into their toothless mouths while you were at work. Grace had four Nest cameras set up throughout the house that cost $199 apiece and a monthly subscription that allowed her to rewind the day's tape to make sure that Julieta wasn't pinching her daughter or kissing her on the mouth. She never checked. For what it was worth, she did believe that Julieta was meeting all of their agreed-upon requirements: playing classical music for at least fifteen minutes a day, reading two books before each naptime, never microwaving breast milk, speaking Spanish, sterilizing bottles, scheduling two hours of tummy time, and holding up black-and-white images for her baby to stare at.

Grace still felt like a terrible mom.

She sank into the sofa and turned on the TV straight away. Emma Kate tilted her head, her eyes staring up at the flashing images, while Grace mentally quoted the message from Dr. Tanaka's pamphlet: *No screen time before two!*

If asked about it, she would lie.

What if we miss our old life? Liam had asked when she was four months pregnant. The sweet freedom of taking walks around the neighborhood after dark was the thing Grace didn't know she would long for afterward. *What if I love my job as much as I love my baby?* she should have asked back.

For a few minutes, Grace sat glassy-eyed in front of a *Friends* rerun that she could quote by heart, reminding herself how, in a few months, when Emma Kate was just a little older, she'd stop doing this. Bobby pins dug into the back of her skull as she relaxed her head into the couch cushions and kicked her bare feet onto the leather ottoman that she'd recently purchased from Pottery Barn for a thousand dollars.

This reminded her: she still needed to set up Emma Kate's college fund.

A commercial came on at twice the volume, technically a regulatory violation that Grace thought deserved a lot more enforcement than Dodd-Frank. She muted it and crawled on her knees to where Emma Kate was sticking her tongue out and drooling. If there was one thing that Grace reliably loved about her daughter, it was her breath — inexplicably sweet. She pressed her nose to Emma Kate's face and her daughter pushed her feet in the air and smiled.

Emma Kate looked like Liam. Everyone said so. Grace had read in one of her prenatal books that it was an evolutionary adaptation, meant to reassure the father that the child was his, so she had decided not to take it personally.

Rug fibers were already collecting on Grace's black dress. If she'd been wearing pants, she would have already changed by now. Emma Kate seemed to be having a burst of unexpected energy and she was scooting along her back and then crossing one leg over the other. Her tiny face wrinkled in concentration, her mouth puckered into the size and shape of a single Cheerio.

"You've got it," Grace found herself saying. She watched her baby kick and wrestle, trying to make her body do what she wanted it to do. How hard it must be to have so little control. Grace gripped the threads of carpet, realized that she was resisting helping Emma Kate not because she didn't want to but because she was rooting for this moment of tiny triumph for the little person beside her.

Emma Kate squirmed. Her onesie bunched. And then, in slow motion, Emma Kate flipped onto her stomach and Grace clapped. Unintentionally. She was applauding Emma Kate, who looked disproportionately pleased with herself, and then — because, why not — Grace lifted Emma Kate and spun her around shouting, "You did it! You did it! You are the champion!" in that whispery baby voice that she'd previously believed was only mildly less obnoxious than when moms spoke to their children in syrupy tones at a decibel level designed specifically to invite eavesdropping: *Oh, no, Timmy, decorations are to enjoy with your eyes not with your hands!*

Grace pressed her hand to her baby's in a miniature high five and — she didn't want to jinx it, but she thought that the two of them had possibly shared what some might call (not Grace, Christ) a "moment."

Without feeling guilty, she turned the volume back up on *Friends* and relaxed into the sofa again, this time with Emma Kate's chin on her shoulder.

The doorbell rang. Grace bounced her baby as she padded still barefoot over to the door and slid open the lock. On the other side, Detectives Martin and Diaz stood, wearing matching slack faces, as though those were also department-issued.

If you think of anything else, give us a call, Detective Martin had said.

Well Grace had thought of something. She had thought and thought and thought.

Detective Martin blinked. A shimmery blue powder coated her eyelids. Brown hair burst like cotton candy out of the back of her head. "You said you remembered something that could be relevant, Mrs. Stanton?"

TRANSCRIPT OF INTERVIEW OF GRACE STANTON
PART I (B)

27-Apr

APPEARANCES:
Detective Malika Martin
Detective Oscar Diaz

PROCEEDINGS

DET. MARTIN: Mrs. Stanton, you called us because you remembered something that may be relevant to Ames Garrett's death. Can you repeat for the record what you told us?

MRS. STANTON: Right before the time Ames died, Katherine came into my office to tell me that Ames wanted to talk to her.

DET. MARTIN: Do you know what Mr. Garrett wanted to speak with her about?

MRS. STANTON: Not exactly, no. But she implied that it was related to a falling out the two of them had recently when, as I understand it, she rejected his advances.

DET. MARTIN: You're aware that Katherine contends that no such advances were ever made.

MRS. STANTON: She's lying.

DET. MARTIN: You believe she's not telling the truth and that Ames Garrett made sexual advances to her.

MRS. STANTON: I believe she's lying to one of us. Either she wasn't telling the truth to us back then or she isn't telling the truth to you now. Which do you believe is more likely? Especially given that Ames was helping to pay for her hotel room at The Prescott. Did she tell you that? Not only that, but I saw a Prescott key in his wallet. I'm not sure if it would have still been there when he . . . when he died. But still. It was there.

DET. MARTIN: Why didn't you mention this bit of information in our initial conversation?

MRS. STANTON: I didn't remember until later. There was a lot happening. I hadn't collected my thoughts. I did share it with my lawyer. Recently. The part, at least, about Ames paying for Katherine's hotel.

DET. MARTIN: So the timing has nothing to do with the fact that, since our initial meeting, Katherine sided with your employer, Truviv, and is providing witness testimony in direct opposition to your and your colleagues' claims?

MRS. STANTON: No, of course not.

DET. MARTIN: Grace, do you smoke?

CHAPTER FORTY-FIVE

27-Apr

Sloane rarely came home to a dark house, one of the small luxuries of being the last one home, but tonight the house looked spiritless, as if it belonged to a family on vacation, a few lights left glowing in strategic rooms to ward off burglars.

"Abigail!" she yelled.

"Up here," a faint voice called back. Sloane could hear the sound of a television. She stared up through the ceiling, as if she could see Abigail through it. Her mom brain filled with all the ugly things that a young girl might start to get into if left to her own devices. Forget baby-proofing, Sloane would like to pre-teen-girl-proof her home. She'd take out the razors, the scissors, anything sharp, the toilet bowls and trash cans, the girl's magazines and instant messenger apps and cell phones and pills and liquor bottles and cameras.

Sloane stripped off her blazer and kicked her shoes underneath the lip of a cabinet.

"The school district superintendent called me." At the sound of a voice, she spun around to the darkened living room, her heart thumping like a trapped rabbit's.

"You scared me," she told Derek. The silhouette of her husband blackened the couch. The streetlights that filtered through the shutters lit the outer edge of a beer bottle sea-glass green. "He said he was disappointed to receive our complaint."

"I never said 'we'," said Sloane, resting her hip against the granite counter.

"You know." Derek raised the beer to his mouth. He always sounded more Southern when he'd had a beer or two. "He wished that we didn't threaten litigation and he hoped we would change our minds. Change our minds. Ours."

"You didn't see the text messages that Abigail was receiving."

"Yes, I did." Derek pointed the bottle's neck at her.

"There were more."

He laughed and pushed himself up off the sofa to pace the rug. "And you hid them? Gee, Sloane, that's so unlike you."

She would not take the bait. "I wanted to keep your hands clean," she said. "I didn't want to involve you. So . . . I made an executive decision."

"This is my *job,* Sloane." He thumped his chest.

"I understand that."

"Do you?" He twisted on his heel to face her. "Because I think that you think just because you make more money than I do, that makes you more *important* to this family. The *executive* decision-maker, right?"

"I don't think that."

"You may make more money, but we both work equally hard. We both have full-time jobs. You could work other places, Sloane." He aimed his finger at her, tipped his chin. "You don't want to, but you could. There aren't a lot of other school districts in this town."

"They're not going to fire you and even if they did —"

"Even if they did, what? What, it wouldn't matter?" He raked his hands over his face. He'd put together the swing set in the backyard with those hands.

"Of course it would *matter.* I'm sorry. Like I said, I wanted to keep you out of it. The problem is not in the saying of the thing, Derek, it's that the thing is happening in the first place." Why did nobody seem to *understand* this?

476

"Right, well, I hope that Ardie and Grace know what they've gotten into with you." And there it was. Her worst fear laid bare by her favorite person. She was a terrible ambassador for the cause. She was a liability. She had told herself that she might be an imperfect envoy for their message, but that she was the only one available and so she had to be better than nothing. But now there was a lawsuit, a counter lawsuit and, well, maybe even more. Maybe even real, permanent, life-altering ramifications for her or one of her friends. And she didn't know how or where any of this would end. Only that it had just begun with Ames dying. And the women were left to deal with it, whatever *it* was. In the end, what if she *was* left with nothing? Nothing could be worse for her than nothing.

477

CHAPTER FORTY-SIX

28-Apr

She lived in a house that would cause Rosalita's abuelita to exclaim, "But the property taxes!" as if it were the waste of exorbitant amounts of tax dollars that kept Rosalita's family out of these neighborhoods. Rosalita's car, a disintegrating ten-year-old Kia, looked out of place parked on the curb and she wondered how long it would take the neighbors to call the cops and, in turn, how long it might take the cops to arrive, given that they had nothing to do in Highland Park other than hand out speeding tickets. Rosalita stared up at the house. Charming white brick. Topiaries climbing out of terracotta pots. Iron lanterns that framed a cherry red door. A sweeping circle drive that didn't even need to be used because of the attached three-car garage.

But the property taxes!

Rosalita set her mouth and dragged her

heavy-bottomed purse off the cloth-covered passenger seat. Ivory curtain backs blocked the windows. Her sneakers had bitten through the hems of Rosalita's jeans so that they scraped the ground with damp, white threads. The chafe of the denim was the only sound her shoes made up the walk.

She tried to imagine the woman behind the cherry red door, who lived in the perfect white brick house with plants that received more grooming than Rosalita's legs. Probably she brushed her teeth first thing in the morning, was purposefully loud during sex, wore matching pajamas, and read health food articles. Rosalita didn't want this life, though she understood this thought was like calling to break up with a man who had already stopped calling her months earlier. It had never been offered to her.

She clutched the heavy iron knocker — a ring through a lion's mouth — and clomped it against the door. She waited, counting quietly under her breath. She knocked again. When no one answered, she shoved her thumb into the doorbell, which had a stretch of Scotch tape covering it. The chime reverberated through the house. Rosalita could hear it from here as well as the footsteps that followed. She glanced up idly and noticed a pinhole camera fixed to the corner of the door. Rosalita imagined the shape of herself reflected in the fisheye lens, warped and rounded, the opening shot of a true crime show.

And then the door opened and the two women stood on opposite sides of the threshold.

"My name is Rosalita Guillen. I need to talk to you." She held out an envelope with clean writing on its face.

The woman had pink skin covered in freckles. She had hair that looked as though someone gnawed on its ends. She looked at Rosalita once and, gently but forcefully, snapped the door shut.

CHAPTER FORTY-SEVEN

1-May

Two news vans idled in the fire lanes with two different anchorwomen who were hooked to camera and microphone cords. Every female news anchor Sloane had ever seen, no matter the city, looked like she was from Dallas, but the Dallas news anchors were by far the Dallasiest of them all. Big sprayed-in hair, pink lips, tailored dresses in one of four jewel tones, paired with platform heels that made them walk like baby deer. Sloane had once seen a segment on the *Today* show about how there was an online Facebook group where anchorwomen shared good deals on TV-appropriate dresses and, honestly, nothing had ever made more sense.

Had it really been less than two months since Desmond's passing? The words "shareholders hate hearing 'no comment' " still rang fresh in her mind.

481

Sloane covertly slipped a compact mirror from her purse and checked her teeth. The moment she began walking, the nearest anchor — a woman with voluminous black hair — started in at an angle to cut off Sloane's course.

"Sloane? Sloane Glover?" She pushed the bulb of a microphone out at Sloane. "How do you answer allegations that you and your co-plaintiffs are responsible for driving a man over the edge?"

"I didn't push anyone off the side of a building," Sloane responded, a statement which she hoped would serve to be both thought-provoking — *Well, of course, you didn't* — and sassy. People could get on board with sassy.

"I was speaking figuratively," said the reporter unnecessarily. Sloane saw dimpled Cliff Colgate slouched against the side of the building, taking a puff out of an e-cigarette, which he then slid into the pocket of his satchel. "Mrs. Glover?" The reporter leaned into her line of vision.

Sloane's attention snapped back and she looked directly at the reporter, who really did wear entirely too much mascara, and that meant something coming from Sloane.

"I don't answer them," Sloane said. "Those allegations are a distraction meant to keep us from being able to focus on the original issue, which was a company that allowed a man like Ames Garrett to behave with a lack of discretion for years unchecked because no feasible options for women existed to complain outside of the legal system without fear of retribution."

"So you think Truviv is out for revenge?"

Sloane considered this. "I think this situation has gotten out of control and I think we need to ask ourselves why that is."

Cliff was casting his chin, gesturing for her to head in his direction. He wore black-rimmed glasses and a white button-down with no tie. She wondered if it was possible for someone his age and in his position to have never actually *worn* a tie. We were entering the age in which every child had grown up on smart devices and wasn't casual work wear in some ways part-and-parcel of the same trend? She excused herself from the reporter.

Cliff kicked his weight from the building, pocket-sized notebook in hand.

"What now?"

He stuffed his hands into the pockets of gray chino pants. "Follow-up piece," he said. "Your former colleague, Elizabeth Moretti, just came forward as the creator of the BAD Men List."

"She *what?*"

Cliff drew the golf pencil from where it was balanced on the top of his ear and jotted something down. "Don't write down my face." She wagged her finger at the notepad.

He grinned and winked and she wondered if she would ever see someone wink without thinking of Ames.

"A magazine was preparing a piece. It was going to out her. She's getting ahead of the story. She suggested you."

Office buildings: strangely devoid of places to sit outside, Sloane was realizing.

"So, I guess it's safe to say you didn't know she'd masterminded the spreadsheet?"

She cut him a look without saying a word.

He lifted his palms. "Not writing down your face." Sloane hadn't felt this dizzy since Abigail fell off the monkey bars at preschool and the school sent her an email — an *email* for God's sake — to let her know that her daughter was in the emergency room, the details of the broken arm and, not, say, a neck injury, only coming once Sloane arrived at the hospital and spoke to one of the very competent, patient doctors on staff.

Her mind spun. On balance, perhaps she shouldn't have been that shocked, given all that had happened, all the things in this world that mattered more than Elizabeth Moretti starting a spreadsheet.

But she might have told her.

"Care to comment?" The point of his pencil, sharpened to draw blood, hovered at the ready.

Whatever she chose to say in this moment certainly wasn't going to be wise. She took a deep breath. "I'll get one to you by end of day. I have your card."

The corners of his mouth sagged, but he flipped the pencil around, so that it was blunt-side down. "Fair enough." She began to leave, to extract herself from the circus of which she was either ringleader or clown. "I spoke to my source in the Dallas PD, Sloane." She went cadaverously still. "They think they've got new information on Ames's death."

"Ames's suicide," she corrected.

Cliff looked out at the street. Sun glinted off his lenses. "Ames's death. Somebody who knew something, might have seen something. Someone. I don't know."

"Who?"

He scratched his temple with his pencil. "That's all I got."

Sloane hiked her purse — heavy with broken crackers, wet wipes, checkbooks, and ten expired credit cards — further up her shoulder. "That's ridiculous. Ames jumped off a balcony. Everyone knows that."

Naturally, that wasn't true. Not even she *knew* it. It was just, *Dear God, could anything else go wrong?* And that wasn't a dare.

Sloane was a good person when it came down to it. Mostly. And she had friends. Lots of them. She shouldn't be in the middle of a . . . of a *murder* investigation.

Why hadn't any of her friends brought casseroles?

"Methinks the lady doth protest too much."

"*Hamlet,*" she answered. "You . . . have the tragedy part right."

Sloane pushed the revolving glass door.

"Email me!" He cupped his hands around his mouth to call after her. "I'm one of the good guys, Sloane."

She pushed her weight so that the door slid backward and she was nearly encased in the cylinder of glass. "Are you sure that's not an oxymoron?" she called back.

Sloane slammed her fist into the pad held by Oksana and pain fired up her shoulder. Jab, cross, hook, and jab. She followed the pattern, one after the other after the other, wind bursting from her lungs.

With every punch, the image of Ames flashed. Crimson seeping from his head, splattering up into the air, raining down on the sidewalk, a river flowing from the shattered bone in his leg.

She punched harder, faster. Forgot to breathe. Sweat dampened the hairs underneath her ponytail. What if she were responsible? What if this were all Sloane's doing? She hit. Fire up her elbow. Her muscles burned. Someone knew something or saw something. Or someone. It could be Grace — why had Grace never *mentioned* that she smoked cigarettes with Ames on that balcony before? It could be Ardie — had Ardie lied about the time she received the payroll signature and, if so, why? Or Katherine — what had caused her to change her story so abruptly?

What *was* this new information? Could it even point . . . to her?

Oksana called time and Sloane collapsed in a heap. She hung her head between her knees. Oksana draped a clean towel around her neck and Sloane dragged it over her face.

" 'A' for effort today," said Oksana.

"I ate a sandwich. With the bread."

Oksana nudged Sloane with the toe of her Truviv-branded sneaker, pushing her into a plank position, which Oksana joined because she was a sadomasochist. Or at least, that was probably the reason.

"Ames was coded red on the appointment book." Sloane barely lifted her head because her torso was in grave danger of being split in half. "None of the female trainers would work with him anymore."

When a wet drop plopped on the yoga mat below her, Sloane didn't know whether it was sweat or a tear, only that it seemed fitting that she'd lost the ability to tell the difference. She'd lost control of basically everything else in her life — her marriage, her daughter, her friends, her career. She was 99 percent sure that she had been trying to do the right thing when she filed that lawsuit. But there was that pesky remaining percentage that made her worry that actually she had just been meddling. That she'd been a bored, middle-aged woman masquerading behind tailored, wool pants and a fancy-sounding title so that no one suspected how completely boring and middle-aged she really was.

"You're going to be okay."

But Sloane didn't know how much stock she could put in the words of someone who smelled so strongly of coconut-banana tanning lotion at three in the afternoon.

Cliff,
Here is your quote: "Elizabeth Moretti believes in one central tenet: knowledge is power. She made knowledge available. She shared her power. We're all trying to protect each other in the ways we know how and this was hers." — Sloane

28-Apr

APPEARANCES:
Detective Malika Martin

PROCEEDINGS

DET. MARTIN: Grace, did you see Ames Garrett on the day that he died?

MRS. STANTON: I did, yes. I did.

DET. MARTIN: How did he seem?

MRS. STANTON: He seemed agitated, on edge. He felt misunderstood. Like he hadn't done anything wrong and he wanted me to understand that.

DET. MARTIN: Did you?

MRS. STANTON: I don't know.

DET. MARTIN: What do you mean?

MRS. STANTON: I felt conflicted. None of this stuff is as black-and-white as people want it to be. I — I don't know. At the time, I felt angry. I felt that Ames had misled me. I wanted him to know that I wasn't the type of woman to ignore bad behavior. I wanted him to feel remorse. I didn't know that he was in such a dark place.

DET. MARTIN: Did something happen that you think upset him further?

MRS. STANTON: Yes.

CHAPTER FORTY-EIGHT

2-May

The news came that Truviv wanted to meet the next morning. A general consensus had been brewing that the depositions had not been going well. Grace received the call from Helen Yeh on her way to work. "I'm going to tell you what I think," said Helen without introduction. "I think we need to hear them out. Find out where they're coming from. After that, we don't need to make any rash decisions. But, we should . . ."

"Listen," Grace finished as she took the Pearl Street exit to downtown. She still hadn't gotten used to speaking into a hands-free device, so her voice came out at a decibel closer to a yell.

"Exactly."

Grace checked her blind spot. "Have they listened? To us?"

She turned onto Main, driving past the park, in the center of which sat a thirty-foot statue of an eyeball — most noticeable for its red capillaries and startling blue iris and the fact that it was an impossibly huge *eyeball* — known as the "Eye Sore."

"I hear you, Grace, I do. But, look, my job, as your attorney, is to protect your interests. You all are lawyers, but if you were doctors, you wouldn't perform your own heart surgery, okay?" Grace might have been a doctor were it not for all the blood. But look where she'd ended up now. "I have to advise you to do what I think will be best for you in the long run. Maybe they're ready to drop the whole thing. We can hope. But you all are in free fall."

So this is what Ames felt in those last few seconds, Grace thought.

Free fall.

Helen met them at the office. Twentieth floor. Grace reminded herself that it was Helen's job to tear them down, prepare them to accept whatever was being offered to them like starving dogs. It was a classic strategy used on unsuspecting clients to make them feel as though their lawyer had gotten them a great deal. Grace ruffled at the thought of Helen having a quick "chat" on the phone with Cosette before the meeting: *I think I can try to sell them on it.*

Maybe Grace was being unfair. Maybe not.

She took a seat next to Ardie while what Grace had come to think of as the "usual group" gathered. "How are you doing?" she murmured. Ardie had lost at least seven pounds, by Grace's estimation, probably without even noticing.

"Okay," Ardie said. "I — well, I don't know what I'm going to tell Tony, though."

"We don't know —" Grace started.

"Please."

Grace didn't have an answer. *She* had Liam. She was the lucky one. If she didn't want to work, she didn't have to. Liam had said as much the moment that Emma Kate slid out of her nether regions headfirst. In fact, he'd probably be pleased to see her home. *No more washing bottles for old Liam!*

Moms were only supposed to work if they *needed* to work. Grace knew this. That was why she'd never let on exactly *how* secure their finances really were. If they gave up now, Grace would be giving up her career forever. She could see the future spinning out ahead of her as she twisted the diamond ring — newly back on her finger — around and around and around.

Sloane arrived.

"Thanks for coming." A mint bobbed on

the back of Cosette's tongue. "We'll keep this brief. Ames is dead." She folded her hands on the table. "We have a key witness on our side that has gone under oath stating that not only did she experience no sexual harassment at the hands of Ames Garrett or anyone else, but that the three of you harbored a personal vendetta against Ames, a sort of mob mentality stemming from a failed romance between Sloane and Ames Garrett." Grace pictured Cosette practicing this speech in the mirror of her hotel bathroom. "Grace's own words support the idea that he was a good, capable boss for whom she was willing to vouch. Ardie Valdez seemingly didn't like that she wasn't promoted in line with her colleagues. The timing of the lawsuit, on the cusp of Mr. Garrett's ascension to CEO, was designed to effect maximum damage, to pin the company to the wall. None of these facts are good for you. Ames Garrett killed himself because of your unfounded accusations and actions."

"You know we take issue with literally all those conclusions, right?" Sloane said.

This was what frightened Grace most: Sloane. Sloane hadn't barreled into the room. She hadn't made a flippant remark about running five minutes late. She sat subdued. Tranquilized.

"Noted. But Truviv is prepared to fight this one to the bitter end if need be. The shareholders, having heard the testimony and the facts of the case, are ready to back this up with a sizeable trial budget. It just makes financial sense, frankly. But here's what I can do for you. Give up your stock options. Resign. Settle with Truviv for five million dollars to cover the cost of legal fees and reputational damage. Walk away from this and Truviv will provide letters of recommendation and sign a non-disclosure agreement prohibiting anyone at the company from speaking poorly of you either personally or professionally."

"Five *million* dollars. You want *us* to pay *you* five million dollars?" Ardie scoffed. "Where do you think we would come up with five million dollars?"

Grace didn't volunteer that she could come up with the money. If she had to. At least, her share of it, perhaps even the whole thing, but she'd have to go to her parents and, well, that wasn't a particularly attractive option. And besides, it was the "resign" part of Cosette's proposition that made her blood run cold. And nondisclosure agreement or not, there'd be no keeping quiet the whos, the whats, or the whys within the legal community.

The diamond ring spun and spun and spun around her finger. She had been so stupid. She would be her own undoing.

"We can set up a payment plan. If we need to negotiate on the total number of years for payment, I think that's something I could probably sell to the board." Cosette checked over her shoulder at the thick-bodied man, the board member from the independent review committee, and he pressed his eyes closed and frowned: *Sure, sure, let's let them have this one.*

"This is vindictive," said Sloane. "It's extortionate."

"No," Cosette said, evenly. She was already placing papers back into her briefcase. "It's preventative. The terms will be on the table until tomorrow. After which Truviv will plan to move forward with its case against you."

It was clear that if you cut open Cosette Sharpe's veins, you would find them crusty with freezer burn. And really, who in this room wouldn't like to try?

The room emptied except for Grace's team. Helen sat at the back end of the table, her mouth pursed, waiting.

"There is a special place in hell for women who don't help other women." Sloane ground her teeth.

"Madeleine Albright," said Ardie.

Sloane moved to stand at the window and stared down the face of the building. "Really? I always thought it was just something Taylor Swift said to Tina Fey. But still."

But still. Grace felt a rush of love and nostalgia for her friends. Maybe this was exactly when people felt rushes of both love and nostalgia. Necks in the guillotine, as it were.

"You would be free of the wrongful death suit." That was just the lawsuit, though. It'd have no bearing on criminal charges. However, the optics wouldn't hurt.

What if I love my job as much as my baby? What if I love it just a tiny bit, a tiny bit more?

Sloane spun back around. "Five million dollars, Helen."

Helen was a small woman, a body like one of those space-saver bags, vacuum-sealed from fat. She ran insane distances on the weekends for fun. "I know that sounds like a lot of money. But for Ames Garrett, that's actually cheap." A sale on Ames Garrett's life. It was their lucky, lucky day. "If you lose a wrongful death suit, you'd be on the hook for a lot more. At least — *at least* — three times that."

498

"And Katherine?" Grace asked, trying to keep her voice neutral. Ever since she'd spoken to the police, she'd harbored a hope that they would find Katherine to be at fault for Ames's death. Grace felt wicked, but that was the bare truth. She was further from God than she'd ever been in her life and it wouldn't bother her if they crucified Katherine. She supposed on some level they were both Judas now.

"As I understand it, she'll be getting a . . . promotion. I'm not privy to the details. Sorry." Helen took a deep breath. "My firm says I can't keep representing you on contingency. I'm sorry. You know I want to. But this wasn't even what I initially signed on for." Grace looked to Sloane for some reaction, but Sloane's face shut down. "Honestly, I seriously doubt that any other high-level employment firm in town is going to want to grind through this volume of work for free."

No one said anything. It turned into the longest silence that Grace had possibly ever experienced with her two friends, who also happened to be the smartest and most capable women she knew. But in the end, it wasn't about intelligence or competence. It never had been. And because of that, they were going to lose.

499

CHAPTER FORTY-NINE

2-May

Sloane found two voicemails waiting for her after that horrible meeting:

The first: "This is Principal Clark. Something's happened at school involving your daughter, Abigail. I'm afraid she hit another student. We need you to come in as soon as possible."

The second: "Mrs. Glover, we've been trying to contact you for an hour. We really do need you to come in as soon as possible due to . . . the severity of the incident."

The severity! Of the incident!

That was twenty minutes ago.

Sloane had never been sent to the principal's office in her life, not even for cheating or talking back or some other *normal* indiscretion. Teachers loved Sloane. She'd been Vice President of Student Council. She'd made buttons, for fuck's sake.

Abigail, on the other hand, had *hit* someone. Only hooligans hit people. Grubby kids with sticky little jelly hands and dirt clogged beneath their fingernails. Other people's kids.

The thought struck her on the frantic drive over: Was it possible that her daughter had been the bully all along? And that was why she'd received the text messages? *Oh god,* what if Sloane was one of those awful parents that believed their child was a sweet little angel baby, and meanwhile she was out kicking puppies and pinching other children behind the teacher's back? *Oh, shit, oh, shit.*

Of all days, Abigail, she would say when she saw her. *Of all days for you to do this.*

At the double doors leading into the administration office, Sloane checked her reflection in the tinted glass, shimmying her skirt into place and pulling her blazer tails down over her hips when Derek jogged up, appearing behind her in the distorted image.

"Sloane," he said, breathless. "Jesus, what the hell is going on?" His hand was on her back and she felt her mouth go crooked. "Sorry, I had a hell of a time finding someone to watch my class."

"I was in a meeting," she explained, with sympathy. "Came as soon as I heard."

Seeing Derek's face, it made it all worse. And better.

He shook his head in disbelief. "Our daughter *hit* someone."

"Our daughter hit someone," she agreed.

They held hands. Though neither of them acknowledged it. And they went into the meeting a pair.

Everyone was waiting for them. That was the first thing they were told when they entered Principal Clark's office. *Everyone's been waiting for you!*

That seemed like a bit of an exaggeration. There was Principal Clark. And Abigail's English teacher, what was his name? Mr. Tawley? Tully? Derek would know. Derek, whose hand was still grasping hers firmly. And then another mother, whose name Sloane had never known. She was wearing hospital scrubs with the name of a veterinary clinic embroidered above the left shirt pocket. A boy, with sweaty, cowlicked hair and Under Armour sneakers that could blind you, hung his head. Dried blood ringed his right nostril. And then there was Abigail. Sloane's pulse faltered at the sight of her daughter making herself small in a corner chair. Fresh tears silently streamed down her beautiful, freckled face at the sight of her parents. Derek and Sloane gravitated

502

to her, flanked her. This was their daughter. They would love her no matter what. Even if she *killed* someone.

"Allow me to introduce you to Steve Lightner." Principal Clark presented the boy like a trial exhibit. Steve Lightner. She recognized the name from the text messages and instantly felt her heart grow teeth. "Abigail here punched Steve in the nose — twice — outside of her English class."

Surely, Principal Clark thought he'd uncovered the smoking gun. *See, Mrs. Glover, your daughter is not so innocent after all.*

Derek touched Abigail's shoulder, so gently, as if scared she might otherwise shatter. "Is this true?"

Abigail sniffled, but nodded.

"He was bleeding," said Steve's mother. "Gushing blood from his nose." The mother's face was grave.

Sloane peered down at her daughter, at the bony blades jutting out of her shoulders like stunted wings. "*Why,* Abigail?" she asked, voice pressing. "Why did you hit Steve?"

It all felt so dire. As though the death penalty were still on the table and everyone — Sloane exaggerated too apparently — was holding their breath to see what the jury would decide.

Abigail swallowed and looked up. "He kept making fun of my underwear. Him and Grady. Every time I bent over to get a book out of my bag, they would shout, 'Granny panties, granny panties.' " Her cheeks pinked. "And then Steve would kind of nudge the top of my underwear each time it happened and tell everyone what color I had on that day and tell everyone that I didn't wear thongs. I asked him to stop, but he kept doing it for, like, three days." Even now, as her daughter slouched, Sloane could see the little peek of underwear showing below the waist of her jean shorts. Purple cotton. "So I went and told Mr. Tully, but Mr. Tully told me to ignore it and that would make him stop. So I tried, but then he grabbed my underwear and . . ." Her gaze dropped. "He gave me a big wedgie. It hurt. So, I turned around and I — and I —" She started to tear up again. "I punched him. Twice," she mumbled.

Sloane's eyes went wide. "She came to you?" She directed the question at Mr. Tully, who, let it be said, was not nearly as handsome as Derek. These people had caused her to question her own, sweet, kind child. Sloane felt wild with anger.

Mr. Tully cleared his throat and shifted

his weight on his feet. "We like to discourage tattling. We think the kids working it out among themselves fosters better life skills."

"Oh, you do, do you?" Sloane folded her arms. "So my daughter was being sexually harassed and she came to you — the adult in charge — and your big life skill advice was to ignore it?"

"Now, let's not overreact." Principal Clark spread his hands out like he was giving the benediction. *Heaven fucking help him.*

Mr. Tully scratched behind his ear. " 'Sexually harassed' is strong terminology. I don't think it was that serious."

"Okay, then." Sloane turned. "Let's hear it. Steve, what life skill did *you* learn?"

Steve's mom — bless her heart — at least had the good sense to look embarrassed. "Steve, she asked you a question," said the mother.

The boy's mouth fell open, fishlike and wordless.

"Derek?" Principal Clark lifted his eyebrows. "Do you want to jump in here?"

Derek frowned and took a step back toward the window. "No, Ian. I, uh, think my wife's got this one." Her chest swelled. She seemed to feel her heart actually inflate. Sloane had long ago stopped giving blow jobs in the name of feminism, but she was reevaluating this stance, considering.

"So, what would you suggest she have done?" Sloane asked Principal Clark and Mr. Tully. "After she used her words to ask him to stop and then went to the person in authority who refused to help her. What was her course of action next? Because," she said, when no one offered a suggestion, "it seems like your preferred course of action would have been for her to, what, take it? Let him touch her? Let a boy push her, grab her, reach into her shorts because he thought it was funny, because no one would stop him, because he wanted to? And not fight back? Have I about got the plot of it?" Wild blinking, nostrils flaring, thank the good Lord there were no cameras recording her now. But there was Derek, who would surely comment on it afterward. Only, no, actually, she saw him watching her, following her every word, with soft, kind Derek eyes.

Principal Clark. "We're just trying to say that violence is never the answer."

"Oh, well, that's good to know. But violence against little girls is more of, what, a gray area? Mostly okay? Fine, as long as we're all good sports about it? It seems to me you're mistaken about who was being violent and who was acting in self-defense. Abigail, get your things, please," she snapped, not taking her eyes off the two grown men standing on the other side of the room.

Abigail climbed out of the chair and sullenly collected her bag and her lunchbox from under the chair.

Derek held the door open.

"Don't ever touch her again." She pointed her finger at Steve. "Do you hear me?"

Steve could not bring himself to look up from those frightening tennis shoes. His eyes must be throbbing.

"I won't," he grumbled.

Outside, the parking lot asphalt was a Teflon frying pan, set on high heat. Sloane was breathing heavily like she'd just won a boxing match. She walked in a tight circle, hands on her hips, letting the throbbing of the vein in her neck slow. She shook out her arms. "The nerve of them," she exclaimed, at intervals, until she was able to stand still with her little clump of a family, heart still on fire for them.

"Are you mad at me?" Abigail asked, her backpack a tortoise shell too large and loaded for her tiny frame. She was no longer crying, but her lower lip looked unsteady.

"No," Derek said. "No one is angry with you." He ruffled her blonde hair.

"But I punched someone," she told them, as if she needed to be clear on this point. She turned her hand over and examined her knuckles, which were an aggravated shade of pink.

"I think you got that impulse from your mother," he said. "And it's a good one. Mostly." He held out his hand and she turned her heavy bag over to her dad, who slung it easily over his shoulder.

Abigail ventured a guilty grin. "I don't think he'll try that again, Dad."

Derek laughed. "I should think not."

With more caution than ever before, Derek wrapped his arm around Sloane's shoulder and kissed her temple.

She pressed her nose into his neck. "Derek." Her voice was low. "Derek, I'm afraid I have some very bad news."

Transcript of Interview of Katherine Bell

28-Apr

APPEARANCES:
Detective Malika Martin
Detective Oscar Diaz

PROCEEDINGS

Ms. Bell: Two of my brothers are cops.

Det. Diaz: Great, then you know the drill.

Ms. Bell: Not exactly. Not like this.

Det. Diaz: At least one person has told us that Ames Garrett had requested a chance to speak with you prior to his death.

Ms. Bell: That sounds right. I don't recall exactly.

Det. Diaz: You didn't mention that you had spoken to Ames Garrett minutes before he fell off an eighteenth story balcony?

Ms. Bell: He may have asked to speak, but I didn't see him.

Det. Martin: Why not? I thought

you and Ames Garrett were on good terms? That's the gist of the statements you've given in the sexual harassment suit against Ames and Truviv, right?

Ms. Bell: We were on good terms, yes.

Det. Martin: So, why not meet with him?

Ms. Bell: I couldn't find him.

Det. Martin: You couldn't find him . . . So, to get this straight, he asked you to speak with him, then when you went to speak with him, he wasn't there. Why would he do that?

Ms. Bell: I waited a bit. After he asked.

Det. Martin: Were you stalling?

Ms. Bell: No, no I wasn't stalling.

Det. Martin: Because you were on good terms.

Ms. Bell: No. I mean yes. We were. I don't know why we didn't meet. He clearly wasn't in his right mind at the time.

Det. Martin: Where did Ames want to meet you?

Ms. Bell: I'm not sure. I don't

think he specified.

Det. Martin: Hm. That would be strange, wouldn't it? Did you find that strange?

Ms. Bell: I figured it was an oversight. It happens.

Det. Martin: What do you think he wanted to speak with you about?

Ms. Bell: I don't know.

Det. Diaz: Ms. Bell, Grace Stanton mentioned that you had a fear of heights. That true?

CHAPTER FIFTY

2-May

Failure was a luxury we couldn't afford, all chained together as we were, our fates locked up tight. One box office flop from a female director and no one wanted "girl" movies, one stock market plunge from a company with a woman CEO and women couldn't lead, one false accusation and we were liars, all of us. Because when *we* failed it was because of our chromosomes, it wasn't because of a market dip or an ineffective advertising campaign or plain bad luck.

One wrong move! As the saying went.

Ardie lay on her couch, a smorgasbord of takeout containers opened, the stink of failure all around her as she watched an old episode of *Community.* "The Last Supper," she was calling it. The last night she could afford UberEats to deliver, more like. The tax attorney in her hadn't been able to keep from doing the math. Oh, how she'd wanted not to! She would owe a little more than $1.6 million after tomorrow. Even on a five-year payment plan, the yearly amount would equal far more than her annual salary. She had three hundred thousand dollars in savings, which would almost cover the first year's installment. After that, she'd have to sell the house. That should make a dent in the second year, but Michael would hate staying in an apartment when Tony and Braylee had a lovely home with a backyard, a soccer goal, and a pool. It was only a matter of time until she became the chore. *Yes, Michael, you have to go see your mother,* Tony would say and he'd feel like a good person for it.

She'd have to go back to a law firm. That was obvious. She hated law firm life, the billing requirements, the face time. She was already too old for partnership track. By the third year, she wouldn't be able to pay. She'd fall behind, owe interest, the hole deepened and deepened. She ignored the chasm opening and took another swig of Coca-Cola, full calories.

Her phone buzzed on the table, underneath a foil hamburger wrapper.

One of the worst changes that had come with being a single parent was phone-ringing anxiety. If Tony had rung unexpectedly during their marriage, her first reaction would have been to feel pleased and a little special. But now it was different. Her first instinct was to answer the phone, *What's wrong?* No matter who called. If one thing could fail, everything could.

But it was Rosalita calling. Ardie watched the phone vibrating in her hand, probably an accident. Or maybe Rosalita was calling to gush more about Salomon's acceptance. Ardie didn't think she was up for gushing tonight. But then the call ended and, seconds later, it started up again.

"Rosalita?" She jammed her finger into the spongy remote buttons to turn down the volume.

"Ardie? Miss Ardie?" Rosalita sounded as though she'd been jogging. "I need you to help me fill out Salomon's financial aid forms. Please."

"Okay, sure. I can help you." She regretted picking up the phone. She wasn't in the mood. "We can meet at the Barnes & Noble later this week." She would have plenty of time then.

"No, now." Rosalita's accent read thick over the phone. "I need you to come now. I don't understand what happened. I — the deadline — I got confused. I thought I had more time. I don't know."

Ardie dragged her hand over her face. She'd already taken off her bra and she hadn't even had dessert. Were it not for the desperation in Rosalita's voice, she would have said no. Or maybe were it not for her own, quieter desperation seeping into the couch cushions. She rolled the paper bag containing warm cookies and stuffed them into her purse.

"I'll meet you," Ardie said. "Send me your address."

CHAPTER FIFTY-ONE

2-May

Saint Ardie, Tony had called her. It hadn't been a compliment.

Ardie arrived at the apartment complex where Rosalita lived and cut the engine. She sank into darkness and, at the same moment, a switch turned on inside her to high alert. She pressed the point of a key between two fingers, a self-defense tactic she'd read about in a chain email that had been passed between dozens of email addresses she hadn't recognized. It was the sort of unsubstantiated advice that she followed because it felt mildly useful and disproportionately empowering. She stared out the windshield at the distance between her car and Rosalita's apartment.

It was impossible to remember a time before this instinctive and immediate fear for our safety had set in, the need to glance over our backs when crossing an empty parking lot, to check beneath our cars, to bristle when a strange man walked behind us too closely, to startle when he stopped us to ask the time. The realization that this fear was particular to us came later, that, unlike the boys with whom we played in cul-de-sacs when we were little, we would never outgrow the cautionary tales. There would forever be strangers offering us candy.

Ardie looked both ways as she stepped from her car and made her way up the metal stairs that Rosalita and Salomon navigated every day.

Ardie knocked and Rosalita answered with a stack of papers and an instruction sheet, plus a worried frown that aged her. Ardie still had only the vaguest notion of Rosalita's age.

A sagging sofa took up a third of the tiled living room. It was spaced too closely to a television set, the size that Ardie and Tony would have gotten rid of ten years ago because it looked "dated." Salomon waved from the couch. It was late, but he hadn't changed into pajamas yet and still wore his favorite cap — a blue Mavericks hat with a green brim, an illustrated cowboy hat hooked over the "M" of the logo. It was too big for his head and he lifted his chin up slightly to see the television.

He held up his hand and she gave him a high five. "I got three wrong on the math portion," he said, but he was grinning. "Not fractions, though."

"Is a high five really all I get? I haven't seen you since the big news. Are you sure you don't have something *else* to tell me?"

He pressed his fingers to his cheeks and peered up at her. "I got in."

"Of course you did." Ardie felt an aching tenderness that Salomon wouldn't need tutoring any longer. He was a sweet, quiet kid with a round face and a love for illustrated books like *Diary of a Wimpy Kid* and *The Wild Robot* that was close to insatiable. She'd asked him to write down a list of his favorites for her so that she could share it with Michael when he was older and Salomon had taken the task so seriously that he'd come back with two pages of recommendations, poured into neat columns. She kept it in her nightstand.

Rosalita was making impatient noises and Ardie released her hand from the boy's cap.

"You see?" Rosalita led Ardie into the kitchen where a builder-grade iron fixture hung over the breakfast table, its ceramic tulips diffusing the light from the bulbs inside. Papers and torn envelopes littered the tabletop. "I don't understand." Rosalita flicked the papers. "I don't understand what they want from me. I can't pay. What else do they need to know? Salomon has to go to the school. I can't pay."

Frustration wafted off Rosalita as Ardie surveyed the task at hand. She imagined Rosalita's annoyance was roughly equal to hers when she'd tried to piece together IKEA furniture.

"Okay." Ardie scanned the instruction sheet, which described what needed to be included in the numbered boxes. "We can do this. No problem. We can do this." She turned over the form, biting on her thumbnail for concentration. "We'll need your federal income tax return, W-2s, some other IRS forms, and your most recent pay stubs. We've got those?"

Rosalita's hands shook as she cast about over the loose papers strewed across the table.

Ardie flattened her palms over the table, leaning in. "No worries. I'll find them." Salomon had begun tossing up a ball and catching it, tossing it and catching it, and Ardie could tell that this, too, was wearing on Rosalita's nerves. "Maybe you could make us a cup of tea? Coffee?" Ardie suggested.

Rosalita smoothed the frizz that had

gathered at her temples. "I'll make both."

Free to rifle through the pages, Ardie began searching for the applicable forms. She cleared a square of space for the ones she actually needed.

She wished she could convey to Rosalita that, no matter how many years of education one had, everyone felt like an idiot when it came to filling out government issued forms. But there was no way to say this without sounding patronizing and so Ardie made herself comfortable in a wood chair that wasn't comfortable at all and began filling out the required information in the tiny, notched squares provided.

"What's Salomon's father's name?" Ardie called over her shoulder.

"No father."

Ardie turned in her chair. "It's important to be accurate," she said as gently as she could, given the biological impossibility of Rosalita's claim. Rosalita made eyes at her son, who was throwing the ball with less frequency and making an obvious attempt to overhear.

"Go watch your movie, Salomon," Rosalita barked, her hands on her hips. Ardie didn't scare easily, but if she were a kid, she'd have listened, too. Salomon obeyed his mother with a readiness that Michael, her tiny king of distraction, had yet to emulate and went to sit on the couch. The television blared.

Rosalita set a teakettle on the electric stove. "Salomon's father is dead," she said quietly.

"Oh, I'm so sorry. I had no idea."

Rosalita rolled her eyes. "Salomon didn't know him. But I thought . . . I thought maybe he'd pay for this school. Sometimes he would help if I asked. Here and there. Not much. But." She shrugged.

Ardie turned back to study the forms. "There's a box to check for deceased, but it looks like they still want a name." Ardie had slipped the heels of her shoes off under the table.

Rosalita's eyebrows folded inward and she pulled a dishrag between her hands. "He wasn't included on the birth certificate. He didn't leave Salomon a single thing. Why should I have to?"

Ardie held up her hand, sensing the roadblock up ahead. "Okay, okay. Fair enough. We'll leave that blank and hope for the best."

She waded through the paper trail of someone else's life and tried to corral it into order. She pulled the pay stubs and set the last three out in chronological order. She read the amounts listed in the little white box at the right. And then read them again.

"Rosalita." She beckoned without turning. "Your most recent paycheck is less than half the amount you were previously being paid. Look." She pressed her finger below the number.

"No, it's okay."

Ardie turned the stub backward and forward. "Why would your pay have dropped that much?" She tilted her head, puzzled. "Did they cut your hours? Is this what you're making going forward or what you were making before?"

"I make that for future now, I think. It's okay," Rosalita said again, briskly, then returned to the teakettle, which was beginning to whistle.

"No." Ardie bit the back of her pen and pushed herself out of the chair. "This has to be an error. There's too much of a discrepancy. I'll talk to accounting for you, or HR. This is ridiculous."

"No. It's fine." Rosalita slung the dish towel over her shoulder and removed a white mug from an upper cabinet. "This is just how much it is."

"Rosalita, this is serious. You can't live on —"

Rosalita pushed the unfilled mug back

onto the counter. "You're a rich person. You don't know what I can live on. You have no idea. Salomon — stop playing with that ball inside!" she snapped.

"I didn't mean —" Ardie extracted her hands from the table in surrender, then turned in her chair to watch Rosalita. "I didn't mean anything by it." Ardie sank back into the chair. "We'll have more in common than you think after tomorrow. Rich? Not so much." She gave a weak smile.

Rosalita laughed, a bit unkindly, Ardie thought, but that was fine, she could understand why. Ardie had a law degree, assets.

Ardie pulled out the cookies, slightly broken in her purse, and set them out to share with Rosalita, who wouldn't take one at first. "Did you know we sued, um, that we filed a lawsuit," Ardie searched for the word, "*demanda judicial* against Truviv, the company."

Rosalita's lips tightened. "I know something of it, yes. I . . . see things. Why?"

"Against Ames Garrett, too. That man who died. Off the building. Sexual harassment. He wasn't treating women in the office well. It wasn't right and we decided we had to do something about it." She lowered her voice and crooked her arm in a parody of themselves. *Do something about it!* They'd done something all right. "As you can probably guess, it wasn't a great idea." Did she believe that? In hindsight, it had been a terrible idea. But at the time, with the same information, she did think they'd been trying to do the right thing. Without the BAD Men List, without Ames dying, without either one of those two things, maybe it would have turned out differently.

Rosalita came to the table, pulled out a chair, and selected one of the cookies. A crumb fell into her lap. "I saw him in his office with that . . . short hair." Rosalita mimed. "Katherine."

Ardie snuffed out a breath and shook her head. To find this out now, a witness. Did it make her feel more or less crazy? "Katherine has changed her tune." She lifted her eyebrows and took a bite of the cookie. "Said that nothing ever happened between her and Ames. We're going to lose. The company's taking everything. I won't even work at Truviv after tomorrow." She smiled, just now fully realizing this. "But you have my cell number. You'll be able to reach me."

"No." Rosalita's forehead folded. She shook her head. "No, that's not right. How . . . how would they do that to . . . to you?" She gestured big, spirited. "Salomon!" Rosalita barked. Both women looked at Salomon, who was tossing his ball against the popcorn ceiling. He tossed the ball and it slipped away from him, deflecting off his fingers. He lunged to get it and the too-large cap dropped from his head.

CHAPTER FIFTY-TWO

2-May

All this time. This was the extent of Ardie's thoughts for those first few minutes, the silence ringing in her ears residual from the sound of her car door slamming closed in the dark.

Ardie kept the seat in her car heated because it soothed her lower back, but tonight, the warmer left a thin layer of slime, the fabric of a Pink Floyd T-shirt sticking to her as she drove. It was ten-thirty and she considered whether to call Sloane or Grace or both.

Eight years.

It had been after Sloane, even. The details hardly mattered. Once, twice, three times, more than anyone could count? They were all just spokes on a wheel.

Ardie rolled down her window and flicked her fob over the keypad so that the metal arm lifted. Her black Lexus tilted on its axis, climbed the Truviv parking garage and slid between two yellow lines on the second floor. She hit the "lock" button and the horn blared twice, echoing against the concrete pillars. Once in the garage elevators, no soundtrack played and she felt the eeriness of being scraped along the edges of a cement shaft inside a coffin box attached to a manufactured pulley. She waved to the security guard on duty, crossed the lobby, and rode the elevator in the next bank up.

The industrial air-conditioning unit hummed through the vacant halls. Around the corner, a young, white woman with anemically brown hair poked her head around a cleaning cart and relaxed when she saw that the intruder was Ardie.

Like a kid on a pool deck, Ardie had to will herself not to jog. The spirit of anticipation prodded her faster. The chance for vindication — a strong word maybe, but one that was nearly within reach.

When she was in law school, Ardie had wanted to investigate white-collar crime and practice forensic tax analysis because it had sounded glamorous in the way few jobs actually were. But a month after her on-campus interviews, she'd been offered a job at a law firm that paid almost two hundred thousand dollars a year. At twenty-five, she reasoned she could go on to practice criminal law after she'd paid off her student loans. And this, she learned, was probably the way most career dreams perished.

Ardie used her keycard to access the room in which the personnel files were stored. The idea that she could parse through the enormous volume of information contained in this room and find nothing hollowed her as she flipped the light switch and locked the door behind her.

Beige file drawers lined both sides of the long, narrow room. Beams of fluorescent lights turned the air antiseptic. In here, she might never know the time of day. Her cell phone didn't even have service.

The personnel files were arranged by department. Cleaning staff had a place in the back third, on the right. Alphabetized. Neatly arranged for easy reference. It was good housekeeping. They were a public company, after all.

It was exactly the type of meticulous analysis that made Ardie a damn good attorney. (*Mirror, mirror on the wall, who has the most boring superpower of them all?*) But it was a useful one and, an hour into her search, her fingertips were dry from rifling through pay stubs and W-2s. Her back slid against the aluminum file cabinet as she sank onto the floor, the typed and signed confirmation of what she already knew clutched in hand. Ardie understood now why she hadn't called Sloane or Grace. It wasn't her story to tell.

But Ardie did have a story and hers had gone like this:

A pianist played movie scores in the corner of the hotel bar. A few minutes ago, she'd put a five-dollar bill in the jar and asked him to play the theme from *Jurassic Park*.

"Another round?" Ames had asked, sliding the company credit card over to the bartender. They were drinking expensive champagne. They'd closed an expensive deal. Tomorrow, she would have a headache that cost more than her handbag.

"I'll be right back. I need to call Dan," she said. "Order me the same."

She excused herself to the lobby, where a canopy of ivy grew overhead. She called her boyfriend. "You sound drunk," he said.

"That's because I am." Her head felt pleasantly heavy, the tip of her nose and her cheeks had begun to go numb. "Good news: I have my life back." The moment the deal had been signed, she felt her body instantly lighten, as though she'd just finished a juice fast instead of two months of eating takeout Thai food from a Styrofoam container in the conference room.

"I'll believe it when I see it." Dan laughed. He was a serious young analyst at Deloitte and Ardie had recently been wondering at what point she would know if he was The One.

"It's true," she insisted in the petulant manner of someone too many drinks in to be convincing. "I'm a new woman."

"Congratulations," he said. "Enjoy yourself. I'll see you tomorrow, or whoever this new woman is that I'm dating."

She returned to the bar and picked up the champagne flute, the bubbles still spinning their way to the surface.

"Drink up," he said. "Then I'll walk you to your room."

CHAPTER FIFTY-THREE

3-May

We had long seen the problem at the heart of it all: being a woman at work was a handicap that we'd been trying to make up for by erasing our femininity in just the right ways. We pretended to agree that an interest in makeup and romance novels and Real Housewives was any more empty-headed than an obsession with sports and craft beer and video games. We joined Fantasy Football leagues. We policed ourselves into removing verbal upticks from our sentences and erasing the word "like" so that we could sound more "professional," when what we were really trying to do was sound more male. Since sexual harassment was a thing that happened to women, believe it or not, we didn't want to admit that we had been harassed. It would be admitting that we were women in a way that mattered. So our insistence on speaking up at last ought to have been a clue of what was to come. *We were going to start mattering.*

Likewise, the fact that Sloane wasn't a puddle should have been a clue, too. It was, at the very least, a goddamn miracle. She was waiting for someone in this room to remark: *Sloane, you are so stoical. How do you do it? And, oh, by the way, can I get the number for your hair stylist?*

But instead, everyone besides her and Grace looked like their stomachs were upset. She considered offering them Pepto-Bismol just to be cheeky, but, well, she probably shouldn't.

They occupied the twentieth floor conference room, the Important One, as Sloane thought of it because this was where she'd done her legal liability presentations for Desmond and the board. She herself had become a legal liability, she realized. She would have made the presentations. Life was funny that way.

Puffy leather rolling chairs circled the slick mahogany oval around which Cosette, her two henchmen (whom Sloane had named Peggy and Brad without having ever actually learned their names), a staunchly spectacled member of the independent review committee, Al Runkin, Helen Yeh, and Grace sat. From the corner, an enviable fiddle leaf fig fanned impressively large leaves from its trunk and probably retailed for five hundred dollars, a fact which Sloane had learned the hard way when she killed two of them in her own living room.

Cosette made a big show of checking the time on her Rolex, as if that were the way anyone really checked the time. Sloane figured the Rolex was probably like purchasing a boat. Once you bought it, you were required to log the number of times you used it to justify the cost. "Have you heard from Ardie?" she asked, like they were waiting for one of their friends to arrive for brunch. *A mimosa might be nice.*

"I'm sure she'll be here soon." Sloane drummed her fingers on the countertop while a silence that threatened Sloane's conversational impulses stretched.

To occupy herself, Sloane wondered at Cosette. Silly things, like whether she was the sort never to have dirty dishes in her sink. (Probably.) Her apartment in New York presumably was *feng-shui-ed,* a copy of Marie Kondo's *The Life-Changing Magic of Tidying Up* half-read on her pristine nightstand, as though the reason her home was in such immaculate, anally retentive order were that she was enlightened and not, say, because she billed twenty-five hundred hours a year.

Cosette gave a perfunctory double-tap of the diamond-rimmed watch face. "Maybe we should go ahead and get started on the housekeeping parts of today's meeting." She pushed three sets of documents over. One for Sloane, one for Grace, one for Ardie. "We've gone ahead and put together the settlement papers. I've used yellow tabs to mark where you need to sign. We wanted to make this as pain-free as possible." Her lips pruned as she leaned across the table.

"How considerate of you," Grace said, her tone minty-cool.

Cosette, bless her, crumpled her face in an appreciative nod, apparently taking it as an actual *fucking* compliment.

Sloane had read somewhere that it would be impossible to kill someone with a thousand paper cuts, despite the old saying, "Death by a thousand paper cuts," but that a million might actually do the trick. She probably shouldn't think about that sort of thing after all that had happened.

"The thing is, Cosette," Sloane started, "you could have just offered to let us drop the lawsuit. We *might* have considered that."

"Sloane, I wish." Cosette clicked open her pen. "Given our history. But the board felt very strongly — and I agreed, to be honest

— that we needed to set a precedent. To discourage frivolous lawsuits."

"Right. Precedent." Grace frowned at Sloane, shrugged. "Makes sense." In another room, Grace and Cosette might have passed as sisters.

Sloane wondered how cocksure — we hated that word — one had to be not to wonder why the two women who were preparing to fork over a gut-churning sum of cash, along with all their stock options and their jobs, didn't have an eyelash out of place.

And then Ardie pushed the door. She held her back against it. "Sorry we're late."

Cosette glanced up and did a double take as Rosalita and her son, Salomon, entered ahead of Ardie. "Excuse me." She tapped the table. "This is a private meeting. We're live, here. Cleaning later, please." Cosette licked her finger and flipped a page on the documents before her.

"Hello, Ms. Sharpe." Rosalita came to a stop in front of the conference table. "My name's Rosalita Guillen. My son, Salomon, will wait in the hall while we talk. Salomon, come, come, manners, please. Take off your hat when you come inside."

The boy removed his hat. "Nice to meet you," he murmured, staring at the floor, ears turning red, while the room turned in on him.

It was like an invisible atomic bomb had gone off — silent, foreboding, billowing — swelling out to transform the faces of everyone in the fallout radius. The silvery line shone like lightning through the boy's dark hair.

Even having expected the explosion, it took Sloane's breath away.

"Cosette," Sloane started as Ardie helped to usher Salomon from the room, "the truth is we never would have uncovered our friend's story if it weren't for you."

Cosette's lips parted, teeth white as a shark's.

Sloane was surprised to find that she didn't feel the jolt of triumph that she'd been expecting. Mostly, Sloane felt a tired melancholy worsening in her bones. It was like declaring your favorite war was World War I when what you meant was that World War I was the one you found most fascinating. No one actually had a *favorite* war. So yes, it was that way with Rosalita. It was an inability to stop staring at the woman she had looked over so many times. (Though Sloane *had* been nice to her at Michael's birthday party. Everyone had to give her that much.)

And, of course, this had happened to Rosalita in Ames's own office, with its hulking desk and that navy leather chair. If she thought about it too long, she swore she wanted to kill Ames. But, well.

Rosalita pushed a slim folder of documents over to Cosette, whose mouth had converted into a pin. "I came today because Ames Garrett assaulted me in this office building eight years ago. He told me he knew I wanted it. I didn't. I never did." Sloane imagined what it must be like for Rosalita to address this room, to address these people — a member of the board of directors, New York lawyers, an HR officer — and not only to address them, but to say these words in this order. Ames Garrett assaulted her.

But Rosalita showed no signs of distress. She seemed perfectly collected. The woman had moxie. Then again, Rosalita had already said as much to Desmond Bankole, the CEO of a Fortune 500 company, all those years ago. She'd had practice. Unlike the rest of them.

"Ames Garrett was Salomon's father," explained Rosalita.

Ardie leaned in. "Are you familiar with Waardenburg syndrome? It's a hereditary syndrome. Relatively harmless, though it can cause discoloration in the forelock and some hearing loss. Ames, as I'm sure most of you are aware, had Waardenburg syndrome."

"So, Ms. Guillen could have had a consensual relationship with Mr. Garrett." She looked around the room to show how completely obvious this was. But if Cosette was treading water now, no one came through with a life preserver.

"A consensual relationship for which Truviv paid her more than twice her previous income?" Grace asked. "A consensual relationship that caused Desmond Bankole to personally sign off on a single cleaning staff member to receive an unheard of spike in pay following the assault? I don't believe that CEOs are usually *in* the business of reviewing cleaning staff pay, do you?"

Sloane had been sad to hear about Desmond. She'd expected more from him.

"Not to mention," Ardie pressed, "that if you review the company's history surrounding the time at which the increase in pay occurred and the time at which Salomon," she lowered her voice, "would have been conceived, Truviv would have been at the precipice of closing on the Run Dynamics acquisition, a process which Ames Garrett himself was leading at the time and which, as projected, has been astronomically lucrative for Truviv."

Rosalita intertwined her fingers and rolled her chair closer. "I love my son very, very much." She searched each of the faces. "That's why I have not said anything until now. Until Ardie." They shared a look. "Until Ardie and I spoke and I decided — *I* decided — that I want to come forward to tell my part of this story. I let them speak because of my English. But I am here because I know what matters. And I know what's right. And what you are doing, it's not right, Ms. Sharpe."

Sloane's throat felt suddenly swollen. If Ames had sought to put Rosalita in her place, he'd failed.

Cosette looked as though she were waging an internal battle in deciding whether she should say what she wanted to say next. "Because you want to get *paid,*" she spat out.

Even Al Runkin twitched.

"Yes, it would be nice to get paid. Sure. But they are telling the truth. I cannot let them lose their jobs and money and everything because they tell a truth that is also my truth." Rosalita pushed a fist into her heart. Sloane's eyes watered, goddammit.

Sloane pushed the small pile of papers

back across the table. "So, while we do appreciate the extra time you put in flagging where we needed to sign, we're going to go ahead and not. The press has already been contacted. In case you had any ideas about — I don't know — going on the offense again."

The woman whom Sloane had named Peggy chose this moment to speak up. "You're under confidentiality agreements with the company." She glanced sideways at Cosette for approval. "You're not allowed to say anything. You'd be in material breach."

"That's right," Cosette added hastily. "You are."

Rosalita raised her hand from the table. "I'm not."

Rosalita had made the call to Cliff Colgate first thing this morning. It was their turn to take control of the narrative and this — Rosalita — would change it. Plus, Sloane thought, it would be a pretty nice scoop for Cliff, too. *(You're welcome.)* He'd promised to handle the article tastefully and with discretion and, as a result, they'd have to put their faith in him that he really was, as he'd claimed, one of the good guys.

"Right, well, we'll leave you to it," Grace said.

Sloane shook her head solemnly. "Sounds

like a real PR nightmare."

There was absolutely no world in which Cosette was not clenched down to her toned rear end. "We'll of course advise Truviv about how best to approach this publicly. They're in good hands."

Sloane paused. "I meant for your firm . . . and for you. Women in law have to stick together," she said. "Thanks for the advice."

Chapter Fifty-Four

Two pink lines. Rosalita had sat on the
toilet, pants still around her ankles as she'd
watched the second line steadily darken
until there was no mistaking what the test
had decided: she was pregnant.

She'd had a scare once before when she'd
phoned her then-boyfriend and told him
her period was late. She thought she knew,
in the back of her mind, that she wasn't
really pregnant even before she'd held the
test up to the light, squinting to see if there
was even the faintest hint of a line forming
along the grayish indention printed into the
white strip. She'd wanted to see her boyfriend's reaction and, for a couple of days,
it had all been very mature and romantic,
playing at the idea of a family with him.

Now, there was no need to squint.

She'd placed the test into a plastic bag
and zipped it tight, beads of urine clinging
to the clear sides. Rosalita was Catholic, but

that wasn't the only reason she wouldn't get an abortion. Over the next nine months, the baby's father would be haunted by the sight of her growing belly, of her fat swollen body, ballooning and forcing itself out into the world. Without a word from her, he'd remember *exactly* what he had done.

Before that night, he'd been the man with silk ties, the odd white streak in his hair like a skunk, the fading blue tattoo mostly obscured by thick, masculine arm hair and the rest by his rolled shirtsleeve, empty cigarette cartons in his trash can. Before that night, she had disliked being invisible, hated the way men like him looked straight through her as though it were a machine and not a person that was dusting the blinds and emptying trash cans. After that night, she would never feel invisible enough again. She would crave the ability to go unseen. But she'd always feel naked.

He had been working late, night after night, so many of them strung together that it felt as though she and the man were working the same schedule. He took power naps on a couch in his office, which had quietly impressed Rosalita. A couch in the office! The word "acquisition" was tossed back and forth and she once thought she'd heard "billion" with a "B" and didn't know how anyone could sleep at all, even on an office sofa, if he was in charge of something that cost over a billion dollars.

At first, she had liked the companionship even if they never actually spoke. The hours stretched and the number of upstairs attorneys who hurried back and forth from the printer and shoved sushi into their mouths over their keyboards dwindled until each evening he managed to be the last. This went on for ten days, maybe more. Once, he did register her and had lifted his head to say, "How's it going," in a gruff voice that didn't invite more than a mumbled response. On another occasion, she watched him standing in front of the floor-to-ceiling window, staring out into the bottomless pit of night, where buildings pressed their jagged teeth into the navy sky. Just standing there. Staring.

The night that it happened, voices carried in the empty halls. If there was a buildup, Rosalita didn't hear it. To her, it sounded like a stereo switched on, the volume too loud so that it crashed into the nerves and made the listener rush to dial back the knob. Rosalita kept her head down and worked through the row of offices, her cleaning partner somewhere off on the other side of the floor.

The fact that she was eavesdropping couldn't be denied, but that was primarily a function of her having ears. She couldn't miss the sound of the two men arguing any more than she could have missed the sound of barking dogs at night. In any event, she understood little of what was being said between the man and the other man, whom she gathered was the first man's — her man's (as she had come to think of him) — boss. She would have forgotten it altogether, if not by morning then maybe in a week or two. She felt sorry for the man who'd been working so many hours only to be yelled at by his boss. Maybe that was the problem — her impulse to feel sorry for him. Because she would always wonder what the man saw on her face that night and she guessed it was pity. What in her eyes had been intended as benign sympathy, in his had already metastasized into something mean. She supposed that was because there was already meanness inside him, swimming in his blood like cancer cells waiting to glom onto something. He had an underlying condition. Where would it have gone if he hadn't noticed her seeing him? If he hadn't already felt the humiliation boiling inside him and acted on that fateful impulse to make his

545

humiliation hers instead.

If a tree falls in the forest and no one's there to hear it . . .

Or, *That's the million-dollar question!*

She'd heard those phrases on TV.

The boss had been gone fifteen minutes or so when Rosalita entered the office, her head down. She would leave the office fifteen minutes later, having learned the difference between being invisible and feeling invisible. She'd have a white scratch puckering along her forearm, transforming itself to red. It would take another nine months for the scratch to scar, having found its way to the soft bit of skin between her hips.

Between those two points in time, she would finally memorize the name on the silver plate in front of his office. She would call a free lawyer that she learned about on a hotline, because Rosalita was not the woman that he had banked on her being. She would meet with the CEO of the company. She would be told that the man — her man — was in charge of a critical acquisition strategy for the company, that it would be her word against his, that the stockholders would push back hard. She would be given a choice, which would be more than she'd been given before.

The wrong place at the wrong time!

Another phrase.

Eight years later, she would want the man's money more than she would want him dead. He would wind up dead anyway. She would show up to his wife's door, something that she had never done before, no matter how many times she'd been tempted. She would have a door closed in her face, telling her to go away and be quiet. And one of those things she would do.

CHAPTER FIFTY-FIVE

3-May

"Hi, Katherine." Ardie hovered in the door, her hands stuffed into her roomy pockets.

Katherine stared at her from behind the makeshift office on the twentieth floor. A private office on the upper level. *Moving on up,* Ardie thought, glancing around at the two walls and the pane of glass, blinds drawn, behind her.

"Hello."

Ardie tried to imagine meeting Katherine in another context. In an interview, perhaps. What would she have thought of her then? Would she have hired her? She found it impossible to say. Too much had happened in the in-between.

"I just wanted to let you know that we didn't accept the settlement offer." No inflection. Just the facts. Like an unbiased news source, if those existed anymore.

The tip of Katherine's tongue slipped

onto her upper lip. "Do you think that's wi—"

"There was a shift in the case," she interrupted. "I think it's safe to say that we'll be receiving a settlement offer ourselves shortly. Maybe even today, and that it will be considerable."

Katherine blinked up at her. Three red blotches had begun to spread up her long, perfectly postured neck. It was no easy thing being on the losing side of a moral battle, especially when you'd chosen the pragmatic one, the upper hand, when you had sold a piece of yourself for the safer bet. Katherine's mouth formed an "O" of surprise.

"Why, Katherine? Why did you lie?" Ardie asked finally.

Katherine took in a sharp breath. "I — I thought it was obvious. I needed distance."

Ardie crossed her arms. "From what? From us?"

"No." Katherine massaged her temples. "Not just from you. From all of it. From . . . what happened." She swooped her hands wide to demonstrate. Ardie waited. "I don't expect you to understand," she said. "At Frost Klein, I didn't look out for myself and look what happened. And there was even *more* at stake here. I did what I had to do. Not just for me. It was better — it *is* better

— for me to have been on good terms with Ames."

Ardie remained calm. Ardie's other superpower. "At Frost Klein, no one was looking out for you. And you weren't just 'looking out' for yourself. You tried to ruin us, Katherine."

"No." She looked down, shaking her head. "No, it wasn't personal." Supposedly, no one was the villain in their own story, and Katherine, Ardie now knew, could make up stories. What she didn't know was whether she was spineless or calculating or a liar or whether it was possible to be all of those things under the right circumstances. "I never asked for this. I never *asked* you guys to sue your employer for me, okay? In fact, I specifically said as much." Katherine rubbed the back of her head with too much aggression.

"Okay," Ardie replied.

Katherine looked through her eyelashes at her. "It's not like, it's not like I went in there planning to say . . . planning to say what I did." Ardie made no motion. "I walked in there, and before I had a chance to say a word, Cosette told me I should know that they were going to sue you guys." She whispered now. "That the detectives were looking closely at anyone who was known to be fighting with Ames. They hoped" — she laughed a little — "they hoped I'd be honest, because they saw such a bright, promising future for me here, and they knew I'd had some troubles before."

"And so that was enough to throw us under the bus."

"They were going to crucify me. Again. My name would be smeared through the papers. I might never work as a lawyer again. For years anyone googling me wouldn't see how I've busted my ass. They wouldn't see that *I* was an editor of Law Review or how far I'd come. They'd *see* that I accused some man of harassment and now he was dead. You didn't hear Cosette. The detectives were going to be all over me. And I wasn't going to be at the center of this house of cards." Ardie thought: *You weren't the center; you were the wind that knocked it down.* "They were asking questions, Ardie."

"I know." Ardie had moved not so much as an inch. "They asked me, too."

"Your name was already on the filing. That was done before he died."

Before he died. Okay, then.

"So why not tell the detectives more?" she asked. "Why not tell them everything?"

Katherine fell silent.

"Ames wasn't a good person," Ardie said. What she would remember most about Ames was that conversation she'd had with him in his office, a day or two after they'd returned from the closing in L.A. It was their last conversation of any substance. Buyer's remorse, he'd called it. Sour grapes. He said she was just mad he didn't call after. It was a one-night-stand; people had them all the time. He was right. They did. Only she hadn't. She knew that. She did. She had been drunk, passed out even, sure. But — "Let's be real for a second," he'd said. "Look at you. You think I'm just dying to sleep with you? I didn't do anything that you didn't want. If anything you came on to me. How many drinks did you order again? You could have just left if you'd wanted to." The sting of shame that lingered over the years wasn't that she believed him, it was that she let him believe she had by not telling anyone — other than that worthless Al Runkin — about it. She looked through the years of experience and across the desk at Katherine. "He might have tried to be occasionally," she continued, "when it suited him or when it wasn't too difficult, but he wasn't."

An almost imperceptible nod.

"Anyway." Ardie brushed her hands. "I

just wanted you to know from me."

"But" — Katherine's neck contracted as she forced a swallow — "it's not over. The rest of it." Her voice was a thin rasp.

"That I don't know." Slowly, she walked over to the window. The great, glass hole. She drew the blinds up. Katherine shrank. "But you and Ames were on *such* good terms. What do you have to worry about?"

The redness had crawled up Katherine's jawline, fingering its way up like a rash. "I know they think I met with Ames."

"You did meet with Ames."

"Ardie. What do I do?" She pressed her palm lightly to the spot where her ribs met. *Hadn't she done enough already?*

Ardie shrugged. "You wait."

"Ardie, I —" She saw the hope in Katherine's expression. The bright lift, the small plea written on her pretty face, asking Ardie to save her again.

"Katherine." She stopped her. Because Ardie had chosen well. She'd picked the choice she could live with, no matter the outcome. She'd picked her friends. And now Katherine had to own her choice. Whether or not she could live with it was none of Ardie's business. Ardie's only business was the secret they shared between them. "We are not friends."

CHAPTER FIFTY-SIX

4-May

The next day, Rosalita returned to work. Returned to spray bottles and latex gloves and clear trash bags and empty toilet-paper rolls. To the concrete box in the belly of an office building and up into its arteries that were the empty, channeled hallways connecting the floors. It was the same thing she'd done for ten years. No one here knew what had happened in the last twenty-four hours and she sank into work because it was hers and because she needed to.

Beside Crystal, she checked off the boxes, office by office, while the night breathed around them.

At odd moments, she saw her young self in Crystal. Like when Crystal contorted her body to pick up a trash bin. Or when Crystal rolled her eyes at some conversation going on inside her head. Rosalita saw these things and worried that she was already becoming soft. Success did that to people and Rosalita had won and won big. With Salomon and against Truviv and, though she still showed up to work, already the difference was creeping in and it boiled down to this: Rosalita would not have to be here. Remove the "have to" and it changed everything.

As they worked together to wipe down the glass of a conference room, Rosalita asked for the first time, "When's your baby due?" It was becoming painfully obvious that Crystal was pregnant to anyone with eyes.

Crystal didn't respond right away. She stood on her toes and rubbed at the window. "August." She lowered herself down to her heels. She swayed slightly and Rosalita resisted the urge to steady her. Crystal smiled, then, embarrassed. "My birthday's in August, too, and I hope she's born on my birthday. I think that'd be cool. I'm turning twenty. So we'd be exactly twenty years apart." She smiled, a mouth full of crooked teeth. Rosalita had never noticed.

Rosalita aimed the Windex and sprayed. *Twenty years old.* "You're having a girl?"

She returned to working. "Yeah. Doctor told me when I was about four months along."

"You have everything all ready?" Rosalita

asked. It was good Crystal had a steady job, but the foreman never would have hired her if he'd realized she was pregnant. She hoped that Crystal wouldn't be fired once he paid attention enough to realize that she was. Things like that still happened down here occasionally.

"Kind of. Well, no. Not really. Her dad can't decide whether he wants to be, you know, *around* after she's born, so I'm going to wait to figure out where we're gonna be." She avoided looking at Rosalita when she said this. Rosalita remembered her own stomach getting bigger and the way she'd lifted her chin anytime someone had glanced — always so obviously — down at her ring finger. "Don't worry. I knew I wanted her either way. I don't have any family." Crystal touched her stomach. "Now I do."

Rosalita tossed a paper towel into the bag hanging from the back of the cart. "I raise my son by myself. It's okay. You'll be fine." Though, of course, no one could know this for sure.

Crystal chewed the inside of her cheek. Rosalita had been there. Alone. Unsure. Most of the time angry.

Rosalita sighed. "Write down your address," she said. "On the clipboard. I'll bring over some of Salomon's old baby things. I've got old bottles and onesies and a bouncer and toys. I have so much stuff, you won't believe. Almost everything you need." Rosalita had saved all of Salomon's things thinking someday she might want another baby, but that time had come and gone.

Crystal shook her head and turned away. "No," she said quickly. "No, I don't need no handouts. I'm not a charity case."

Rosalita stepped closer, so that their personal spaces bumped into one another's uncomfortably but she stayed, unmoving. "Stop. You hear me? You stop that. When another woman offers to help you, you take it. You understand?"

Crystal looked at her out of the very corner of her eye. Rosalita raised an eyebrow, waiting, refusing to take a step back, until at last Crystal nodded.

CHAPTER FIFTY-SEVEN

18-May

"Thank God, y'all are here." Sloane foisted her heavy purse onto the empty chair. This restaurant had a thing and that thing was plants. Vines cascaded from terra-cotta pots; succulents topped reclaimed wood shelves; miniature white orchids sprouted from handmade ceramic mugs centered on the tables. It was where Pinterest came to vomit, trading in the sort of motif that seemed so effortless and natural that it had to be attainable, only it absolutely was not and Sloane lived for it. "I feel like I haven't seen you in ages." She leaned over to hug Ardie and Grace, in turn, before dumping herself into an artisanal Wishbone Chair. "I'm jonesing. Physically. Look at my hands." She held out her hand, which was trembling slightly, though it might have been low blood sugar.

"It's been four days." Ardie looked up

from a concise paper menu that had been nailed to a small plank.

"*Which* has been the longest since . . ." Sloane waved her arm.

"Since my maternity leave," offered Grace.

"Exactly." Sloane nodded solemnly, picking up her own plank menu and scanning down for the wine list. Something cold, white, and crisp was in order. "And we all know I barely survived that." Sloane flagged the waitress, a woman dressed in all white with forest green suspenders. "I'll have a glass of the Starmont Chardonnay, please. Anyone else?"

"Same, please," said Grace.

"Me, too."

Sloane raised her eyebrows. She had an appointment with her dermatologist to fix that next week, but for now . . . "A round, then. Thanks." Sloane took a sip of room temperature water served in a squatty mason jar. "Gracie, look at you. Have we *freed* the nipple after all?"

Grace wore a floral shirtdress with a primly creased collar. "If you must know, yes." Well, of course, Sloane always *had* to know. "I'm even letting Emma Kate use a pacifier."

"Scandal." Ardie trailed her finger down the list of appetizers.

559

"Hey." Grace flapped a white napkin over her lap. "It was a *hard* decision."

"Of course it was." Sloane leaned down to stow her oversized sunglasses in her purse. "So. Tell us." She leaned in on her elbow. "Was she still there when you went back to get the last of your things?"

"Not sure." Grace's glance flitted toward the open kitchen and then back. "To be honest, I couldn't bring myself to check."

So. No one had spoken to Katherine since. Sloane might think that she'd never existed, so completely had she been excised from their lives, except for the fact that everything had begun to change the moment she arrived. Three days ago, Sloane had called Grace and Ardie with the news that Ames's death had officially been ruled a suicide. There wasn't enough evidence of foul play apparently. Detective Martin had called her personally, bless her. This was the news that Sloane had been hoping for and yet it carried with it a mixed legacy, because there would always be people that agreed with Cosette, believed that they'd gone too far. That they'd been unfair. That they were at least partly responsible for Ames dying. This despite the settlement agreement and large lump sum check currently making its way through the bowels of the law offices of

Helen Yeh, who, by the way, was now happily collecting her 40 percent (eye roll).

"Derek's back," Sloane announced when the wine arrived to keep her mind from racing down closed paths.

"From the mountains?" Ardie laid her menu over her plate.

"The Appalachians. He has a beard."

"And?" Grace prompted.

"*And,* a week hiking and eating beans in a can later — I don't want to jinx it but — he says he's ready to *move* on." She did hope that he meant it. She felt sorry for Derek. Since the lawsuit had settled and Rosalita's story had made papers, there'd been requests for interviews, talk show spots, podcasts, even a few literary agents sniffing around. People loved their adjectives right now: harrowing, heroic, painful, courageous. And here Derek was just trying to be mad at his cheating wife in peace. "Oh," she said, just remembering. "And Abigail made a friend at school. Lottie Silverman. She's come over to play exactly three times, so I'm pretty sure it's serious. Even her name sounds nice. *Lottie.* She reminds me of you, actually," she told Ardie. Ardie was wearing all black, which was completely not in line with the fresh décor, but *that* was Ardie for you.

"I'm not going to even ask what that means." Ardie angled in the chair.

"Oh, I know." Grace took a long sip of the wine.

It was delicious. Sloane knew her wines. "Well, guys." Sloane lifted her own misty glass. "Cheers. To our first official working lunch." They clinked, even Ardie who hated toasts. "First things first. What kind of office should we have? Like Southern chic? Mid-century? Is that still cool?"

Ardie pulled a pocket calendar from her bag. This made Sloane feel safe and smart, to have a partner who ran around with little leather-bound pocket calendars. "I looked at the spaces in Uptown that our realtor sent over," said Ardie. "I liked them, but are we sure we feel okay about Uptown?" Sloane opened her mouth to speak, but Ardie pointed the business end of the pen at her. "Do not start singing 'Uptown Girl.' "

Then, honestly, what was even the point?

"Fine. Do we offer Rosalita a job? I don't know the proper etiquette. Or whether she'd even take a job. Or . . ."

"Yes." Ardie straightened the cutlery around her plate. "We offer her a job. Not necessarily as a cleaner. But we offer her something. Your guess is as good as mine as to whether she takes it."

The settlement money would be split four ways, not three. Rosalita was the only one of them remaining at Truviv so far. She wanted to see the money in her account before she considered jumping ship. From the beginning, Sloane had insisted to herself that she was doing all of this — the list, suing Truviv — so that she could have a future there. But after all was said and done, she found that she couldn't work for the company that had tried to ruin her with an unlawful death claim, that had tried to destroy them all.

Grace chewed on her lower lip. Her thumb and pointer finger twirled the stem of her glass.

"Ok, what?" Sloane asked her. "Why so silent over there? You hate mid-century, don't you."

Grace took a breath. "Okay." She folded her hands in her lap. Sloane felt a chill run up the back of her neck. "I don't want to be the buzzkill here. I just — I know we're all excited about starting our own practice and I just . . . I don't know if I can. Right now, anyway." She delicately pressed two of her fingers on the spot between her eyebrows.

"What?" Ardie asked, scooting her chair back so that it made a loud screech in the serene restaurant. Ladies-who-lunch turned.

Grace looked skittish for a split-second, then calmed. "I want to come with you, I do, but maybe part-time? And after some time away. But" — she took a gulp now of wine — "I understand if you guys need to move forward without a spot for me. I'm just on a new medication and I have some health stuff I need to sort through." She spoke too quickly, using her hands like a traffic cop.

Sloane's jaw dropped. "You're dying, aren't you? Is it breast cancer?" Sloane asked, steeling herself. "It's breast cancer, isn't it?"

"No, no, god. It's not. I have . . . I have postpartum depression." She said this low, like she might have said "leprosy" instead.

"Oh, honey," Sloane said, sharing a look with Ardie. She didn't usually call her friends pet names, but perhaps there were moments that warranted it and this was one. "Why didn't you tell us?" Though would Sloane have known, deep down, if she weren't so distracted?

"It just didn't sound like *me.* So I figured it wasn't. Ames actually pointed it out."

Ames. That hit hard. The fact that Sloane had been too distracted, but Ames Garrett had been able to spot it.

"Anyway, I'm sorry. I just —"

"Please." Sloane butted in. "Please, you come when you're ready and not a minute sooner."

They relaxed. Sloane could feel it. The way everything was click-click-click-ing into place. Sloane actively despised the notion that the universe might be telling her something, that everything happened for a reason, as if the universe gave a fuck about the comings and goings of middle-aged blonde women, but she would say this much: things felt right.

"While we're making confessions . . ." Ardie shifted in her seat.

Sloane looked up sharply. "Are you *dating* someone? I knew it. I could feel it."

Ardie squinted one eye shut. "No. What? Actually, I do have a date. Tonight, in fact."

"See?"

"Oh, is he nice?" Grace asked.

"I don't — I don't know. I met him online. I — no, it's about something else." She looked suddenly flustered, then, just as quickly, centered herself. Sloane had about a dozen more questions. Still, she knew better than to pepper Ardie with them now. "I need to tell you both something. Okay?" Grace and Sloane waited, expectantly. "I think you both deserve to know, after all that we've been through, that — I mean, I think you realized that Ames and I actively didn't like each other, but, see, there was more to it than that. Ames sexually assaulted me." She sat back. Let the information land.

"I'm sorry. *What?*" Grace's pretty blue eyes narrowed.

"Ames Garrett sexually — he raped me. I'm embarrassed it's taken me this long to admit, but I thought you should know, so there it is. And I'm sorry, Sloane. I'm not great at saying that. I should have tried harder to warn you."

"Wh— when? What?" Sloane felt that blind, unseeing look take over her eyes, confusion and anger, searching for a place to settle. But that place was, unfortunately, dead.

"I was drunk," Ardie said, out loud. "Really drunk. Do you remember I'd come back from L.A. right before you started? From closing that sort of hellish Fiter deal that everyone was talking about? We stayed in the same hotel that you and I stayed in when we worked on Matrix Band a couple years ago actually."

"The one with the ivy on the ceiling?"

"Yes, that one."

Sloane did not like this factoid. She felt a sudden onset of nausea. Like the room was

566

spinning.

"Anyway, I can't remember all of it. I just wanted to put it behind me and forget that it happened. My dad used to tell me the best way to keep a secret is to pretend that you don't have one, so . . ."

"So then I slept with him?" Sloane nearly shouted.

Ardie's glance skirted the room. "Sloane. I know. I'm —"

"But — but — Ardie, you must have *hated* me," Sloane interjected.

At this, Ardie let out a genuine laugh. "I did try," she admitted.

"No, really." Sloane's hands gripped the edge of the table and she leaned her chest in, hissing at Ardie. "You must have absolutely hated me."

Sloane felt her face flush, as if she were coming down with something. She needed another mason jar of water. In fact, Ardie slid hers over to Sloane and she drank.

Once quenched, Sloane sat heavily, weighed down by the effort spent on *those* words — Ardie's words — and felt exhausted down to her bones, this despite the fact that they weren't even hers.

"It was complicated," Ardie said. "I'd hoped you would hate him right off the bat. At that point, he was so hatable to me, I figured it'd be obvious to everyone else, too. Then, for a few months there, I thought maybe I really was just a one-off. Maybe it was a misunderstanding. And you were so persistent in trying to be my friend."

"I wasn't." Sloane dabbed her mouth with the napkin, accidentally staining it pink. "Okay, I was. That does sound like me." She smiled, shakily. "Why didn't you say anything later? Like with Katherine?"

"It felt too late. Like it would appear convenient more than helpful, I think. Among other things."

Ardie hesitated, her eyebrows folding in. "Grace, are you all right?"

Oh god. Poor Grace. She was crying. Of course she was. This was too much for her. Hormones. Postpartum. She shouldn't be hearing this. *PG-13!* They needed to keep the conversation PG-13 for Grace.

"I'm fine," Ardie assured her. "Really." How would Sloane ever know now whether or not that was true? "Why are you so upset?"

"Because he *did* that to you. And because I feel so guilty. And then I feel guilty for feeling guilty." Grace stifled a sob. It looked physically painful. "He's dead and, after hearing that, I should be glad. Right?" She pressed the back of her knuckles to her nose. Of the three of them, Grace clearly had the hardest time getting on board with hating Ames, with believing Katherine, but the point was that she had. She'd chosen to believe them. She was being too hard on herself. "The thing is," she said. When she swallowed, it looked as though her throat hurt. She closed her eyes. "I killed Ames."

CHAPTER FIFTY-EIGHT

18-May

Grace killed Ames. Had Ardie misheard her? Grace. Grace said she had *killed* Ames. Sloane had spouted wine like a whale, which Ardie couldn't even pass off as Sloane overdoing it, because Grace Stanton had confessed to killing Ames Garrett. Which wasn't at all true, of course. Had Grace actually *met* Grace before?

"Why would you say that?" Ardie asked, tentatively.

Grace's eyes were slightly unfocused, as though the wine were working double-time. "Because I *did.* I was the last person to see Ames," she said. "I — oh —" The word escaped as a sad, little moan. An animal giving up the fight.

"Grace, you're not making sense." Sloane's chest rested against the tablecloth as she tried to get as physically close to Grace as possible.

570

"I am," Grace said. "I finally am." She pinched her chin down for a moment, collecting herself. "I was so angry with him, for being fooled into believing that he actually cared about me. Or maybe it was just my pride hurt that he thought I could be fooled. Anyway, I told Sloane that much. But then . . . but then that morning — the one that he died — he messaged me, something ridiculous, baiting me: *I thought we were friends.* That was what he said. It should have been me saying that to him, you know? So I went up there." She tilted her head back now, for a second, stared up at the exposed beams of the ceiling. "When I couldn't find him in his office, I knew he was up on the balcony, smoking. And I swear, I just thought, I'll go speak my mind to him. Well, I *did.* Or I was and I was smoking and I felt very together. I mean, I was sort of shaking but I felt good. Strong. You guys have always been so good at standing up for yourselves and I just wanted —"

Ardie let out a burst of laughter. "Really? After what I just told you? You think that?"

Grace looked sober. "Yes. I know that." And in response Ardie just pinched her lips together and felt an uncharacteristic squeeze on her heart, because they would never see themselves the same as they saw each other and that was a gift. "Anyway, I was talking and he sort of leaned in to light his cigarette off of mine and — I don't know — I freaked out. It spooked me. I had this weird spasm and I don't know how but my ring snagged his eyebrow. One of the prongs was loose." She examined the shiny rock on her left hand that sparkled brightly in the natural light. Ardie missed wearing a ring. She'd sold the diamond and wished she hadn't. "Gosh, there was this bright gush of blood on his face." She covered her eyes, recalling. "Seriously, it dribbled down." And Ardie wondered: Had *she* seen the gash on his eye? "He wiped it with his thumb and smeared it all over the railing and he called me . . . he called me a bitch. No one's ever called me a bitch before. At least not to my face. I still don't know what came over me. It was like I was a different person. I saw black. I said, 'Go take a flying leap.' *Who* says that? On a balcony?" Grace wiped the film of tears from underneath her eyes. "I was afraid maybe Katherine saw us talking out there, saw me hit him. Then I left. Well, anyway, you know the rest of the story."

Ardie did. But not the same one that Grace knew.

Sloane hadn't touched her wine since Grace started talking. "You cannot put that on yourself, Grace," she said. "We have no idea what was going through his head."

"Sloane's right."

"Trust me, I —"

"You weren't the last person to see Ames," said Ardie.

Sloane's glance quickly tracked up, the question written clearly on her face: What had happened on Floor Eighteen?

Ardie only knew for sure what happened to her, *because* of her, and what might have happened without her, after she'd, by chance, gotten on an elevator with Katherine and seen her get off on the eighteenth floor.

She only knew this: A payroll officer would confirm that Ardie had received a signature on payroll tax documents around 1:30 PM, although the payroll officer hadn't checked the exact time, which would explain why, shortly after Ames's death, she would be seen riding an elevator and she would be cleared of any possibility of wrongdoing. Ardie, on the other hand, knew that she'd received the signature of the payroll officer closer to 1:25 PM, a discrepancy of five minutes.

What happened in those intervening minutes before Ardie inserted herself into the scene? She imagined Ames pacing the balcony, sucking on the end of a cigarette, an image that wasn't difficult to conjure because Ardie had seen it before, though it had been years now. She imagined Ames trying to justify himself to Katherine, trying to explain how he'd never done anything that anyone didn't want him to do. A speech that she'd also heard before.

Ardie had felt uneasy the moment Katherine had left the elevator and had been thinking of Sloane when she made the life-altering decision to stop off on the eighteenth floor herself. She intended to ease her conscience. Just to check. She watched through the sliding glass door, drawn by the rising voices — or the rising voice, rather, which was Ames's.

Ames raked a hand over his face. Katherine tried to push past, but his arm went out, blocking her.

The slap was a shock. Electric. Polarizing. Ardie's chin flinched inward in sync with Ames's own. Katherine's hand had struck out like a viper.

If Sloane had been accused or if Grace or even if Katherine had, Ardie would have told the next version of events. She would have said that it all happened so fast. She would have gone to the police then, no matter the fact that it was too late. She would have told all of it.

But that hadn't happened. Something more insidious had taken the place of those would-be events. Instead, Grace had been privately blaming herself, spiraling, and so the question became: What should Ardie do now?

"You saw Ames?" Sloane asked and it felt as if the restaurant around their table ceased to exist. Grace's tears stopped. She stared.

"Not just me," Ardie answered slowly.

And it was then that the waitress showed up to take their orders. Ardie imagined how they must look to this poor woman with the green suspenders. The strange thing about delivering bad news was how it was rarely new information to the messenger. So Ardie had to allow for her words to take the color of revelation for the sake of Sloane and Grace. She had to choose what to say. Carefully.

She ordered seared rainbow trout with soba noodles and sprouts.

Meanwhile, Sloane and Grace held their breath until the waitress left. Ardie had meant to ask for another refill of her water.

"What are you saying?" Grace's fingers wrapped tightly around her cross necklace.

"Ames asked to speak with Katherine and she went. When I found this out I was, understandably, concerned."

There was a fascinating tidbit Ardie had once heard: Women walked around the world in constant fear of violence; men's greatest fear was ridicule.

"And you're sure that this was after I talked to him." Grace's forehead wrinkled. There was a new expression on her face: hope.

In reality, it didn't happen as fast as Ardie would have liked. When Ames's hands were around Katherine's throat and he was shouting at her, spittle flying into Katherine's eyelashes, there must have been words, but Ardie couldn't remember which ones. Katherine's eyes bulged like a cornered deer's, her back to the balcony's cement barricade. The flare of heat in Ames's face purpled.

The sliding glass door peeled apart, the sound cutting like a blade.

"Ames." Ardie hooked him by the shirt collar, grabbed his elbow, and pulled him off. *What on earth did he think he was he doing?* She remembered, even knowing Ames the way that she did, being surprised by him in that moment. Like, *Oh, and he's capable of this, too.* Katherine's hands pressed to her windpipe, her chest collapsing.

And in the next second, Ardie felt her

insides explode. She wondered what he saw in that last second of his life. Blind rage, teeth bared, curiosity, cold intent, or pent-up frustration. She knew what she saw in his eyes — hatred and carnal fury and a how-*dare*-she. She felt the struggle. Felt his arms on her. Felt his strength and her own and the fact that they were both holding back just a bit, out of some instinct that cleaved them to propriety.

And then the thought struck her: there was no *returning* from this moment.

They'd passed the point. The moment she had grabbed him off Katherine.

She pushed him, again, this time with her shoulder in his chest. Grunting in surprise, he staggered. One leg left the ground as he struggled for balance. And then — and then — the weight of him simply dissolved.

Gone, windmilling backward through space.

Katherine kneeled down, panting where his feet used to be, and it seemed nearly impossible, too far-fetched to believe what she'd just seen: Katherine — a woman in a crisp black pantsuit — grabbing Ames's standing leg and . . . heaving.

She was actually *trying* to throw him over the ledge. Forcing his center of gravity too high.

And Ardie understood that Katherine had experienced the same revelation. No going back.

Thank you, Ardie had whispered, hands on her knees as she caught her own breath. Sweat coated her forehead.

The truth: Ames *might* have caught himself. Or Ardie, with her hands full of his shirt, *might* have pulled him back. Were it not for that one. last. push.

Afterward, they took the stairs.

"I'm absolutely positive," Ardie said.

Grace started to speak and then stopped herself.

"Oh," was all that Sloane had to offer.

A bomb goes off and pieces fly out in unpredictable directions, causing destruction of varying degrees. Collateral damage.

If she went over the story enough times, she could nearly convince herself that, in the end, he'd chosen to jump. Sloane stretched across the table and squeezed both Grace's and Ardie's hands, and Ardie felt a little sorry for men because they never got to hold hands with each other.

EPILOGUE

We had been programmed to trade in secrets. Our leading deodorant brand promised not to tell. Our magazine covers hocked the secrets to clearer skin, better hair, toned legs, and longer orgasms. Our mothers passed down recipes with secret ingredients. Even our feminism — second-wave, couched as it was in our feminine mystique — felt purposefully (smartly) veiled in secrecy.

Our motto had long been: Keep it between us.

And we did. For generations. Passing along old wives' tales, telling each other how to relieve cramps, cautioning one another never to leave an open drink unattended, not to wear a ponytail, not to open the door to strangers, not to be in a room alone with him. Our tactic was avoidance, to mark landmines and encourage each other to step around them so that nobody went *kaboom.*

It wasn't only the warning that kept us safe but our ability to keep that warning quiet. Like secret agents operating behind enemy lines, we couldn't afford to get caught. And yet we risked it anyway. With voices hushed, we reached out to each other to offer our knowledge. We tried. Because we'd always wanted the best for each of our friends.

We wanted her to dump that loser. We wanted her to stop worrying about losing five pounds. We wanted to tell her she looked great in that dress and that she should definitely buy it. We wanted her to crush the interview. We wanted her to text us when she got home. We wanted her to see what we saw: someone smart and brave and funny and worthy of love and success and peace. We wanted to kill whoever got in her way.

We started to wonder: By whispering, *whose* secrets were we keeping anyway — ours or theirs? *Whose* interests did our silence ultimately protect?

The answer came to us gradually. As we began to strip off our pantyhose and ask for more money and march in pink hats and hold megaphones. As we built digital platforms and watched handmaids and demanded that companies advertise sizes that fit our bodies. As we took up space.

As we grew *tired* of whispering because what were *we* hiding, after all? We had stories, all of us. Would speaking up cost us? Maybe. But maybe it would cost them, too.

And so, when one of us spoke up, it was never just for *her.* It was for *us.* If anything, she was the willing sacrifice. Another log on the pyre stoked by us, our stories, our voices. And we would fan the flames. Spread the truth. Join the chorus. Burn it to the ground. Raze the earth, if we had to. Start over on level ground.

Our legacy would be our words. Shouted out loud. For all to hear. We were done petitioning to be believed. We were finished requesting the benefit of the doubt. We weren't asking for permission. The floor was ours.

Listen.

ACKNOWLEDGMENTS

I have been gifted with the most incredible network of people that helped dream this book into existence.

A loud and heartfelt "thank you" to my agent, Dan Lazar, for opening (and holding) the metaphorical door like a true gentleman. After countless reads, notes, calls, and emails, Dan thrust my words into all of the right hands and I am eternally grateful.

Of course, two of those hands belonged to my lovely editor, Christine Kopprasch, who asked all the smartest questions, in all the kindest possible ways, and understood right from page one how this book should feel when it ended (and how to help me navigate the in-between). By that same token, I feel fortunate to have landed at Flatiron Books for the opportunity to work with outstanding people including Amy Einhorn and Amelia Possanza. Thank you, also, to Bryn

Clark, Robert Van Kolken, Nancy Trypuc, Katherine Turro, and the rest of the Macmillan team.

I deeply appreciate the input and hard work of my film agent, Dana Spector. (You and Dan make a formidable pair.) And to Jon Baker, for championing my book (and being patient when I accidentally made a beeline for Astoria . . .).

Same goes for my foreign rights agents, including Maja Nikolic and Peggy Boulos Smith, who found *Whisper Network* homes across the globe. Speaking of "across the globe," I'm particularly indebted to the Sphere and Hachette Australia teams, with special thanks to my biggest cheerleaders and savvy editors, Cath Burke, Robert Watkins, and Rebecca Saunders, as well as to Maddie West, Ed Wood, and Louise Newton.

I have wonderfully supportive friends who read and commented on drafts: Wendy Pursch, Julia Jonas, Emily O'Brien, Lisa and Joyce McQueen, Charlotte Huang, Lori Goldstein, and Shana Silver — not sure what I would have done without you. In addition, I'm incredibly lucky to have the women in my book club, who embody sisterhood and women supporting women (and books!). Thank you to Jeremy Coffey,

Elizabeth Stork, and Hue M. Flex for answering my research questions. And to the many, many women who shared their stories with me — writing this book has created its own quasi–whisper network and I've enjoyed getting the chance to lean in and listen.

I'd be remiss if I didn't mention that I work at a law firm with amazing attorneys who have been kind enough to give me the time and space to write: Thank you.

And finally, the biggest thanks goes out to my husband, Rob. Being a working mom is next to impossible without the full support of a partner. You continue to step up so that I can reach for my dreams.

AUTHOR'S NOTE

Reader,

I reaped the benefit of my first whisper network when I was a summer associate at a law firm. At a work event, a much older partner was giving me an uncomfortable amount of attention. The other associates were leaving, but this partner and his friends kept encouraging me to stay with them at the bar. "How old are you?" they asked. (Twenty-four at the time, while they were over fifty, in case anyone wants to do that math.) "Do you like older men?" I was in a tricky situation — a summer associate is sort of like a well-paid intern vying for a full-time position, and networking is key. But in that moment, I felt more like a target, someone they hoped — assumed, really — would be a "good sport." I felt myself doing that smiling and fake laughing thing that we all turn to in these moments. I wanted to leave, but I also wanted a job. And wanted to make sure this man felt — *I don't know* — appeased? At the very least, not rejected.

Really, though, I remember less about those men and more about the woman who extracted me from the situation with a lot more grace and social skill than I possessed at the time. She had a charming Southern accent, a big, shiny smile, and as she joined the group she put her arm around my shoulder and told me quietly, "Go ahead and leave, I'll take care of this." So, I listened and I let her. The next day, a senior associate, having heard a version of what had happened, asked if I'd like to speak to HR. Answer: Absolutely not! Sure, his behavior was bad, but — *sorry* — this very influential partner was about to take part in the decision to hire me — or not. I later learned I wasn't the first young woman to have a run-in, but because of the kindness of a few savvy women, I — and my career — survived unscathed.

It's been like this as long as I can remember. Many years ago, I was the only woman on my college's men's rowing team. I was the coxswain (a.k.a. the person who yells at the rowers and steers the boat). As the only woman on the team, I was preoccupied with ensuring that I fit in. Nothing would ever bother or offend me. No way! Not me! One day, I sat around with the team. Admittedly, I'd gotten crossways with one of the boys over the previous few weeks and he'd been annoyed with me for reasons unknown. I reached for a slice of pizza and this boy — who was 6'5" — kicked me hard in the jaw, causing my teeth to snap together with a loud *clack*. His laugh was mean. Everyone else sat slightly dumbfounded, but silent. I was, of all things, mortified. As my eyes pricked with tears, I knew only that I didn't want to do the "girly" thing — *overreact*. I clung desperately to the notion that I was the kind of girl who could hang. So I quietly got up, went to a different room, and never said another word about it. Little did I know that versions of this dynamic were playing out in bigger and smaller ways for so many women, and an echo of it would follow through my and every woman's professional life — *Play along! Don't cause a scene!*

Three years ago, I had a baby. Becoming a mother opened a whole new set of challenges at home and at work. Twelve weeks after my daughter's birth, I returned to work. On my first day back, a new partner asked me to stay late. Around 7 PM, when I told him more insistently I really did need to feed my newborn, he — a father of three

— said, "How old is your daughter?" I said, "Oh, she's three months." And he responded, "Well, she's not really a newborn anymore then." I explained that either way she needed to eat. He magnanimously granted twenty minutes, completely oblivious to the fact that "feeding" meant with my breasts. That night, my husband drove thirty minutes to bring our daughter to the office, and I nursed her in the parking garage.

These are the kinds of things I discuss with my girlfriends, while I'm walking Town Lake with them at lunch or at book club or working out. I found myself discussing these stories so much that I started writing *Whisper Network.* As the story grew, I realized the book deserved a chorus, a voice for the collective women, beyond the women of my novel and beyond me. I called my best friend from law school, who told me about a compliance hotline that often threads complaints directly back to the very person complained about. I talked to my friend who returned from maternity leave to more than two thousand emails because no one helped while she was away. I spoke with an attorney, struggling with infertility, who was told point blank by a male partner that women are no longer useful to the firm once they've had children. All these stories became the book's "we" narrator, a means to talk about the working woman experience, of which sexual harassment is certainly a piece, but not the ONLY piece.

As I was writing this book, I was — and still am — hopeful about how our attitudes toward sexual harassment have been changing. Interestingly, one of my good friends called me while I was finishing the first draft and asked if I could recommend an attorney to handle a sexual harassment claim for her. She told me an incident had occurred at a conference and, while she didn't want to offer details, she hoped I could connect her with someone. I'm embarrassed to say that my first reaction was: *Are you sure you want to do this?* I felt terrible. I'm a lawyer and a writer who has spent countless hours contemplating speaking up about harassment, but I also cared about her wellbeing and knew that speaking up could still come with a high price. Particularly if a woman isn't someone with a platform or any other ostensible form of protection, or if she holds other marginalized identities. But. Things are changing. Slowly, definitely unevenly, but I do think they are changing, thanks largely to the many brave women who have stopped whispering.

As women shared their stories with me, writing *Whisper Network* became a quasi-whisper network of its own. I look forward to sharing this book with readers who I hope will continue to expand the network in new ways.

Best,
Chandler

ABOUT THE AUTHOR

Chandler Baker lives in Austin with her husband and toddler, where she also works as a corporate attorney. She is the author of five young adult novels. *Whisper Network* is her adult debut.